# GOING UNDER

*Also by William Luvaas*

THE SEDUCTIONS OF NATALIE BACH

# GOING UNDER

## William Luvaas

G. P. PUTNAM'S SONS    New York

G. P. Putnam's Sons
*Publishers Since 1838*
200 Madison Avenue
New York, NY 10016

Library of Congress Cataloging-in-Publication Data

Luvaas, William, date.
  Going under / William Luvaas.
    p.   cm.
  ISBN 0-399-13968-0
  1. Family—United States—Fiction.
PS3562.U86G64   1994                94-14231 CIP
813'.54—dc20

Printed in the United States of America
1   2   3   4   5   6   7   8   9   10

Although it is a myth we often foster, it is never true that a writer works in isolation. Grateful thanks to all those who have given me support and encouragement during the writing of this novel, especially to my wife and muse, Cindy, and my father, John Luvaas; to my editor, Stacy Creamer, for her fine suggestions; and to my agent, B. J. Robbins, for her enthusiastic belief in this book. Also to Jerry Bumpus, Tom Nelson, Laurie Edson and Stuart Borden.

FOR MY FATHER

# 1

---

# Aunt Debbie

It was raining like it always rains in Oregon: by the week and the bucketful. That spring it had rained seven weeks straight. Dogs grew mildew behind their ears. Cows stood up to their knees in mud, stock still, rain slicking their backs. Only the occasional eye blink indicated they were alive at all. They lost interest in eating, while grass grew around them in a green fury. Up at Dorena reservoir, they released water from the spillway, fearing the dam would bust. It was wetter than piss in a snowstorm. Every morning, the weatherman on KOIN woke me, apologizing he couldn't do better this morning. Like it was up to him, the horse's butt. I kicked the clock radio off the chair beside my bed. Kapockety. Forty-eight straight mornings. It never did break, but toward the end it began to sputter when it hit the floor. This was back when they advertised "shock proof" and meant it.

That was the year I stayed with my sister, Jerri, and Don, her husband, in the house on Walnut Street. My first year in college. My last. In a grandmother's room under the stairs behind the kitchen, painted slug yellow. The ceiling sloped forty-five degrees one side. I stuck my desk under there. Good a place as any to store a desk. What little studying I did was at the library. Just enough to spoil Mom Sally's conviction I'd flunk out. I quit before giving her the satisfaction.

I'd hear the boys scurrying upstairs to bed, Olson and Jeffrey. More scamperings later when I returned to my room from a washup. Olson's eye glued to my keyhole (I couldn't imagine Jeff there; the little fart wouldn't have known what to look for). Not that Olson saw much—his step-aunt in her undies. Whoopdy-do. Ten years old and trouble in his pants already. Like father like son, they say. He was Don's.

One night I sprang the door open and sent Olson sprawling on the floor at my feet, little shit, staring up at me like I'd caught him sleepwalking. Lids hung at half-mast, eyes the buff yellow color of tanned deer hide. Slicked-back big-boy hair.

"You'll go blind," I said. "Guess you didn't know that."

"Bee ess," he said with a smirk. He seemed a bit worried nonetheless.

"Virgin's honor."

He grinned at that. You could count on Olson for a grin. I rolled him out the door, hung a pair of drawers on the door-knob. Enough is enough.

Long after midnight, I'd be awakened by Jerri clattering dishes, scrubbing a kitchen already spotless. Just the thought of dirt wouldn't let her sleep. I'd open my door and my sister would look at me, surprised. "Are you still awake?" she'd ask, really asking: "What are you doing in my house?"

"Do I look awake?"

"Dummy me," she'd say, "I thought I left the oven on. I laid there for two hours worrying about it. Too lazy to get up and look I guess."

"You're about lazy as China needs more babies. Why not put a cot out here so's you wouldn't have to get up?"

"How's about coffee?"

"You can't sleep and you want a cup of coffee?"

"Backwards I guess. It'll knock me out cold." Still a beautiful gal, my sister, when she smiled. Her nostrils flaring.

So we sat across the dinette table with our feet up on benches, backs against the wall, sipped coffee and talked about girlhood dreams. You could almost see them flit and fly away in the damp kitchen air, smelling of coffee, yeast and cinnamon. Misty reckonings. Hopes we, neither of us, had courage to envision. Even then. Years before I got stuck flying for the airlines. Before Jerri began watering down her coffee with cheap vodka.

It was during all that rain we got a call from Walter and Sally out at the farm on the Rogue River. They could use some help, Walter said. "River's up three feet over my pasture and the cows is stranded wherever they can find a patch of high land. Afraid we may lose some."

Don got out his fly-fishing waders. Jerri thought they should leave the kids home with me. We wouldn't hear of it. Jeff and

Olson hadn't ever seen a drowned cow before. Little Meena hadn't seen a flood. Wouldn't miss this one for the world. I think she expected to see Old Noah loading camels on his ark.

The river had broke free of its bed, swelled a quarter mile wide in places, reached up into the woods and pulled out what timber it wanted. Boat docks, fishing cabins, tombstones . . . whatever suited its fancy. Already, it was within three feet of the county bridge when we crossed over, dark and thick as cocoa, a white scum of marshmallow swirling atop. A logjam of spider-legged stumps, torn branches and an old outhouse was jammed up against bridge pilings. You could feel the shove of it as we went over. "Lord-eee." Don gripped the steering wheel in both hands. The kids stood on the seats to look. Jerri crying, "Are you out of your right mind? Don't even think about crossing." But we were already on the other side.

The river had reached up slope and taken half the apple orchard, Mom Sally's vegetable garden below the house. It licked the scarecrow's knees. He tilted, forlorn. Straw stuck out stitching in his head. Might take the plunge any minute. The house was still high and dry. But you never knew. God had been breaking records all winter long.

Walter stood out in the rain in his yellow Duckies (well, it was Dad, but we called him Walter). You saw right off he wasn't the real item, only a retirement farmer. He couldn't decide, he said, whether to rescue his cattle first or the Chevy flatbed parked down below the house. Two more feet and it was a goner.

"Better get our cows," Sally said. She wore her straw gardening hat, brim wilted down with the wet so it looked like a lamp shade. Or worse.

Walter's plan was to take out the flat-bottomed Rogue River boat with the ten-horse outboard. He had lines rigged up with snaphooks at the end. "A cow swims all right"—he spoke to Jerri like it might interest her, raindrops sputtering from his lips—"Trouble is, the moment it finds a current it forgets about direction and follows dumb. Any cow can swim a lake, but put it in a river it's going to drown. Follows the current, you see, until it is exhausted." Like he knew a damned thing about it. Worked all his life as a dock master in Portland.

Talking to a wall. Coulda been. Jerri didn't pay him the

slightest mind, though he leaned half in the car window. She was scolding Sally about her knees. "You shouldn't be out here, Mother. You shouldn't even be up. I know you're in terrible pain in all this humidity."

There was a new wonder drug: cortisone. They had her on that. Sally grinned, silver tooth caps cheery in all that green gloom. "I feel like I could go dancing."

Walter said he needed four good hands. "We'd best leave Mother out of it. That's Don, Debbie, Olson and young Jeff. You're man enough, young fellow. Unless Jerri planned to go . . . I didn't think so?" Asking not Jerri but the rest of us. They had conversed that way long as I can remember. Never asked a direct question of the other. Never answered one.

"Don, you aren't taking those boys onto that river," Jerri said flat. "Over my dead body."

But the boys came. Jeff, too. Onto a river wide as a lake. Rain pelting on our hats and ponchos, half-deafening. Jeff's job was to keep a lookout for cows, snags and submerged logs. He did. Screamed bloody murder at every board spotted downstream. His eyes wide as pumpkins. A plump imp in an orange life vest, hair fanned flat across his skull. With each false alarm, Olson called him a "bonerhead."

The current, lazy here, frantic there, whipped us past brown whirlpools, rapids flushing over rocks, streaking around snags. Foam frothed yellow in branches of huge spruces. Firs bent right over in the current. From somewhere down below came an ominous bellygrowl.

We found cows. Three of them on a narrow rocky island midstream. Forlorn and bawling. Walter told us, normal times that island was a crag rising twenty feet out of the channel. He'd be damned how they'd got onto it. We landed Don at the upstream end and circled while he approached the cows, stooped at the waist, scared of them as they were of him. They milled nervously together in a willow scrub. Lowing mournful. Heads down as he approached. Walter shouted, "Goddamnit all, Don, you've got to walk right up to a cow else it don't trust you." Those cows weren't all that stupid. Olson said he could do it. I bet. Don managed to slip loops around the necks of two cows. The third, a huge, splay-hipped Guernsey with sad eyes and a suspicious disposition, retreated to one end of the promontory, her back hooves in the stream.

We passed close. Don threw me the lines and I secured them quick to cleats on board. Walter pointed the bow into the current and throttled off. Cows plunged off their island behind us like twin sea lions, swimming for all they were worth behind the boat, eyes wild, muzzles bellowing in the air. Jeff shouted pure glee. The lines made tortured squawks against the gunnels. The third cow gave the forlornest bellow you ever heard. Seemed she might follow her sisters, but didn't. Don approached her, arms spread wide like a football tackle. The big fuck. She turned to face him, head lowered. Seemed she might charge. Don arched to one side to protect the family jewels. Take a dive if need be.

"You go on," he shouted, "I have to reason with this one." Walter wasn't about to leave him out there. Those silly cows swimming for all they're worth behind the boat in a bellowing wake. Like horned seals, black muzzles in the air. Round and round that island. I knew already it wouldn't work: two cows following a boat is two too many as it is.

"Hurry up," Walter shouted.

Don did. Tiptoed up and dropped that rope around the Guernsey's head pretty as a roper. Trouble is he caught a single horn. She panicked, stepped backwards off the rock and sank down in the river slow as a walrus. Don went in behind her, gripping the rope. The cow caught the current and went with it for all she was worth, while Don spun like a top behind, dog-paddling with one hand, holding the rope aloft with the other. His red wader toes sticking up. The boys screamed bloody murder. I seized their waistbands, afraid they would go in after their dad. While Walter tried to turn the boat to follow. Not so fast he drowned what he had on the hoof behind.

"Let 'er go, Don," he was shouting. "Let 'er go."

Trouble was, our cargo served as anchors. We couldn't catch up. Don's Guernsey cow bobbed downstream toward white water frothing at bridge pilings, toward that roar in the river down below, dragging Don along behind on his back. Funny, if you weren't caught in the middle of it. They hit a riffle where trees had been or rocks. The cow bobbed left then right into a chute. It picked up speed.

"Oh Jes'chris'," Walter grumbled at the wheel, eyes fixed on bridge pilings two hundred yards downstream. I knelt beside him, line in hand, ready to throw it. Lech or no, I didn't want Don to drown. Jeff clawed at the gunnel, would have gone in if I'd let go of his seat pants. Ahead, the roar loudened above the general rush of water. A white line across the stream below the bridge.

"Heaven'sake let 'er go," Walter shouted.

But Don had followed the cow into the riffle and disappeared. Ducked under. Came up again, not moving, snagged on a tree branch, maybe eighty yards above the bridge. He'd released the rope, struggling to keep his head above white churning water around him, the whole time shouting God knows what. Poor Jeff chiming in with him. And Olson. *Daaaddddyyyyy.* The Guernsey had turned now and tried her damnedest to swim upstream, wanting no part of Walter's theory. She lost ground against the current. We watched her skirt the logjam and shoot around the bridge piling on a sheet of smooth rapid water, no more substantiai than a cork. Walter made a wet noise with his mouth.

I will say this for my father: He can handle a boat. He used that riffle somehow to pivot around Don. Cows and all. Sidled up beside him to port, bow upstream, and nursed the engine. We seized Don's arms and dragged him aboard. He lay wet as a sewer rat on the planking, silty water pouring out his waders. Laughing and crying both. Tears streaming from his eyes. Cuddling a son in each arm. "Thought I'd bought it," he kept saying. "Know what! You don't swim too well in waders."

Walter laughed, threw one forlorn glance at where we'd last seen his Guernsey cow, then throttled forward and took us out of there. "Two thousand dollars' worth of cow," he muttered.

We got those hoofers to shore. Alive somehow. The fourth, wherever it was, would have to wait. Actually, Olson spotted it later on a tussock not twenty feet from shore, swam out himself and herded it back with a stick.

"Dad almost drowned," Jeff shouted at his mom as we approached. "It was a water rodeo. The cow bucked him off and dragged him underwater towards the waterfall."

"Sounds like one of your tall tales," Grandma Sally said.

"Bonerhead," Olson said.

"It's a miracle you didn't all drown." Jerri was inconsolable. She chewed out Don, who stood sheepish in his wet clothes. Glared at Dad and me. Someone had shit to pay. That was a thing about my sister. Not that she held her husband guiltless. Only saw in him an impressionable child who fell too easily under the influence of others.

"I believe we've had enough excitement for one day," Walter decided.

But we hadn't. Not by nearly.

The night before, Jerri and I sat up talking till three A.M. She was saying how she'd wanted to sell real estate (we Simonets could sell anything) or study Shakespeare. "I loved Shakespeare. If I had your opportunity, Deborah—" Her lips firming in a miserly frown, eyelids flagging, heavy as Olson's, so's you might take him for her natural son, rather than an extra she'd as soon have out of the house. "I used to lie on the grass in Grant's Park and think: 'I'm going to have a romantic life.' I didn't care fish piss about security." Opening her hands, one corner of her wide mouth curling. "Look what I got."

"A hard-working husband, nice house, two of the sweetest kids on this earth. Three actually."

Jerri stared at a soft halo about the fluorescent tube above the sink. The kitchen hazy, as if moisture had leaked in a fog under the basement door and hung on the spice-laden air. A watery mother-of-pearl glow reflected off ceramic tiles beside the fridge. My sister's face half light, half shadow. If there is a man-in-the-moon, the dark side is female. Aren't we taught to believe? My sister did with all her heart. Her dark side faced me. Light caught angrily at her eye.

"You leave them out of it, Deborah. I love my children."

But they're in it, I thought. "Did I ever say different?"

"Dreams don't mean a thing." She snapped on a schmaltzy ship's lantern mounted at back of the dinette booth. My sister's face suddenly close and pale. Grandma Sally's overlarge mouth, nose and eyes. For a moment, half groggy, I mistook her for Mother. "You'll learn that, Deborah," she said with a near spiteful smile. "All our fancies and silly romances . . . you just as well forget them."

"Which ones in particular?"

She lurched across the table at me. "Forget them!"

"Yes, ma'am."

Wouldn't you know, Jerri nodded out after a few minutes, but I couldn't sleep all night with coffee pushing buttons in my head. I sat watching her nod off, wondering if they had a sex life at all, Jerri and Don. Doubting it. No more sign of it than Oregon going dry. No different that way from Walter and Sally. (You couldn't anymore imagine those two making love than the Virgin Mary dancing topless at a bar.) Although each generation insists it is less stodgy than the last. Difference is, both of them, Jerri and Don, were about as highly sexed as two people can get before going natural. Don's smile oozed sex when I passed him in the hall on my way to the john mornings. Bare-chested, wearing only his pajama bottoms. "You're looking fine this morning, hon," he'd tell me. The fuck. Me with fuzzy teeth, my bladder so full I thought I'd leak. I'd double-lock the door. Still, it's a thing about marriage: dries up the sex organs. By fifty, I'd guess they drop right off.

Walter wanted to rescue his truck. We went down after lunch. The rain had stopped a few minutes. It was the kind of swirly sky lined in high background gray, charcoal dark clouds racing like horse soldiers beneath, wispy white banners flying behind. We all went down, because the mud was deep and Walter might need us to push. It was a great old hulk of a Chevy flatbed, 1953 model, with huge balloon tires, more rust than paint on the cab. Jerri forbade the children to get anywhere near. She did her best to corral Meena. Olson led the rebellion, leaping onto the bed, sitting with his feet dangling over the apron. Jeff and Meena followed, helping each other up.

"Are you deaf?" Jerri scolded. "Don! I want those children off of there this minute." Don and Walter were up in the cab. She approached the driver's side and spoke to Dad, we understood well enough. So did he. He turned to Don, who was telling Jerri to let it rest. "Something wrong?" he asked. "Seems everyone's having a good time."

"Over my dead body," Jerri snapped. "I'm warning you, if anything—" She was drowned out by the truck's backfiring and kids' screams.

"Oh, leave it rest," Sally said. "What harm is it?"

Dad revved the truck. It bellowed black plumes of smoke. The kids shouted delight. The monster inched forward, then settled back. Tires spun in their ruts, throwing back coxcombs of black mud. Digging deeper. With a grinding of gears, Walter rocked the monster forward and back in the ruts. The truck lurched and bucked, kids with it, whooping like cowboys on a huge clunky bull. Tires climbed half up the grooves then fell back, cutting deeper. While we Simonet women stood aside, and Jerri said she didn't know what those idiots thought they were doing.

"Damnblast it all," Walter cried. He slammed the lever forward. The truck shook and bucked like a Brahma bull. Olson hung on. But before our eyes Meena and Jeffrey slid off the rear. They sat an instant midair before gravity took them under the truck as it rolled backwards. Jeff fell down beneath huge double tires which seized him like a shirt wringer and pulled him in.

Jerri was shrieking, while Sally and I ran to him.

Maybe it was the panic and Walter hit the gears just right. Or the truck understood its duty. Completing its pass over the boy, it rolled high up the rear side of tire ruts, then back down over Jeff again, up and over the front. Free. Brakes shrieked. The men leapt shouting from the cab. Jerri dove headfirst under the truck on her belly, slithering across mud like a snake. She pulled Meena out whole. Lifesaver fashion, a palm under her chin. A mother's instincts: to save what remains to be saved.

But Jeff!

I crawled on my knees toward tire trenches and peeked over. Others gathered silently behind me. Jeff's torso was crushed deep into tire grooves, becoming part of them, while his legs, his knees, were crooked in a sitting position over walls of the trench. Perfectly whole. I could make out his slick blue nylon jacket, a hand squashed into muck. But where his head should've been was thick red ooze, indistinguishable from mud around it. Blood, I thought. Dear God! Brains. His head a crushed pulp.

Don made a sound back in his throat. Or maybe it was me. And Walter: "Lordy lordy lord . . . " Instinctively, I grabbed my older sister, who'd dropped to her knees, clutching Meena to her chest.

"Don't look!" Swatting at Olson, who peered over my shoulder. I never saw such wonder in a face. It stopped me cold. He was pointing.

Looking back into the tire groove that had been my nephew,

I saw eyes blink open. Stare up in wide wonder. Snowy white in all that dark muck. Lips moved. Creezus. He rose like Lazarus out of the grave while we watched, our assholes puckering.

"Wow!" he cried. "It ran right over my head."

Jeff struggled to raise himself, extracting one arm with a sucking pop, then the other. Call us dumbfounded or that a miracle. We stared dumbly as he struggled free of the soft mold he had left behind. Only Olson had sense enough to help him. Tire tracks crisscrossed Jeff's jacket, mud packed his nostrils. Then— wonder exhausting horror—hysteria began. Jerri fainted dead away. Don, Meena, Olson began shrieking at once, clambering for him.

Jeff left a perfect impression: a skull-shaped pothole in soft mud, one scalloped ear, his shoulder blades. Jerri, when I'd slapped her awake, couldn't believe he was whole. She insisted we call an ambulance. Though Walter and Sally ran him through his paces: sit-ups, knee bends. He looked like an Oregon tar-baby, I'll say that.

"There's one thick bonehead if ever I saw one," Walter joked.

"Bonerhead," Olson said affectionately, still a bit awed.

"Boney," Meena cried in delight.

"You see, the ground's soft as clay after all this rain," Walter told Jerri by way of Don. "It's a thing could never happen twice."

Jerri kissed the mud off of Jeff's face. Hugging him till he squirmed and wanted to break free. But she was too angry to join in our rejoicing. Like it didn't matter pissall how fortunate we had been. Only that Don and Dad couldn't care less they ran over her children. It was a lark to them.

But Boney had earned himself a nickname. A story he never tired of embellishing. Harmless compared to other lies lived by that family as absolute truths. Those two were the only miracles ever afforded them: Don's near drowning, Boney's near mangling. Both spent in a single day.

# 2

## Jeff

Our favorite thing was the tunnel in those days, before everything went to hell in a pee bucket like Aunt Debbie says. Sometimes we dug all day, and by afternoon we were so dirty our
mothers didn't believe we had been playing tackle football. So
we told them we were down in the storm sewer at the golf
course, which was full of sewer rats and diseases, and I was
never to go down there again, which I promised Mom I wouldn't
ever, since it wasn't any lie to promise her that but the God's
truth. So I didn't feel too bad about lying in the first place.

Steve Weatherspoon said if we dug deep enough we would hit
oil. That's where oil comes from—down deep. He learned this
when his family vacationed at La Brea Tar Pits in Los Angeles.
Sometimes oil bubbles up to the surface and dries out into asphalt and animals get stuck in it. I didn't believe him at first.
But next Christmas when our family vacationed in California I
saw it for myself.

I stood looking at the tar pits in amazement—like round
swimming holes filled with black bubble gum, glazed and shiny
on top. Slowly boiling, seemed like, bubbles rising and popping
across the surface as if the world had a bad case of gas. Tar
clung to the carcasses of sloths, mastodons and saber-toothed
tigers in long stringy fingers, pulling them under, like The Blob
or a huge gooey amoeba which slowly digested them. Their eyes
and mouths were wide open with fear, and they fought against
it with all their might, but wasn't any use; every move they made
gave the tar a tighter grip. They were goners. They were only
models, Dad said, but it looked real enough to me. I could almost hear them hollering: baby mastodons that had fell in and
their mothers went in after them and got stuck, too, tar clinging
to their knees.

"Isn't that just pathetic," Mom said. She leaned on the railing in a blue dress; her sunglasses had pink plastic frames and made her look like a movie star. "All the rage," she called them. She wore them all the time, even at dinner in the hotel restaurant down in Tijuana, Mexico, when the mariachis surrounded our table and played their trumpets and guitars so loud you couldn't even eat, and she put hands over her ears and screamed at Dad to get rid of them.

"That's what mothers do," she said. "They throw caution to the wind for their children." She hugged me, her arm sweat-sticky around my neck. I leaned on the railing beside her and nudged my head into her breasts, liking her smell of Jergens lotion. On the other side of her, my sister, Meena, pushed her face away like she wanted to breathe. She said Mom's lotion smelled like baby poop. She was eight then and had an opinion on everything.

"Would you try to save us, Mom," I asked, "like their mothers did?"

"You bet she would. Anchors away," Dad said.

Mom gave him a dirty look and jiggled me. "Of course I would, honey." Her breath was damp on my cheek, smelling of sour coffee and sweet vodka. "Of course I would wade right in to save you, and I would become stuck just as the elephant did."

"It's a mammoth, Jerri," Dad corrected her. "A mastodon."

"Whatever it is. That's what moms do. Their children always come first."

"All right, Jerri, we get the picture."

Looking up at an angle inside Mom's glasses, I could see moisture swelling in her eyes, and I thought I better change subjects. But the tar fascinated me.

"It pulls them down just like quicksand. The whole family."

"Not me," Meena said. "I'm not going in that yuck."

"No, darling, your brother is kidding."

"I wonder how it feels?" I asked Dad.

He leaned on the railing, arms tanned and his shirt half un-buttoned. He thought you should wear a Hawaiian shirt when you visited California. He said he wanted to stay down there and wear a Hawaiian shirt all year long. "Maybe I could toss you out to the middle somewhere. How'd you like to swim in them waters, Cap'n?" He winked.

"Donald," Mom snapped, "you'll frighten them."

He leaned across me and whispered, "You're going to frighten everyone with those damned glasses." His smell of smoke and earth damp was completely different from Mom's. I thought I would sneeze from the combination.

Mom tilted her head away. "They protect my eyes."

"You promised me, Jerri. Do you remember?"

Dad sounded angry, and I sneezed then.

"Can we go, Don?" Mom insisted. "Jeffrey has hay fever."

Dad looked at me like I had betrayed him, then back at animals in the tar pits, his lips pressed tight together. I wanted to tell him I didn't have hay fever. But it was too late. It was the beginning of something, I knew, right there on our trip to Los Angeles. Or maybe it began earlier when Dad fooled around with Aunt Debbie on Thanksgiving. Mom and Dad had argued every night since then right up to Christmas. Actually, there wasn't much Christmas at all. Just a tree and presents. Mom hardly baked a thing—no minced meat or apricot bars. She said she couldn't be bothered. The Christmas spirit passed right over our house and didn't never look back.

My half-brother, Olson, claimed Dad finger-jobbed Aunt Debbie, even though he wasn't there. He was down at his mother's house. But when I described how Debbie's skirt was wrapped around her waist, he said that's what Dad did. It made me mad. "They were just horsing around," I told him. Maybe Dad goosed her, that's all. Then Mom walked in and dropped the turkey on the floor. So Dad took us to Los Angeles over Christmas vacation. Maybe he was sorry. Maybe he wanted to make up.

Meena pointed at saber tooths, which she called lions. Two of them had jumped a sloth and tore its stomach wide open, but one had got its hindquarters stuck in the tar, and you could see it was a goner. The other one, too.

"The lion's got buck teeth," my dumb sister said.

"Saber-toothed cat." Dad smiled that small way he did, showing a peek of brown dead tooth on top. "Whole happy family going down together—including the house pets."

"Donald!"

"Yeah," I said, "pretty neat."

But it was awful really. Life was awful in primitive times.

Everything ate everything else and the tar ate them all together like the earth's stomach.

"You've heard the expression *tooth and claw*. There's a perfect example of tooth and claw."

An old white-haired couple stood listening to Dad with their heads tilted to the side. Maybe they thought he was a tour guide.

"Are you addressing the children?" Mom asked.

"*Smilodon californicus*, that's Latinate for saber-toothed tiger," Dad told the old people. "We began classifying creatures by Latin names with Linnaeus. *Mammuthus imperator*, *Mammut americanum*, the American mastodon." Dad pointed at the hairy elephant in the pit. He knew everything in those days.

The old man nodded, smiling without opening his lips. The woman stared at Dad's exposed chest. She seemed confused.

"What we have here is the early discovery of black gold. Pretty darned tough way to discover oil." Dad grinned. The old man grinned with him.

Standing between him and Mom, I tried to decide which of them I loved most. They never asked, but it was something they wanted to know, I knew it was. All those extinct animals stuck in the tar made you wonder about things like that. I knew if we fell in I would try and save Meena first, then Mom, because that was the correct order. But I expected Dad to save us all. I couldn't decide how to translate that into love: who you loved more—the one you rescued or the one who rescued you. It was the kind of thing Pastor Nordstrom gave sermons about, the kind of thing you have to think about a long time. But I knew if Mom wouldn't let me rescue her or Dad wouldn't try to save us, I couldn't love them anymore. Because there are basic rules even to love.

"Jeff's got on his Einstein Cap." Dad leaned over and smiled at Mom.

She ducked to look into my face, neck scooping, glasses like tilting, pink-tiled pools with her eyes swimming beneath. "Darling, what are you thinking about?"

"Nothing," I said. "Just thinking."

"Watch it, buddy." Dad tapped my skull. "You'll get stuck and never think another thunk the rest of your life."

He was tan and smiling and full of California, so I couldn't tell if he was kidding. I put it all out of my mind. It was dumb thinking like that anyhow.

Steve's idea was to get rich from the oil. I wanted to find fossils. All I thought about when we dug our tunnel was mastodons with their mouths wide open and their trunks up at La Brea Tar Pits like they were screaming. More than anything I hoped to find curved saber-toothed tiger incisors down below. I picked out a spot on my bedroom shelf to put them, crossed like swords.

"Forget it," Steve Weatherspoon said one day in the tunnel. "If we strike oil it will gush out in a geyser. We'll be black and oil will get in our eyes and ears. So you can just forget about finding fossils." In my flashlight beam (we taped flashlights to our army helmets, which we wore down there), Steve made a Marlboro Man grimace. Fishing a wrinkled paper out of his back pocket, he unfolded it on the bumpy dirt floor. It was a picture tore from *Life* magazine of roughnecks in Arabia covered with black gunky oil like mastodons in La Brea. It rained down on them from a geyser as tall as Old Faithful, and they were trying to fit a pipe over it.

Steve tapped the picture. "That's what it's gonna look like."

"Wow," I said. "I know." I was fascinated. The men looked spooky in our flashlight beams, smears of red clay across their faces—like men dug up from the center of the earth.

"Won't it get over the houses and trees?"

Steve shrugged as if that was part of the deal. His hair was cut in a skin-top crew cut with a tuft sticking up at front, so oil wouldn't clog in it when we struck. I imagined him with oil covering his head—square except the round chin on bottom— and it made me laugh.

"What's so funny, fruitcake?"

"Your head," I said.

Steve slugged me, I slugged back, we both pretended it didn't hurt. We sat cross-legged on the sloping floor of the tunnel with our necks bent. Barely high enough to sit up down there, and it twisted down steeply, the walls bumpy and irregular—like a mole's tunnel magnified. We had dug fifteen feet three inches from the entrance and Steve figured we were nine feet under.

Deeper than a corpse. Up top, little hairy roots stuck out like spider legs, but farther down was solid red dirt crisscrossed by black streaks and rocks thrown in. Completely dark down there, because we covered the entrance when we went below so no one would discover us. It smelled like the inside of a trunk that had been closed a long time. The air was thick, and we had to surface regularly to revive our breath. Steve rammed his shovel tip into the wall and scraped some dirt into a gunnysack.

"Shhhh," I said, "I hear somebody."

We stopped to listen.

"Turn off your beam," Steve whispered.

Maybe it was footsteps. Our third-most worry was Meena would find us and tattle. Second-most was our moms would find us and make us quit digging. First-most was the Double Dutch Clutches. We were the Long Loop Boys. Without the rest of our gang, they would whale on us. There was a scratching sound up by the entrance. I could sense Steve's eyeballs popping from their sockets, but I couldn't see them. Then came three long knocks and two short on the hatch.

"Di-dow," said a small voice, far away.

"Dow-di," we both answered.

The lid came off and sunlight turned around the hairy corner, blinding us. Buck's round head was silhouetted against blue sky, his ears stuck out. You couldn't mistake it for anybody else. Steve pushed past me; I crawled up on my hands and knees behind him.

"You scared the pee out of us," he said up top.

"I come to dig," Buck said.

"You can't dig when you scare people like that. Whewy, I thought we were done for." Steve was red as a maraschino cherry.

"Me too."

Buck looked back and forth between us. "Double Duth-ths?" he lisped. We nodded. His eyes squinted across blackberry vines and bushes surrounding us. Dad called him "old cue-head" 'cause his noggin was perfectly round, his crew cut even shorter than Steve's, and his hair was only slightly darker than his skin. In the summer when he had a tan, you couldn't tell where skin stopped and hair began. He got so dark that teenagers rode by in their cars and shouted "nigger." That made me mad. Nigger callers are niggers theirselves.

Nobody could spy on us from the blackberries, but the rest was little leafy stuff that could hide an army. Still, it was the best place in the neighborhood to mine for oil: Old man Ashcroft's empty lot beside the compost heap. You had to crawl through bushes on your belly to get inside there, so nobody would find the entrance in a million years—unless they followed us or it was Meena. She could find anything. We were digging under the compost heap, because Steve and Olson agreed we would find oil under there for sure. Compost heaps always produce oil if they rot long enough. Everyone knows that.

"We got to change the password," Steve said. "Before Long Loops come in the circle they got to whistle." He stuck two fingers in his mouth and made a shrill thirr-rrr sound. When Buck tried it, it came out lispy.

"Who says you say so?" I asked. "You're not honcho."

"When Olson's gone I am." Steve had piggy eyes when he looked determined. "Right, Buck?"

Buck looked at his feet and nodded. By age, he should have been number two, but it was a common fact Steve was smarter. Besides, the tunnel was his idea.

"Still," I said, "we got to vote."

"How can we vote when Olson is at school and Gary Seamore has baseball practice?"

"Olson will be home this weekend," I said.

"Okay," Steve said, "but until then we got to whistle."

We agreed. Buck said he could dig a booby trap while we worked below—only he called it a "boobth trap"—which was a hole covered with twigs and leaves that a spy would fall in before reaching the tunnel hatch.

"You know what a booby trap is?" Steve asked. "It's your mom's bra." We laughed; it was a good one. But I was worried Meena might fall in the trap by mistake.

"Wouldn't hurt a Double Dutch or a grown-up much, but she would prob'ly get killed or something."

"Nah, it won't be tho deep," Buck said.

Steve and me crawled back into the tunnel and pulled the hatch overhead. Down below was a damp, mushroomy smell like a grave; it filled your nose and made you dizzy and drowsy—only except the stale underarm smell of Steve and his butt in my face.

"Turn off your flath-light a thecond," he said, mimicking Buck. I was afraid he might goose me or fart, but I did it anyway. Up top, we could hear Buck digging, making huffing sounds; the clank of his shovel came right down through the ground. "The amazing thing," said Steve in a quiet voice, "we're the first human beings to feel this dirt—even back before the Indians."

"Yeah," I said, a little awed, touching the wall with my hand. It was cool and greasy.

"I figure at thirty feet we'll strike oil." Steve snapped on his beam. He looked like a small, serious, square-headed underground mole-man.

For a second, I wondered if I was dreaming. Then my beam passed in front of him. A face stared back at me from the bumpy dirt wall. A woman's face buried inside the dirt, her eyes glowing like mica, looking right into me. I yelled and my beam went crazy across the walls. I scrambled for the top, clawing at dirt with my fingernails. Behind me, Steve was hollering, "Shuddup . . . *Shuddup*," our echoes fighting each other down the tunnel.

When I looked back the face was gone.

"Criminy," Steve cried, "you almost bust my eardrums. Are you a gonad or something?"

I was staring at the spot where the face had been. Maybe it was a vision, like when people saw Jesus or the Virgin Mary. Only this was shaggy-haired and bug-eyed like a picture I saw of a bog man in the *National Geographic*, who fell into a bog in England ten thousand years ago and turned into a mummy.

"Who was it?" I whispered.

"Who was what?"

"A face. I saw a face in the wall."

Steve looked where I shined my beam, then back at me. He frowned. "Dirt. Just red old dirt."

"It was my mom," I said softly.

Steve stared at me kinda weird. It surprised me too when I said it, because, really, it looked more like Mom's kid sister, Aunt Debbie, who was a stewardess in Portland.

Up top, Buck peered down at us, his face hung upside down, crinkled by concern, his eyes slit. He prob'ly thought we had struck oil with all the hollering, and he wanted to get us out of there before we drowned in the tar.

# 3

# Meena

She hid, sly as a spider, flat on her belly on a dry nest of bayberry leaves, feasting on the boys' secrets. Boney would say something silly like, "Meena would probably be killed if she fell in." It was all she could do not to giggle, pinching her nostrils between thumb and index finger, scarcely breathing in the dusty old-slipper-pelt-on-a-dog's-back smell of her secret places. Careful, very careful not to move. Branches poked her through the T-shirt, finger-tickled soft zones behind her knees. Jeff (she'd nicknamed him Boney the day truck tires rolled over his head) told Steve she was a ghost. You'd turn around and presto! She appeared out of thin air. Steve said Boney was always saying gonadal stuff. After scoring highest in school on the Stanford Achievement Test, Steve thought he was smarter than Mark Van Doren. He was a boner. Later, when she had breasts, she would enjoy teasing him. But that was later. Now she wanted to tear his ears off. He was telling Buck how Boney had seen his own mom's face buried in the dirt. Buck's features bunched together accordion fashion, all wrinkles and crinkled eyes, laughter squawking out of him.

"Only a spas would see something like that," Steve said.

"But I saw it," Boney insisted.

" 'I saw it . . . ,' " Steve mimicked.

"I did." Boney was on the verge of tears. He stiff-armed Steve, but Steve, who was learning jujitsu, seized her brother's arm and spun him around, forcing it up behind his back. "Uncle?" he demanded. Boney grimaced. She wanted to pounce on Steve, go for the soft places with her fingernails—his ever-peeling nose and armpits. But spiders could spin her hair into their webs, millipedes could tickle paths across her skin, she wouldn't move. This was her secret power: making people talk about her.

Once, in the old house on Walnut Street, she hid in the hall closet outside her parents' room, scrunched in with the Hoover and ironing board, listening to her parents' muffled voices beyond the thin wall. Daddy told Mommy she couldn't imagine the pain of losing a daughter. Meena's heart quickened, but gradually it became clear he meant the daughter who had come before her: Sitka, who went off with Daddy's first wife when they divorced. Mommy said she was sick and tired of hearing about her. "You've started a new life, Don. Maybe if you forgot the old one you'd stop neglecting your family. Your little girl."

"Meena? Meena knows I love her."

"Neglecting me," Mommy said in a strained voice.

Bedsprings heaved. "Sitka is my daughter, for crissake."

"I'm your wife."

"Well . . . sure," he chuckled, "sure you are." He made cooing, smothered sounds. Mommy was snuffling . . . or giggling. That was still a time she might do either. Daddy suggested Aunt Debbie come live with them while she was going to college. "We have room. Hell, I'd be lonely, too. Just the kids around all day."

"Don't you say a word about my children," Mommy snapped.

That was the earlier time, before Mommy became angry for no reason, before some unnameable force entered their house, bringing with it a gloom of depression and unhappiness that emerged out of nowhere and cast its spell over them—gray storm clouds that sneaked up from the cellar and pressed outward against windowpanes, so she couldn't stand in their brightness without being swathed in shadow. The time when her brothers slept upstairs in the attic, beyond the storeroom where her half-brother Olson said a bear had its den. It was safe up there, above murky waters below, where storms arrived unannounced, whipping up froth.

When the boys had gone, she emerged from her hiding place, lifting aside the lid Olson had cleverly disguised with twigs and leaves. The cave's breath was moist and moldy as a basement. Her Brownie flashlight cut a trail through snaking darkness as

she inch-wormed on knees and elbows over the earthen floor.
Near the entrance, walls were pocked with the cross-sectioned
burrows of gophers and moles. She half-hoped, half-feared a
buck-toothed rodent's snout would poke out of a hole as she
squeezed past. She'd watched gophers working the field above,
snuffling dirt from runways into crescent-shaped mounds like
tiny bulldozers. Perhaps gophers considered the Long Loop Boys
a larger species of burrowing rodents.

She was hurt that the boys excluded her from their search for
oil. The Long Loops had let her join them as a junior member;
they wanted her on their side in games of steal the flag, since
she was best at finding the other team's flag. She had assumed
that when she was old enough they would make her a full member. But in the tunnel she saw for the first time a code at work
in the world: Boys were boys and girls were girls. The tunnel
was a boy thing. Carefully guarded. She felt an illicit thrill invading it, violating a taboo. Getting even. Steve Weatherspoon
would be furious if he found her there, Olson, too. But Boney
would forgive her. After all, he had given her the flashlight.

She searched for her mother's face in the wall—bulging cod-
fish eyes, lower lip jutting out in a perpetual pout, like her
own—staring out from a hatching of nicks and gouges. She
didn't doubt it was there. Like Daniel in the Bible, Boney often
saw signs and wonders, while she smelled them. Would it be
pasted there like the baseball cards lining walls of the boys' bedroom? Hovering like a black-and-white image on TV? Embossed
as in a dream? She pushed her fingers into silky crevasses, feeling
for her mother's profile. Pushing her nose against hard pack, she
inhaled its clean earthiness: a smell of growth and trickling water, spicy ozone damp, or the dank cellar smell of the house on
Walnut Street, Daddy's workbench littered with burnt match-
sticks, the night-crawler smell of time itself, a time she might
label "happy" before that war which seemed pointless and end-
less had begun between Mommy and Daddy: terrible screeching
battles after the kids were put to bed and she sneaked up to be
safe with her brothers in the attic bedroom. All three of them
huddled at foot of the attic stairs, listening. Olson interpreting:
*Now he's pee-o'd, now she's gonna throw something.* That terrible time the door was flung open and two red straining faces
loomed overhead, veins taut at necks, hands reaching down to

pull them out, though Olson managed to flee into the bear closet, where neither she nor Boney dared follow.

Children like you, nosy children, must have their ears washed out with soap. Mouths too.

Even in that earlier time, she would come to understand, there was nothing like stability. Or happiness. Only sudden manic flights when Mommy led them outside in her negligee and they did a giddy impromptu Maypole dance, round and round, holding hands under a warm rain that soaked them to the skin and turned Mommy's nightie to transparent cellophane clinging to her breasts and stomach. She tossed back her blood-black hair and piped out shrill arpeggios of laughter, Olson giggling, Boney delighted—along with grinning old Mr. Carpenter, whose face was cupped between his hands in the window next door. Round and round until Daddy came out and asked if they'd gone loopy, laughing in a husky, nervous way.

Even then she knew nothing could be predicted of her mother's flighty moods. By afternoon, Mommy would be sullen again, pointlessly angry. She might bend them over a knee for setting a place mat crookedly on the supper table, slapping bare flesh until her palm was too hot to continue or she grew bored with their wailing. It didn't mean she was angry any more than a silent quadrille in the rain meant she was happy. What it meant Meena wanted desperately to understand. Before it was too late to reverse what begins as moodiness or fickle experiment, then becomes habit, and finally destiny.

Her small roving hands explored a stain black as India ink on the red clay wall, glazed and angry, recessed a little, like the charred oblong weal in Daddy's workbench from the time Olson tried to burn down the house. She was afraid to see what Boney had seen: a visage pieced together of taut cartilage and knotted red flesh, eye and nostril sockets gaping—Mommy's face that first time she had "lost it," seizing Olson's arm, dragging him clomp by clomp up cellar steps, smoke wisps trailing behind, and two younger children screaming bloody murder for their half-brother, whose mouth was clamped in defiance.

Her hands skittered over embedded rocks. She was awed that the past could be recorded there in aggregate—the future, too, maybe—locked in images like those glazed in crockery . . . if you knew how to see them. Her flashlight beam leapt across bumps and gouges to a damp zone in the wall, behind which lay a hidden spring. Moisture oozed surfaceward, forming a wet blister which swelled around her fingertip until a single drop separated and trickled down the wall, adding to slushiness beneath her knees. It had rained two days before and water continued to trickle down to the huge ocean at the center of the earth, which she had heard her brothers talk about.

Placing her tongue against the wall, she tasted mineral dampness tart as a dime. Like rain on her tongue that terrible morning she stood in back of the house on Walnut Street, peering up through branches at her mother sitting half-naked in the tree house. Water dripped from leaves and shone like shattered glass across the lawn. The night before, after a terrible row, Mommy had fled out into the storm in her underwear and had remained missing until Mr. Carpenter called next morning to say Mrs. Tillotson was sleeping in the children's tree house in the rain and wasn't that odd. They found her in the crotch of the huge old oak "amphaloola" tree, her teeth chattering so violently she couldn't speak, but wouldn't let them bring her down. So Dr. Byrnes had to stand up on a rickety wooden ladder and administer a hypodermic in her thigh. Even then she wouldn't come down until Aunt Debbie climbed up into the tree, holding an umbrella over their heads.

Afraid the tunnel would close in and swallow her, Meena fled, replacing Olson's lid and crawling on her belly through the path she had burrowed in the bushes. But footsteps and muttering beyond the circle of brush made her freeze. Someone poked the bushes with a stick. Double Dutches, she thought. Walt Whitaker or Jerry Stitt, who picked on her at the bus stop and threatened to whale on Boney when he defended her. No matter what they do, she decided, I won't tell them about the cave.

It wasn't a stick at all but the shiny poking head of a golf club. Its owner muttered soft curses. Through the foliage, she made out green slacks, an unbuttoned vest from which spilled fleece stained the yellow of smokers' teeth. Glasses slipped down old Mr. Ashcroft's nose, wispy white hair scattered across his forehead, his legs splayed at awkward angles; from below he looked like a wobbly gateleg table about to collapse. The boys told stories about what Mr. Ashbutt did to kids he caught in his lot. Girls especially. He was a fruitcake, a D.O.M. From her low angle, he looked it: his face steamy red, rheumy blue eyes peering intently down through the bushes at her.

He poked at leaf litter with the golf club. She realized what he wanted was the round lump under her belly. He often came to chip golf balls into gopher holes on his empty lot. The club head whacked blindly at branches just inches from her nose. Keeping her eyes on it, she wormed a hand under her stomach, seized the golf ball and threw it in the path of the probing club. There was a sharp click. Mr. Ashcroft tilted his head like a robin.

"What?"

Meena licked her lips. The club had knocked the ball deep into blackberry vines. Mr. Ashbutt steadied himself on one leg and leaned down to peer into the bushes. His eyes, the luminous blue of a cold winter sky, looked blankly into hers. Cautiously, she reached for the ball through a tangle of sharp thorns, grabbed it and rolled it out under Mr. Ashbutt's feet.

"What?" he asked again, nearly stumbling. "Well, I'll be, I'll be." Propping himself—club angled out to one side like a cane— he looked again into the bramble, features stretched in a wide grin, lines in his face cinching taut. "Golf leprechauns in the berry bushes," he chuckled, reaching gradually down and gripping the ball in his huge hand.

"My father's hands were big enough to cover both my knees at once," she remembered. "He smelled of Old Spice, pressed shirts and pencil shavings. He would cup my forehead when I sat on his lap and brush my bangs away with a finger. I loved that; I wanted him to stroke my head all day long. Such huge hands . . . to a child. I loved the veins: blue cords roping over parallel bones. I would be cupped there entirely in those hands— my knees, my head. And while he stroked me I stroked those veins. He liked that."

There was a time when Mommy would stop and smile. She saw her mother's face framed in a television screen: smiling, placid. When Meena thought back on those days, memories were always in black and white, as if that time was made for TV. The time and the tube had invented each other. She saw Mommy smiling, glad her husband had found another daughter. She wasn't sure when the smile faded, when Mommy had first busied herself whenever her baby sat on Daddy's lap—clattering dishes, banging cupboards, her back squarely to them. But she remembered the smile. It faded about the time Aunt Debbie came to live with them, the time of thunderstorms when Mommy taught her to hide.

A vivid image struck her as if framed in time. A flash of truth that blinded in its stark simplicity. A veined hand, large as Mr. Ashcroft's, hopping from her knee, hanging in flight like a locust before lighting hungrily on Aunt Debbie's ass as she passed in the kitchen—round and firm in the khaki Capri pants she wore about the house that summer. For a moment, Daddy's palm cupped her bottom. Meena giggled: just a silly game, she thought. Aunt Debbie paused, the dip above her buttocks hollowing, shoulders rigid. She was beautiful, Meena thought.

Both Debbie and Mommy turned as if connected by a single nervous matrix—two sisters. Upper lips beaked and pouty, pulling disdainfully away from teeth. "Would you mind?" Aunt Debbie asked. Mommy's eyes asked more angrily. The smell of maple syrup hung on breakfast air, bacon sizzled and left its greasy streaks across memory. Daddy's Adam's apple bobbed, he grinned foolishly and opened his hands as if to say: They're only hands, what do you expect of them? Mommy lurched forward and yanked her from his lap. Always the right arm, wrenched again and again from its socket. Years later the body remembered: It was her bursitis shoulder.

My mother taught me to hide—she was certain of that.

On Walnut Street during one of those violent thunderstorms that came each September. She couldn't recall a single electrical storm when her father was home. It was always just after the boys had come home from school. The sky grew dark and Mommy moved anxiously from room to room, making certain they were away from windows. Then, as thunder rolled and grumbled in the distance, she stood, head craned sideways, eyes straining, humidity puffing her hair in a dark mousse. Mommy moved quickly to switch off the lamp, throwing the room into gloomy darkness, perhaps fearing domesticated electricity would attract its wild ancestor.

"Take off anything metal," she commanded in a hushed, ominous tone. "Olson, Jeffrey! Belt buckles. Quickly!" Seizing Boney, who was moving too slowly and pulling his belt through hoops with an angry hiss, while he stood rigid. "Lunch money!"

She stripped his pockets inside out; they hung dumbly, like elephant ears. Olson leapt beyond her reach, muttering something about mixed nuts.

"Meena, move!" Mommy shrieked. "Take off those shoes this instant, those are metal buckles."

Mommy fell on her, yanking bobby pins from her hair and gobs of hair with them. But what started Meena shrieking was a palpable scent of fear coming off her mother, like scorched flesh, filling the cramped attic room. She clung to Mommy's pants creases, front and back. Mommy leapt for Olson, who had put his hand on a metal lamp, as a thunder crack tore air to shreds overhead.

"You little idiot. Lightning follows metal."

"What's your problem?" he lipped, ten years old.

"Quick, children!" Mommy shouted. "Down to the basement, hold hands, keep away from windows and sinks."

Passing through the kitchen, Boney slid against the wall to avoid the refrigerator, Meena slid behind him. Olson stepped forward and planted a kiss against it just as a flash lit up the dark house, all the scalding light of heaven pouring through windows and walls. Mommy framed in white light in the doorway behind as if she had stuck her fingers in an outlet. It seemed her skeleton was visible within her skin, like the X-ray machine at the foot doctor's. Then it was dark again. Mommy gripped the thick tail of hair at the nape of Olson's neck and hurled him headlong down the stairs.

Boney was afraid of the brass knob on the basement door. Wasn't it metal too? He grasped it with his shirttail.

"Pansy," Olson scowled, elbowing him aside.

Then they were in the earthy dark. Safe from lightning that zigzagged across the sky above in search of metal and flesh. "Water, too," Mommy warned. "You boys keep away from those pipes." It followed them down into the ground, where it cooked small creatures and earthworms in their lairs. Meena could smell their tiny steaming corpses.

Mommy had brought down matches and candle stubs in her pockets. They huddled on fruit crates in a circle, staring at feeble blue and yellow flames, while thunder stalked through rooms overhead. Meena hugged her mother's chest—occasional rapid tremors translating from mother's body into daughter's. Daddy was dead, his car cut in half by a lightning bolt on his way home from work. Later, when they opened the cellar door, they would peer up through black smoldering remnants of the house at a gray sky flushing buckets of rain on a charred landscape. Already, she could smell wet ashes combined with the mildewed cold concrete fishy earthworm gut yeasty sewer trap smell of the cellar.

The boys were amusing themselves hunting salamanders in dank corners when Daddy opened the cellar door. He must have thought they were holding a séance. "What in the name of common sense? You scared the daylights out of me, Jerri. I saw your car but no one was in the house."

"The lightning, Don." Mommy's eyes blinked against bare basement bulbs; she composed her face in a smile. "I was just about to go see if it was over."

Daddy watched her carefully. "You had to hide in the basement?"

"She made us take our belts off," Olson said peevishly.

"Your belts?"

"Buckles, Don. There's metal in the buckles."

"I suppose. What's metal got to do with it?"

"For heaven's sake, Donald. You were in the war. They must have taught you these things in the war."

"Well, I dunno." He seemed leery of her, his eyes narrowed. "How's my little beauty?" he asked, pinching Meena's cheek.

"Know what else, Dad, she said we can't touch the pipes." Olson wore what Aunt Debbie called his wise-ass frown, pale lips forced together in a jagged line. His nostrils scooped in underneath, tip of his nose beaking sharply, so that his upper lip seemed unusually long and sarcastic.

"That's something I've heard." Daddy nodded. "I've heard people say keep clear of pipes and windows during electric storms. Kind of an old wives' tale, I guess."

"This old wife happens to be young."

"I didn't mean . . . Look, Jerr, no need to scare the kids," he said in that mock whisper adults use to inform children they shouldn't be listening. "You're white as sheets."

"She practically broke my arm," Olson whined.

"Okay. Let it rest, buster. Go on, you guys. Upstairs." Behind them, they heard Daddy tell Mommy she should call his office next time there was a storm. "You could talk to one of the girls—if I'm tied up. Might make you feel better."

"Oh, could I? . . . If you're tied up," she mocked. "Over my dead body. You know as well as I do that you can't touch a phone during a thunderstorm."

On the landing, Olson's mouth fastened hot and obscene over Meena's ear. "I'm glad I don't have a fruitcake mother."

"You're the fruitcake," she shouted back at him.

Boney leapt on his back, smacking wildly at his big brother's head with small fists. For a moment, Olson tottered, nearly toppling down the steep stairs. Then he chopped back an elbow and Boney went down, clutching his belly. "Nut case, nut case"—Olson leered over him—"your mom is a nut case."

Daddy whacked his butt from behind. "Can it, Olson." Lifting her under the arms, he cuddled Meena to his chest. "Nothing to be afraid of, Princess." He smiled. "All safe."

But Daddy's smile wasn't safe; it looked yanked out crumpled from the closet and thrown hurriedly on. He treated Mommy cautiously that night, as you might treat a sick person. Maybe he thought she was a fruitcake, too.

Through that time she visited, Aunt Debbie refused to hide in the cellar during thunderstorms. "It's your funeral," Mommy yelled, rushing the kids down the steps ahead of her.

"Okay if I take a bath?" Aunt Debbie shouted back.

When the storm ended, Debbie would come for them, making an "All clear" sound. "Time for a body count." Boney would play dead, lying on the cold concrete floor, while his sister screeched excitement. Debbie leaned over him, tight slacks bunching at hips, smelling of Woolite and bubble bath. They would probe under his ribs and armpits, while Boney squirmed and giggled, holding his breath until his neck flushed vermilion. Olson stood by with a transfusion of water, waiting for the right moment to splash the glassful in Boney's face. Finally, Mommy would tap Aunt Debbie's shoulder. "Don't you think that's about enough?"

"Oh c'mon, Jerri, they love it."

"I don't. Jeffrey, get up off that cold floor. You'll catch your death." Turning icily to her sister. "I don't appreciate your disrespect."

"Pee whiskers, and you know it is."

"Watch your mouth around the children, Deb-or-ah."

"Do you know how you sound? Do you?"

Standing face-to-face beneath bare basement bulbs, unmistakably sisters: identical slope of foreheads and uptilted nostrils, Mommy's face fuller, Debbie's elongate like Grandpa Walter's, cheekbones prominent but hollowing to near concavities in the sweep to her chin; Mommy's cheeks tended to puffy at that time of the month, while Debbie, when fatigued or periody or ill, became gaunt. Both possessed the same thick hair, so red it was black or so black it compressed to a rubicundity full of purple lights. Mommy went in for fancy perms, but Debbie piled long straight hair atop her head in a simple coil. She was the trimmer, Mommy hippier and more buxom—hers a woman's full figure— while Debbie possessed the lithe figure of a girl, high pointed breasts and shallow hips. Meena would always feel inferior before their beauty—the older sister's distinctly Anglo-Saxon, while the younger's seemed proof of Indian blood said to run in Simonet veins.

The sisters faced off, while the children drifted upstairs, wanting no part of this, hearing Mommy demand: "Who needs another kid around here—I have two of my own."

"Three," Debbie reminded her.

"I meant . . . technically. Three."

Olson kicked the riser before him as he went up the stairs. Below, the sisters argued, voices rising and falling, bickering. Debbie's voice curt and rapid, Mommy's slurring vowels. They argued over what was allowed and what wasn't, and Debbie kept telling her not to have a "conniption."

Daddy thought Mommy would enjoy having her sister around the house to help with chores and chew the fat over coffee. But Mommy didn't want her in the kitchen, was reluctant to leave the children in her hands. Behind closed doors, Meena heard her say she didn't trust the girl.

However, it was Aunt Debbie who'd climbed into the tree house to rescue her sister on that horrible Sunday morning, wrapping a raincoat around her. Below, Meena watched, her own teeth chattering uncontrollably, as Debbie bent over her mother's ashen face and ink-dark hair clinging like a shapeless cap to her skull. Daddy stood looking hopelessly upward, lost, defeated, eyes bruised with sleeplessness, the dimples in his cheeks hollow pits. While Boney kept asking why Mommy didn't come down, why she wouldn't answer him, bewildered by the desperate, obsessive ways of adults. Overhead, Debbie repeated, "But you can't stay here, honey. You know that." They held hands—younger and older sister—and Mommy must have trusted her then, because after a time she lifted her head and said it was all right, they could bring her down if they must.

# 4

## Aunt Debbie

Meena Cybele Tillotson. My niece.

Alfred Olson Tillotson. Chip off the old block.

Jeffrey Ronald Tillotson. I love that little fart.

Jerri Lee Tillotson. My big sis. I do love her, but at times it's f'ing hard.

Don Tillotson. Smooth talker. He could sell stupidity to the Russians. I've never blamed him for marrying Jerri. He was Mr. Up-'n'-Coming, he needed a beautiful wife. He had a son. Maybe he loved her.

Imagine naming your kids Olson and Ophelia. Americans love their airs. Ophelia vamoosed with Don's first wife (I've only seen pictures). Isn't that cute? Divide the kids like household goods: her to Mom, him to Dad. Guess I can't get modern. By ten, I hear, she'd changed her name to Sitka (for the spruce?). Name your kid Ophelia, see what you get. I won't pass judgment; it's passed often enough on me.

I haven't had to live through the mess—only the one year of it before I quit college and started flying, while things were still Norman Rockwell cozy . . . at first! Shit crystals, they were so cuddly-lovey. At twenty, I wanted to puke. Don hadn't started to fondle me yet, only ogle. Men learn to be dogs step by step. Sniff and drool. Later they pant. If it runs unchecked, you see

fantasies on mucousy surfaces of their eyeballs; they lose control
of their hands. Even dogs paw more elegantly. It's progressive,
like Parkinson's. But he's Jerri's problem. She's his. What a f'ing
disaster.

Olson worried me. He was the odd man out as soon as Jerri
had her own. She was like a girl with a pair of dolls. Couldn't
be bothered with someone else's. Those first years, he threw
screaming tantrums, and she locked him out of the house. They
honed nerves on each other, those two, until they were sharp as
flint. It was like two high-strung horses in the same stall.

Women learn to give up step by step. It's ingrained as doggy-
bonkers for the boys. First, small insecurities, little odd obses-
sions. Then the bury-my-heart-in-my-children routine. Jerri
played at mothering: changed their clothes a dozen times a day
if it suited her whim, dressing and undressing them like Barbie
and Ken dolls. Then the regretting began: quitting college,
housework, having kids so young—whole shitty ball of wax. In
truth, I never remember Jerri happy. Not even as a girl. I try to
understand her pain. She's my sister after all.

She says I've been lucky, thinks stewardess is a Ka-reer, thinks
glamour is living out of a suitcase in six American cities at once.
Jerri envies my collection of a-holes' apartment keys, spinning
and clattering on the mobile above my bed. Honey, I tell her,
these studs carry a pocketful of spares. Every time they meet a
girl in a bar they offer her a key, like their sexual business-card
thing. Come up and see me sometime. Sure thing. Walk right in:
half a dozen gals lined up across the bed like grilled wieners. Oh
boy! Roll over, girls, make room for me. They make a good
mobile, turning and jingling. "Jupiter's nuts," I call it. Every
now and again I wink at some Mr. Hornytoad in first class and
present him a key just given me by an a-hole in tourist. I flick
my tongue at his ear. "Come up and see me tonight, hon."
That's the only fun there is in it. Imagining one a-hole unlocking
another's door. You've got to be getting a bit desperate to see
any glamour in that.

Then Jerri embarks upon that one big obsession to which all
others magnet like lint to a sock. Drink, Miltowns, uppers or
ice-cold hysteria. Homebound bitchiness. Or a combination.
Used to be. Now it's got more complicated: eating disorders,
spas, workaholism. Drink, in Jerri's case. You try to recall a time

you first noticed. How old the kids were then. Whether you were living sixty percent in Boston or Portland. Was it before they moved from Walnut Street to Ro-day-o loop? Before Don grabbed me in the kitchen that Thanksgiving and pushed his hand in my drawers or shortly after?

The kids and everyone in the dining room, chattering. And I thought for a moment I would let it happen, curious to see how bad a case he had. Then Jerri appeared, framed in the dining room doorway behind him, carrying a platter with the half-devoured bird. Her eyes hard-shrunk gimlets in the general gravy of their sockets. Boozed. Jellied. They shrunk smaller into cold points. No use pretending we had bumped accidentally or Don was picking a flake of turkey from my blouse collar. He'd got it open and was feasting on my bra. My skirt hitched up. Jerri dropped the platter. Smithereens. Grandma Sally's best hand-me-down hand-painted Syracuse china with the trout and water hyacinth. All to bitty bits.

I didn't smile. Didn't speak. Just backed off. I tried to communicate: He's your hound dog, hon, you should train him better. She had the carving fork in her hand. For a moment, I thought she would dig its tines into Don's back. I would have. He leaned forward into the vacuum between us, back hunched, eyes droopy-stupid. Goofy as a puppy. But the children were behind her. You wouldn't murder a child's father in front of them. Besides, it was me she wanted. She came on jiggling the fork at chin level.

"Dirty little hussy, get out of my home."

"Don't do anything foolish," Don said.

"Careful," I said. "It's my tender spot."

Jerri's feet crunched on porcelain shards. I stared down at her stockinged toes on the glass—one foot had caught the pope's nose and pinned it to tiles. I was thinking how clever it was she'd done her toenails the color of blood oozing around her feet. Jerri was smart that way. Don looked, too. The doggy phase had passed. He was people again. The kids stood either side of their mom gawking at my dress tucked into my pants. It was a picture they wouldn't never forget. "If that's what you want to believe," I said. "Happy Thanksgiving." I went without a fight. It was their mess after all.

There's a saying they have in Gamblers Anonymous: A house

of cards is not a home. But when it crashes all comes with it. Isn't a thing wrong with drinking, or maybe drugs, or wagering. It's all the mess to clean up after. By then it was something had already come to live with them. I'm pretty sure of that.

Already, that last summer on Walnut Street, the house was rigged with booby traps. Mornings, a vaporous breath of vodka rose from Jerri's coffee mug. Sitting across the dining nook table, I'd ask if there was anything, you know, she wanted to discuss. I was flying by then and thought I could help take anything off the ground. A marriage maybe.

She'd titter like it was the stupidest question.

Olson maybe? Our beloved brother, Chuck?

Jerri's eyes would spook—and I'd think it hadn't been a smart thing to say—then they glazed over. She had a way of recovering, my big sister. Dropping low as Lazarus, then springing back. Laughing. "Did you enjoy your sun bath yesterday?" she might ask. "I was watching out the kitchen window."

She didn't know the half of it. That was right out in the open sunlight: her hubby rubbing suntan lotion on my back, while his womenfolk watched. Jerri in the kitchen window. Meena hidden behind a row of beans in the garden. Not the half of it. How he knocked on my door at two A.M., asking if I'd like a shot of brandy. While Olson was less subtle. He'd hop right in the sack with me. Two mothers already and the poor duffer was love-starved, wanting to crawl between my tits. I'd dump him on the floor. Feeling like a f'ing family confection. Jeff wanted nothing but to cuddle. Little mutt. Already sensing his mama's distraction, resigned to it in that perplexed, accepting way of children. He would be all right. He possessed his mama's bounce, his daddy's glide. His big halibut eyes, features overlarge for a child. So gawking ugly with his mop top of dusty hair he was almost cute.

It was Meena who worried me. She turned up like a spider in impossible places. If a light bulb burnt out with a flash, she'd run screaming holy terror for the basement stairs. There was the Christmas Don hired a private Santa. Grandma Sally was there; Dad, too, that Christmas before he died. Don's brother, Alfred. Eggnog and a beautiful tree chockablock with gifts. A jolly moment. Santa roly-poly and jocose, his cheeks the color of good bloody beef when he come in from the cold. Whiskers cascading down his red belly in a white spume, yellowed at mustache tips. He stank of perspiration clear across the room. Meena refused to sit on his lap. Who could blame her? His jellied blue eyes and big lumpy baker's hands! She sat at Grandma Sally's feet and shook her head, no. While Don and Jerri coaxed and cajoled. "Meena, honey, be nice. Santa came clear from the North Pole to see you." Olson's sarcastic polecat grin.

"Santa flew on a broomstick," he said.

"Don't be scared," Jeff encouraged her.

Meena sat tight, shaking her head.

"I've had just about enough," Jerri said.

"Oh, leave her be," snapped Grandma Sally.

But Jerri finally lost it. Grabbed Meena by the arm and sat her bodily upon a worn red terry-cloth knee. Santa chuckled nervously. Ho ho ho. "Smile," Don cried, "Daddy wants to get a picture." His f'ing Kodak. A flash. Meena hunched, eyes red and wild as a hurdy-gurdy monkey's, knowing it was a put-up job. You couldn't fool her with as shabby a Santa as that. In the snapshot, she has pivoted, a knee forced into Santa's groin, fingers tangling in his beard. Trying to tear it away and prove him a phony. He was but the beard wasn't. Poor man. He screamed hell's bells while she tore out gory chunks. It took three of us to disentangle her fingers. A f'ing free-for-all. Santa went stumbling and cursing for the door. Stewed, we realized then. Skunk drunk. But it worried you: a kid who would mug Santa Claus.

Walnut Street. Bad history and booze. Disappointment maybe is what it was. Jerri's and Don's both. Though ask them what was missing and they couldn't have said. Just another little portion of the American dream, facing the street with a waist-high picket fence. Geraniums in the right season, delphiniums. Friendly neighbors. Prosperity. Your own private rent-a-Santa Christmas Eve. How could anything go wrong in a place like that? Who can explain it?

# 5

---

# Meena

She opened the door to their bedroom just as a tiny jet of blue flame snuffed out the match Boney was holding up to Olson's butt. Olson screamed and slugged him.

"That burned."

Boney's eyes widened. "It was like a blowtorch. Really neat."

"How'd you like it if I singed the hairs off your asshole?"

"You told me to do it," Boney protested.

"Six inches, not one inch, bonerhead. Un-oh." Olson yanked up his underwear. "Little Miss Tattletale."

"I am not," she insisted from the doorway.

"We're lighting farts," Boney said cheerfully.

"Is that what you do all day at your dumb boarding school?"

"Nah. We have burping contests, only we call it borking." Olson gave a demonstration, incorporating a drawn-out, toadish *booork* into the burp sound.

Meena frowned. Boys were disgusting. It wasn't any effort for them to invent the grossest pastimes. Maybe she didn't want to be a Long Loop after all. Sure, it would be fun to help dig the cave or hook sleighs to the rear bumpers of their dads' cars during snowstorms and play crack the whip around the loop, but she suspected they did disgusting things down in the tunnel, things no girl would invent in a million years. Nonetheless, she had come to ask if she could join. "I'd make six," she reasoned, "only one less than the Double Dutches."

Olson flopped on his bed in exasperation. "You're a girl, Meena. We're the Long Loop *Boys*. We supposed to change our name or something?"

"Yeah," Boney echoed. "What we gonna call it: the Long Loop Boys Plus One Girl? That's dumb." She hated how he parroted his older brother when Olson was home.

"We could call it the Long Loop Kids," she said.

Olson groaned. "Gimme a break."

"It's still better than the Double Dutch Clutches."

"Anything's better, except a bad fart in a small closet." Cupping a palm over his armpit, Olson pumped his arm vigorously, making sounds identical to wet disgusting farts.

"I don't want to join anyway and dig your dumb cave."

The boys stared at her. Hitching up his undies, Olson approached, making a fist with one hand, rubbing his ass with the other. He was boyish for fifteen, skinny and loose-jointed, a hollow at center of his bare chest, but too swaggering for a boy. His dirty-blond hair was slicked back in a ducktail and curled thickly behind his ears, his eyes deep set and thick-lidded, red and sleepy-looking, even when he was tense with energy (as he usually was). There were two Olsons: one alert, pulsing with electrical energy—as if that lightning bolt really had entered him through the refrigerator long ago; the second Olson drowsily reptilian, suspended in that semi-stupor which precedes sleep. He didn't resemble Dad. People were always saying (right in front of him) that they couldn't believe all three children had the same father. Nothing made Olson madder.

Both she and Boney were dark-haired and dark-eyed like their mom. Boney's eyes were toad-wide, full of wonder at the world. Whatever you told him he believed. Whatever excited you was sure to excite him. He was smart, Boney, in a stupid way. He quickly forgot what he didn't wish to remember. When they fought and she dug fingernails into his wrist and drew blood, he would soon be back repeating what had made her mad in the first place, as if he had forgotten all about it—like those magic tablets you wrote on, then lifted the plastic cover to make the writing disappear. But Olson never forgot. His skeleton would rise up from the grave to knock on your tombstone and remind you of his box kite you had once crash-landed in a tree.

She stared at his Adam's apple, fascinated and disgusted—a sharp, obscene lump like Dad's . . . his Dad's. She hoped Boney didn't grow such a disgusting knob, a huge filbert in his windpipe.

"Dirty little sneak," Olson hissed. "If you tell anyone about our tunnel I'll put a venereal disease on the toilet seat."

She didn't know what a venereal disease was but it sounded awful. "I won't tell," she promised.

Olson turned to Boney. "The two most dangerous things you can do is catch the clap and smoke on the can. Once Aunt Debbie lit up while she was on the john. If I didn't rush in to put out the match the whole house would've blown to hell from sewer gas."

"You went in the bathroom while she was pooping?" Meena demanded.

"No big deal. She used to invite me in all the time for lessons in female anatomy."

"Sitting on the toilet?" Boney's eyes were popping.

Olson shrugged. "It was an emergency deal. Usually we just took showers together."

"I'm going to ask her."

"Who cares. Ask what size jugs she's got while you're at it." Olson made a gross face, turning out his lips at her.

"I'm gonna."

Seizing a rubber band from the dresser, he advanced, aiming down its taut length at her face.

Meena curled against the door. "Don't," she begged.

"You gonna tell?"

She shook her head, no.

"Can it, Olson." Boney asked more than demanded. If it was reversed, she would have leapt on Olson's back and dug her nails into him.

"Had enough?" A corner of Olson's mouth looped open.

Meena nodded.

"C'mon, Olson. Pick on somebody your own size."

"No problema, bonehead." Olson swiveled and fired the rubber band point-blank into his half-brother's chest.

"I'm telling." Meena escaped out the door.

"So what," he yelled behind her. "Who cares what that pantywaist tells her. She ain't my mother anyway. I never listen to her. She's on the rag all the time anyway, unless she's drunk. My mom says she's going through early mentalpause."

Outside the door, Mommy placed a hand on Meena's shoulder and steered her silently back inside the boys' room.

"Is that what your mother says, Olson?"

His mouth fell open.

Mommy stood in the doorway, smiling. "What else does your mom say about me?"

"Nothing," he mumbled.

Mommy sat on the desk, hands clasped between her knees, looking down at pictures Boney had drawn of the clubhouse he planned to build inside the tunnel. It looked like a rabbit warren: crisscrossing passageways linking many nests. Beside her, Meena smelled the vague rubbing-alcohol odor of the clear hooch Mommy kept in a Joy detergent squeeze bottle on the kitchen counter. Mixed with the baby poop smell of her hand lotion, it was nauseating.

"If you don't care what I think, you might just as well talk in front of me as behind my back." Mommy folded one knee across the other with a silky sound. "Does that make sense?"

Olson's eyes shifted about the room. They were pale, almost gray like his dad's. When he was nervous, his eyes became sleepier still. They never looked directly at you unless he was mad. Then they devoured you. He stared at Mommy's knees.

"She says you're a lush."

Mommy's eyes blinked; she opened her hands for him to continue.

"She says I should learn a lesson from you about the dangers of alcoholic beverages."

Mommy released a high-pitched chortle, ear piercing, not a real laugh but like something she had practiced. "Well, isn't she a good Girl Scout. What does your mom say about menopause?"

"Nothing," he mumbled.

"Let's see, your mom's over forty. She could probably teach me a thing or two about menopause. Not too shabby in the drinking department either. Has your mother been back to Tranquility Acres?" Mommy pushed her chin forward, smiling. Meena hated when she was like this. Better if she got mad all at once and got it over with: a squall rather than a protracted storm. This way there was no telling how large her anger might grow, piling up by frowns and simpers.

Olson pretended to be interested in Boney's latest matchbooks: a Thunderbird Inn and Caesars Palace. Rows of them were strung across the room from wall to wall. Mommy opposed the collection, citing Olson's bad history with matches, but

Daddy insisted he'd outgrown that: Many kids are fascinated with matches. Many kids don't try to burn down the house, she had argued. Olson kept opening the covers and closing them again, as if fascinated by their tight fit. Boney traced a finger along the raised parallel cords in his bedspread, kicking his feet against the springs. Daddy would have made him stop.

"I'm speaking to you, young man."

Olson ignored her.

"Olson?"

"None of your business," he said softly.

Mommy's smile tightened. "No, I suppose not. I suppose your mother isn't my business. And I suppose I'm none of hers. Maybe you ought to tell her so. Don't you think?"

Olson grunted noncommittally.

"I've told you boys I want you to get rid of those matches. If one of them were to—" She cut off abruptly, smiling down at Boney's sketch. "What's this, honey?"

He looked up, startled. "Just . . . something."

"I see it's something. I'm wondering what it is."

Boney was thinking, skin bunching between his eyes. "I know," he cried, "it's a submarine."

"Bonerhead." Olson grinned.

"Olson!" Mommy snapped. "Is that any way to speak around your mother?"

He shrugged. "She doesn't care."

"*This one* cares. Get your feet off that bed, young man. You don't put your loafers on my bedspread. Over my dead body. Now! Olson."

Instead, he crossed his ankles. Tension crackled in the air. Mommy glared at his feet; he at her knees. Meena saw he was about to blow it. She remembered the time Mommy caught him playing with matches behind the house on Walnut Street and Olson called her a bitch. Mommy had dragged him inside by the hair and spanked his bare bottom with a yardstick; when it broke she used a hairbrush, until it broke, too, then her bare hand. Daddy had come in and pulled her off, horrified at the welts and gashes on Olson's butt. "What's the matter with you?" he'd demanded. "When would you have stopped? When, Jerri?"

Perhaps Boney remembered that time, too. His fists were pressed hard into his legs, eyes squinted at his half-brother—as if to visualize all this differently. Olson would ask politely if Mommy would let him make his famous Boy Scout baking powder biscuits for dinner; they would laugh together over some stupid thing David Brinkley said on TV, as they sometimes did, Olson squatting on his haunches before the set, superimposing his face over the screen to mime Brinkley's—frowning and duhing and putting words in his mouth, and they would split a gut laughing.

Instead, he scowled straight ahead at Mommy's nylons, pushing off his shoes with his toes, one by one, letting them clunk to the floor. Mommy's mouth worked through quick smiles and frowns; she regarded his stockinged feet on the bed, unable to decide whether this was compromise or double dare. Olson's sleepy eyes glinted, proclaiming: I hate you more than you could ever hate me.

"Olson, are you making fun of me?" she asked softly.

He shrugged, then grinned. "I can see your underpanties."

Mommy's cheeks flinched. She clamped her knees together. "All right, we'll just see."

There was a long silence. The air full of flapping, noiseless wings. Mommy's hands clutched the edge of the desk, knuckles white as bone china. Olson's knotted into fists. Meena thought she would flee—run downstairs and call her father at work.

At that moment, Boney leapt from his bed and ran over. "Yeah," he cried. "See! This is where they sleep. This is passageways and stuff. This is where they keep torpedoes."

For a moment Mommy stared at him uncomprehendingly. "Darling?" She ran a hand through his thick hair, smiling, distracted, glad as anyone else for his intervention. The air was made of hard, glaring glass and he had shattered it to pieces. Slowly, the blood retreated from Mommy's skin, draining back inside of her. "Oh," she cried, leaping up. "I almost forgot my pie." She swiveled in the doorway on her way out. "Friends again?" she asked Olson.

"Sure," he said. "No problema."

But when she had left, before she called back to Meena to stay out of her brothers' bedroom, he muttered, "She hates my guts."

Later, while Mom and Dad were having their after-work drink and the boys passed a football back and forth on the street,

Meena hid beneath a window outside the living room. "He's never given me half a chance," she heard Mommy complain.

"I don't buy that," Daddy said. "It's a chicken-and-egg-type thing."

"Meaning?" Mommy asked.

"Meaning you're both wrong. You're the adult here, Jerri. You have to take the first step. He has a mother. You can't force the boy to love you."

She laughed a bitter laugh. "Oh yes. He often reminds me."

"Olson's my son, Jerri. Maybe if you tried to see me in him, you'd find something there you could love."

After a while Mommy said, "Maybe." Her tone hollow, mocking, as if she meant to add: *Over my dead body.*

# 6

# Jeff

Our biggest problem was getting rid of the dirt. Old man Ashcroft might become suspicious if we dumped it all on his compost heap. Besides, Steve Weatherspoon said it caused spontaneous combustion if you mixed dirt and compost. Germs and microorganisms in the soil got it hot and the leaves and grass and stuff caught fire by themselves. Poof. It was a stupid idea and I didn't believe him, even if he beat me by forty points on the Stanford Achievement Test, mostly in science. He was the smartest kid in seventh grade. Big deal. Dad says Albert Einstein was slow in school; he was always thinking genius thoughts his teachers couldn't understand. So maybe Steve would turn out to be actually dumb when he grew up, and his earlier brains was a misdiagnosis. Besides, when I asked Olson about spontaneous combustion, he said only a pansy would think up something like that.

We were down to eighteen feet and still hadn't hit oil—not

even tar or anything black. In fact, as we dug down through it, the dirt changed from dark brown to red, and we were afraid it might arouse suspicion when we dumped it out on top. We hauled it up in gunnysacks. Since we had to drag them behind us, it was like huge snail tracks across the grass. It was a miracle nobody ever caught us. Soon there were red gopher mounds all over the field—biggest gopher mounds you ever saw. Prob'ly surprised the gophers. Buck saw Mr. Ashcroft sitting in the lot one day on a fold-up stool with a twelve-gauge across his knees, waiting for a gopher to stick its head up. Every once in a while, he walked over to a mound and rubbed red dirt between his fingers. Buck said he looked funny sitting there in his brown slacks and vest with a shotgun on his lap, like a banker waiting for robbers. Soon after that, old Mr. A. stopped coming on Saturday mornings to hit golf balls. We thought he was scared away by the huge gophers. It wasn't until later we learned he had croaked.

Buck said we could mix the dirt with pine needles and mold it into bricks; he saw it in *Spartacus*. We could use the bricks to build a fort against the Double Dutches. It was a genius idea, which made me wonder if it wasn't true about intelligence tests, since Buck was second from dumbest in seventh grade, next to Gary Schmidt. Maybe he was smarter in the real world than in school. Only problem was, where would we build our fort? Second, the bricks fell apart. Steve said it had to be clay to make bricks. So Buck had a second idea, which wasn't quite so smart.

There was a widow lady whose back fence was at one corner of old Mr. Ashcroft's field. She only used her yard to grow vegetables, so we decided—Buck anyway—she prob'ly wouldn't notice if we dumped dirt over her fence. I went along with it. On dump nights, I'd wait until Dad went off to a meeting and Mom started talking to the TV set or on the phone (which Meena said, if you listened in upstairs, there wasn't anybody on the other end, but she's a liar; it was prob'ly Grandma Sally), then I'd sneak out through the garage and run across the loop to Buck's house. I'd whisper "Di-dow" outside his window, very softly because his sister's bedroom was next door. Once I even saw her take off her top. Her tits stuck out like bullets in the bra, and I wondered if her actual breasts were like that. But when I pressed my face against the glass to see better, she lunged forward and yanked the shade down, so I never did find out.

Buck would open his window and stick out his head. "Dowdi," he'd say, like I didn't know it was him. We'd run over and grab the gunnysacks we'd left in the bushes and drag them across the field to the widow's fence. We had left a crate there to stand on, and it took both of us our full strength to push the sacks above our heads to spill over the fence. It was quiet out there. Spooky. Nothing but crickets and the sound of someone's TV or a dog barking in the distance. The widow went to bed early—even in the summer when it wasn't dark till nine—and her house was always pitch dark. Except one night I noticed a flickering light inside her sliding patio door. Buck was grunting and mumbling beside me. "Hush up," I said. We let dirt slip out the end of the sack and slush down on the pile inside. I couldn't see much through the fence slats, since they were splintery and you couldn't put your eye up against them to look.

"I see a light," I told Buck.

"That'th juth your invaginathon," he whispered, his spit exploding like cold popcorn against my cheek.

"If I get caught I'm done for."

We dumped the other sacks over. Nothing happened. I wondered how high the pile was inside. Prob'ly didn't matter since grown-ups rarely notice things like that, especially widows. Meena said she was a witch who poisoned people's dogs and hung chicken bones on her apple tree like Christmas decorations. If you had to dump dirt in someone's backyard, that was the best place in the neighborhood to do it.

When we returned a couple nights later, Grandma Sally was staying with us while Mom and Dad were on vacation in California. Aunt Debbie came, too—"on the sly"—to see us kids, since Mom said she couldn't set foot in our house again. "I'll bring my daughter if I like," Grandma Sally told us. "Since when has your mother paid any attention to me?"

It was riskier to sneak out with Grandma Sally there. She always stuck her head in my room to see what I was doing. She read social studies over my shoulder, reaching down to stop the page if I read too fast. "Bullshit," she would mutter. "What do they know about the Depression? Why, I lived through it. I never saw a thing of this CCC and such. The war ended all that when we went to work in the shipyards." Grandma had been a welder and had maggoty white scars on her arms where sparks had fell down in her gloves. "The Japs ended the Depression, it had nothing to do with Mr. Roose-velt." I was smart enough not to argue with Grandma Sally. "You'll learn more from *I Love Lucy* than from your silly history book," she'd say. But she liked mountain-climbing stories. If she caught me reading those, she would ask me to read to her, since her eyes weren't much good anymore, even with her glasses.

I knew I had to dump the dirt and get home before Grandma noticed I was gone. There were six sacks that night. We lined them up along the fence like sacks of beans at the end of rows.

"Isn't it a little much?" I whispered to Buck. Inside, the pile had to be at least to our waists already.

"You got a better idea?" he asked.

I didn't. We were balanced on the crate, side by side, pushing a bag over our heads when I saw the light again. Not in the house at all but reflecting off the glass patio door outside, forming a flickering pool across a white patio table, spooky. "Freeze," I whispered. My eye was pressed up against a fence crack. "It's a candle," I said.

"Pig ballth," Buck lisped. "C'mon and dump. My armth ith tired." We had the sack pushed straight up over our heads and our arms were shaking. Buck's head beside mine smelled more like dirt than dirt itself. "Dump!" he said.

Just then I saw a figure lying on the grass. "Stop! you jerk," I whispered. "Don't you see it? I'm getting outta here."

Buck's arms made the final push upward. Mine, too, or else it would have spilled down on my head. Dirt showered over the fence with a tinny racket and clatter. In our surprise, we dropped the whole sack over the other side.

"Who's there?" cried a shaky voice near the house. "Is that you, Gerald? Hullo!"

Buck made a sound like air leaking from a tire. He gripped my shirt. "Shhhush," I said. I was never so scared in my life, not even when Mom took us to the basement during lightning storms.

"I know you're there," the voice came across the lawn toward us. "I've suspected all along. Who else could it possibly be?"

Buck clawed me—my ear, my arm. Plum petrified.

The widow's voice was right by the fence now. "Hullo, Gerald? Dear, I wish you would come out. I've been waiting for you. Really, dear, I won't be frightened. Who else could it be?"

"Get rid of the evidenth," Buck stammered in my ear.

"Run, stupid!" The pukey smell of his earwax made me gag. Buck jumped down from the crate and grabbed another bag of dirt by himself.

"There you are," the widow cried. "Woo-hoo. I see you, darling."

Buck slung the sack up onto the crate and knocked me off, the jerk. What was he doing?

"I've visited you every day, dear. But there's no sign of disturbance on the surface. I suppose it comes from down below. But there you are," she chirped. "A wonder."

Her voice, just over the fence, was syrupy and creepy. She must've been peeking between fence slats. I could just make out her outline moving along; her dress glistened like mother-of-pearl. With a grunt, Buck heaved the sack of dirt over his head all by himself and let it spill over the fence. The widow shrieked. The dirt had fell down on top of her.

"Who is it?" she screamed. "Who's there?" Her fingers reached through the fence, gripping the slats like white grubs. The whole fence shook. Buck's arms went out beside him like a scarecrow. He jumped off the box and smacked into me.

"How dare you . . . Gerald!" she cried. Her voice wasn't shaky anymore, plain mad.

We stood like posts in the dark, too spooked to run, knowing anyhow she couldn't get to us. But we forgot the gate on the side of the fence. When it opened and she came wiggling toward us in tiny steps like a caterpillar, Buck lit out for the bushes. But I couldn't move. It was like a nightmare where you stand watching a giant lizard coming for you and you can't run. The widow seized my arm in one hand and the back of my neck in the other. Her fingernails dug in and I knew Meena was right: She was a witch. It was human bones hanging from her apple tree. I was done for. She leaned close to study my face. Her face was small as a baseball, moonlight hopped off her glasses. I tried not to smell her breath or even breathe.

"You're a boy," she cried.

"Yes, ma'am," I squeaked.

"Little monster. Dumping dirt in an old woman's yard. Is that how you get your kicks?"

"No, ma'am."

"Why'd you do it then?"

"We got to," Buck said from the dark.

The widow shrieked. She clutched me to her bony chest, suffocating me in a smell of Geritol and mothballs. "Another one," she said in a wispy voice. "I thought you were my Gerald."

We sat at the widow's dining table waiting for Grandma Sally to arrive. Over the phone, the widow made it sound like we were hoods who dumped dirt on her on purpose. There was red smears of it on her forehead and little piles on her shoulders. She wore a quilted blue bathrobe that buttoned clear down to her feet and made her look like a bumpy worm or a mummy. She gave us both a glass of milk, which neither of us drank. We weren't that dumb. Besides, I had a stomachache.

Her house was crammed every inch inside with fuddy-duddy furniture and knickknacks, china in glass cupboards and lace doilies on polished wooden tables. Soft, floppy rag dolls perched on lamp shades and windowsills, straddled doorknobs and laid in cut-glass bowls like they were taking a bath. There were red-haired, freckly farm children, old-men dolls with buck teeth, funny potatoey-face trolls, dark-skinned dolls with kinky hair, Swiss children with apple cheeks, bronze Indians wearing Mohawk haircuts. Even more amazing were the tiny wooden signs occupying every inch of dining room walls, cut in odd shapes and varnished to a glitter, each with a different saying (what Aunt Debbie calls "proverbs and rhubarbs"): GOD BLESS OUR HAPPY HOME. TIPPECANOE AND TYLER TOO. MONEY TALKS . . . BUT NOT AS MUCH AS MY WIFE. HOWDY DOODY, FRESH & FRUITY. That one baffled me. So did GERRY A. TRICKS NUDIST COLONY (OLD FARTS ONLY). The widow saw me looking.

"That was Gerald's last sign," she said. "It was my husband's hobby. The dolls are mine."

"There's prob'ly a thousand of them," I said.

"Three hundred seventy-six." She smiled. Her face small and wrinkled as a witch doll's on the windowsill, her teeth brown along the bottom row.

When Grandma Sally arrived, she wasn't as mad as I expected her to be. She stood in the doorway surveying the room with an amused glint in her eye. Aunt Debbie and Meena came in behind her. Debbie winked at me. "Have you been getting Jeffrey in trouble again, Buck?" Grandma Sally asked.

"No, Grandma," he mumbled, scared to look at her.

"We'll see."

She towered over the widow by a foot. Dad said for a woman he could see eye to eye with, he never agreed with Grandma about nothing. Grandma Sally's face was square, like Meena's; her glasses frames stuck out like plastic wings on the sides, making it seem even broader. Her skin was paper white—she believed sunlight was bad for you—and her hair was the color of caramel, not gray like the widow's. You wouldn't know she was an old lady at all if it wasn't for lines above her mouth, which Aunt Debbie calls her "smoking lip"; others fanned like sun rays across her cheeks, disappearing completely when she smiled. But she didn't smile much. Nobody could stare Grandma Sally down. It was a way she had of focusing narrower and narrower till the truth popped out of you like pus from a pimple. My best hope, I knew, was not to look at her. To try and think up some good reason for dumping dirt in the widow's yard. But I couldn't think at all.

"What's this you've been up to, Jeffrey?" she asked.

I could see she was amazed by all the signs and dolls. Her brow furrowed trying to read them, and I was afraid she would ask me to do it for her. Behind her, Aunt Debbie stuck out her tongue. The widow didn't see, but I did. Meena giggled. Grandma Sally reached back and whacked her. The widow was saying how we had been dumping dirt in the corner of her yard for two weeks now. When she first noticed, she couldn't believe her eyes. "Not local dirt," she said. "This soil is red and comes from a distance. I thought it was an animal at first, you see, but the color puzzled me. Besides, the pile became quite large. So, you see, I thought my prayers had been answered."

"Afraid I don't follow," Grandma Sally said.

"Have you been married, dear?" the widow asked.

"I don't see what that has to do with anything. You say my grandson is dumping dirt in your yard?" Grandma Sally wasn't in a mood for nonsense. She glanced over at Buck and me, her eyes frowning—the exact same color as Mom's, "Indian brown" Dad calls it, and her same bags underneath.

"I'm trying to explain," the widow said. "I wouldn't wish you to think me odd."

Grandma Sally looked at the signs and dolls. "Now why would I think a thing like that?" My sister giggled.

The widow told how she would light a candle on her patio table and lay out under the moonlight on clear nights to have a chat with her "deceased" husband. "At times I heard him plain as if he was sitting in that chair. Other times I couldn't. So I would just lie there. They say moonlight is good for the complexion."

"You were sunbathing under the moon?" Aunt Debbie asked.

"That's a twist," Grandma Sally said.

Aunt Debbie had sat down and was studying the widow with a worried, sad expression. Meena stood beside her, staring.

"I wouldn't say sunbathing exactly," the widow said. "Well, there's some believe a wall falls down between the living and the dead, but I believe it is a curtain that may be drawn aside. Do you see? There's living souls have a foot on the other side. Same with the dead. Don't you see? Gerald and I were very close. If it's anybody could communicate—" She faltered; moisture appeared in her eyes, then evaporated again. "Don't you see?"

"It's all right," Debbie said quietly, giving me a dirty look, and I looked down at a huge doily like a flat spiderweb at center of the table.

"One night I heard the dirt spill over my fence; I was sure I did. So I decided I would lay cookie sheets atop the mound to warn me when it happened again."

Buck looked guilty: teeth clenched, features bunched up. Grandma Sally was watching us.

"Tonight I'd connected very strong with Gerald. Well, I visited his grave yesterday, you see, and couldn't find a sign of disturbance, but I thought he might be digging out from underneath. So I had to know what he wanted me to do—to help him, you know. So when I heard tins rattling—"

"Crud's horses," Grandma Sally interrupted her. "You're nuttier than my pecan stuffing. Come on, boys, let's go home. I don't know what you are doing out this time of night, but I intend to find out."

Buck looked even scareder now.

"Mother!" Aunt Debbie scolded.

"Mother nothing. You expect me to believe Jeffrey has been dumping dirt in this crackpot's yard? Why, I never—"

"I know," the widow said, "I know what you must be thinking. But I can show you the mound. They've left their sacks behind."

Grandma Sally removed her glasses and let them hang from leashes looping over her ears, down over her bosom ('cause when they're big or your grandmother's you don't call them tits). Naked, her eyes were red and pouchy. "My grandson is not a boy who would torment a poor woman who has lost her husband." She reached forward and whisked dirt off the widow's shoulders. Then looked up at the GERRY A. TRICKS sign and put her glasses back on. The widow's mouth opened; she looked like she might cry.

"Maybe I'd better go see," Debbie said.

"You'll do no such thing." Grandma Sally shot us a look. "Were you boys dumping dirt over this woman's fence?"

For a second I couldn't answer. When I did, my voice came out hoarse. "We never knew she was standing underneath or else we wouldn't of."

Grandma Sally's mouth opened with a wet, annoyed sound. "I don't know who's nuttier here. Young Buck?" she demanded.

He nodded.

Grandma came over and thumped us both on top of our heads, like she was shooting spit wads. Then she bent down to pinch dirt out of the widow's hair. Meena and Aunt Debbie glared at us like we murdered somebody. Debbie asked why would we do something so goofy. I knew we would have to make something up fast, but I couldn't think of anything. So I said we were only storing it there; we planned to move it.

"Likely story," Debbie said.

Grandma Sally told the widow she needed a bath. Nailing a finger at me. "You have a whipping coming, young man."

"Heavens no," cried the widow. "I won't be responsible for that. They're nice boys. Children are to be cherished not whipped." She pointed to a sign with bark around the edges: ABUSE THE ROD, MISUSE THE CHILD, it said. "My husband and I couldn't have children. It was our biggest unhappiness."

"A good thing you didn't," Grandma Sally muttered.

But I could see Meena was watching the widow with a look of amazement, and I knew she would never call her "witch" again; I wouldn't neither. She wasn't any witch. Except maybe a good one.

The widow said she wanted to keep the dirt if she might, turning to Buck and me like we owned it. "Maybe you fellows would be kind enough to scatter it over my garden. It could use the iron—red soil, you know. Besides, I would feel there was a little of my Gerald there."

We agreed, delighted at this prospect instead of a whipping.

"When you've finished that, you will help her plant," Grandma Sally said. "No more sneaking out nights. Understood?"

I knew we were off the hook then. Mom and Dad or Buck's folks would never hear a word about it.

"What I want to know is where all this dirt comes from." Aunt Debbie rested her chin on a fist, looking at us amusedly.

Buck and I glanced at each other.

"Gopher mounds," I blurted.

"Gophers!" they all said at once.

"Yeah," Buck said, his face lighting up like a flashbulb, "gopherth."

Meena nudged Debbie with her elbow and whispered something in her ear, and no one said another word about it. Though I guessed that little sneak told Aunt Debbie about our tunnel, which was okay; you could trust Debbie with a secret.

That's how we found a way to dispose of the dirt. Mrs. Grazziola ('cause that's the widow's name) had the biggest garden in history that year, and Buck and me had two rows of our own.

# 7

## Meena

She hid in the garden on Walnut Street between rows of pole beans, which she and Boney had planted three to a hill, twining in thick leafy green up teepee'd poles, earthy and pungent in the sunshine. Beyond, in the yard, Aunt Debbie lay sunbathing. Meena peeked through leafage, admiring her aunt's sleek one-piece Jantzen swimsuit—stretchy sky blue, clinging to curves of her body like Esther Williams's did, denting at her belly button. *Her* own stomach was hard and resonant as a drumhead, convex instead of concave like Aunt Debbie's. Sunlight glared off the house's white shiplap, winked back from the square-framed kitchen window, which looked out onto the strip of lawn and garden, with the huge amphaloola tree at back. Mommy was out shopping. Daddy at work. So it astonished her to see him standing suddenly on the back porch: creased slacks, generic white shirt and bow tie to match burgundy suspenders, which he always wore in those days, claiming they kept his shoulders straight. He smiled broadly coming down the steps, telling Debbie he thought he would find her out here on such a beautiful day. He was tall and more handsome, she thought, than Clark Gable.

Debbie frowned and flopped onto her belly, but didn't protest when he knelt beside her on the blanket and offered to "do her shoulders." The sweet cool smell of suntan lotion spread over the yard, mixing with the sharp green of snap beans and waxy chard and the sweetness of petunias which formed a purple trim around the garden. She loved the sipping sound the lotion bottle made as Dad squeezed a snaking white bead down Debbie's legs. He rolled up his sleeves and rubbed it into her skin, and a warm glazed fleshy odor mesmerized them . . . circular motion of his fingers, which she could feel across her own scalp, moving down her knotty spine. Not twenty feet away, Aunt Debbie's dark eyes squinted shut, a cheek rested against the back of her hand, the other bronzed cheekbone glistened. She smiled a tight-lipped, sensuous smile. Daddy knelt rigidly on the blanket beside her, glancing periodically at the house, a loose lock of sandy hair fanned across his forehead. Lying there, Meena felt a sleepy, slow current of excitement enter her belly through the warm earth. She closed her eyes, imagining the warm fingers of sunlight on her bare legs were Daddy's hands. Shrinking very small, she crawled across the grass like a spotted garden spider, joining her aunt on the blanket.

It was still. Daddy worked silently, his fingers moving in slow spirals toward the hem of Debbie's suit, pushing in between her legs. She swatted at them, more peevish than annoyed.

"You're incorrigible," she said.

"Wooh. Big word." His hand closed around one taut hemisphere of her ass.

Meena caught a giggle, pushing her chin forward into lacy carrot greens, fascinated to learn what would happen when Mommy wasn't home to say "No." Would he spank her bare bottom? Stick his finger up her bum, as Olson said grown-ups did? She watched Daddy bend stiffly forward to kiss Debbie's neck. She laughed and so did he. "Dirty old man," she teased. Daddy's eyes closed, his mouth opened; he was smiling.

Something was wrong. Meena boosted onto her elbows in alarm and stared at the reflective metallic eye of the kitchen window. In that suspended moment, Debbie's eyes connected with her own. An instant of recognition. Debbie's hand went back with a loud smacking sound against Daddy's hand. She pushed up into a crouch and twisted away from him. "Leave off," she snapped. But whether she spoke to her father or to her, Meena couldn't tell. Aunt Debbie's eyes fixed on her in the garden, where she lay absolutely still in the smell of dust.

The tunnel smell. Or the smell of dust mice when she hid under the bed in the master bedroom years later. If they had dragged her out by the stocking heels, she couldn't have said what she was doing there. Merely curious? Testing the horizons of her power? She didn't know why Mom and Dad shut their door at night. After all, she and Boney never closed their doors. She expected that her parents feasted on special dishes which

Mommy never made for supper. A trap door behind the shoe rack in Dad's closet opened and a stainless-steel kitchen appeared. Or, conceivably, they argued about Aunt Debbie—beginning in soft, insistent whispers, which enlarged into violent shouts that shook the household, and they didn't care, as though children were an abstraction, shut out beyond the walls of their rage. Or Mommy dressed Daddy up in nylons and camisoles and he dressed her up in tie and suspenders and they played house. Or—and this prospect thrilled her most—they discussed the children. Olson's lipping. Boney's nightmares. Her own secret ways. She wanted to lie beneath the bed while they spoke in the sober, commonplace voices of adults about the secrets behind her secrecy.

She slipped quick and quiet as a heartbeat into their bedroom, wriggling sideways into the few inches between carpet and box springs, not knowing she would do it until she heard Daddy on the stairs. Just under when light spread across the floor and slippered, then bare feet plodded from place to place like foxtrotting partners who avoided touch. Once his large hairy feet approached Mommy's smooth smaller ones near the vanity— just visible as Meena craned her head hard to the right. But smooth feet turned and moved away. The feet didn't interest her. She closed her eyes, better to hear the whisper of sliding closet doors, small tapping sounds and unscrewing of lids that Mommy made at the vanity over her head, Daddy's hands slapping out a rhythm on his bare chest. He yawned, then bedsprings yawned beneath his weight.

She nearly cried out in alarm. His full weight had sunk upon her, pinning her to the carpet. Not painful, but sandwiching her there so that every breath was an effort, and if he bounced . . . Thank goodness her head was turned sideways. A bedspring grid impressed upon her cheek; she felt curlicues digging in where metal wound about metal. Just inches away from her nose, a huge gray dust mouse crouched on hairy paunches. She blew it away.

They didn't speak. Daddy yawned and made ha-haing sounds, deep and speculative. Mommy's toothbrush whispered response. Then he stretched out and there was the slithery, satiny sound of bed sheets, and his weight lifted from her abdomen and settled over her like a heavy winter coat.

"Did you lock the front door?" Mommy asked.

"Yup."

"The children are quiet tonight."

"You bet."

Her heart beat wildly. It seemed the bed heaved with it; Daddy was sure to notice. But he ha-ha yawned and said he would like to move to California. Up above, Mommy turned her head to regard him (eyes closed *she* saw it perfectly: lanolin blotches across Mommy's cheeks, Kleenex in hand, thin cinnamon eyebrows making peaked accents over her eyes; her hair covered in a shower cap to assure no lotion touched it).

"You're dreaming, Don."

"No." He must've propped up on an elbow; she could feel his contour. "I just might swing it. There's talk of opening an office in San Diego. It could mean district manager for me."

For a time there was no reply, just the whisper of tissue scraping flesh. "Wouldn't that be fun," Mommy said.

"Jerri! It's a big deal. The kids would love it down there—the beach and zoo. They have a terrific zoo."

"What about wifey? Would wifey like the zoo? Maybe you could put her in it." Mommy laughed harshly at the mirror. "Maybe she could have her own special cage."

"Not funny, Jerri. Not funny at all."

"Not funny at all," Mommy yammered.

"I believe you would like it down south. I honestly do."

"Maybe I would," Mommy said after a time.

"Nothing certain yet. Still in the talking stages." He settled back.

"And maybe I wouldn't."

"I've got a hellish day tomorrow. Some people haven't the sense to settle. They insist on the impossible."

"Nothing is as pathetic as an animal in a cage—back and forth all day long." Mommy spoke in a monotone, as if to herself.

"You don't survive with your head in the clouds," Daddy said. "But some people thrive on fooling themselves."

After a time, Meena thought he had fallen asleep. Her right knee ached; she managed to straighten it out. Her neck had begun to stiffen.

Then Daddy said, "I believe Olson would like California. Surfing and all. He's doing much better this year." His voice hovered overhead. She wondered if they often spoke out loud to themselves when they were alone together. Suddenly the tone changed. "I'm worried about Meena. All the sneaky stuff."

She lay still, sensing the fingers of his thoughts reach down through the scaffolding of bedsprings to discover her.

"She's like my sister, Debbie," Mommy said, her voice turned away from them.

"I don't like the spider stuff. That can't be healthy."

Mommy laughed harshly. "Look who's talking about healthy."

"Sneaking around the way she does. Do you suppose she does that sort of thing at school?"

"Maybe she's learned a trick or two from her dad."

"I'm serious, Jerri. What will people think of a little girl who prefers to huddle on the transmission hump rather than sit up in the backseat of a car? She spends more time on her hands and knees than on her feet."

Mommy laughed again. "Elbows and knees—her dad's favorite position. What do they call it? Missionary position."

"This is our daughter we're discussing, for Pete's sake." Her father's voice hummed vaguely in the bedsprings.

"Don't you take a self-righteous tone with me, Don. Do you think you're the only one in this house who worries about that little girl?"

"Look, I don't know. It's something I thought we might agree upon. That's why I brought it up."

"Oh you did. How fatherly of you. How husbandly. Maybe the Chamber of Commerce will give you an award."

"Sorry I did," he mumbled.

Bedsprings heaved, his weight centered under his buttocks, nearly crushing her. She caught a shallow breath, placing small hands against the springs and pushing upward with all her might.

"Why can't a father express concern for his daughter, I'd like to know. Seems a natural enough thing to me. You always seem to find something—I don't know—illicit in it. You want me to reject her. Is that it? Would that make you happy?"

She sensed her mother's head turning, eyes slit over broad cheekbones, glassy, glistening at her father.

"Did I say a word?"

"It's what you don't say. Everything sneaking in between the lines. You should see yourself, Jerri. Go ahead, look!"

"Did I?" Mommy repeated.

She would have to breathe soon and could not. It would be terrible to suffocate beneath her parents' bed while they discussed her. Only after they had looked everywhere else would they find her there: dried up like an insect husk. Her arms had begun to shake with the effort of pushing.

"It's natural for a daughter to be the apple of her father's eye. You've told me how fond your dad was of you at Meena's age. How jealous Sally was. Maybe it runs in the family."

"Don't you dare!" Mommy said, her voice sharp and jagged. "Don't you say a word about my father."

"All right, Jerri, take it easy."

"*Don't you dare!*" Mommy shouted. "You bastard."

He moved atop Meena, stretched out above her on the bed. Air rushed into her lungs as into the rubber bulb on a bicycle horn, with a nearly audible expansion. For a time she was dizzy, sipping breaths.

Silence was long, far too long. Meena knew it was all very delicate now—papery eggshells made of dust; you had only to breathe. She hoped Daddy wouldn't. Hoped he wouldn't dare get anywhere near but let Mommy's feelings settle by themselves. Else there would be yolk everywhere, blood-splotched, screaming yellow across walls and carpet and in her scalp. She would be caught between them as they rubbed it in each other's faces. She moved her lips carefully to tell him: "No. Not another word." Sometimes he didn't seem to understand.

Then a miracle: Mommy began humming at the mirror.

Silence was unbroken after that. Daddy began an even breathing. Mommy turned the spigot on and off. Sometimes it sounded like she laughed softly to herself, but maybe it wasn't laughter. Meena waited under the bed. Her legs turned pins and needles, and she was sure Mommy knew she was there and punished her sneakiness by keeping the light on. Any moment she would call in a cramped, hard voice, like a marble was trapped under her tongue: "Meena! You come out of there, young lady."

She would have to come out, of course.

Mommy's mouth would shrink, she would speak with her

teeth—crooked in the bottom row, leaning together like old maids—no longer beautiful but transformed to an evil witch. "Come here, young lady." Grasping Meena's arm and pulling her hard against breasts, a flush creeping down her throat into the fissure between in stippled pinpricks. Mommy pinned her between her knees, a claw at back of Meena's neck forcing her face within inches of the sink enamel. Meena watched a hand reach out to turn on the faucet, the palm swishing round and round atop a bar of soap, its saccharine bouquet so close and acrid it burned her eyes. "Your mouth doesn't need a scrubbing," Mommy hissed. "Your eyes do, young lady." She rubbed suds into Meena's eyeballs, her fingers pushing back under corners of the lids. The small girl's screams brought her father out of bed.

"Jerri! What in Christ's name are you doing?"

He yanked his daughter away and rushed her to the bathroom, where he carefully rinsed out her eyes. Even next morning they were red and swollen and the world a little blurred. But her secret remained intact: They were moving to California. More important: She was the apple of her father's eye.

But this isn't true. This didn't happen. Not on this night. After a long while, vanity lights went out and the room was left in near darkness. Mommy's footsteps padded across the carpet. Meena couldn't turn to watch them leave, but she heard. They would go on—tiptoeing down the hall and downstairs to one of her secret caches. Meena knew them all. Bedsprings heaved and she sensed Daddy sitting up in the dark. He cursed and fell back again, rolling to his side. It was her opportunity: weight had lifted just enough. She slinked sideways on her butt and shoulders in caterpillar movements, face forced against bedsprings, hardly noticing metal curlicues that snagged her bare arms and tore twin gashes across her left cheek just below the eyelid. There wasn't much time. Daddy's back faced her, his hair rumpled on the pillow. She wished to lean down and snuggle her face against it, but tiptoed quickly to the door instead. Something made her hesitate before stepping into the hall. Placing a hand on her cheek, she felt wet sticky fissures the bedsprings had torn, then peeked around the door frame.

Mommy stood at the top of the stairs, illuminated by nightlights in the hall. Erect, Valkyrian, a tiny smile on her lips. She stepped forward with a sweeping movement of her nightgown as if in a trance. Breath froze in Meena's mouth. This was not Mommy at all. It was a spook spirit that sometimes occupied her mother's skin, and now looked directly at Meena but didn't see. A creature that roamed the house in the dead of night. With that frozen smile, it turned mechanically and entered Boney's room. Meena shot across the hall into her bedroom, into bed and under covers. Turning her scratched cheek against the pillow.

When the spook spirit finished with Boney, it would enter her room. Maybe it would just arrange covers around her dark head. It would smell like soap and vodka, and it might, Meena feared, clasp the back of her neck with a hand that was cold and tallowy. And she would be frozen in sleep.

# 8

# Meena

She was taking ballet then. In the secrecy of sleep, she would pirouette, perfectly erect on pointe, magically spinning, zigging to one side of the polished wooden floor, zagging back in miraculous fouettés, her left leg whipping, while other girls stood at the barre watching, skinny and spidery-legged in white tights, faces jilted in wonder: Sherry Frost and Imogene Davis (the double snots, she called them, because every nose has two nostrils). The nose of the instructor, Madame Chevaux, was so sharp you could slice potatoes with it, her forehead wide as a California sky, lips a little disapproving even as Meena spun.

Meena would drop to her arches and do multiple entrechats, ankles crossed, hop hop hop . . . a gazelle in a pink tutu. The double snots' mouths hung slack and stupid. But eventually she must stop and lean panting on the barre. Then Sherry and Imogene took the floor, graceful as china dolls, long necks extended, bowing to one another, beginning with mincing pliés, each finding in the other a fixed point, like a dancing husband and wife. Their behinds inverted pink valentines, hard as wood. They would arch their backs, pretending to have breasts—Imogene actually did, Sherry nearly. Madame Chevaux's eyes would sparkle, her feet and shoulders making a reprise of their movements, hands clasped before her lips. "You see, *mes chères*," she would say breathlessly, "*sub-til. Élé-gant.* Ballet is not the dance of a rock and a roll."

Sherry and Imogene tilted their heads side to side in pretentious self-imitation. Meena despised them. Most of all she hated Madame Chevaux for loving them. (But Madame Chevaux couldn't have guessed then that Sherry would soon look like a pepperoni pizza, with her face full of pimples, or that Imogene would never outgrow her skinniness, so that in adulthood she was not graceful but gawking.)

Some nights Meena wore her leotard to bed so that others wouldn't laugh, seeing her in her nightie in ballet class. But this night she woke realizing she had been dancing in her nightie, not in ballet class but down aisles of the County Art Museum in Los Angeles—which the family had visited last Christmas—past Vermeers, watery Cézannes, Degas bathers with puffy pink faces. She twirled and her legs were wet with anxiety. So that when she woke it didn't surprise her that bed sheets clung to her knees and she must peel them off like moist bandages. She went to shake Boney awake, risking the nocturnal perils of the house.

Leaning down over him, she whispered, "I peed in my bed."

Boney yelped and sat straight up, scooting away from her on his rear end. His eyes big as half-dollars in the night light. He smelled rubbery and moldy at once—the odor of sleep combined with the red-earth smell of the tunnel, which he carried around everywhere like his own secret. His teeth gleamed.

"Meena?" he asked.

"Shhhh," she hissed.

"Meena, you're all bloody. All over your face."

She felt her cheek. It had dried now, no longer sticky but powdery and flaking. Although the ruts were gooey and sore. Boney got up and led her by the hand to the bathroom, closing the door behind them. Seeing her, his face turned in on itself like a barnacle, serious and big brotherly. "It's bloody all over," he whispered, incredulous. "Your arm, too." He ordered her to take off her damp nightie. "Don't look," she said, wiggling it down over her hips instead of pulling the yucky pee-soaked gown over her head, curling a hand like a leaf over her place. Boney began sponging away dried blood with a washcloth, working gently around the scrapes on her cheeks.

"It's gashes," he said.

"Something scratched me."

"A bat?" he asked, eyes wide. "A vampire?"

"Mommy," she replied, immediately sorry she had, for this seemed to frighten Boney more than if it had been a huge hairy ugly bat, its leather wings crinkling in the dark.

"With her fingernails?"

Meena nodded, then shook her head.

"Her teeth?" His voice barely audible.

"We're moving to California," she said brightly.

"Liar. You did it yourself, Meena. You know you did."

"I didn't either. Honest."

"You're a liar. You stink like a toilet. You peed all over yourself." He pried at the concealing hand.

She shook her head. "Mommy scratched me. Then I peed."

It wasn't altogether a lie; they both knew that. Boney rinsed the washcloth under the tap, cringing as her blood spun away pink down the drain, fascinated and horrified—as she was—to see part of her vanish. She watched his eyes in the mirror and knew Boney saw what she was seeing (it worked that way between them): a pale bat with Mommy's face and hairdo flapping through the quiet house looking for something to quench its thirst, alighting on the upstairs landing to listen to them sleep. Passing over him, it perched atop her headboard and flexed its claws.

"You did it yourself, Meena," he insisted. "You got mad and did it yourself."

"Shhhh, stupid, you'll wake her up."

"That's dumb. Only a boner scratches himself, even if we do have to move to California."

Angrily, he pried away her clamping hand and worked the cloth down her legs, averting his face, scrubbing her knees and ankles. The cloth was cool and tingly on her brown thighs. Reaching the top, he said she had to do that part herself. She knew he was right, but liked the scratchy feel of the cloth on her legs. She was beginning to be cold with the evaporating wet.

"They have a zoo in California," she said.

"And tar pits." Boney's eyes lit, then collapsed on themselves. "I'm not going," he insisted.

"I know, 'cause of your dumb tunnel."

Boney wore a pained, cornered expression—as when she dug fingernails into his arm and wouldn't let go. It wasn't fair fighting. "You stay out of there. Don't even think about it. It could cave in and you would suffocate down there." Suddenly tensing, listening, his brow knit. "Hurry, Meena," he whispered. "Get your nightie on. Fast."

"It's full of pee," she whined.

"Hurry up." His face was spooked.

The door flung open and Mommy stood framed in the doorway. "Meena . . . Jeffrey? What are you two doing up?" Mommy's face undecided between fright, concern and anger. Her chin thrust forward as she took in her daughter's nakedness and scratched cheeks, the cloth in her son's hand. "Jeffrey! What have you done to her? What on earth have you done to your sister?"

"Not . . . nothing, Mom," he mumbled.

"Nothing!" she snapped. "Meena, put your nightie on. What has your brother done to you?"

"It's wet," Meena protested.

Mommy leapt forward, eyes bulging hard as marbles in their soft sockets. God alone knew what she was thinking. She knelt on a knee and hugged Meena close, seized a towel from the rack and wrapped it around her.

"She scratched herself," Boney managed in a tense, unconvincing voice. "Meena wet her bed."

Mommy's breath came in short, rapid inhalations. Turning her face aside, she closed her eyes a moment. In cold bathroom light, her hair glinted auburn within coils of black, like light spiraling down glazed walls of the tunnel when the trap door was lifted and dark was chased inward. It fascinated them, Mommy's hair. They stared at its soft coils and lights, inhaled the sweet familiar creme rinse smell as her head bobbed close. Maybe, if they focused hard enough, Mommy's face would grow safe again—instead of a stretched, unrecognizable mask. They would all laugh together at Meena's stinky nightie. Boney wanted to reach out and touch Mommy's hair, Meena knew, but didn't dare any more than he could touch Angel Hair spun of glass fiber.

Instead, Mommy seized the elastic waistband of his pajama bottoms, yanking him forward, glancing quickly down at his thingy. It wasn't the unexpected strangeness of it that startled, but her contempt, lips puckered and disdaining. "My own little boy. What's got into you?"

"I washed her off," he protested, blushing violently.

Mommy slapped him across the mouth. Hugging Meena close, she clawed into Boney's scalp with her other hand, bringing him into breath sweetened with vodka, soured with sleep. Side by side, brother and sister. His lip bled. A congealed ruby of blood clung to a gash in Meena's cheek. Mommy's mouth formed words precisely, but her voice fluted high and wavery.

"You won't ever touch her again. She is your sister. Do you understand me? Your sister!"

"I didn't do nothing."

"You call *that* nothing?"

Mommy twisted Boney's hair in a clawing hand; he cried out.

When she let him go, he slammed against the wall as if pulled by an elastic cord. Mommy pursued him on her knees, dragging Meena along, with a hand clamped to her place. Boney rose to his toes, peering helplessly into Meena's face, she into his. Bewildered, not knowing how to protect each other. That was beyond them now. Mommy shook her head mechanically. When she spoke, it was in a dull monotone.

"My mother stood by. I won't. Do you hear me? Over my dead body will you touch your sister again. You will not. You will not. My own little boy. My Jeffrey. Over my dead body." Her face coiling in grief. Breaking through it appeared a second face, transposed over the first within her transparent skin: boozed, tile-eyed, cheeks cinched tightly to lip corners, nostrils flaring. Meena pulled away, hoping she might wake up now. The dream had gone too far. Let it be Madame Chevaux's short white teeth and razor nose, all the girls opening their mouths and laughing at her for wetting herself.

"*Do you hear me?*" Mommy screamed.

Before Boney could move or even nod his head, the hand seized him inside his pajamas, wrapping his soft parts in a fist, twisting so hard that he cried out and nearly fainted. Meena felt his pain reach into her belly and turn her guts to green jelly, like Olson said it did. She was screeching. Boney mewling. Something had given way inside Mommy: screaming bloody, splattered egg yolk everywhere. She wouldn't permit . . . wouldn't stand idle . . . would take away what she had brought into this world. Hugging the naked girl to her, she shoved Boney violently away. His back slammed the wall. He jerked to the side, his head whiplashed. It hit the toilet bowl with a sickening crack as he went down.

Boney's eyes did a pas de deux in their sockets, shuddering and rolling. Meena watched his feet do a spasmodic tap dance against the wall, like he was dancing to heaven. Boney was dying, his head cracked open against the toilet bowl. When Mommy gathered her in her arms and fled the room, Meena went dead limp.

They collided with Daddy in the hall. "Jerri, what in the name of common sense—"

"Get away," Mommy shouted. "Don't touch her."

"Jerri, get a hold of yourself."

Meena was screaming, reaching for her father. But, as in all dreams, her words went quiet on the air. When Daddy reached for her, Mommy slapped him. An awful red smacking sound. Waking her daughter to the stern truth that she was already awake. Wide awake in a reality that had entered a dream. She squirmed, but Mommy's strength was supernatural. Clutching her daughter to her belly papoose fashion, she fled down the stairs and out the front door into the night.

# 9

## Aunt Debbie

The message awaited me at check-in in San Francisco:

CALL URGENT. JERRI'S FLIPPED. LOVE, DON.

The worst ever this time, he whispered on the phone once I got through. Fear just everywhere, skit-static through the line. Jerri had been boozing after he hit the sack. And it wasn't clear: the kids naked in the bathroom, Jeffrey mauled Meena up some, dicking his kid sister. Right there I said, *No way.* Something's off here. It was a whacham-a-call-it, a non sequitur. Jeff was too shy, if he got it up, even to look at it. You'd think they would realize that, word one. But Jerri was piss-plastered. Don too much a chip off the old self to see his son any different.

"Where is Jerri now?" I asked him.

"She took Meena, that's the thing. You know how she drives."

"You need to relax, Don."

"I've never seen her this bad, babe. I woke up and all hell had broke loose in there. Meena was wrapped around her and Jeff down beside the toilet. Convulsing pretty bad, eyes rolled up in his head. I thought she'd killed him. God, Deb, I was never so scared in my life. Didn't wait for an ambulance, rushed him down to the hospital in the backseat. He came around before we reached Emergency. Sat up in back and asked, 'What happened, Dad?' just like that."

"Don, is he okay?"

"I think so. Concussion. Took twelve stitches to close his scalp. She left him like that. Can you imagine? Her own son. I don't know what is happening in our lives."

"Don't bullshit me, Don. You need me, I'm here. But don't give me the innocent Willie crap."

"It's the kids, Deb."

"Balls. It's you. Kids, too . . . Okay."

He got control of his voice. "Jerri could use a little steadying when she gets home."

"She may throw me out."

"I don't think so; I was just on the phone with her. She scared herself good this time. I mean, Jeffrey . . . What got into her head?"

"We both know exactly what's in her head."

There was a silence. "Good Lord, I mean Jerri suspects something like that might have happened to her, it's no reason—"

"Not suspect, Don, she knows. I was right there."

"You understand a thing like that. Maybe a man can't. Maybe you could get a hold of this trouble in her, Deborah."

"I can't fix her life if that's what you mean."

"Just help us get sorted out again. Once we're past this, I intend to make a fresh start. All of us."

"You could just about convince yourself. One condition: Keep your hands in your pockets."

He was offended. "I'm trying to rescue a family here. I think you might understand that, Deb."

"I do. Really truly. I had a father spent his adult life rescuing. When he wasn't ruining, he was rescuing."

"I think imaginations have run far enough on this deal. I don't need you adding to that."

"Fair enough. We agree not to molest each other."

It was pissing rain in Millford. Always pissing rain. Didn't much dampen the stench of the paper mills. The smoke of slash from tepee burners south of town hung thick and low over everything as the cab dropped me in front of the house. The kind of lodged-deep smell that set loose things you hoped were tucked safely away. Sealed and filed. I stood in the rain looking at cedar siding, lighter near the eaves, darker where rain had soaked through. Juniper hedge, rhodies posted like sentries at each corner of the house, Jerri's blue spruce that Don decorated with lights Christmas. He hadn't taken them down yet, though it was March. They loop-the-looped, dripping and forlorn, through its branches. I sensed the Tillotsons had already abandoned the place in spirit. They would leave those lights behind.

I wasn't eager to go in. I walked up the drive past Jerri's

station wagon, Don's Impala. Family cars, they call them.
Maybe they hadn't seen me arrive; I could turn around and walk
away with my flight bag and nobody would be the wiser. Past
neighbors' houses with their own rhodies and blue spruce, ga-
rages docked out front like gunboats. Nobody ever saw a thing
in those places. You could do a striptease in the cul-de-sac, set
up a guillotine, throttle the kids. Nobody would be the wiser.
They huddled inside around TV football and miniature pool tables. Minded their own. Didn't give a f'ing fuck what happened
across the street. Why should they? This is a democracy after
all. I didn't see how they could stand it. All that emptiness. Then,
maybe it was better than what we had coming up. I couldn't
find any difference.

I stood in the rain, surprised to see Jerri looking out at me.
Her face half-mooned: pale one side, shadow-hidden the other.
Rain a curtain between us. Time opened it. That same face, but
younger, leaning close. Half light, half shadow. She had snapped
on the bed lamp. I watched her lips work, furious it seemed.
What had I done now? Too groggy to remember. Borrowed her
orange lettermen's cardigan again? I intended to sit up, protest
my innocence. But she clamped a hand over my mouth and
looked wildly behind her. She dragged me from bed. Caught a
nail file from the night table and snapped out the light. I thought
she had gone bonkers. Jerri pulled me into the closet, into a
crush of dresses and skirts. I resisted, afraid she might stab me
in there. But her tone of voice was commanding. "Trust me."
Closing the door from inside.

In the close, fragrant dark, I couldn't see a thing but vague
vents across the closet door. She whispered at me. But wasn't
her words that alarmed me so much as her smell. Because that
is a sense will intensify with nothing but dark to confuse it. She
smelled of Daddy's Prince Albert pipe tobacco. But I couldn't be
sure because our brother Chuck had begun smoking, too. It
overwhelmed her eau de cologne and the vague woolly scent she
carried with her. The thing is, Jerri didn't smoke.

"Over my dead body," she kept saying. "He won't make a
whore out of you." She clutched the file hilt to her stomach,
point facing the door. Blubbering, hysterical. I knew something
had happened but vaguely. Balls! I understood well enough even

then. That part of me already a woman understood instinctively. Though I was just eleven years old, how could I know all of it?

After a time we came out. Jerri sensed the danger had passed. She was becoming concerned about herself, saying she must get to the john, and I would have to come. We did not mention that night again. Not ever. Though I watched closely next morning, I couldn't tell which of them it was—Dad or my brother, Chuck. She was ice to both. That wasn't possible, I thought: not the both. I expected one day I would learn.

Me in the rain, Jerri in the window watching me walk up the steps. Two sisters, inside out. Regarding each other in the glass like separate sides of themselves. She looked like shit. Baggy-eyed and sunken-cheeked. Looked guzzled in and upchucked out. Her hair matted one side like she'd slept against the car window. It wasn't like Jerri to face the world without her face on—in the soiled nightgown she wore into International House of Pancakes at seven A.M. to call Don. Even shitfaced, she still required makeup. The Grim Reaper himself would have to hold his horses until she'd been to the beauty parlor. Don was right: never this bad. It was the Jeff thing, I understood that.

After I'd rung the doorbell eight times—with her standing right inside watching my finger on the bell—she decided to open.

"Glad the doorbell works," I told her.

"Look who the cat dragged in."

"Donald asked me to come."

"I just bet he did."

I gripped her elbow and led her inside her own house. Into darkness, turning on lights as we went. "Don't you think you've been angry enough for one twenty-four hours?"

Jerri nodded solemnly, too haggard to reply.

I made coffee and the two of us sat at the kitchen table, while Don and Meena slept upstairs. It felt late of a Sunday morning. Jerri in there fighting: her face punched this way by tears, chopped the other by defiance, holding her own. She gripped the coffee mug in both hands. Did fine bringing it to her lips, but on the table it jittered. Her nail polish was chipped, hair hung like a dowdy shawl across her scalp. Overnight she'd lost it. A beautiful woman nonetheless. I told her so. How proud I was as a kid to point her out to classmates if we saw her with a boyfriend on the street (more often a gang of them) or out on blacktop behind the high school practicing with the rally squad. We'd line up along the fence like monkeys, fingers gripping the mesh, and oogle-augle.

"You were the prettiest of the lot."

"Oh chicken piss." Jerri frowned. Or pretended to. Pleased in spite of herself. She couldn't resist a compliment.

"Seven of you, I remember."

She got a faraway look, her forehead smoothing. "Silly McCallister, Sharon Baumgartner, Sharon Howard, Suzie McCormick, Sissy Wollitzer, Samantha Higgins . . . isn't that a kick? I was the only gal whose name didn't start with an *S*."

"You could do the splits. That inspired me. I tried and nearly tore out my yoni."

We laughed. Something we hadn't done together in ages.

"Gawd I was sore after those games. We leapt and kicked and split-ted. And I didn't get my voice back till Monday. Kind of dumb when you think about it."

"I remember lemons. The fridge was half lemons."

"Oh! If I caught anyone after my lemons . . . " Her voice rose. "Dumb. Really dumb. Meena won't do rally squad—over my dead body." She touched fingertips to her eyes. We had entered rugged terrain. It happened suddenly like all unhappiness does: One moment things are hunky-dory, the next life is the shits. Jerri was suddenly cornered, seeking escape. Or a drink, I guessed.

"Maybe you ought to hit the hay, huh?" I touched her clasped fingers.

She jerked hands and coffee mug away, sloshing some onto the table. "We're a big girl now, we can make our own decisions." She leaned forward to whisper, her eyes almost rakish. "How about just a nip?"

"Over my dead body," I snapped.

Jerri's eye corners twitched, her cheeks. How dare you, her eyes said. How dare you, little slut. Shit whiskers, I thought, now she's going to pull one of her stunts. Shrieking and breaking things up. Instead, she gathered knees in her arms and hugged her forehead to them, rocking. Leaking whimpers.

"All right, honey," I said. "Jerri?"

Her face, when she looked at me, was pale as cold putty.

"I don't know how I will look him in the eye . . . my own baby."

"You will, hon."

"How could he do it? Olson maybe. Not Jeffrey."

"He didn't do one damn thing. We both know it."

"Look at her!" she snapped. "Go up and look at her."

"Did you ask her, Jerri?"

"What's the matter with you? You don't ask about a thing like that. Why, it could ruin her. Look what it's done to me. Deborah . . . just look at me," she said in disgust.

"I am looking at you. I don't see anything different. Sleepy maybe, a bit fusty is all."

"You think you see a thing like that? The scars are all inside. It's just torn her up. She refuses to admit any of it. Meena defends her brother. Imagine! Doesn't surprise me one bit; I went through it myself. Everybody does. Denial." She looked blankly ahead. "I think we will have to separate them."

"Over my sweet ass you are going to separate those two."

Jerri stared at me, incredulous. "She can't live in the same house with that boy."

"That boy is your son." I gripped her shoulders, wanting her to know my steadiness. "I don't believe it. I don't believe word one of it. We're going to find out. That's why I came. To find out what happened and avoid all this craziness."

Jerri nodded. Her life tottered like a tower of building blocks constructed in a stupor. You saw that.

"They're your children, but that's as far as it goes. Your history ends when they are born, theirs begins. Hon, you can't confuse that."

"Oh, we know all about it, don't we?" she said bitterly. "We don't have our own, but we know all about other people's."

"Are we going to do this?"

"Can I see him?" she asked meekly. "Will you take me to see him?"

"Sure I'll take you . . . soon as Don gets up."

"Now."

"Hon . . . I don't know."

She smiled. Wasn't pretty, I will say that. It wasn't pretty. The tiny beak of her upper lip gone thorny. "I won't make a scene if that's what worries you, Debbie."

"I want to clear this up. That's all there is to it. I want you to go in reassured. He'll need that. You will, too, hon."

I thought she'd go fetal and weepy again. Dynamic, you could call Jerri. Like a bumpy Land Rover ride over rough terrain. The emotional bounce could wear out a saint. But she gathered herself in one of those remarkable about-faces of my big sister. Sat up. Stretched her chin to one side, then the other.

"I'm fine," she said. "If you're afraid to be seen in public with your dummy sister, that's your problem. I guess you and Don have discussed me. Kid gloves." She wiggled her fingers.

"Balls. And you know it is."

"I've had my coffee and I feel fine. So I'll take a shower and you can drive down with me or I'll drive by myself."

"It's your car." I shrugged.

"It's my family." Her smile sweet and sticky. She busied herself with kitchen chores, then went upstairs—a new woman. Perhaps she had suddenly remembered the vodka secreted away in a plastic creme rinse bottle in the shower. That's unfair. You want a person to change, you have to believe change is possible.


# 10


# Jeff

My hair was even shorter than Steve Weatherspoon's. On top my head felt shiny and smooth as a doorknob, except for the stitches in the back. There were twelve of them, like stitches on a football. The nurse said I shouldn't touch them. "You don't want to work them loose."

"Would my brains spill out?"

"Land's sake," she said. "You are a live wire, aren't you?"

"It's sore."

"I should say so. You took quite a spill, young man."

"Are you mad at me?" I asked.

"No." She looked puzzled. "Why ever should I be mad at you?"

"My mom calls me 'young man' when she gets mad."

"I see."

"I slipped and fell down in the bathroom."

She shook her head, her eyes like blue boulders buried in a puffy fist before someone shoots them.

"That's God's truth," I said. "I smacked the toilet."

She didn't say nothing, only pinched her lips. I knew she didn't believe me. She was the grouchy type, like Miss Parkinson at school. On top her hair was black and combed back under her cap, but it was cotton balls above her ears. I wondered why she didn't dye it so it would be all the same color.

"All right, young man, let's see if you can sit up." She came over and flicked my arm with her finger. It stung.

"I can sit up myself. You don't have to snap me."

"We'll see."

She snapped me on the other arm, the old bitty, not even warning me this time by saying "young man." I sat up anyway. Skin stretched tight on my scalp and pulled at my stitches.

"If you're going to be sick again, I want you to use the bag. Can you manage?"

"I don't feel sick anymore."

"Good. Maybe we'll try some breakfast then." She always said "we." When she brought the pudding, she said, "Should we try some tapioca?" I thought she was going to eat out of my same bowl. "Would we like some Cream of Wheat?" She smiled just like Miss Parkinson, which means: You better like Cream of Wheat, young man. I already learned you had to say yes. If you said no, she'd flick you and say you didn't know your own mind. But I hate Cream of Wheat. Meena says it looks like birds' diarrhea.

I already hated that place, too. Not just grouchy nurses but the smell. Across the room was a curtain on a metal frame; behind there someone kept moaning. Gave me the creeps. When I asked the doctor what was wrong with him, he said it was a gallbladder patient. I knew I didn't ever want to have a gallbladder. It smelled awful, like vomit they tried to cover up with bathroom deodorizer.

"Your family will be here soon," the nurse said. "Maybe the doctor will let you go home."

She went out into the hall, and I heard her tell somebody I was afraid my brains would spill out. A tall nurse in a pale blue uniform grinned at me as she went past the door; she was a nun. They kept nuns around for people who were dying, so they would have someone to confess their sins to at the last minute. I wondered what I would confess if I died last night.

They had put me on a stretcher with wheels on the bottom and there was two Negro men pushing it, which was weird because I never saw Negroes in our town. So I thought maybe they all worked in the hospital. That's why you never saw them: They were too busy.

The one pushing behind was short and rubbery-cheeked and kept saying, "You gonna make it." In front, the man burst through doors and said "gangway" when nobody was there. Every time we went around a corner he said "gangway" and nobody was there.

They took me through a large room that smelled of Lysol and Mercurochrome. A woman sitting behind a desk reading a magazine pointed and said "Over there" without looking up. They brought me into a cubicle and closed the curtain. Dad was with me the whole way, walking beside Mr. Rubber Face. His head looked different from underneath: His chin was bony and his face spread up from it in a triangle toward ridges in his forehead. His eyes were milky like always when he was emotional. It scared me that he looked so scared.

"Am I going to die, Dad?" I whispered when they closed the curtain.

"Of course not." But it wasn't Dad who answered, but a doctor in a white coat who swished the curtain aside and asked Dad to wait outside, please. "Not enough oxygen in here for three of us." That's what Steve Weatherspoon always says in the tunnel. Only two at a time, not enough oxygen for three. I thought then maybe Steve would become a doctor. He's curious about the human anatomy, and he has a way of ordering people around like doctors do.

The doctor smiled in an unsmiling way, like fingers pulled up his lips either side. "How do you feel?" he asked me.

"It hurts, but at least it stopped throbbing."

"I hear you took a spill."

"I tripped on the bathroom rug," I said, trying to sit up.

"All right. Relax now . . . Jeff." He glanced down at a paper.

I was afraid he didn't believe me. His face had no expression, like pancake dough when you first drop it on the griddle, just his nose sticking out. A big no-nonsense nose.

"My sister wet her bed and I went to wash her off."

"Sir Galahad of the bed wetters. That a mite tender?"

"Ouch!" I said. He was poking and pushing on my head.

"Sisters are a nuisance," he said. "Baby sisters in particular."

"She's okay. She's not really a baby anymore. She's old enough to know better."

"Old enough to wash herself after she wets her bed?" His eyes watched me through granny glasses.

"Yeah." Closing my eyes because my head started to throb. I wondered if Mom took Meena away for good. At least they didn't have a car wreck, which always worried me when Mom left like that. They would be at the hospital if they did.

"Jeff, I want you to raise your arms. Can you do that?"

First arms, then my feet, then touch my index fingers together with my eyes shut—easy stuff (except I didn't know you could do that). He leaned close with a spy scope in front of his eye, a pointy black weevil's snout like doctors use, and asked me to look up and down. I was scared he might see I was lying by watching the blood vessels in my brain. Doctors can tell. Blood pounded behind my eyes like surf on a beach. But they would never get that out of me. It was an accident, that's all.

He snapped the spy beak shut and dropped it in his pocket. "Think we better get some pictures," he said. Maybe they wanted proof in case my head healed up. The police took pictures of dead bodies and stuff at the scene of the crime.

"It was only an accident," I insisted.

"Yes, Jeff, you've told me that. You tripped and fell. Would I have any reason to doubt you?"

He saw me gulp. That's the most spastic thing you can do, Olson says, if you have to tell a lie.

"How's the belly?"

"Quivery," I said. "I'm afraid I might throw up."

His eyes were battleship gray, like radar dishes magnified twice normal size behind his glasses. "You were roughhousing a bit, is that it?"

I boosted up on my elbows. "I didn't do nothing to her."

"All right . . . relax."

I watched the stethoscope hose jiggling from his pocket; any second, I knew he would pull it out and listen to my heart. Then he would know. But he swished the curtains aside and Dad stood there. "Nothing to worry about. Mild concussion," the doctor said. "We'll take some X rays."

Dad smiled a little. He was chewing his lip.

"My heart's okay, too," I told Dad. "He didn't have to check it."

"Uh-oh, better not jump to conclusions." The doctor pulled the stethoscope from his pocket; I thought I was done for. The cold metal like an ice cube on my chest. "Seems to be working." He winked at Dad, then turned on his heel and walked away, and I whispered to Dad that I didn't tell him anything. He winced and patted my arm.

They took X rays, and a funny fat man with a lisp and huge hairy fists shaved my head. His lisp wasn't the same as Buck's, which was almost a stutter. It seemed like the fat man lisped on purpose, making wet smacking sounds as he spoke. He told me he had a concussion once when his brother hit him with a base-ball bat. "I thaw thtarth. Firtht, a red flath, then bright twinkling thtarth, then nothing. Ouch, it hurt. What did you theee?"

"My mom," I said, because I knew he wouldn't tell anyone; I just knew. "Her hair looked like flames and smoke, and my sister was clinging hold of her."

"Wow," he said. "I never thaw anything like that. Very freaky. My mama wathn't violent, juth my brother. Your mom knocked you down?"

I nodded.

He nodded.

"Now you tell me if thith hurth. I hate hurting people." He used a gleaming straight razor that made scraping sounds across my scalp. I was sure he would cut me—his hands were so big. "Goodneth, that ith nathty. The hair'th all matted."

"Why d'you think she did it?" I asked him.

"Well, I couldn't thay. My brother found any little excuthe to be angry. He wath like a pot boiling over; juth throw in a little thalt—and watch out."

It pinched as he worked around the wound, but I didn't pay any attention. I asked if he thought they would put Mom in jail for pushing me down if they found out.

"I don't think tho. Thometimeth they remove children from a home where there'th violenth . . . loth of violenth."

"This is the first time it happened, honest. I'm not mad at her or anything."

He leaned down close, his breath smelled of cinnamon. "We'll make it our thee-cret."

Thinking back on it later, I decided it wasn't a sin to lie if you told someone the truth. Telling him erased the lie I had told the doctor, and I wouldn't have to confess the sin to anyone, 'cause I already did. But if you held it inside and let it rot, then it would be like a bad potato in a sack, rotting all the rest with it. So when the nuns came to hear your confession the stench would drive them from the room—even in a hospital where they were used to bad smells.

My worst sin was when I stole a bra from Mom's drawer and didn't bring it back. It was for the dummy the Long Loops had in Buck's basement. His father stored window dummies down there from his department store. Most were missing a leg or head or something, so it looked like bodies piled up after a war. Pretty neat. But this one was beautiful, with a Japanese face (which was why he didn't use it, because of the war veterans). She had tits and hair and eyelashes, everything, even nipples, which Olson colored brown with a crayon, because that's the color Asian nipples are, he said. We cut off hair from another dummy and pasted it on for her pubes, and it looked so real you couldn't believe it. Made out of plaster or something, with smooth skin and a tiny red mouth, one hand on her hip and the other facing palm up like she was holding something. We called her Tokyo Rose.

Then all of us had to bring something. I got a bra and Olson got see-through panties from his mom's, where he visits summers. Only he was scared she suspected him. Steve got nylons and Buck got a garter belt, because his mom was the only one who wore them. Except we never figured out which way it fit.

Gary Seamore stole a negligee from his sister. That was our hottest item, because Ginny Seamore was the sexiest girl at Millford High. We dressed Rose up and sat in the dark basement shining flashlights on her, so it was like a striptease show. She was more beautiful than Marilyn Monroe, though she looked like Gina Lollobrigida. Then one of us would take off a piece of her clothes. We took turns. It was *Playboy* magazine down there in Buck's basement. All the Long Loops imagining it was really Ginny Seamore—except maybe her brother. Disgusting when you think about it.

Sometimes, one of the guys would jack off, mostly Olson. Once he actually humped her. Gary Seamore got furious, because he had to take the negligee back each time, and now it was covered with Olson's slimy jism. Really gross. So they washed it in the machine before Buck's mom got home. Only it shrank about three sizes in the dryer. Ginny Seamore never guessed what happened. She just found her nightie shrunk mysteriously in the drawer. Gary said she told her friends it was a sign from God that he wanted her to lose weight to enter the Miss Oregon pageant (she was very religious). Why else would your nightgown shrink like that in your own drawer? After that, I could never look at Ginny Seamore again without giggling. Sometimes you know people's secrets better than they do themselves.

But I felt really bad about Mom's bra. I think it was one of her favorites. I kept wanting to take it back, but Olson said, "Don't be a jerk. One day her bra disappears without a trace, then it reappears again. She'll know somebody took it." I think he was scared she would blame him.

"Why would anybody take it?" I asked.

"Stoo-pid." He grinned and ran a hand back through his hair, long and slicked back like surfers' hair in California. "Why'd you take it, bonerhead?"

"It wasn't my idea."

"She'll think you use it to jack off."

I wished he hadn't said that, because before that I always thought of Ginny Seamore down in the basement; after that, I kept imagining it was Mom. I would hide my head while the guys whistled and cheered. The worst torture was when it was my turn and they chanted at me to take it off. I hated that. It was like undressing your own mom in front of the guys. I decided as soon as I was old enough to walk into the Bon Marché and buy a bra without arousing suspicion I would replace the one I'd stole. But that wouldn't be for a long time. Maybe never. It was a relief, anyway, to know I wasn't dying, and I wouldn't have to confess my sins. There were lots of smaller ones. But Mom's bra was the one that would prob'ly land me in hell.

When Aunt Debbie poked her head in the door, I was on my third bowl of tapioca. "Brain food!" She winked. "Rat whiskers, it stinks in here." I was never so happy to see anyone. She kissed me and sat down on the bed. "You look like Yul Brynner," she said. "Ol' chrome dome. Kinda sexy. Except the Frankenstein ties in back. What's that, so you can take your brain out and air it?"

"Yeah," I said. "You could pour sawdust into my head."

"It's already full, buster. Pee-you it's rank." She threw a hard glance at Mr. Gallbladder's curtain. "Fella could use a bath." She leaned close and her face recomposed to Debbie seriousness. "Everything's going to be hunky-dory," she said. "Sometimes there is bad history in a family and that causes trouble long after it should be forgotten. I can't tell you about that now, but someday I promise I will. I know what happened last night. I know it all. Meena told me, and I told your mom and dad. Little spook! I had to drag it out of her. I told her you would go to jail if she didn't tell me. So she did. She took Chester into bed with her again and he scratched her. Then she peed. That suit you okay?"

I nodded.

"The truth ain't worth fish piss in some families, and yours is one. It's like you all tilted sideways and can't walk straight anymore. Except you." Debbie poked my nose. "I don't blame you. Criminy, pretty soon you don't know which parts of you are real anymore. Maybe it's a cracked head, but at least you know who it belongs to." She smiled and bent down to kiss my forehead. She smelled like sweetened tea leaves; I breathed her in. But I knew I didn't deserve her compliment. I was going sideways, too.

"Is Mom still mad at me?" I asked.

"No, hon, she isn't mad. It was never really you she was mad at in the first place."

"I didn't do nothing." Motioning her close. "I told Meena she had to do that part herself . . . you know?"

"The girl part?"

I nodded.

"You're red as a beefsteak tomato. It's nothing to be ashamed about. That's where all the trouble starts."

"I think the doctor is suspicious. I told him I tripped and smacked my head."

"Doctors make a living being suspicious. Your mom's outside." Debbie straightened up. "She'd sure like to see you."

I already saw her—standing like Meena in the corridor with her back to the wall. Her chest rose and fell, she seemed to be catching her breath. Then she turned to look at me. I waved. She waved back. "Honey," she asked timidly, "can I come in?"

She never asked before. She was dressed up in the velvety purple skirt and jacket she wore to church, which Dad calls her Jackie Kennedy outfit, and looked very smart. Except her eyes were red and puffy. For a second, I was afraid they would go wild again like last night. But mornings were safe, I knew. Dad says, "After three cups of coffee your mom could wrestle the devil."

"It kinda stinks," I said.

She came straight over like she didn't hear me, and I told myself not to but I tensed when she kissed my cheek. "Darling," she kept saying, "my little boy." She rubbed a hand over my forehead, and I was afraid she was going to cry. Her mouth formed a small round wound. She kissed my forehead, then the top of my bald head, and I knew she hesitated before kissing the rest, because I had seen it myself in a mirror the doctor held up for me after he finished stitching: puckered purple, stitch ends sticking out like black fish whiskers. "Not very pretty," he'd said.

"Oh, honey, I'm just so awfully sorry. I'm just . . . You mustn't think . . . Honey! You don't think, do you"—she gripped my chin hard in her hand and was looking at me close— "You know Mom didn't mean to, I'm sure you do."

I tried to pull away, but her fingers were too strong.

"Okay, Jerri." Aunt Debbie touched Mom's shoulder.

Mom shrugged her off. "Remember when you used to hurt yourself Mommy kissed it and made it well? Would you like her to do that?"

"That's all right," I said. I was trying not to smell her breath, trying to turn my face away and pretend I didn't.

"You're just so cute with your liddle shaved head."

Aunt Debbie crouched beside the bed, studying me close like she did the back of fanned cards when we played hearts and Dad accused her of X-ray vision; she knew what I was thinking. Her eyes jumped back and forth between Mom and me, squinting like a referee's.

"We'll get you a cap," Mom said. "Your Grandpa Walter liked to wear a cap."

"Jerri," Aunt Debbie said softly.

"Isn't he just the cutest thing? Just darling. Don't you think so?"

"I think he wants us to bugger off."

"Will you stop treating me like a child, Deborah."

"When you stop acting like one."

Mom's fingers skittered atop my head. She straightened up and tugged at the hem of her short jacket. "He can't be in this room. I can't imagine what his dad is thinking. It stinks in here."

"I'm used to it now," I said, glad she changed subjects.

Mom glared at Gallbladder's curtain. "They've put him in with an old person. Can't they put him with someone his own age?"

"There may be a shortage of boys with cracked noggins."

I laughed. But Mom said it wasn't funny one bit.

"It's a try. Creesus, you'd think someone died."

"You should hear it when he moans," I said.

Mom knelt down beside the bed on a knee and took my hand. Her breath smelled half-and-half: coffee and the booze she kept in the Joy bottle beside the sink and when no one was looking squirted it in her cup.

"We'll get you another room, dear. Mommy promises. She knows she can be difficult sometimes, but she doesn't mean it. You know she doesn't, don't you, darling. Sometimes she goofs. Do you think you might forgive her . . . just a little?"

Her hands icy cold, and I wanted to extract mine, but didn't want to hurt her feelings. Just wanted her to sit beside me and we could play hearts or Monopoly. I was thinking about the Joy bottle—how Meena and I worried she might mess up someday and get the wrong one and accidentally squirt in real detergent.

"Mom goofs plenty, but this is the end of that. She promises. The end. Can you forgive her?" She lurched forward and hugged my head into her breasts, gripping hard with both hands, her wool jacket electric-tingly against my stitches—like antennae sending shocks into my brain—while words muffled together in her chest. I couldn't make them out. My cheek squashed against her lungs (Olson calls them) and my nose in the moist, wrinkled fissure between, so tight I couldn't breathe. I began to panic, thinking she was Tokyo Rose come to life when my turn came to unfasten her bra—clutching me with plastery, perfumed fingers.

"Will you forgive me, darling?"

Aunt Debbie shouting, "For crissake, Jerri. Get a grip."

When Mom let go, I admitted I stole it. I did, I took her brassiere. It wasn't Meena playing grown-up or Olson with his dirty mind . . . it was me. "I'll give it back, Mom, I promise."

They stared at me like I'd gone bonkers.

# 11

# Aunt Debbie

Jerri was on both knees beside the bed. I thought she'd pull Jeff right down onto the floor. Damn her. Pawing him. Jeff's eyes spooked. Doing his damnedest to deny he was afraid of his own mom. Fighting the thing, you could see. Promising he would bring it back—the bra, I suppose.

"What are you talking about, honey?" Jerri fumbled a bra strap out of her blouse. "See! I'm wearing it." She looked wildly at me and laughed, afraid Jeff's thinking had cracked with his noggin. "Isn't that a kick! Mommy doesn't want you to worry about it anymore. You've had a rough time, honey."

"Your pink one," he persisted. "I only meant to borrow it."

Jerri looked at me, desperate.

"It doesn't matter," I said, hating myself for not realizing she had been getting pissed while I fed her coffee to sober her up. Or possibly the shower spigot sprayed dry martinis. Couldn't face this thing without fortification, I suppose. I was dragging her up by the armpits when the nurse come in. A face that could sober a bar full of drunk Irishmen. She looked from Jerri's droopy eyes to nylons bagged at her knees. Squinched her lips and left the room.

"Wha's her problem?" Jerri demanded.

"Big mystery. You promised me, Jerri. No scenes."

She straightened up, haughtily. "We're leaving now, honey." Leaning over Jeff, who cringed away. "We'll come back later with y'r dad. Get some sleep."

"Honest, Aunt Debbie," Jeff crooned.

"Doesn't matter fish piss," I said. "Tomorrow you'll be going home and everything will be back to normal. Hunky-dory."

After I'd got Jerri home and put her to bed and returned with Don that evening, Jeff told me about it. I thought it was the funniest thing: four boys sitting around a naked dummy in a circle jerk. "But I don't like all the sneaking around. It's not healthy."

"Is my mom a drunkard?" he asked, little shit, those great thousand-pound questions in the middle of nothing.

"These days they call it alcoholic."

"Can she get well?"

"She can, yes . . . if she wants to."

"Did she try to kill me, Aunt Debbie?"

"Okay, enough. Erase that thought. Just clean the paper." I sat on the bedside. "Your mother loves you. Whatever else she does, she loves you. Do you hear?"

"I have a headache," he said. Didn't surprise me from the looks of his bald head. It was a sight: a cruel black line, crimped and puffy where stitches puckered the skin, gone blue at edges. Like a zipper atop his noggin.

Don and Meena stood in the doorway. He was looking at my bare knees, she at her brother's shaved head. A gauze bandage on one cheek. It was like they had returned from a war zone, those two. Don wanted them to make up and be friends. "We are friends." Meena skipped over to Jeff. "Can I see your stitches? You look awful," she said cheerily. "Ugh, dis-gusting."

Don had brought Jeff an eye patch, made him look like a dwarf pirate—with that baldy head. He asked me to join him for coffee downstairs. We left the kids plotting how to scare the nurses.

The cafeteria was empty but for two white-coated doctors by the dispensing machines and a dour bunch at a far table, Gall-bladder's family. Don stared into his oily dispensing-machine coffee and said he wondered how much more he could take. He went to bed nights and didn't know if Jerri would be beside him next morning when he woke up. She wandered the house or sat up at the vanity mirror staring at herself. "I don't dare tell her to come to bed." He cringed, his eyes rolling vaguely toward Jeff's room. "It's the booze, Deb."

"Booze. Yes, that's part of it."

"What else?" he asked edgily.

"Bad history. Things haven't worked out like she wanted."

"Husband thing maybe?"

"I guess maybe you'd know about that."

"I don't know, damn it. That's the thing. I don't."

Over the Formica table his face cinched up in sincerity, brow bunched. Be fair, I coached myself. The man's in a shit sandwich. So what if he buttered the bread. We all butter our own bread. "Maybe you don't, Don. It doesn't matter. Fault doesn't matter. It's what you do about it. We try to help our friends, even if we're married to them."

His dimples again—but anguished, a pothole in either cheek. His knee bumped mine under the table. He mock-frowned. "What are you suggesting I do, Deborah? I'd like to know."

"Dry her out, for starters. Keep her dry."

Across the room, doctors talked and gestured. Now and again, the lanky one yanked a glistening silver dispenser handle behind him: whank whank whank. Couldn't help themselves.

Don leaned forward, conspiratorial. "Jerri won't admit she has a problem, she won't hear of it."

"You're afraid of her, aren't you, Don?"

"Afraid?" He guffawed. The doctors looked over.

"You know what it does, it about terrifies the kids seeing that. Daddy afraid of Mommy."

"Boy, you are something. Never give a man an inch. Isn't that old Sally's motto?"

"That's only the half of it. Fact is, you won't check her into Tranquility Acres. Everybody in town would know. Isn't that what worries you? Don Tillotson's alcoholic wife! Might better think of promoting someone else. You prefer to keep it closed up at home."

"That's way the hell out of line, Deborah."

"You think people don't know already?"

Don clutched the table; he stared at red crescents of his thumb nails. "I don't give a good goddamn what they know."

"Then get her help."

"I'm telling you she won't take it."

"Balls! You know it is. She's screaming for someone to tell her 'Enough!' She wants it so bad she can't talk about it. Trouble is, you're birds of a feather. You'd rather pretend. So what if Jerri sleeps in the closet; who's going to notice?"

"That's nasty, Deb." The knee again.

"You damn betcha it's nasty." I pointed a finger upstairs.

The lot were looking at us now: Gallbladder's family and the doctors. Don leapt up and brought back Cokes. Stood at the table in his white pullover, lanky, leathery tan, knowing he cut a figure. I wasn't buying into it. Old Walter taught me early: If the fish is hooked, don't pay any mind to its leaps and runs. Adjust your star drag and keep tension on the line. But Don wasn't anywhere near the boat. Not yet. He sat, forcing knees hard against mine, gray-blue eyes turned up full volume. He'd passed bad habits on to Olson. You wondered did they sit them down at puberty and teach them the ropes: *If her lips open to smile, you bet she'll open her legs.* Once I'd caught the little shit collecting pubic hairs from between my sheets. Single-handed, he was a threat to the public school system; they'd had to send him away to an academy.

I ground my kneecaps back into Don's. Legs was my strong point. Maneuvering aisles at 30,000 feet over the bumpety-bumps.

"So what you plan to do, hon?"

Don leaned back and patted his stomach. "We're moving

south. San Diego. I'll manage our new office down there. We're going to start over again. A whole new life."

"Oh you bet. Jerri can buy booze right at the supermarket."

Don's eyes tightened. "You're a cynic, Debbie. That's your trouble. Always was. You don't give the world a chance."

"Balls on the world. I'm talking about my sister." I reminded him that Jerri had had a future before he married her. She'd sold three houses, begun her estate license. Don linked fingers behind his head and said she wouldn't have made it. Just like she couldn't make college. Smug bastard.

"Don't get me wrong, I encouraged it. I said, 'Jerr, you've got sales in your blood, but you've got to make up your mind to do something.' That's her whole trouble . . . always was."

"Is there ever five minutes of a given day you don't lie to yourself, Don?"

He took my hand, shaking his head. His cheeks glowed red hot. "You can't imagine the pressure, hon. Two families to support. Sitka won't talk to me, her mom's poisoned her that bad. Olson—Jesus, I don't know where he's headed. There's a boy he's picking on at school, smears shit on the kid's sheets; principal thinks it's a homo thing. They've separated him to another dorm. Good Christ! . . . a queer. How do I talk to him about a thing like that? And now Jerri's problems—"

"Alcoholism!" I blurted. "Can't you say it?"

"Jerri's . . . She abuses, that's all it is."

"She's supposed to face it when you can't?"

All the flaw was in his chin, his neck draped straight away from it. Dad said a man's character is in his chin. Don didn't have beans of it. New environment, he was saying, new climate, palm trees, Jerri hates the damned rain, maybe she could sell real estate again, new school down there for Olson. "The kids are going to love it. We'll have a guest room, anytime you want to visit—"

"You're babbling, Don."

"Dreaming. Guess you don't know about dreaming." He worked his knee up my thigh, hitching my skirt.

"Maybe not. But people ought to keep dreams to themselves." I clamped his knee between mine. "I move dreams across the continent two hundred a load. Funny thing, people think they'll leave their troubles behind, but they take them right along with them. You see that."

"Never give a guy an inch." Don grinned. Like something he practiced in the mirror. Taking every inch he could with my skirt. Occurred to me I might jab a spiked heel into his crotch.

"You want to stop hoisting my skirt."

Don's eyebrow jerked up as if snagged by a fishhook. "Little brotherly affection, that's all. Hey, I'm trying to avoid desperation here." He slid a hand up my forearm, the back of it grazing my breast. "You're a comfort to me, hon."

My instep caught the edge of his chair; using it as a fulcrum I eased my toes into his crotch and bore down. The look on his face! Shit whiskers. His neck flushed bright. All that charm doing back flips. My shoe sole thin enough I could feel squirmy living flesh trapped beneath. When I eased up, he scooted straight back across the floor in the chair.

"F'r crissakes, Deborah," squealing an octave higher than normal. His eyes darted wild about the room. "No more of that," he said hoarsely.

"It's a deal." I lip-smiled. "No more."

But something I hadn't seen before in his expression: ruthless, vindictive. Not surprising maybe. He was a clipboard-toting company gun. I only knew the home side of my brother-in-law. The look he gave me was another side completely. Frightened me a little, I'll say.

# 12

# Jeff

Meena laid on Gallbladder's bed. I told her she'd prob'ly catch a foul disease and they would have to cut her open, but I think she wanted to be cut open. She was jealous of my being in the hospital. "This bed stinks," she said. I told her Gallbladder had bedsores. Meena only wrinkled her nose and covered her ears with her braids like she does when she's creeped out, but she didn't move. Aunt Debbie burst in.

"I'm outta here, hon," she snapped, like I'd done something wrong. Her hair mussed and talking fast like she does when she's mad. What was it, I wondered: telling her about Tokyo Rose? When she kissed my forehead, her blouse was open so I saw her red bra, her whole neck blotchy and perspiring. She asked me if I could forgive her for hurrying off like this. Her breath tasted of tea leaves as always, but her eyelids were puffy like Mom's.

"Aunt Debbie, your blouse is unbuttoned," I said.

She gripped it together and spun on her heel. "Meena, you get off of there. Shit whiskers almighty."

I could tell Meena was nervous even though she pretended to be asleep. "He used to fart in his bed all the time," I said, "the moist, disgusting kind."

"Ugh." Meena jumped up like she got a shock.

"All right, kiddos, I'm off. Fly United." Jerking up her thumb, but her eyes antsy, leaping around. Sister Paul Marie had come in. She gawked at Aunt Debbie's blouse like she hadn't never seen a lady in her bra before, her mouth pinched in disapproval like Grandma Sally's does. She smiled the gimpy way nuns and nurses do and asked, "Are you the mother?" Debbie looked her over from her white collar to the square nurse's shoes and the blue barrel in between. "I'm outta here is what I am. Bye-bye, sugar pies, wave to me in the friendly skies."

"Bye, Debbie," we cried.

"What a peculiar woman," Sister Paul Marie mumbled after she left. "That's our aunt," Meena told her. She wanted to follow Paul Marie to the nurses' station to find out if nurses steal dead people's hair to make wigs. "Tapioca is dead people's snot," I told her. She said Sister Paul Marie smelled like toilet disinfectant (she knew about people from their smell). Later she told me Dad smelled like Aunt Debbie's cologne. He peeked around the corner before coming in my room, like we always did before entering Mr. Ashcroft's lot.

"Just us," I said, "Aunt Debbie already left."

Dad threw me a stern look. I wondered if he was mad at me for being in the hospital and costing him so much money. Hospitals seemed to put adults in a bad mood. I asked him was

Debbie mad at him, too. He came right over. "What did your aunt tell you? Jeff . . . Meena? Don't you kids believe a word she says."

Something weird was happening. It was like the adults were all experiencing personality changes: Mom, Aunt Debbie, now Dad. Like the mean self they carried inside them had broke loose in bad hospital air.

Debbie didn't say nothing, I told him, except she had to leave. Dad rubbed my head. "How's the old nogger?" But when I asked him if Mom was coming, he opened his mouth with a wet exasperated sound like he does when he and Mom have an argument and he doesn't know what to say. He sat on the edge of the bed and explained I had to stay there another night "for observation." I had a convulsion last night and they wanted to make sure. Then he and Meena left. We never even got to play Monopoly. What good is being in the hospital if you can't have any fun?

That night the hospital was full of bleeps and shoe squealing and sick people's moans. I concentrated on the tunnel to distract my mind. Digging had got hairy. Great chunks of roof caved in and dirt dribbled down on our heads as we crawled past. We were afraid the whole thing might collapse. One day a cave-in blocked the tunnel twenty feet down. Lucky nobody was inside; they would have been buried alive. Meena, for example. That weekend when Olson was home, the Long Loops held an emergency meeting. Steve Weatherspoon had read in a mining book where they braced the roof with timbers and dug air shafts down hundreds of feet for air exchange. We had to do that, he said, or give it up for a lost cause. Olson called him a total and complete gonadotrope: Where would we get timbers, or how would we put them up since it was so narrow? We'd have to widen it, Steve said. Steve, Buck and me were all for widening and sinking down an air shaft and whatever else it took to do the job right (Steve said they laid down railroad tracks in the deeper shafts), but Olson and Gary Seamore said, "No way, hosay."

It's true the dirt was a problem. The widow had took all her garden would hold, and we'd dumped so much in the drain sewer at the top of the loop that it flooded the Weatherspoons' lawn on the last rain. People were getting suspicious.

That's when Gary Seamore had a brainstorm. His dad was in

construction; there was always bags of portland cement lying around his garage. We could borrow a few, mix it with sand and gravel and pave the sides of the tunnel as we went. We needed re-bar, he said, to reinforce it. So we snuck out nights to get portland cement and re-bar from the Seamores' garage. Sometimes we wheeled it in a wheelbarrow down neighborhood streets, but that was risky. So two guys would tote a fifty-pound bag between them. A real bitcheroonie. One night when he was home from school, Olson discovered a crack in Ginny Seamore's curtain, and we climbed all over each other trying to watch her undress. She stripped to her bra and panties and stood at the mirror, turning left and right and boosting out her tits. Ten thousand times sexier than Tokyo Rose. We were all whisper-chanting: "Take it off, take it off" (except Gary, who pouted because it was his sister). But she didn't, and when she returned from the shower she was wearing her nightgown—like she knew we were watching. So I thought to myself: What if it was Meena? After that I stopped spying. When Buck sneezed one night all the guys had to stop.

We pushed buckets of concrete along planks on the tunnel floor. It was hard work, mixing and hauling and plastering, and bending re-bar to fit the curve of the cave by placing it over Buck's booby trap hole and jumping on it. Olson thought we should give up on finding oil and advertise the tunnel as a cave-man dwelling place. The walls were full of our handprints from plastering cement—which dried and expanded and looked like huge, gnarly Neanderthal hands. We could sell tickets to neighborhood kids and show them the handprints and the huge rock, where the cavemen were buried behind, he said. But we knew his real reason was to feel up neighborhood girls down there, so we vetoed the idea.

Olson's theory was that the rock came straight up off bedrock. It was warmer than clay walls of the tunnel because heat from the earth's core got conducted up through it. Steve said it was a boulder from a glacial moraine or the edge of some ancient cliff from millions of years ago when the ocean came in this far; sediments had filled in around it. That made sense to me, because the soil down there was sandy and compacted some places into soft sandstone like at the beach just above the shoreline. We had to break it up with a pick, and when it crumbled it smelled like an ancient oceanic fart. Foul and mysterious. When the pick rang up against something solid one afternoon, I thought it was a dinosaur skeleton. Instead it was a monolith. Better than anything.

A loud buzzing woke me up: on and off, on and off. I was scared they'd brought a buzz saw to cut open my skull. I peeked out from under the covers, could see the privacy screen, a chair by the window—which I thought somebody was sitting there and nearly shit my shorts, but it was my clothes. The buzzing came from Gallbladder's bed. Maybe they'd put someone in an iron lung. Then I realized it was the phone. Stitches pulled against my skin as I got out of bed, blood throbbed between them.

"Mercy Hospital," I answered.

"It's me," the phone whispered.

"Meena? It's the middle of the night." I was afraid a nurse might pass my half-open door. Battleaxe would flick me clear back to bed.

"Mom killed Dad," Meena whimpered.

"Bee ess, and you know it." A chill went down my spine even though I knew she was lying. "What happened?" I whispered.

"They were yelling and it woke me up. Daddy told Mommy Aunt Debbie had to fly out unexpectedly, but she didn't believe him. Mommy says he has a heart-on for Debbie."

"It's booze talking," I said.

"Shhhh." Meena was quiet, except her breathing. When the danger passed, she told me how she'd went down and hid in the hall closet to listen. Mom said Dad didn't give a damn about her; she kept yelling a dirty word at Dad and see if she cared.

"What word?"

"*Fuck her.* Go on and fuck her."

Someone in the hall stopped to listen. I crunched back in the corner behind the screen and held my breath; they walked on. It was like in prison where the guards kept passing to see if you were asleep. Meena said Mom had screamed so loud she couldn't block it out with her fingers. She heard feet running past the door, and when she looked out Mom was chasing Dad with the fire poker, yelling she would kill him. She was a rotten liar, I said. I was afraid my stitches would pop out and blood would squirt over the ceiling. Meena said it was worse than when Mom pushed me into the toilet. She'd gone completely fruitcake.

"Are they still hollering?"

"They stopped. I think she killed him," Meena squeaked.

"She didn't either, Meena. You're imagining." Because I knew how strong my sister could imagine things. Sometimes she lied and sometimes she imagined, which is the same thing. I told her to sneak outside through the garage, straight to the tunnel. I would meet her there.

"Y'r in the hospital," she whimpered. "Your head's broken."

"I'm leaving right this minute."

Meena's voice tucked up, hardly a breath. "I think she's coming upstairs."

There was a muffled sound. Then nothing.

"Meena . . . Meena! You listening?"

"Hello . . . who is this?" a voice demanded—hard and cold like it was cut out of tin. Mom's voice. The receiver leapt out of my hand onto Gallbladder's bed. A small, tinny voice kept saying "Hello . . . Hello . . . " I stared at it, backing off. I knew Meena was done for now. And I knew where Mom would come next.

It took me two seconds to dress. The coast was clear; I tiptoed out into the hall, past rooms with their doors open. In one an old lady turned her head and smiled at me. Patients were asleep or maybe dead in their beds. I was afraid one would make a death rattle when I came by or buzz the nurse. The nurses' station had windows facing the elevator, which was the only way downstairs. I didn't know how I would escape yet but hoped I would invent a plan. Inside, nurses were talking; yellow light spilled into the hall. Somebody laughed, and I heard Battleaxe say, "Well, I know what I would do." Another said, "Oh, I bet you do." Just then a buzzer rang. "Whoops," said Battleaxe, "that's mine."

I heard her shoes squeaking. No time to think. I slipped into a room that said ISOLATION on the door and crouched beside the bed. Someone was breathing heavily—a smell like yeast when Grandma Sally bakes bread. Meena would have puked. I watched Battleaxe pass in her squeaky nurse's shoes, her legs fat white pickles. She glanced left and right into rooms, but never saw me. My cheek was pressed to metal bed bars that burned cold as dry ice. I knew I had to move fast. She would come right back.

My stitches tingled. When I reached to scratch them, another hand reached through the bed bars and scratched for me. So big it held my whole head at once. Fingers poked at my stitches like fingers of a blind person, and I wanted to scream for Battleaxe to save me before it poked through the crack into my brain— like the soft spot in a baby's head. When I squirmed it gripped tighter. A dead man's hand which had froze into rigor mortis was clutching my head. The widow's husband! I just knew it. Slowly, I reached up to touch the hand. It wasn't cold like I expected but warm and veiny, covered in small bristly hairs. I scratched between knuckles, like the top of Chester's head when he was overexcited. Gradually, the fingers released their grip. I bolted to my feet.

What I saw on the bed was a million times scarier than the hand. The room was half dark, like black-and-white TV. The corpse's eyes flickered, but they were asleep—rolling and asleep wide open, 'cause they didn't have eyelids. Or eyebrows. The eyeballs rolled. His cheeks looked like melted cheese. His hair was white but he wasn't old. Then I realized it wasn't white or even hair, just dead dry grass coming out of his skull. Where should have been a nose was a hole: white jagged spines stuck up like shark fins. I fled out of there and caught the wall across from the nurses' station, panting.

Inside the station, a candy striper and nun were talking. The nun looked up. I dropped to my knees and crawled across tiles under a gurney parked against the wall beneath nurses' station windows. The nun's shoes squeaked and I knew I was done for. She paused at the nurses' station door. From under the gurney, I could see her blue skirt and white seamed stockings. "Well, I could have sworn—" She was too plump to bend over far enough to see me. My heart pul-lump-eted like I'd done the fitness run at school. If she came any closer, I would run down the hall to the freight elevator. She was too old and fat to catch me, but she could call the guard downstairs . . . who I hadn't even considered yet. Any second I knew Battleaxe would return.

The nun stood beside the gurney, white sausage legs close enough to touch. I prayed she wouldn't guess I was there, even

though it's prob'ly a sin to pray against a nun. Veins made blue
spiderwebs under her stockings; her feet were so small I was
amazed she didn't tip over. She told the candy striper how your
eyes play tricks when you get older. "Sister Jean Baptiste sees
floating boxes. Imagine!"

The candy striper said she hated old age.

"Well, it can't be helped. That's God's plan," said the nun. I
heard more foot squeaks. When I crawled farther under the cart
wheels, it inched forward. The nun reached out to grip a handle.
"Deteriorating rods or some such, I've forgotten my anatomy."
She gave a little laugh. "Why, my memory is worse than my
eyesight."

If she went inside, I'd make a dash for it. The squealing got
louder: Battleaxe, I knew. It stopped with a clank directly across
from me. Elevator doors jumped open and Mr. Gangway
stepped out. I was looking right at him from under the stretcher.
Meena says you can make yourself invisible: If you pretend you
are the color of the wall, people won't see you. Mr. Gangway
grinned and walked toward the nurses' station, scuffling his feet.
"Who's the sweet thing visiting with you this evening, Sister
'Lizabeth."

"One of our little angels, Mr. Simms," the nun said.

"She's pretty enough, that's God's truth." Suddenly his voice
tightened. "Uh-oh, here comes trouble."

Battleaxe came around the corner thirty yards away. I thought
I'd pee. She would drag me by the ear clear back to bed, thump-
ing the whole way, like Mom did when she was really pee-o'd.
Instead, she stopped in a doorway to talk to someone.

"Let me get inside here before she ask me to clean up somebody's mess." Mr. Gangway and the nun disappeared inside the
station. Battleaxe's butt stuck out of the doorway down the hall
like a giant cassava melon. I couldn't make a run for it; there
was nowhere to go but back into Skeleton Man's room. I'd
rather die than go back there. Slowly, I stood and peeked in the
window. Gangway was saying what good it would do him to
see a pretty girl dressed up like a candy cane if he was sick in
bed, the candy striper blushed, Sister 'Lizabeth tapped his shoulder. No one was looking my direction. In a flash, I stretched out
flat on the gurney and pulled the sheet over me. Just in time.
Battleaxe's shoes sounded like the executioner coming down

death row: squeak squeak squeak. "Uh-oh," said Gangway, "I got business elsewhere."

Battleaxe's voice said, "Hello, Mr. Simms. Where have you been all evening? We've missed you." Through the thin sheet her silhouette looked like The Blob's mother, right beside the gurney.

"Busy. Real busy. People dying and being born all night long. St. Peter got his hands full this evening."

"Is that so?" Battleaxe's hand rested beside my leg.

"Oh yeah. Regular Grand Central Station on the first floor. I had my hands full all night. I got to be getting back there now."

I breathed so shallow it didn't budge the sheet. Fluorescent tubes along the ceiling pulsed in and out, shadows shuffled through the weave. Battleaxe's hand crawled like a snake; I had an awful feeling it would crawl under the sheet to snap me. But suddenly I was moving rapidly ahead, gurney wheels whirring like an eggbeater.

"Later, ladies, I got to get this wagon to the basement," Mr. Simms said over my head. "They took Mr. Phelps down from ICU. Ain't Mr. Phelps no longer only this coil of flesh." His head swayed above me like a dark moon, lights ticked past.

I was done for now for sure. He would take me down to the corpse freezer and shut the door. "Gangway," he said, and I knew we were at the end of the corridor by the freight elevator. I was invisible. You could disappear in a hospital. If you were very quiet and played dead, you could disappear.

# 13

# Meena

She slid quick as an eel between dresses in Mommy's closet. Hidden there amid fragrant fabrics, she could just make out a shadow hunched, muttering over the phone in the darkness beyond the open door. Then it fell across the bed, eyes aglow,

looking directly at where Meena had taken refuge. She burrowed
silently deeper into evocative suedes, gaberdines, worsteds, cor-
duroys and synthetics that formed a vestmental bouquet of memories around her, until she was sheltered deep in her olfactory
past: that redolent autumn following their move from Walnut
Street to Rodeo Loop, when all was nose-tickling plaster dust
and the sweet chemical pungency of paint, a blue denim skirt
retaining an ammoniac taint of hard bubble-gum tar chunks
roofers had left behind, deliciously oily, like the exhalations of
La Brea Tar Pits. She sidled along the closet's back wall through
musky seductive perfumes, foul tobacco, old men's pig breath,
morning coffee and lemon verbena, a musty, wintry, nostril-
stopping whiff of snow, ski wax, leather boots, the scorched sour
mildewy reek of the warming shack, where mittens dried atop
the stove; Mommy's stretch Bogner ski pants abraded her cheek,
then she turned and found Chester sunk into the bosom of a
rayon blouse . . . yuck! To her right, a silky tangerine burst—
bright and evanescent, like spray clinging an instant to the air
when an orange is torn open: Mommy laughing gaily, moving
among cocktail party guests in a red satin dress that brushed
Meena's cheek; she sat on the stairs between her brothers watching grown-ups graze each other like cattle—Daddy's business
friends, important people—but the boys began horsing around,
shooting peanut bits into the burgundy punch through cocktail
straws; Olson shied a nut off Mr. Parnel's bald head, and her
dumbcough brothers crawled over each other laughing; Mommy
came for them, nostrils fluttering, face the steamy red of her
dress, seizing Olson and Boney by an ear and dragging them
upstairs. Below, guests exclaimed in alarm and Dad cried, "Jerri,
for Pete's sake!" Mom turned and waved to them from the top
landing, smiling as if to say, "They're only children, I can do
what I please with them."

Above the naughty, drowsy, forbidden scent of hot flesh under
the sun, the pedal-pusher-gardening-smock odor of moldy soil—
prehistoric decay deep in the cave beside the rock—and the
dried, powdery sachet of Mom's chrysanthemums and rhodies,
there hovered that loveliest of odors: the tart clabber smell of
Daddy's cheeks after he'd shaved, the Old Spice he splashed on
to mask it. Above that, pervading all, was that pungency which

supposedly lacks a breath, but the whole closet reeked of it, the room, the house—half turpentine, half pollen.

Vodka.

It wove clothes together in a gummy ravel, the viscid web of some huge, gluttonous spider . . . watching her now from the bed. Motionless, its eyes alone glowing to betray it, as they glowed at night perched over Meena's bed. So even in sleep she smelled the decaying detritus of old victims snarled in the bristles of its cephalothorax, could hear spinnerets whispering on its abdomen—weaving gossamer twine to bind *her* to the bed while it feasted, its fangs so sharp they punctured the skin painlessly, so its victim felt only the tickle of working mouth parts. Her dreams full of crawly, joint-legged things, and she would gag in her sleep on the effluvium that flowed up from its gizzard when the spider burped—a fetid brew of cockroach guts, the rotting paper smell of moths, all fermented together.

Slowly, very slowly, Meena stooped to seize a spike-heeled pump from the closet floor, whispering into her family's rank, gently smothering history—into the leathery, perspiring smell of the shoe's instep—what she would do: If the spider hops at me, I will crack open its skull. Like it did Boney's. She pressed her free hand against the wall, using it as a spring to launch herself. Leapt forward out of her mother's ambient history with a shriek and a great jangling of hangers.

Mommy screamed reply and sat straight up in bed. Not any spider at all but her own mom, hair awry, eyes wide open. Instead of running downstairs past Daddy's mangled body, out to the cold dank of Boney's tunnel, as she had planned to do, Meena ran straight into outstretched arms. Mommy cooed and stroked her head, mumbled what a fright she had given her, what an awful fright.

Years later, she would tell women in her therapy group that there was security in her parents' screaming. "It was the long silences that frightened us. We never knew what to expect then." Other women nodded. Except Elise, who said that it was when glass started breaking she wondered who would be cut up and how bad.

Years later, too, Aunt Debbie would tell her how she and

Don had ridden the elevator to the basement floor of the hospital that Sunday evening when they came to visit Boney, instead of to the fourth where he had a room. Just one of those clues Debbie offered her niece in the painstaking reconstruction of her past.

The bell rang, Debbie said, and she had looked up at the floor indicator. "Wrong direction," she said. The door slid open to a "lab" sign on a door across the hall, an orange triangular RADIOACTIVITY sign. Don glanced left and right down the hall and jammed his wallet between the rubber fender and metal jam to prevent the door's closing. Then turned to face her, his lips tight, all the Paul Newman charm fled from his blue eyes. In its place the thin cold rind of the sky at 30,000 feet. He flung Debbie against the back wall. A handrail caught the small of her back, a metallic kidney chop that left her woozy. He was kissing, biting, groping under her skirt, inside her panties, raping her with his fingers, tearing buttons from her blouse. Keeping up a running babble: how he didn't want to do it this way, babe, *believe me.*

Debbie remembered the cold metal against her bare shoulders, the door jerking spasmodically, pain creeping in a needling cloud across her lower back. Yet she was strangely collected, nearly detached. Waiting. She reasoned with him not to do this, to come to his senses before he'd gone beyond what could be forgiven, though he already had, of course. The door jerked. He pulled her underwear aside and unzipped his pants. She had thought—as she told it years later and his daughter listened, with a hand to her eyes—that she would seize hold of him. Or wait until he was inside, then gouge his eyes. She felt capable of that.

But he merely prodded her with the tip of his dick, mockingly nudging her labia, then withdrew. Stepped away. Like some silly fucking grown man's game of paint ball tag. He smiled sheepishly, trying to shove that tire iron back inside his pants. Peevishly, he straightened her blouse and bra beneath and promised he'd buy her a new one. Dimples veritably winking. (Meena could see them, could see all of it too vividly.) "Can you forgive me, Deb?" he asked. "Afraid I lost my head there a minute. I'd like to kiss you if you don't mind." That's what he had said— as innocently as if this were their first date. Debbie had stepped

quietly forward, pulled his wallet from the door and hurled it
into the hall, then shoved him out behind it.

"That's all I was able to manage," she said almost apologet-
ically those many years later.

# 14

## Jeff

Gangway was humming. The elevator door shut and he was
humming. Then he said, "That woman is bad news." I wondered
if he was talking to me. By now, he must've seen my shoes sticking up under the sheet. Maybe he thought I was dead and he
was accustomed to riding in elevators talking to cadavers. Sometimes I talked to the rock when no one else could hear. Didn't
make any difference that it didn't talk back, I knew it could hear
me.

"Bad, bad news. Don't give a body time to breathe . . . What
inna hell!" The elevator stopped. Next instant, Gangway yanked
the sheet from my face and stared down, his face huge, dark and
upside down, cheeks pitted from acne, eyes stretching wide in
surprise. I stared back, I didn't dare blink.

"Lord awmighty, what they did to you, little man? Damn!
Nobody tole me nothing 'bout you." The gurney jerked ahead
into the hall. I stared straight up at white acoustical tiles. Knowing this was my chance—before he wheeled me down the hall
to the corpse freezer. But I sensed his eyes glued to my forehead
and didn't dare move. It would give him too big a shock, he
might have a heart attack. Once you're dead, you have to stay
dead. Still, it worried me the doctor would come down and feel
my pulse with his stethoscope, then he would guess I was lying
about slipping on the bathroom rug.

Gangway prob'ly read my thoughts. "Don't you go nowhere, hear?" His footsteps hurried off down the hall. He was
shouting for Dennis. Another voice joined Gangway's, hurry-

ing toward me. I knew exactly what would happen: The doctor would tell the cops and they'd arrest Mom for child
brutality. Besides, they might discover she had cold-cocked
Dad with the fireplace poker . . . even if I didn't believe she really did.

They were looking down at me—Gangway and Dennis, the
guy who shaved my head for stitches, his face shaped like a light
bulb from underneath, broader at the bottom. "Good grathious,
they juth brought him in lath night. I prepped him."

"St. Peter been hyperactive tonight. Young boy like that."

Dennis laid a hand on my forehead and snatched it away.
"Goodneth! he'th thtill warm. Quick! Get him upthtairth.
Th-tat! Code red," he cried, "code red." He began kneading
my chest hard with both hands. "Hurry, Lamar, page Dr. Ker-
ner . . . thtat!"

Gangway hovered over me a moment, and I knew what Dad
meant when he said "pulling a long face"; I never saw a face so
long in my life. "Stat," he shouted, then ran off. Dennis was
CPRing me so hard I thought he'd crack my ribs. The loudspeakers were calling, "Stat . . . Code red . . . Second floor . . . Stat."

"Hurry, damn you," Dennis muttered at the elevator. When
he put his ear to my chest, I knew it was now or never—before
they rushed me upstairs and cut me open. I touched the top of
Dennis's head.

"Excuse me," I said politely.

He yelped and leapt away, nearly fell backwards into the elevator when the door jerked open. "I'm in kind of a hurry," I
said. "I got to get home and rescue my sister." Poor Dennis was
trying to talk but his vocal cords was stuck; he motioned his
hands low for me to lie back down again.

No way, hosay. I was off the stretcher and through the stair-
well door. I ran up two flights. Through safety glass mesh, I
could see the parking lot outside, but a sign on the door warned:
ALARM WILL SOUND. So I went through the opposite door—into
the emergency room. Walking right past cloth-curtained booths
and people reading magazines toward double doors where they
wheeled me in last night. Calm and steady like I didn't just rise
up from the dead or have my head busted or nothing, looking
straight ahead. I wished now I had a cap like Mom said. I slipped
on my eye patch for a disguise. All around me, loudspeakers

were announcing: "Code red . . . Stat . . . Second floor." I was already famous.

"Hold on!" a doctor barked from one of the cubicles. I froze. He was talking to the loudspeaker. "Hold your horses." Him and two nurses stood in a puddle black and thick as motor oil, working frantic over a man whose chest was caved in. His shirt was cut open and his eyes rolled back. A tube led to his arm from a transfusion bottle. I wanted to watch. All I could think was that song about the car wreck: "Transfusion, transfusion." But I hurried on past a lady whose hair stuck out like red wings, a great dark splotch on her dress. She held the *Ladies' Home Journal* crumpled in her hands. Her eyes followed me blankly— not surprised to see a bald-headed boy with an eye patch. She must've been the crushed guy's wife. I felt sorry for her.

I walked right toward the receptionist, sitting behind a desk facing the entrance and talking rapidly on the phone. *Hit Parade* magazine lay open before her. Downstairs, I guessed, they must be having a conniption. Dennis would tell them how I rose up like Lazarus or the *Invasion of the Body Snatchers*, and they would call the guards. If I was ever invisible in my life, I had to be now. Walk right out past her like a wraith. She was my last obstacle before I was in the parking lot. Home free.

But as I reached the door, the receptionist snapped, "Just a minute, buster! Where do you think you're going?"

I walked on, arms stiff at my sides like a bald zombie, never looking back. The automatic door slid open.

"Hold on right there!" I heard her chair scoot, her shoes squealing across the floor behind me. (That's one advantage to hospital shoes, you can always hear them coming.)

Zombies can run if they got to. Especially if their dad is bleeding to death like the car wreck man. I lit out over the parking lot, zigzagging between cars, across Grant Avenue and down the alley beside the doctor's clinic, ran five blocks before stopping to catch my breath. Pulse beat at my stitches, I felt dizzy. No sign of anyone chasing me. The whole town was asleep, not even any cars on the street. I was on McDonald by the Millford Music Company, which sold instruments to the school band. If a police car passed I was done for, so I stuck to dark creepy alleys behind the stores, then crossed a corner of the river park. My footsteps clacked on the walk bridge over the river. It was spooky out and beautiful in a lonesome way. Nobody around: just the river and its friendly fishy smell mixing with the aroma of spruce trees. Half a moon. I stopped to watch current whirl and scatter white over rapids below. It made a splashing happy sound, the best noise I heard for a long time. Then I remembered Meena.

When I lifted the trap door off the tunnel and called inside, there wasn't any answer. Just my hollow echo swallowed up in its damp dirt breath. I knew only a corpse could be down there alive. I was scared then. Mom would never hurt Meena. But then I remembered her face right before she shoved me against the toilet bowl—like someone else's face was trapped inside, teeth gleaming like river rapids. Our real mom went transparent and it was someone else lurking inside her—that same face on the tunnel wall, which would do anything to escape.

Chester charged the fence, but smelling me he began to whine and quiver. The house was dark as a butthole in hell. I slipped into the garage through the lawnmower door. The inside door popped open with a loud click and I froze, arched like a crab over the lawnmower, while dumb Chester tried to crowd in behind me. "Shuddup, numb nuts," I whispered. Mom and Dad's bedroom was right upstairs.

Inside the house was darker and spookier than the Halloween haunted house at the Elks club. Cold and creepy and stinking of wet ashes. Moonlight painted rectangles across the cork floor. Furniture was blubbery sea lions slouched in the corners, all breathing quietly at once. I thought one might waddle toward me any second. I felt my way around the corner into the family room and bumped into the La-Z-Boy, its hide moist and rubbery. Decided to sit down a minute on the couch and reconnoiter. Nearly sat on Dad's head—lying on his stomach on the couch, his face buried in a cushion. "Dad," I whispered, "Dad, it's me." He never budged. He was dead. His hair was matted like after he showered, but I couldn't make out where his skull was broke.

I backed into the coffee table, shaking all over with the jumping heebies. Hair standing in bristles on my arms, my jaw trembling, and stitches pulling open on my skull; I felt them crawl out through the skin and my brains begin to spill. I still couldn't believe Mom would do it—even the crazy lady trapped inside her. Maybe robbers had broke in and were hiding somewhere.

White curtains glowed phosphorescent across clerestory windows. I considered making a run for the patio door, but the fireplace opened its mouth to catch me if I did. Where was Meena? Upstairs in her bedroom? Or maybe Mom wrapped her in a sheet and took her away. I hadn't noticed if her car was parked in the garage.

Just then the refrigerator stepped forward, beyond the counter separating the kitchen and family room. I grabbed the heavy glass ashtray from the coffee table. Fast as a wink, I tiptoed back into the entry and hustled upstairs.

Up there was familiar smells in the dark: the funky smell of people sleeping, wet bathroom shampoo aroma and Mom's flowery cologne, Olson's Delco model airplane glue, Meena's school paste smell, my sweat . . . My whole shirt soaked, even my undies. I was never so scared, not even in Skeleton Man's room at the hospital. Under my toes, the hall carpet was spongy as pine duff. I reached the T fork—Mom's bedroom to the left, Meena's to the right. I had to find out.

Meena's bed hadn't been slept in. I dropped to my knees on the rug and whispered under it. Water dripped in her sink, the faucet Dad promised to fix every weekend. Now he wouldn't be able to ever. I begun to cry. Hard sobs coming up like burps from my chest. How could they all have died while I was asleep in the hospital? It didn't make sense. If I was home I wouldn't let it happen.

I went back into the hall. A stair creaked. I had the ashtray ready, discus style, remembering what my sister said about the spider lady who roams our house at night. How she perches at top of the stairs, body transparent and glowing like phosphorous. Nothing there but empty darkness.

I tiptoed into Mom's room to the bed, praying I would find her lying asleep and Dad next to her like always. Downstairs on the couch it was really a burglar they had killed or someone they ran over on the freeway. Early in the morning, they would dig a hole in the yard and bury him. Meena had went to sleep in Olson's empty bed like she always does when she's really freaked.

I was right: a big hump on Dad's side, a smaller one on Mom's. I leaned against the closet divider and caught my breath. Hair relaxed on my arms, I felt sweat turning cold on my chest, and I smiled. My hand flopped back into Mom's open closet, feeling for clothes whose smell filled the room. It was empty. I leapt forward. Across the bed all her clothes were lumped in a huge mound. My fingers brushed scratchy tweed and the smooth slickness of a silk kimono. Then I realized Meena's small head lied sideways on the pillow, her whole body buried under Mom's wardrobe, one hand clutching a blouse in a death grip.

I wheeled away from the bed, really panicked. My last hope was my bedroom window: the escape route Olson and I figured out in case the house caught fire. Fifteen feet to the flower bed below. But the hall light snapped on and a silhouette blocked the doorway. White as fog. Not transparent at all but solid real, nightgown wavering like the aurora borealis. Naked underneath. Not Mom but a caricature like cartoonists draw—her mouth too big and hair scattered in a halo, eyes sparking mad from booze, clutching the fire poker over her head. It bobbed there, back and forth, as she approached me.

"Ged away from hersh," she snarled. "Ged oudda my housh." Not like any voice I ever heard before.

I bolted, trying to dodge past, over the bed, smacking into the vanity, tripping over a chair, whamming my knee hard, so I nearly woozed-out and stumbled back into the nightstand, trying to get out the door. But she was bearing down, her teeth clenched, crooked and savage as a wolverine's. I saw her arms fly back over her head and bring the poker savagely down. At the last instant something changed in her face. It was Mom again, the startled expression she makes when she messes up a golf shot. She swerved her aim to the side. Beside me came a loud pop and flashing explosion of light and glass. The crockery lamp on the nightstand shattered, spraying Meena and me with sharp confetti.

Through the door, Meena's window curtains pulsed red, then white, then blue. Just like in a movie: The cops had followed me home.

# 15

## Meena

"Yes, sir," they said. "No, ma'am." Hands clasped behind their backs, lips pressed together; when Mommy slurred her words, the older cop's chin wrinkled grimly. He did not look at her but anywhere else. His eyes watery hazel, sad and somewhat hound-ish, like Chester's after he'd been scolded. The flaccid skin of his cheeks and jowls heavily porous as if liquid could pour through, snarled with blood vessels more blue than red. The younger one's eyes kept roving from Dad's rumpled trousers and ribbed, sleeveless T-shirt to bright intersecting swaths of blood on Mom's chiffon nightgown under the open robe, like a check mark at her waist. He was trying to figure it out.

"We could take her to have that sewn." The older one nodded at Meena, though didn't look at her. She wouldn't go with them. But Boney would have to; they'd come for him. "Escaped from his bed," the older cop said. Her brother looked like a prisoner standing between them, bald-headed, eyes on his feet.

"I thod he was a burglar," Mommy slurred. "Wasn't thad dummy of me?" Red raw tear grooves either side of her nose. The officers stared uneasily ahead at the entry way hutch—black marble top and silk flowers that never lost their bloom. "Funny liddle bald-heady man, so I followed him ubstairs with the fire thingy . . . the poker thingy. I saw him leaning over my baby girl. Meena . . . my baby. No he wouldn', over my dead bodysh. Be-cause I thod he was . . . I thod he wan'ed to . . . "

"Yes, ma'am. We understand."

Mommy gripped her brow, squealy-voiced. "Thad's when I hit the lamp. Didn' I do, honey? I saw who it was and I . . . I swerved." She gripped Boney's chin. "Didn' I do?"

The policemen exchanged a nervous look.

"Honey, you know Mommy didn' mean to . . . don' you? You know she never means . . . Mommy—"

"Jerri!" Dad said softly.

"We should be getting him back," the older cop said.

Muscles knotted at the back of Boney's neck, skin crawled about his stitches. He looked like a funny, puny Elmer Fudd. Without hair, his ears stuck out like handles on the Moscow Mule mugs Dad kept in the basement. She had never noticed they were so big. Meena was afraid Mommy might push her thumbs into the puffy edges of his wound and squeeze out his brains like pus from a pimple. She was in that might-do-anything mood, eyes spook wild.

"Ma'am." The young cop touched her elbow, one eye tweaking in a nervous tic.

The older one looked at Dad. "Sir?" he said.

"Boney," Mommy said. "Honey?"

Carrying on a conversation in single words as grown-ups do.

"Jerri Lee," Dad said, his voice warbling. He was afraid of her, Meena knew, afraid she would start chasing him again with the fire poker and he would have to run round and round past the policemen, who would stand grimly watching, hands clutched behind their backs, waiting until something terrible happened. Then they would lead Mommy to their squad car by the elbows and drive away. Meena would huddle quietly on the floor in back, legs tucked beneath her.

"They want to get him back," Dad said.

"Oh, do they?"

"Yes, ma'am."

Meena saw how anxious they were to go. The older cop's jaw tight, skin puckering at his chin. Secret anger worked in him.

"He's my son." Mommy kept a hand on Boney's shoulder. She appeared suddenly sober, flip-flopping.

"They have to release him over to Mercy. Someone authorized has to sign the discharge. That's state ordinance." The older cop spoke to Dad. Mommy stepped toward him.

"I know whad y'r thinking."

"No ma'am, you don't. Not by a long shot."

"Oh, I do. Whad a terrible nasty woman," she yammered. "A fil-thie awful per-ver-sed mother."

"No, ma'am," the younger blurted.

Mommy turned on him, her eyes had that crazy glazed look, smiling like she did at such times, upper lip beaking above her teeth, her face inches from his. He stood perfectly straight, eyes straining downward at her in their sockets.

"I know . . . a drunk dreadful pig who neglegs her chil'ren . . . aren' yoush?" she cooed mock-seductively.

"Not me," he managed.

"Oh, c'mon," she laughed, "admid it. Y'r par'ner won'. But y'r young an' pretty."

"Jerri, for the love of God."

"Tha'sh my husban'," Mommy grinned. "Isn' he a shiddy liddle doggy do? Liddle waggy doggy dog . . . Bark! Bark!"

"All right," snapped the older cop.

"Ooowlllll." Mom threw back her head, then lurched toward the young cop's ear. "I scare the piddle pee oudda himsh."

"Goddamn you to hell, Jerri. The kids are here."

But Dad was a liar. When he clamped a hand around her neck, Meena shrugged him off and went to stand beside Boney. They were in the tunnel, they had pulled the trap door over their heads so no one could find them, they had disappeared.

"Will you shood me?" Mommy cooed.

The young cop lurched away at the waist. Seemed at first she had grasped his thingy. But it was his gun butt, its handle curving forward in the holster. He clamped a hand atop hers and they did a lurching, hip-heaving fox-trot across the cork floor.

Daddy seized Mom's arms from behind, just before the older cop moved. Now somebody would get shot. The young cop had backed against the front door, flushed and panting, his cactus-green eyes dodging from one to the other, hand fixed on the gun handle, seeming undecided whether to draw it.

"She's crazy drunk," he said hoarsely.

"That'll do," said the older.

But Mommy was laughing, a greedy bitter chortle that soon turned to wailing. Daddy guided her to the steps and sat her down on the bottom riser, face in hands, bawling. Now and again, incomprehensible phrases burbled out—something about taking away her babies. Meena wished she would close her knees.

The older cop took Dad aside, his large jaw working solemnly. "Dry her out," Meena heard him say. "Don't you realize . . . for the children's sake." His eyes not evasive now but holding Dad's with paternal warmth and authority. While Dad stood nodding, contrite as a boy. "Alcoholism," the cop said, "now that's a disease I know something about."

It was the first time that word had been uttered in their house.

One night, a few days after he had left the hospital, right after they finished washing the dishes, Boney said he had to show Meena something—swearing her to secrecy on the pain of never talking to her again. Mom was watching TV in the family room.

"She'll kill us if she knows we sneaked out," Meena whispered.

Boney assured her it was worth it. "We can say we were bringing Chester some water."

Poor Chester had to sleep outside ever since she had ratted on him and said he clawed her face. Some nights he howled and whined in his high-pitched boxer's voice, and she pulled covers over her ears, sorry she had told a lie on him. Determined to make it up to him, she saved a dime of her lunch money every day to buy a Hershey's bar. Chester was nuts for chocolate. He'd be waiting for her by the fence when she came home from school, leaping straight into the air upon seeing her, turning circles and punching the air with his front paws. Dummy dog. Devouring his half in one slurpy gulp, then whining and nipping for hers, like he'd forgotten his the moment it slid down his throat. So she had to hold her half high above her head. His pink ticklish tongue a careful washcloth finding every wrinkle of her fingers when she had finished eating it.

Chester charged at them from across the yard as they slipped out of the utility room door, punching Boney's chest, his whole body wagging with his tail. "Watusi dog," Aunt Debbie called him.

"Down," Boney whispered, "you dumb dope."

She threw arms around Chester's neck and smooched his black rubber mouth, which smelled of a butcher's shop.

"We found something," Boney said as they opened the trap door and slid down inside the cave. "Now I know what we were digging for all along."

Both pretended she had never seen the rock. They crawled on

hands and knees over bumpy, uneven ground and puddles of
water that had percolated down through the soil after a heavy
rain. The sound of dripping echoed along walls, adding eeriness
and an impression of vast expanse to the cave. Their flashlight
beams skidded along rough cement walls that began halfway
down, like the Roman catacombs. Boney's pants cuffs dragged
in the mud. They were going to catch it for sure. But she forgot
about that the moment they reached the rock: a scintillant wall
of granite which the boys had brushed clean. Quartz and mica
crystals winked pink and blue under her beam, like geologic glitter trapped in solid rock. The Long Loops had begun digging a
side passage, clinging to the curve of the boulder.

No one knew how deep underground the rock was; Boney
said twenty feet. They placed their cheeks against the rock's
moist surface and tried to feel the fire burning at the earth's core.
Shé heard it grumbling far away. Boney whispered—because
they always did down there—"That's just the heartbeat in your
ears." That was gonadal. Boney couldn't hear because his skull
was cracked, but she could hear people screaming in hell far
below. It gave her the creeps, made her feel claustrophobic and
panicky in her stomach, like that feeling when a roller coaster
suddenly dips. She wanted out of there.

But Boney was telling how he'd hoped to find tar down there,
mammoth bones and saber-toothed-tiger teeth, but the rock was
even better. Gray-pink, stolid and inexplicable, gently curving
like the hip of some huge buried idol. Someday, he said, he
would return with excavating machines and dig it up. That was
just Boney. Dad said you could fill his Christmas stocking with
horse manure and he'd call it gold nuggets. If you cracked his
bonehead skull, he would show off the scar snaking through his
hair stubble like a badge of honor.

They emerged filthy as pigs. Mud had worked into the weave
of their jeans. Boney proposed they prop a ladder against
Meena's window ledge and crawl inside. They could wash their
clothes in the shower and Mom would never know. But they
heard shouting inside family room windows as they passed:
Mom and Dad arguing so loud they didn't need to place ears
against the glass to hear them. Dad said if things didn't work
out down south they could come back. Mom said they couldn't

just pull the kids out of school. Dad said there were great schools in California. "And oodles of sweet yum yums in bikinis," Mom yammered.

"F'r crissake, Jerri, what has that got—Have you been drinking?" As if it wasn't plain obvious.

"Never touch the stuff." She laughed bitterly. "Answer me, Donald, have you been fucking?"

Boney firmed hands over his ears and hurried around the house. Meena heard Dad telling Mom, *For crissake, the children*; Mom asked if he ever gave one damn for them in his life, or her. Something crashed inside and Chester began howling. That was their cue to slip in through the utility—around through the living room and upstairs without being noticed. They showered individually in their clothes, wrung them out and threw them in the hamper, knowing they mustn't be seen in the bathroom together again as they always had been before. It might push Mom over the deep end.

# 16

## Aunt Debbie

Truth be told, Grandma Sally wasn't up to it: Meena crawling about the house like a goldarned insect, up on furniture, hiding in corners, scaring the living wits out of us when we passed. Besides, "Jeffrey isn't our same jolly boy," she grieved.

"His mom's in a detox," I reminded her.

"Well, we don't call it that," she corrected me. "It's Tranquility Acres."

"Don't matter fish piss what you call it, Mother, it's a fancy drunk tank."

Don had left for California—his firm asked him to find office space down there, so he said—else I wouldn't have considered going down to Millford. As far back as I can remember he'd talked of moving south. Sweeping out his arms and squinting a little: palm trees, seventy-five degrees in December, his own swimming pool, bougainvillea climbing up one side of the house, a view of sunburnt California mountains . . . That's the life! Don's wet dream, dry as it was. No harm in it I suppose, unless you begin to believe it and expect others to believe it with you. He'd hung his Hawaiian shirts and pin-striped white cotton Casual Cruise sports jacket on the rack across the backseat of his Impala, I expect, and drove south. Like the itch had got so big he had to scratch it.

We emptied the house of hooch. Meena led us from stash to stash, leaping about on all fours like a spider. That house kept no secrets from her. Turn her upside down, all the lousy lies and jealousies of that family would trickle out in a smelly slush. Four Joy detergent bottles under the sink, an ice tray full of gin cubes in the freezer (I didn't know the stuff would freeze; I'd often wondered how Jerri got tipsy on straight ice water) and her desperation stash: a mayonnaise jar suspended in the toilet reservoir. Sally said the important thing was starting out clean when she got home. But she could always buy more.

To hear Sally tell it, as we drove out to visit Jerri, I wouldn't recognize my sister. Four weeks dry, ten pounds lighter. Regular sleeping habits. "She's not the same girl. It's all the secret drinking was her trouble. She says so herself."

"And the rest of it, too."

"You might give her a chance. A person don't change if their family won't permit it."

"I wish her my best. I really do."

Mother removed glasses and rubbed her eyes, smoking lip puckered like she'd bit into a green persimmon. "There's not a man in this world attracted to a skeptical woman, Deborah. That's half your trouble, you want my opinion."

"Not much."

TRANQUILITY ACRES.

At the main gate, a hand-scrolled sign in looping gothic script welcomed "all who seek inner peace and sobriety." Gave me the creepy-jeebs already. Like some feely-touchy hippie thing or a plaque stolen off the loony-bird widow's wall. The kids squabbled in the backseat. Nervous, I guess you'd say. Couldn't blame them. Last time they'd seen their mom she was trying to remodel the house with a fireplace poker. Lindburgher, the sobriety czar, had refused to accept Jerri with a blood-alcohol content above flat zero. So Don checked her into hospital to detox first. Though it was hard to imagine Jerri reaching blood empty in short of a month, truth be told.

The drive wound up over folding green lawns, state-institution style. But upscale. Alcoholics' country club. We passed Cottage A, a Cape Cod with weathered wooden shingles; B was imported from Bavaria, shuttered mullioned windows and overhanging eaves; there was a Norman farmhouse, a miniature replica of Monticello . . . whole f'ing drying-out theme park. All told, it reminded me of Beverly Hills.

"Is Mom in an iron lung?" Jeff leaned forward on the seat.

"Who told you a thing like that?"

"Who else?" I said.

Sally gripped the wheel; the outrigger glasses gave her a triceratops look. "You're too old to believe everything your brother Olson tells you."

"They had to pump out Mom's old blood and put in new blood to get rid of the booze," Meena said.

"Why, there's not a thing in the world wrong with her blood. It's all in her mind." The kids nodded. I poked Sally's hip. That's all we needed—talk about replacing Mom's brain.

Only distinction between Tranquility inmates and guests was the lapel pins they wore: loopy smiling sunshine faces indicating the number of weeks they'd been dry—purple, red, blue or yellow. Couldn't say if they were intended as a badge of courage or a scarlet letter. Or both. I felt sorry for them—on display like that. Jerri still in the yellow zone, about to graduate to blue. Grandma Sally had brought her a tiger-throated orchid. "Late Easter celebration?" I asked. It might just as well have been, Sally said: her daughter returned from the dead. You couldn't argue with that.

We found Jerri beside the pool with her pals. Tan and glowing, black hair gleaming like volcanic glass in the sunshine, a body would give some eunuchs a full erection. She looked great. The kids were delighted to see her whole and healthy. No iron lung. But they held back, awkward, shy before all those expectant eyes. Their mom's mostly. "C'mon," she coaxed from a recliner, "Mom won't bite." They moved closer then. Kisses and hugs all around; Sally and I shook hands. Some kinko crew, I'll

say. Regular rogues' gallery of hard-core habituals lounging half
naked about the pool. Made the rest of us seem almost normal.

A lank, gravelly-voiced woman kept repeating what a lovely
family we had. Eyebrows thick smears of butter. Hair the color
of smokers' teeth spilled indifferently from her bathing cap and
swimsuit crotch. The Tranquility motto was "The Truth Shall
Set Ye Free" (set in wavering tiles at bottom of the pool). I saw
they meant it. I wondered what the tall buttery gal did out in
the world of shaved crotches. A dry, leathery woman named
Faye told us she wished to hell she could see her kids. "Don't
hold your breath," George quipped. Real fatso, that one. A mo-
ronic purple sun pinned lopsided above an obscene bulge in his
nylon trunks, big enough you could fit two normal-sized in there.
His gut a brown hairy blimp, face wide as a tree stump. He
winked lewdly at me—one eye the size of two.

"Go to hell," Faye told him.

Meena leaned on Mama's shoulder. Jeff kept his distance, two
taut cords reaching up the back of his neck into hair just filling
in. I could make out a puckered crescent where stitches had been.
Maybe he'd forgiven her, but hadn't forgotten by a long shot.

"It don't look too shabby here at all," Sally said.

"I'd settle for a margarita," the tall buttery gal replied.

"Naughty naughty."

"Just kidding."

Jerri had coaxed Jeff to her side. He knelt on one knee, looking miserable in his sport coat and white shirt. She ran fingertips
through his bristle and told her buddies how she'd "freaked out"
that night, had seen a funny little man in the house and followed
him upstairs. "I had the fire poker and I could see his baldy head
leaning down over my baby, this funny little baldy-headed man,
and I raised the poker"—swinging both arms overhead to dem-
onstrate—"and heaved down with all my might. When I think
now what I might've . . . what y'r dummy Mom—" Nuzzling
Jeff's scalp with her chin.

"That's over and done," snapped Sally.

"I'm telling it, Mother. Thank goodness I swerved and clobbered the lamp. Dummy me," she lilted. Then huddled her shoulders, dark eyes wavering.

"You weren't that far gone," Faye decided.

"That's when I cracked and said, 'You've got to stop this,

Jerri.' So here I am." Spreading her arms wide. "Over my dead body."

"She's told us that story ten times, but it's a whole lot more dramatic now I see her kids."

Jeff and Meena stood looking abashedly down at wavering green pool water, black lane lines snaking along the bottom. Wasn't open for swimming, too early in the year yet.

"I'm still trying to figure out why the kid was bald in the first place," fat Georgie puzzled.

"It was an accident, that's all," Jeff insisted.

"That's right, honey, an accident. Y'r mom pulled a boo-boo."

I wondered if Jerri had forgotten she shoved her son into a toilet bowl and cracked his skull. Had she ever known? She was telling how police had arrived and a rookie cop drew his pistol on her. "Can you imagine! Threatened me with physical bodily harm in my own home. Isn't that a riot."

"Sons of bitches." Faye scowled.

Jerri's lips pursed, eyes like bright splinters of glass. "They threatened to take my children away from me."

"I'd sue." The buttery gal nodded at me, smiling in a way made hairs stand on my neck. Georgie watched Jerri's crimped navel like he might a steak sizzling on the grill.

"Entered my home and called me a good-for-nothing drunk and child neglecter. As I live and breathe."

Sally drew up her bosom. "I believe I've heard enough."

"Ask my children. He threatened me with his gun. Ask them, Mother! Didn't he, honey? Didn't he do?"

"No he didn't," Meena replied, bold as you wish.

Fatso boomed laughter. The rest of us stared. The air brittle as clear glass. A man lying on the deck rolled over and slapped his belly—pale and hairy on front as he was smooth and sunburnt behind. Jerri was smiling. Mouth wide, but eyes squinting like fingers had caught heavy lids either side and stretched them tight.

"Mom grabbed his handle," Meena said.

"Which handle?" Porgie gripped his blimp belly and shook. I wanted to smack the tub of shit. Jeff told his sister to shut up.

"That's right, honey, I did. I grabbed his pistola handle. We danced, didn't we?"

"No one got shot," Jeff insisted.

"That's good, sweetheart," the tall gal said, "but I still believe I'd sue."

She could go on believing. Enablers, I believe they call them. Closely related to hyenas and vultures, you ask me.

Jerri's "suite" was in "Bavaria"—a bright, spacious room with a balcony, tulips in pots on the ledge. The kids closed their eyes and Jerri produced a scarf for Meena, a beanie for Jeff. About to pee from excitement. "Made them with my own hot little hands." Jerri crocheting! You might believe a leaf could have intercourse. Jeff turned the cap around in his hands, not knowing what to make of it you could see, trying to be enthusiastic. Grinning sheepishly, he tried it on. Pie slices, yellow, red and purple, a short blue bill. Tranquility colors. Truth be told, it made him look glum: His long narrow face and ears stuck out.

"Nerdso," cried Meena, the new scarf tied under her chin. Yellow with green misshapen polka dots. Looked like a pair of elves Santa had let go for a lost cause.

"Mom knows," Jerri sighed. "Dummy dummy Mom. She knows what you're thinking. Go on and laugh." Hurt, because you could see it mattered to her. She'd tried her damnedest. Sally insisted that wasn't it at all, they were lovely really. The kids piped in, terrified they'd shove Mom over the deep end.

We sat on the bed and played hearts. "You've got to keep your hands busy," Jerri said. "They make a big deal of that."

"Your grandfather liked a cap," Sally mused. Not knowing when to quit.

"Drop it," I told her.

Jerri frowned. "A John Deerey thing."

All of us tense as nails. A funny thing: Put people in an artificial setting doing artificial things it makes you more uneasy than their normal craziness.

The kids skittish all week long, waiting for their mom to come home. Jeff disappeared hours on end, and Meena claimed he was outside, although weather had turned from the spring heat wave to squally bluster that slashed rain across windows. Oregon typical. One day she went out in driving rain through the back gate, dead center of the arborvitae hedge, and returned with her brother a few minutes later. "Well, what d'you suppose?" Sally was put out. He looked like those years ago when the truck ran over him: jeans stiff with mud. Regular Oregon tarbaby. Sally caught him sneaking up garage steps. She stood at the top, her arms folded.

"Where have you been, young buster? If I may be so bold."

He gaped up at his grandmother, mouth working for an excuse. Wasn't short on one long. "Playing football . . . in Mr. Ashcroft's lot."

"In the pouring rain? You've been over to the golf course, I expect, crawling through drain sewers again."

"No, see"—looking uneasily about—"I wasn't s'posed to tell anyone."

"You better . . . The God's truth, Jeffrey."

"There was this hole, see, in Mrs. Grazziola's backyard. Maybe fifty feet deep. It just appeared out of nowhere. Buck and me had to find out what was down there for her."

"Oh, you did." Sally frowned, eyes gray as cold mush. "I expect it was the Devil's staircase or some such. You plan to tell me you crawled down into a hole in the pouring rain?"

"See, we think it's an old ancient well from prehistoric times. There was these funny pictographs on the walls inside—bisons and mastodons and saber-toothed tigers, and people's hands traced with red dirt."

"You took an elevator down I expect."

"No, see, we used an extension ladder." Warming to it. "It was a bit hairy, but we made it."

"From a fire truck I expect." Sally turned to me. "Or made of skulls and crossbones."

"Yeah." His eyes gleamed. "A whole stack of bones was piled at the bottom." Sally inclined her chin for him to continue. "Honest, it was all muddy down there, and bones—"

"I called the widow; she hasn't seen hide nor hair of you."

"Well, it wasn't . . . see, not exactly in her backyard. Behind, in the lot. We got the ladder at Buck's."

"Young Buck is sick in bed with the flu. I called there looking for you."

Jeff gulped. "He's feeling a bit better. He thought the fresh air might do him good." Turning to me for succor.

"Face it, buster, you're caught."

"I can't tell," he whispered, "I promised the guys."

Sally seized his collar and marched him upstairs to the john. Zipped his belt out through loops and popped it taut in her hands. Had seized the band of his shorts when I caught her arm from behind. "Would you use your head. Can't anyone in this house ever use their head?"

Jeff stood there in his skivvies, looking pathetic, jeans forming a filthy halo around his ankles. Absolutely colorless. Blood zero. Like a shock victim I'd had once on a Denver flight. He'd already had too much bad history in that room with female members of the family. Sally slapped me then. Yellow roots of her teeth showing. *That will be your punishment, young fellow, who ain't man enough to take it himself.* But he was, that's the thing. Carrying secrets in his drawers. Somebody needed to help him declare it.

But Meena defeated us both. Three days before her mama came home she spun a web of yarn across her bedroom door—crisscrossing blue threads. Just enough room for her to slip beneath on her belly. "To catch flies?" I asked. She hissed at me, her face against the web inside. Wearing white wax Halloween fangs stained red at the tips. Meena hunched her back, lank dark hair hanging down in snarls. I dropped to my knees outside and hissed back. My niece lunged forward and sank fangs into my bare knee. I scooted away. Staring down at white dents she'd left in my flesh. She slid under the door after me. Licking my wounds with a tongue red as a cardinal wing. I couldn't decide which spooked me more—the spider's bite or its apology. I stroked her head, scooping greasy curls from behind her ears. Assuring her Mommy would be just fine. Cured. Daddy would be home tomorrow. But I didn't say I'd be out of there before he arrived.

# 17

## Jeff

Meena's room smelled worse than the tunnel on a rainy day—
a dirt clod smell, or the smell of moldy peanuts. She dumped
her clothes any old where, mixed in with school papers and
Kleenex and dirty socks and Hershey wrappers. Aunt Debbie
said it smelled like an old wino in there. Meena just grinned her
dumb tarantula grin: gimpy white wax teeth. Olson had given
her a whole box of them because he thought it was funny.
Grandma Sally said a granddaughter was no problem, but she
didn't know where to begin with a spider. I think she was scared
Meena would end up at Tranquility someday like Mom.
Grandma Sally made her sit at the table for dinner and straighten
her legs under her like a human being.

Grandma ordered us to clean our rooms before Mom came
home. (My half was messy, but if I got even one dust ball on
Olson's side he'd slug me silly.) "You hang up those clothes on
hangers, young miss," Grandma told Meena. "I want your trash
picked up." So Meena hung her dirty shirts and pedal pushers,
even dirty undies on hangers from drawer knobs and curtain
rods—like a bonerhead flea market. She swept up dust balls and
put them on top of her dresser. "Cool," said Olson, who was
home from school for spring vacation. "It looks like a scale
model of the city dump."

I warned my sister she could only push Grandma so far.

"Spiders live in dirty houses," she said. "After they suck their
victims' blood, they leave their husks jimble-jamble in their
webs." But Grandma Sally had no appreciation for science. She
stood at the door with Mom's exact same frozen-mouthed smile
which Mom inherited from her, then walked about tapping
hangers. While Meena crouched on her bed, lower lip tucked
under wax fangs like spasmo Miss Dracula. Electricity pulsed

off Grandma like the hand-cranked static-electricity generator at school. Her right hand opened and closed automatically.

"Very cute." Grandma folded her glasses and dropped them in her apron pocket, then heaved Meena over her shoulder like a sack of oats and walked into the shower with her legs kicking the air. We stood watching Grandma Sally in her bra sudsing Meena, until she snapped, "You boys scoot." She was one person Olson didn't mess with. Funny how our family always took care of its dirty business in the bathroom. That's where we deposited all our filth—inside and out. Maybe all families are like that.

Meena stayed clean after that. But spun a web in her bedroom doorway and hung up a sign: NO INTRUDERS ALOUD.

"That's gonadal," I told her. "Spiders spin webs to catch bugs not keep them out."

She hissed at me.

"Besides, spiders can't write. If they did, they'd prob'ly spell A-L-L-O-W-E-D right."

She hissed again.

"I know who you want to keep out. Think how it's going to make her feel when she gets home from Tranquility."

"Dirty rotten liar," she spit.

"I knew you could talk, bug eater."

Meena grinned. After that she cut up her insect book and Scotch-taped aphids, crickets and ladybugs all over the web.

I'd go sit in the tunnel to get away from Meena's dumb spideriness and Grandma Sally's grouchiness, although it was damp down there and nasty-asty. I could make out rain pattering like ten zillion tiny frogs hopping on leaves. A trickle of water cut a channel along the dirt floor and emptied into a pool by the rock. Dim gray light filtered down in a foggy haze from the entrance. Spooky, but I liked it anyway.

We had almost abandoned the tunnel before reaching the rock. One day while we were plastering the sides, Buck dropped his trowel and sat back in the wet concrete, his mouth wide open. Olson and me grabbed him under the arms and dragged him outside. Buck's eyeballs were jitterbugging in his head. Olson and me had learned mouth-to-mouth in Scouts—where you suck out the mucous then breathe directly into the person's lungs—and we both wanted to be heroes someday, only never expected it would be on Buck, who had dried spit curd at his mouth corners. So Olson flipped a quarter to see which one of us got to save him. But before we could try anything, Buck opened his eyes and asked, "What happened?" Just in time, because I lost the flip.

Steve Weatherspoon said the problem was oxygen exchange. We were down so deep new air couldn't circulate—like standing on the bottom of the ocean breathing through a long straw. You'd suffocate that way in your own carbon dioxide. Steve's idea was to put up an air stack for oxygen circulation. To drill the hole, he invented a pipe drill based on an Egyptian water drill he saw at the Science and Technology Museum in Portland: pipes screwed together in four-foot lengths, an extendable shaft running through washers inside to keep it from wobbling. On one end was a hand crank from an old food grinder, on the other a humongous wood bit. When you stuck the drill shaft into the ground and turned the crank, dirt came up the pipe and spilled out the top. We could add new sections to the pipe and shaft to go as deep as we needed. A genius invention which won first place at the state science fair in Salem. Steve called it "a hand-generated earth-boring machine." When people asked what it was for, he looked them right square with his dull yellow eyes and said, "Drilling for oil." Which was the God's truth. But Steve's drill kept missing the tunnel shaft. His genius only went so far.

Our plan was to dig a room beside the rock big enough to stand up in. We would make a concrete ceiling and carve our names in it for posterity. It would be our clubhouse and message to future generations. Olson wanted to bring girls down there to make out and Buck wanted to bring his *Playboy* collection. My plan was to store canned food and make it a neighborhood air-raid shelter for when the Russians nuked us—prob'ly my best idea ever. All the guys liked it. When the time came, we would tell our parents. But only in a dire emergency. Like Dad says: We all need our secrets. Secrets make the world go round. But who ever guessed the emergency would come so soon?

Dad came home a day before Mom. His Hawaiian shirt with the hula dancers was wrinkled and stunk of perspiration so bad I held my nose hugging him. He drove straight through from

San Diego, he said, twenty-three hours. His eyes were bleary, he hugged his elbows and cussed the damned Oregon weather. When Grandma said he should've worn his jacket, he snapped, "Can't wear it if you don't have it, can you." Someone lifted it out of his car.

"Look who's grouchy," Grandma told him. "I think you'd better get some rest, Don." He was, too. Warned us kids not to touch his car.

Dad was always antsy before we left on vacation, jittery and snappy over any little thing, so it spoiled the fun of going away at all. Mom called it his traveling menopause. But the second we got on the highway he'd turn on the radio and beat time on the steering wheel and we'd play the alphabet game like he didn't have a worry in the world. But I never saw him grouchy after a trip before. Usually he was glad to be home. It was a bad omen. When Chester jumped up on him and started kidney-chopping out of joy to see him, Dad twisted his paw so hard Chester yelped and limped to his basket. But he was happy to see Meena; he kissed her right smack on the lips. "Look, I'm beat," Dad told us. "Can't you see, I'm exhausted." He stumbled going up to bed, and Grandma Sally said he was nervous about Mom coming home, that's all. Everybody's a little nuts, I decided. Even Dad. Better to be a little nuts than lots.

He didn't get up until nine P.M. We ate hot dogs and laughed at Olson's note from his English teacher, which she wrote he was the brightest boy she ever taught. "Also the laziest and most filthy-mouthed."

Dad frowned. "Some dubious distinction." Olson said that he did his best. Dad said in California they drove woody wagons and Caddies with zebra stripes and VWs that had eyelashes painted around their headlights. Everybody in California was weird and had cars to prove it. Olson said his boss choice was a '57 Chevy. Dad put on "Surfer Girl" by the Beach Boys—who piped and warbled like they got hit in the balls—and Dad and Meena danced. He wiggled his hips and shook and swiveled on his heels like on *American Bandstand*, Olson whistled, I tried to imitate Dad, and Meena boogie-woogied with a funny smile on her lips, completely forgetting she was a dumb spider.

They kept dancing until Grandma Sally said she'd had enough "noise" and turned it off. Grouchy her own self. She asked what was this job Dad would be going to down in California. Dad said they were opening a new branch.

"You'll be manager?" Grandma asked.

"We're discussing it."

"It will have to go beyond discussion, don't you think, Don?"

"You bet, Sally. Sure it will. Absolutely." Dad wiped sweat from his lip. Tiny beads sparkled in his beard shadow. He had that far-off guilty look. An awful thought occurred to me: Maybe Dad makes things up sometimes—not lies, just slight exaggerations. It worried me. When dads do that it causes trouble. But most likely he was sweating from exertion.

Later, he warned us Mom might act different when she came home. "We're going to have to be patient. Can't expect her to get well overnight. No arguing, no roughhousing. Understand? She'll need all the love and consideration we can give her."

Meena skipped me a look. It was like Mom had cancer or something. Alcoholism is a weird disease; they can't cure it with medicine or operations, only love and what Grandma Sally calls "forbearance." Maybe it was another stage Mom was in now. She'd leave her trapped, drunken side at Tranquility Acres. Aunt Debbie had sent the fire poker off in the trash. Things would be different now.

When she arrived the next afternoon, Mom wore yellow and blue paper leis like she'd come home from Hawaii. She came in the front door whirling, "Taa-daa, look who's home," hugging and kissing us until we couldn't breathe. "Where's your cap, Jeff? I hoped you'd be wearing it. Doesn't matter. It was a dummy cap." She laughed and dropped the yellow leis over Meena's head. "Yellow represents rebirth, blue is my graduation. Five weeks without a drop. I'm dry as bird pucky." We raised our fists in the air and cheered. All of us, except Dad. He smiled so hard I thought his cheeks would crack. Mom kissed Chester smack on the lips. Grandma Sally was beaming. Everything's going to be different, I told myself. Mom's skin was shiny and dark as a hazelnut. I was glad Olson had left so he couldn't make a crack at my ear about her cleavage. Dad stared like he'd never seen her before.

But when Mom passed Meena's spiderweb and saw the NO INTRUDERS ALOUD sign her face fell. "Is that what you think?" She looked at me. "Maybe you'd prefer I didn't come home?"

"No, Mom," I insisted. But Meena stayed quiet.

"I can ask your dad to drive me right back to Tranquility. Is that what you'd like?"

"Of course she wouldn't," Grandma Sally cried.

But my sister was straightening the bugs on her web.

"Meena, I'm speaking to you," Mom said very properly, but her lips quivered.

"Only spiders allowed, no intruders," Meena mumbled.

"I see."

Mom went off with Grandma Sally to unpack. I told my sister to cool it. "You want her to have a relapse and be nuts all over again?"

Meena slashed me with her dirty long fingernails. So I tore down her stupid web. Eye for an eye, tooth for a tooth. But her screams got me a licking.

When we woke up the wind was howling, lashing pine trees in the front yard, the Christmas lights Dad never took down whipped and bobbed, my windows breathed like sails, which was amazing because it was glass. Olson's box kite, stuck in branches of the Japanese maple, snapped and jumped, one stick clicking at branches like a playing card against bike spokes. A hurricane was coming, the radio said. A double freak: Oregon's first in recorded history and it wasn't hurricane season. "Wacky wacko wacked-out weather," the announcer said. Twelve-foot waves and ninety-mile-per-hour winds were approaching the coast. I was never so excited in my life, not even when the river flooded Grandpa Walter's farm. Oregon is the boringest place on earth, and Millford the boringest town in the state. Even the Oregon football team is boring, even the chicks, Olson says, compared to California, and the rain is most boring of all. But we never had a hurricane before.

Mom wouldn't let us go to school. Dad said he had to go to work hurricane or no; he'd been out two weeks. Mom kept looking up at the ceiling beams like she was scared the roof might fly off. Grandma Sally looked tired, her eye hollows the color of bruised peaches when she took off her glasses. Mom and Grandma wouldn't look at each other. They had a fight last night. No big deal really, they always fought. Like Mom and Meena. Over the same stuff. Because they loved each other didn't mean they liked each other. It's just the way mothers and daughters behave. Mom had told Grandma to go home, she was sick and tired of being treated like a child. She said Grandma never believed she was capable of a thing. Grandma said Mom didn't appreciate the sacrifices she'd made—like taking care of us kids while Mom was at Tranquility. She had her own life to lead. Mom said Grandma was afraid she'd hit the hooch the moment she left the house. Grandma got huffy after that.

Mom's head kept moving like there was bugs in her collar. Meena hopped onto the couch beside Dad and rubbed her nose against his cheek—spider talk for "hello." Dad laughed and they cooed and nuzzled like a couple goofy lovebirds. Dad asked what breed of spider she was: daddy longlegs, crab spider, jumping spider, wolf spider . . . Meena hissed. "Ah-hah, a wolf in spider's clothing." Mom watched them narrowly, fingers drumming on her cup handle. Meena licked Dad's cheek. Suddenly Mom ran over and yanked her off his lap. Didn't he think she was a little old for that? Dad made his I-dunno face, skin bunching around his mouth. "Don't make a federal case of it, Jerri." Mom ordered Meena to sit up like a lady, she wouldn't tolerate any more of this spider nonsense. Meena hissed and showed her teeth.

"All right, you two," Grandma said.

Later, after Dad left for work, Grandma Sally asked Mom why she opposed Dad's friendship with his daughter. "That's the most natural thing in the world, a father's love for his little girl. After all, your dad doted on you, I didn't stand in his way."

Mom's eyes widened, sprayed with tiny red capillaries. I was afraid she had put booze in the detergent bottle again. "Is that what you call it, *doting*?"

"Well, I was jealous at times but I never let it get the best of me."

"No! You certainly didn't." Mom snorted an angry laugh.

"There's many mothers want their children all to themselves," Grandma said. "I don't subscribe to that, it isn't healthy. Children need a father, too."

Mom leapt up and ran from the room.

"Why, what's the matter now?" Grandma's teeth left white dents in her lower lip.

I followed Mom into the hall. She stood looking out into the storm, huddling her arms like she was chilled. She put an arm around my neck and nuzzled my head into her soft breast. And began to cry. Maybe she wasn't a little nutty, maybe she was nutty a lot. Any old thing set her off. I tried to think of something else but couldn't change subjects in my mind.

By noon the storm came inland over the Coast Range, knocking down half the timber up there, the radio said. A school bus with the Corvallis track team was trapped in the Cascades. Nobody knew if they were dead or alive. A billboard on I-5 had broke loose and took out a semi; worse, a Gerry A. Tricks home in Eugene collapsed on top of the old people. The wind was picking up by the minute. It howled around the house and slugged the arborvitae hedge in gusts like an invisible fist. Wind ruffled the fur on Chester's cheeks, who was huddled against the patio window, his eyes white and forlorn, shivering and shaking and snapping at the wind. We couldn't even hear him barking—like TV with the sound turned off. Mom wouldn't let me open the door to let him in. "Are you out of your right mind?"

Everything was in motion. Trees lashed and bent nearly to the ground, then snapped upright, branches flew past and birds, their wings spread out like brakes. The whole sky spun and churned like a blanket in the dryer. Rain blasted the glass in sheets, rolled off in waves and swirls, barrels of it at a time. Meena pressed her cheek against the window and whined with Chester, till Mom screamed at her to get behind the couch. Wind licked the rain right up, and a new squall would come. It blew right through the walls. The electricity went out; it was pitch dark inside. Mom paced and muttered, her eyes like little flashing searchlights, Grandma Sally couldn't get her to sit down. I expected any second for lightning to flash and Mom to rush us into the basement again, like she used to when we lived on Walnut Street—even if there wasn't any. We just had to hope the roof wouldn't peel off. "I could use a drink," Mom said, but seeing how we looked at her, she smiled. "Just kidding."

Right then I realized her whole problem wasn't really drinking at all. It was a storm which kept brewing up inside of her, with lightning and thunder. She was always scared she would lose control. Though I didn't really understand it. Then I got an idea.

I told Grandma Sally about our air-raid shelter. Where was it, she wanted to know. But I couldn't make myself tell. "Anyway, it's prob'ly too wet down there."

Something smacked the side of our house. We ran to the living room windows. The Weatherspoons' patio roof was hurling down the street: four-by-eight corrugated sheets of green fiberglass and razor-edged tin whipped over their house like fighter planes, spun along at head level like huge Frisbees. Just then the school bus pulled up at top of the loop and kids piled off, heads down, trying to run into the wind. Steve Weatherspoon stopped dead in his tracks as a sheet came straight for him, arms spread and his mouth looped open, so scared he stunk his pants. Not knowing if he should dodge left or right. At the last instant, the tin veered off and clanged off the top of the bus.

Mom was outside before you could sneeze, running toward the kids. Brave! You can say that for her. Gesturing at them to get inside. A sheet of fiberglass was coming, warbling like a yodel on the wind. Then I was running, waving my arms, scared it would cut her in two. Meena. Grandma Sally, too. Mom straightened up like she might catch it, but it hung a louie and shattered against a tree. Their whole patio roof was gone—crashed into houses and caught in tree branches.

It was more amazing even than the flood. If you ran with the wind at your back, you broke the world's record, but moving into it was like pushing against a breathing wall. We bent at the waist to keep from being knocked over, like pictures I had seen of explorers in Antarctica. Wind clung hold of us like a sumo wrestler and threw us around. Meena spread her shirt and leapt like a flying spider. Buck tucked a fifty-cent piece against his thumb spinner-style and heaved it into the wind. It went ten feet, then shot back past us, whistling like a bullet. A goner.

Mom shouted for us to get inside, quick! Only her lips moved. Somewhere a tree gave way with a sharp crack and we were running—I was—toward the tunnel. Everybody was following behind me, except Grandma Sally and Steve Weatherspoon, who sussed me out and was lip-screaming to forget it. We would asphyxiate down there with so many of us anyway. Which we almost did. Except we huddled close around Mom at the entrance, sitting in a row like monkeys in the dark. Buck showed me where a piece of roof gashed open his leg, and we used a handkerchief to stop the bleeding. Wind moaned over the mouth of the tunnel like a mournful dog, humming all around us. But we felt safe there, almost cozy.

"Let the roof fall down on her head," Mom laughed, "see if I care. . . . Mom's only joking." She hugged us around her and was having a fine time and could move right in, she said, except she could do with a bit more light. Her hands icy cold against my neck.

We sang "Ninety-nine Bottles of Beer on the Wall" and told Polack jokes. But Mom's eyes kept walling toward where the tunnel disappeared in twisting darkness. Not like it frightened her, just like it haunted her the same way it haunted me. She understood why we had dug it. She'd been here before, I wanted to tell her, I'd seen her face pocked against the darkness.

Dad arrived just after the wind let up. His hair mussed wild, shirt collar open and tie crooked. His eyes were like little gleaming mirrors when he peeked in at us, laughing, saying we looked like a lot of possums down there—just our eyes showing. He helped us up one by one. I never saw him so giddy. "We're on our way," he shouted. "I got the job. California or bust." We all cheered—except Buck, who looked at darkening clouds, gloomy that the storm was leaving.

Mom said Dad had been drinking. Naughty him. But he told us a story about a tree that fell across the road on his way to work and nearly crushed his car. "It's a disaster zone out there. Trees down, radio towers, storefronts demolished. Like the sack of Rome. I've promised to stay long enough to help settle some of these claims, then we're outta here. You kids are going to love it down south."

"They have a fantastic zoo," Meena said.

Dad looked at her funny, then grinned. "That's right. A fantastic zoo."

"Whoopeee," Mom said, unexcited. Though she always hated the rain.

Dad looked around like he first noticed our gloomy cave— just a raw hole in the dirt. Then his smile fell, as if he thought of something he didn't wish to remember.

# 18

## Meena

She spun her second web of sturdy nylon fish line across her bedroom window in California, looking out on scarlet plumes of a bottlebrush tree and a huge prickly pear cactus beside a granite toe jutting out of the parched soil—connected, she believed, to the rock in the Long Loops' cave in Oregon, an underground shelf extending the length of the Pacific coast. Across the city, orange and avocado groves formed terraced steps up low hills, backdropped by the sienna ridge of Burnt Mountain. If it was heaven, it was a peculiar parched paradise, pocked, miserly soil rich in the scraping, burrowing lives of ants, spiders and gophers, but supporting little green. Sunlight beat down tropically at midday, but evenings were chilly, with a scent of orange blossoms on the air. Everything grew here, little naturally.

Her web's concentric rings were joined by radials extending outward from the central bull's-eye, like the elegant webs of the orb-spinning Epeiridae. She'd built it to prevent a Mexican farm worker from slipping through her open window while she slept—men with mahogany dark faces and great toothy smiles who camped in eucalyptus scrub at bottom of the canyon. Never guessing its real purpose was to keep out an intruder closer to home.

But one night an intruder she could not protect against parted strands of her web and crept slyly, chitinously under her skin—bloodying sheets, erupting in strange paddings of flesh. She'd read about such things: mother spiders that carried their minuscule, scuffling brood on their backs or tucked safely inside mandibles, the spiderlings scurrying—she imagined—in games of tag through stubbly hairs. She dreamt of silky cocoons encasing baby masses under her swelling pink nipples: teeming, restless, eight-legged tapioca clumps, countless tiny wrinkled faces looking outward. Numberless spider-legged ballerinas poised at the barre, on pointe on multiple toes, scuttling awkwardly into each other. Upon waking, she itched all over, her hair follicles tingled. Secret imperatives scurried inside her. Gone spider down deep.

Was this how it worked? Homunculi waited in fatty layers under the skin, and when a penis poked you—as Olson explained it to her and Boney—squirting, he said, like a single-shot squirt gun, then *his* share of babies mixed with *hers*, and by arrangement one was elected to represent the mass. She could incipiently remember a time when she was ganged together with a multitude of brothers and sisters who had proudly elected her to go forward into the world to represent them. More popular then than she had ever been since.

Overnight, her flesh erupted and threw her into confusion. It was California, she knew, which causes even cactuses to bloom. Olson teased her endlessly, coming up behind her and pinching her tits. "Just checking." He'd grin and she would kick his shin. She walked with her shoulders hunched, preferring coarse cotton twill to polyester. Arachnids and insects wore skeletons outside their bodies as a kind of armor. It made perfect sense to her.

"Stand up straight, young lady," Mom barked, forbidding any more of this "spider nonsense." She, more than anyone, noticed the change in her daughter, studied every move she made, scolding, correcting, grounding her for coming home late from school, for wearing eye shadow, for not wearing a bra under her baby dolls, for saying "crap," anything! Everything. Mom forbade her to join her brothers' bike explorations down dusty farm roads. Accused Meena of borrowing lingerie. "Don't be idiotic," she'd laugh, "you can't wear my bras," right in front of her sneering bonerhead half-brother. What was her problema? At dinner, she sat staring at Meena with a worried expression, constantly on the rag since she'd quit drinking. Until Meena wished she had never stopped. At least then she minded her own business.

One day Mom took her aside and explained in a hushed, deliberate tone, "You aren't a child anymore, honey. I want you to tell me if any . . . funny business happens."

"What funny business?" Meena demanded.

She wanted to hear Mom say it, to stop all her sneaky, jerk-off insinuations. Remembering, suddenly, the time Dad arrived home from California, while Mom was at Tranquility. He'd come in bleary-eyed, dead on his feet, but had been so happy to see her—and she to see him—that he lifted her and spun her around. But it was his kiss she recalled most vividly: hard and lingering, right on the mouth. His rough wooden lips crushing her soft ones. He'd never kissed her that way before. Grandma Sally's eyes widened in momentary alarm over Dad's shoulder. A thrill of something she couldn't explain had shot down Meena's spine and tingled at her fingertips. A shiver, almost a fright. Was that what Mom meant?

But Mom was unwilling or unable to say; she just wall-eyed her daughter's rebellious body—that haunted, wary, heavy-lidded look. Mom was a jerk. Who was going to talk about it to their mom? Although in health class, in home economics, school hallways, at dances . . . no one talked about anything else. Sex. The in thing, the only thing. Sex. Girls passed around worn copies of *Lady Chatterley's Lover* and giggled over it. Seeeex. Biggo deal.

Even Dad appeared to notice her stirrings. He seemed perplexed by them. Suddenly he no longer knew how to act around her. When they hugged, he leaned away at the waist like a nerd. She would sneak up behind him like a trap-door spider—which pounces upon victims from burrows in the ground—gripping a hand over his mouth and squashing her new breasts into his shoulders. Enjoying how he bolted forward, how Mom got pissed off and demanded, "Are you out of your right mind?" Biggo deal. It was only a game. The more uptight Mom became, the more intransigent Meena got. Was she supposed to stop loving her father or he her just because she was developing breasts? What was Mom's problem? Was she maternally retarded? Just jealous . . . Of what? Who? It was beyond gonadal, it was emotionally spastoid. She couldn't decide which pee-o'd her more—Mom's nutso overprotection or Dad's nerdso passivity.

What began as nubbly stubble on her pubis and under her arms lengthened into dark fleece. Mysterious doings were afoot. As her legs grew nubbly-stubbly, she studied her collection of predators pickled in alcohol—funnel spiders, desert snow spiders (which she found suspended on glistening orb webs five feet across in the semi-arid desert air, nearly an inch wide, white but for speckled brown abdomens), wolf spiders, hoppers, silk spinners and spitters . . . most covered in silken black hair. Terribly wonderful. Or wonderfully terrible. If you play at something long enough it comes true. She was becoming a spider.

California also wore an exoskeleton—hard outside, soft inside. Boney pointed out interlinking mountain ranges in his atlas (here they called them sierras). While, in outings to collect tunnel spiders (*Lycosa nidifex*), which lurked underground in burrows lined in silk, she found that soil was crumbly soft beneath the hardpan outer crust. Hard, cheery faces of neighborhood stucco houses concealed mushy, forbidden truths. Lemon, cassava, grapefruit, cactus fruit, pecan, avocado . . . everything had its hard, shiny exterior. The blondest kids in class had the tannest skin. Girls with the brightest smiles were the gimpiest phonies underneath. Mr. Trump, who coached wrestling and looked like Jimmy Cagney, was a homo. Leela Annibell Hitchcock, whose dad was Baptist preacher, was school slut. Nothing in California was what it appeared to be on the outside.

Mom took three months to unpack the movers' boxes. She kept busy with her new friends—Wendy next door and Donna Evans down the street. They had coffee together after Dad left for work, spent the day sitting around Wendy's pool, playing hearts, Mom reading real estate manuals in preparation for her broker's license exam. Sometimes Meena quizzed her from practice tests at back of the books. Mom would look off with a strange, close-lipped smile and say, "Your mom's going to make a pot of money selling houses. Isn't that a kick?" Then she would lean back in her recliner and cover her eyes with plastic green frog-eye sun blinders and appear to lose interest.

After work, Dad went natural, changing from suit and tie to beach togs. He'd poke around the garden, growing artichokes, zucchini, musk melons, spicy hot jalapeños . . . things she'd never heard of before California. "This is the life," he'd say. He traded his Impala for a flashy red Corvette convertible. Meena overheard Mom complain to the gals: "I don't get it. Does he plan to drag the gut Friday nights and pick up jailbait?"

"Their adrenalines go haywire down here," Donna Evans said. "It's the heat." She had been married four times, worked nights as a registered nurse and stank of hospital antiseptic.

Wendy modeled underwear for Sears Roebuck and was pretty in a pinch-cheeked, low-foreheaded Doris Day way. She told a joke about the man who came to the beach dejected and left erected. "End of story," she said. Meena sneezed. "Meena, are you eavesdropping?" Mom called. She danced on tiptoes back to her room. Spiders never answer. The wisest build a funnel at top of their webs where they can run to hide.

So why was it, in sunshine that had extended nonstop from June gloom through October, in a brand-new life without one detergent bottle hooch stash under the sink (she kept track), in what Daddy called "our paradise on the hill," with its view of Escondido avocado groves so green they were nearly black, why should things feel so shaky? Why did Dad leave for work every morning as if he was going to his execution? She'd heard Mom tell her pals he wouldn't discuss his new job. "I don't even know where his office is, or how much he's earning. I've never lived in a rented house in my life . . . over my dead body." The gals made low sympathetic sounds. To rent in California was unpatriotic.

It was as if the earthquake fault running beneath them in Escondido extended through their lives. Twice they'd heard a brooding rumble—from everywhere and nowhere—a warning from deep earth. Glasses rattled in cupboards, Chester freaked out, Mom shooed them beneath door frames, terrified the whole house would collapse on their heads. On the surface everything seemed hunky-dory, no sign of anything brooding beneath. For the first time Meena could remember, Mom and Dad weren't fighting. Oregon gloom replaced by blond wall-to-wall California optimism in that ranch house atop the hill in Escondido. Why, then, why did she feel a glass had slipped from her hand and she waited for it to shatter on the floor?

If only Mom would stop looking at her as if she knew something Meena didn't know. If the two of them could stop bickering. If Mom would F-off about the way she folded back her bedspread or wore her underwear—biggo deal—about the house, or refused to shave her legs (hairier than Boney's, who must've shaved his). If Olson would grow up and stop being a bonerhead spas who found her breasts the biggest joke in history and swiped her trainer bras to wear like pirate bandannas to hold back his scraggly long hair. If only Dad would relax and call her "little outlaw" again and play "showdown at high noon," where they poked each other with their pistol finger until one giggled. That would never happen . . . which was okay; it was a dumb game anyway. If, at least, he stopped being afraid to hug her. And Mom got off the rag about it.

If only Boney stopped spying on her at school—afraid some ninth grade surfer dude would rape her. (What could he do about it anyway, Mr. Ninety-five-pound Weakling?) It didn't increase her popularity one bit to have Mr. Nerdso following her around—his little-boy haircut and big ears. "Oregon! Where's that?" Angela Vorpos demanded of Meena her first week at Eagle Grove. Gum chewing, books clutched to chest, a pleated miniskirt and sassy blond bob swishing about her ears as she glanced side to side at her gang. Wrinkling her nose. "Millford! Gimme a break." Meena shot forward and hissed in her face—an angry ophidian sound. Angela spun away, hands shielding her face. For a time after that they left her alone. Although she could hear their chickenshit whispering behind her back. Oregon was like a social disease they had brought with them. She had never had many friends—since that time when a horde of siblings had elected her to represent them in the world—and didn't expect to be popular at Eagle Grove. They could go F themselves.

Meantime she began collecting insurance: Mom's green frog eyes, a pair of Olson's Jockey shorts, Boney's Tranquility cap, an ugly necktie Dad never wore and—since she'd been accused of it anyway—a gauzy 36C Olga bra from Mom's lingerie drawer, a gnawed Chester bone, her favorite snap of Aunt Debbie, a turtle-shell comb she stole from Diana Tarantella's desk at school—who was so stuck up her nose tilted permanently in the air (they made a biggo deal of it, saying it was a family heirloom, if anyone had information . . . blah, blah, blah; or drop it in Mr. Danner's mail slot, no questions asked). Wrapping each item in monofilament and stashing all under her bed, because spiders spin their paralyzed prey in silk, while enzymes injected from their fangs dissolve the innards, turning their victims to a kind of pudding. She'd counted up to seventeen wrapped, digesting carcasses in one web.

Late at night, Meena hung her prizes from dresser knobs and curtain rods around her room, shining a flashlight from one treasure to the next, feeling rich. Unexpectedly, one night, Mom opened her door. First sign she'd begun wandering the house again in insomniac restlessness. Meena killed her beam too late. Mom was on her, tearing away covers, insisting she was reading some smut in bed—*Lady Chatterley's Lover*—demanding, "Where is it?" She searched between bed and wall, under the bed, bare now of those items that hung all around them, eerily illumined by bathroom light spilling through the open door so it looked like a voodoo Sabbath. Mom never saw them. She confiscated the flashlight and said whatever it was Meena was doing she would do it no longer. Over my dead body. Thinking it was a sexual thing, because she never gave her daughter a look that wasn't tainted with sexual insinuation, sexual suspicion, sexual fear. But a daughter's treasures, cozied in spider silk and hung about the room—she could never have imagined such a thing.

"I decided I wouldn't forgive her until she returned my light," she told them years later. "I collected webs, carefully, from trees and fences, the sticky kind that orb spinners weave, that cling to your face like a wet handkerchief and give you the creeps. A whole mat of them wound between two sticks. One night I laid it over Olson's pillow before he went to bed. His screams were worth every slug he gave me. You should have seen him! Spiderweb clinging in cotton-candy tufts to his hair. Grrrrosss."

But what she did to Angela Vorpos—after Boney told Angela to lay off his sister and Angela told her boyfriend, Brian, who beat Boney bloody—was sheer genius. She dried her spider collection in the sun (perhaps fifty of them) and brought a bottle of dried spiders to school. Walked right up to Angela in the lunchroom, surrounded by her yackety-yak friends, and smiled as much like Mom as she could manage, brackets cinching her lips taut either side. Gone spider down deep.

"Hiya, Angie," she said sweetly, then sprinkled dead spiders over her sloppy joe. Angela stared down at it a second, then bolted across the table and upchucked over her friends. Meena was a little bit famous around school after that.

# 19

## Jeff

Dad pulled over onto the shoulder and stopped. Dust rose up under the car and settled over us through open windows, leaving a chalky powder on our cheeks. We had been driving nonstop on our way down south from Oregon; the moving truck wouldn't even arrive for another day. Dad leaned an elbow on the seat back and grinned at us. "Well, wha'd'ya think, guys? We're Californians now. Pretty sweet, huh?" The breeze was hot, not like any breeze I ever felt before. Mom said she thought she would die. She wouldn't look up at our new house, only down the hillside to where they were building the freeway, past an orchard with tree trunks painted white.

"You must've gone all out to find a place as dusty as this, Donald."

The house spread across the brow of the hill, ranch-style, like hospital buildings at Tranquility Acres. Palm trees all around, like they towed a tropical island to Escondido. Every type of tree imaginable: shiny-leaf olives, spreading pecans, papery-bark eucalyptus, apricot, orange, grapefruit—which amazed me because I didn't know grapefruits grew on trees. Olson nudged me.

"You ever seen a tree with yellow nuts?" He nodded at tall slim trees marching in a rank along the west side of the house. "Looks like Martians' peckers."

"What was that, Olson?" Mom smiled.

"That's cool."

"Cypresses," Dad said. "A cypress windbreak." He was pleased with everything, I could see. Even licked dust from his arm to test its taste. So I tried it too. A sweet citrus perfume hung thick and sleepy on the air, so different from the smoky sawmill stink back in Millford.

Mom looked up at our new house. "Do I have any say in this?"

"What do you mean? I'm doing this for you, Jerri, you and the kids. You know that. No more Oregon gloom!" Dad kept looking from the house to the orchard to the new freeway, his chin bunched.

Mom looked at the house, play-frowning. "Do the lawn thingies come with it or are they extra? It looks like an old-people's home." Leaping fawns and dumb grinning elf statues.

Dad shrugged. "Hey, this is California. Everyone's kooky in California."

"Well, we ought to fit right in, then."

It was all on one level. Just a regular house, but stretched out like everything in California. Right off, Dad set up a golf tee in the front yard, where he could shag balls across the road into the orchard. Next door lived Wendy and Sandy, who looked like twins. You couldn't hardly tell them apart—except Sandy's eyebrows were darker and her mom hardly had any—or which was older, except for tiny crow's-feet beside Wendy's eyes when she smiled. But Sandy was bigger—all over!—"Sixteen going on thirty," Dad said. Both wore short shorts and bikini tops and blond ponytails and were brown as filberts, both modeled ladies' underwear for the newspaper. I saw them every Sunday, smiling side by side in nothing but a bra and underwear or maybe a girdle. No big deal; they lounged half-naked around the pool in their bikinis anyway.

"SandWitch," Olson called Sandy, 'cause she treated him like a kid even though she was his same age. He hated that. But Sandy bossed everyone around, including her mom, since she got the most modeling jobs. Meena was in love with her. She sat on the pool deck for hours watching Sandy paint her toenails or lift dumbbells to make her boobs stick out, while Mom and Wendy and dummy Donna from down the street sipped iced tea and got browner and browner. California was like living on permanent vacation, so Dad never stopped being jittery. At first he was excited, like when we planned a trip, but soon he began to grouch about all the money Mom was spending. He kept calling the realtor in Oregon to ball him out for not selling our house. When I asked if I could see his new office, he snapped, "Hold

your horses, pal, we're still remodeling." Seemed like they kept
on remodeling forever.

Olson and me went rattlesnake hunting with his pellet gun in
the canyon behind our house which led to the highway project.
You had ten minutes to live after a copperhead bit you, he said,
unless you sucked out the venom. I think he kinda looked forward to getting bit—me anyhow—so he could find out. He
dared me to turn over rocks and called me a chickenshit if I
didn't, so I had to, while he squinted down his arm and I was
scared he would miss and blast my fingers.

We found a winos' camp in a grove of eucalyptus at the Y
intersection where our canyon joined another. Nothing but old
mattresses, Sunkist cartons full of cruddy clothes and wooden
boxes tacked to trees, with a few cans of food in them, a piece
of black plastic tacked up for a roof. Nobody home, but when
Olson walked in and started breaking up the place I was scared
they might come back any second. "Wetbacks," he sneered,
dumping cartons out into the dirt and shooting the food tins full
of holes. "Dirty spicks." His eyes drowsed up, he grinned and
pulled one mattress atop another.

"Let's torch it."

I pleaded with him not to, it was their home. Besides, the fire
would spread right up the dry canyon and fry our house. "Good
riddance," Olson said. He stacked clothes atop mattresses and
stood shaking the box of stick matches at me like an angry rat-
tler. "Poor lidda boy gonna shit his pants." I reminded him how
Dad beat him with his belt after he started a fire in our basement
on Walnut Street. Olson got pissed. He thumped my chest, his
upper lip worming. "Don't gimme that crap. Y'r dad's a fucking
bum, too. Un-em-ployed."

"Liar."

"Ask my mom. Dad stopped her alimony payments out of
financial hardship. She's up shit creek in a leaky canoe."

"Y'r a dirty rotten liar. Dad's branch manager."

"Hah-ha, I'm Mr. Magoo."

"I'm going to ask him."

"See if I care. Truth's the fucking truth. He's a bum and his
sissy son can lick my shorts." Olson lit a match and dropped it
on the sleeve of a khaki army surplus shirt. The weave turned

red like a smoldering lantern mantle then burst into bright yellow flame. I stomped it out. Olson slugged me. "Okay, bonermouth, wanna play games?" He threw the matches at me and ripped open a mattress, exposing white cotton guts. "Light it," he ordered. "Go on." He took a spread-eagled stance, aiming the pistol inches from my face. His eyes narrowed, he jerked the pellet pistol. "Go on. Do it, faggorola." Down the barrel, I saw the gray-blue slit of Olson's eye, like looking up at the hatch from down in the dark tunnel. I shook my head, no.

"You asked for it." Olson raised his arm and lowered to take aim. Flesh tingled along my old scar, my teeth clenched so hard it made my fillings ache. My fingernails scratched automatic at the flint match strip, but I wasn't holding a match. Down on the highway I heard earth movers grumbling, a bird peeping in bushes close by, and I wondered if the pellet would lodge somewheres in my brain, if my thoughts would swell up around it like water around a rock and come out crooked afterwards. Seemed like forever, Olson didn't shoot. When I opened my eyes, he was looking down at a magazine that had fell out of the mattress—naked women with tits so white blue veins showed inside, their legs wide open, showing everything. He turned pages with his toe.

"Boss, mucho boss." Olson smacked my head. "Corruption of a minor!" At least he didn't burn down the canyon. He was satisfied with just stealing the magazine.

When I asked Dad if it was true he wasn't really branch manager, he hit the roof. I shouldn't listen to a word out of Olson's filthy mouth. "You have a question, ask me." I shouldn't worry, he said, we'd get by. "I'm counting on you to play second man around the place. Your mother needs your help if she's going to lick this thing." It was weird, California made everybody weird. The next weekend he took Olson out onto the patio for a talk. Dad's eyes were tight, he jabbed a finger; Olson looked down at the tiles with a smile on his face. I knew I was in for it then, my brother would never forgive me.

In August, Meena and me started digging into the sandy canyon wall behind our house, which was pocked by gopher, owl and skunk burrows like a huge natural apartment building. We dug straight in—more a cave than a tunnel—but after two feet the wall collapsed and half buried us alive. Meena's hair was full of sand. She motioned me to turn my back so she could shake out her shirt. Biggo deal, with her itty-bitty titties. But something scurried in the coyote bush and Meena screamed and clutched the T-shirt to her chest. Only a rabbit, I said. But I thought about the men whose camp Olson trashed, and we high-tailed it out of there.

My dumb sister had turned into a spider—hairier-legged even than me. She crawled around fields with her ear cocked to the ground, listening for trap-door spiders scratching in their burrows. She would pry up the little door with a toothpick and blow into the hole, then when the spider jumped out, she clamped a jar over it. It amazed me that spiders lived in tunnels which they dug themselves and rigged trapdoors (like snug corks of dirt and cobweb, with hinges on the side). They were the Steve Weatherspoons of spiders. Or the Vietcong, who made booby traps with stakes that pierced your guts if you fell in. Meena wanted to be a trap-door spider, waiting in its silky nest for something tasty to crawl past. It was a stage she was going through, like men went through in caveman days. Mr. Danne-meyer, in science, says that when people get really scared they want to crawl back into their mother's womb. What had got my sister so scared, I wondered. Maybe she was homesick for Oregon, which I was myself.

She had spiders of all varieties in jars on her bookshelf, pickled in alcohol. Dad gave her a microscope for her birthday and Meena showed me weird button eyes in rows above their man-dibles and claws on tips of their hairy legs. You could see the breathing slits and markings over their thumping hearts and the epigynum (the female's sex parts) on the abdomen, which looks like a person on the toilet from underneath. She pulled the big cardboard box our new fridge came in out beside her bedroom window and made a nest inside, huddling in there for hours, reading spider books. When someone passed by the flap door, she leapt out, baring her wax fangs. She prob'ly pulled Chester inside a thousand times and sucked his blood.

Once, the man from the electric company was reading the meter and the trap door popped open and Meena scuttled out on all fours, hissing and baring her fangs. He nearly shit a brick. Took off running, kicking his knees high in the air, like she was an actual spider blown up a hundred times. He stood beside his truck yelling at Mom and Wendy how he wasn't paid to put up with "damned loony birds" when they came down from the pool next door. An old guy with a bald head and his face flushing red as his mouth. Mom went in after my sister and dragged her out by the hair. This was going to stop . . . now! young lady. I guess the old guy thought my mom was nutty as my sister.

After Meena dumped spiders in Angela Stuck-up's food at school—whose boyfriend slugged me—and she upchucked all over the Kool crowd while Danner the Banana stood watching, Mr. Danner called Dad and warned next time he would expel her. Mom and Meena got in a huge-o fight; Meena called her a boozer and Mom started crying and said no one cared whether she lived or died, then roared off in her Ford wagon, and Dad went bonkers. Did Meena intend to ruin everything after all Mom's hard work? Was that the idea? When Mom came home, she tore Meena's room apart. Under the bed was like out of *The Brain Eaters*—weird voodoo stuff wrapped in fish line like she had cast a spell on all of us: Mom's pantyhose, my beanie . . . Diana the Tarantula's comb.

Mom went in with Meena to see Danner the Banana, all gussied up in her blue serge Jackie Kennedy suit. I got a glimpse of Danner looking from Meena to my mom's cleavage. Wrinkles bunched up beside his mouth and spread to his forehead in a frowning epidemic. He looked like a funeral director with blue cheeks, tall and skinny as a spider leg. But what caught my attention before Danner closed the door was a lady sitting inside, wearing a Jackie Kennedy suit like Mom's, only pink. Lips dark glossy purple as grape gum after you've chewed it a long time. Stooping over Meena, smiling, trying to make friends. Already I didn't like her.

Ms. Childlove, Mom said, a psychiatric social worker, who came to our house to talk to Meena about her spider thing the next day. "That's not her real name," I told my mom. "People in California invent their names." (Like Sandy next door, who changed hers from Sandy McNutt to Sandy Beach.) "I'll bet her first name is Goona." Mom laughed in spite of herself. She said it wasn't like me to say something like that; I was picking up bad habits from Olson. But when I peeked into the living room, Meena was curled up on the sofa like a wolf spider. Ms. Goona

Childlove had pulled a chair up close. "I want you to trust me," I heard her say. My sister hissed at her. I would have too. She looked like a police lady from another planet.

California drove everyone bonkers. Except Mom. She was so normal after Tranquility it was spooky. You get so used to someone being sick that when they get well you think there's something wrong with them. Sometimes I woke up and thought Mom had come into my room. Nothing but the far-off crowing of roosters at the farm below the orchard. It worried me that the wetbacks from the canyon might come after us for revenge because we messed up their camp. So I'd go in to check if Meena was all right. But one night she wasn't in bed. I thought maybe she'd gone outside to hunt wolf spiders with a flashlight. (Their eyes glowed like tiny emeralds in the beam. Once we saw a mother with big glowing eyes and above them a zillion tiny glimmering eyes of her hatchlings riding on her back. Pretty amazing.) I bumped into my sister as I stepped back into the hall. Scared the doobies out of us. "Mom's in the kitchen," she whispered, "just sitting staring into space. I think she's plastered."

"Bee ess, Meena. You know it is. Anyway, you shouldn't be spying on people."

She said Mom and Wendy put hooch in their iced tea. My sister had itsy spiders crawling around her brain making a cobwebby mess. It was her who claimed she saw Dad at the Del Mar Fair with his Mexican girlfriend. Dad? Gimme a break.

That was August. Mom let us go to the fair on our own with Toby Olsen from down the street. Olson and Olsen, they called themselves. Big deal. A fat kid with a bad temper and greasy hair rolling back over his head in two-inch waves, his cheeks hung in jowls over his chin like an old man's, broader than his forehead. We were in the livestock barns and Olson said Toby looked like "a blue-ribbon Hampshire hog" or a horse's dick head, which he did, too—fatter on the bottom and narrow at top. Toby Olsen pushed Olson's arm up behind his back and forced him down over a hog trough. Even meaner than my stepbrother, which is prob'ly why Olson hung out with him. Olson took it back.

Then they grabbed me and held me by the legs, upside down over the hog pen. "Sooey sooey," Piggy Olsen yammered to fat grunting porkers lying in straw across the pen, "c'mon 'n' get supper." From below, his wide-open mouth was gummy white with saliva. All the blood rushed into my head and it felt like my old scar would burst open. I was yelling and kicking. If I didn't quit, they said they'd drop me.

A fat sow got up and waddled over to sniff me. I nearly peed, looking upside down at its rubbery, sniffling snout and old person's bitsy mean pig eyes. It smelled like all the greasy bacon in the world frying at once. "Ead 'im up." Piggy Olsen was laughing. "Nibble his eyes." Looked like it might, too. Grunting and its little slit mouth open, full of teeth.

Meena screamed and I wriggled and tried sitting up in the air.

"Stop it, asshole," cried Olson, "I'm losing my grip." The last second Toby pulled me up. I leaned back against the fence, while old ladies adjusted their glasses to look at us.

"That was really stupid," Meena said.

But Toby Olsen laughed and Olson cocked a finger at my head and said that would teach me to be a rat fink.

Olson and Olsen had brought squirt guns filled with ammonia. First, they just shot little kids and stuffed bears hanging on midway booths, while Meena and me played steeplechase and dime toss and won three goldfish. We heard a scuffle behind us at the milk-bottle throw; I knew it was Olson and Olsen even before looking.

A stringy-haired, tough-looking blonde lady was shouting at them (she looked like a man with tits, Olson said later: tall and lean-faced, not old but her face lined and creased from the weather, sunset red, like she'd been working carnivals all her life). Piggy Olsen was cussing her out. He whipped out his squirt gun and blasted her in the face. She screamed and hurdled the counter for them, but staggered, her eye whites showing like she was blind. "Come on!" Olson shouted at us, and we hightailed it around the Texas Barbecue tent and hid behind Orange Julius. Me playing lookout. The tough lady came by, cursing and stomping her feet, rubbing a fist into her eyes and peeking out a crack in her fingers, moaning, "Sunnuvabitch blinded me." Beside her was a short husky man with a mustache and a lady in a jeans jacket, meaner-looking than both.

"Couple of punks," he said.

"Four of 'em," said the jeans lady. "I seen four kids."

"I'm gonna stomp shit outta all four and eat their guts. Damn! My eyes smart."

We watched. Toby Olsen huddled up, clutching his arms. Gone chicken. "It wasn't my idea," he said.

"Shuddup, fatso," Olson whispered.

"She looks just like this mean wiener dog my dad used to have. It bit me about a hun'rd times."

We sneaked over to the Mystery House, 'cause Olson said we had to lay low. It was a huge decrepit wooden shack with cobwebs over the windows, and a witch with a bloodshot eye kept sticking her head out a door upstairs. We bought two rides apiece, and Olson said I better ride with Toby. But Meena said no, she wouldn't go then. Until Piggy Olsen thought he saw them coming and that ended it. The ticket collector looked us over suspiciously. He wore a hood and had his face greasepainted gray like a ghoul.

It might've been neat inside if I wasn't too scared for real to be scared for fun. Toby Olsen grumbled and squirted his gun at every spook that popped out at us. Meena screamed in the car behind us when we went through the crinkly guts, again when we passed the kid who had fell onto the tracks and got his leg cut off. Blood squirted out of his stump. "Boss," Olson said, and Toby wouldn't believe it wasn't for real, not even when we went by the second time. By then Meena and Olson were scuffling in the car behind. Stop it, I heard her say, or she would tell Dad on him. "Big chance." Olson laughed.

Outside, the tough lady and her friends were waiting for us when the ride finished (prob'ly the ticket collector tipped them off). Her eyes enflamed like the Devil's. Toby Olsen waddled back into the fun house over the tracks. Two guys went in after him and dragged him out with his heels scraping the ground. The lady reached back fast like she was slamming a Ping-Pong ball and slapped him hard on both cheeks. "See this!" pointing at her oozy red eyes, "y'r fuckinay lucky it ain't got me blind or I'd cut y'r dick off."

"That'll be enough of that, Checkers," the mustached man said. "Cops'll take care of them. Don't you worry none."

"D'you see that?" she yelled at me when I said I was sorry, pulling the lid away from her red eye. She called me a punk and punched my stomach. The lady in the jeans jacket said to piss off, he's a kid, and the guy told Meena and me to skedaddle before he bust our butts. So we did. Pronto. But I felt like I might puke.

When I said I felt guilty to abandon Olson, Meena said it served him right; he was a dirty-minded douche bag. Still, I was scared what Dad would do when he got home. We headed for the O'Brien Gate where Mrs. Olsen was supposed to pick us up at nine. As we passed the Rock-O-Plane, Meena caught my arm and pointed to a couple getting into a car at the landing. "It's Dad," she said, the liar. I saw a Mexican lady in a frilly dress stepping into the oval cage. It rocked back and forth on its pivot and she laughed at someone inside.

"You're crazy," I told Meena. We watched the cars begin to spin overhead, rocking and tipping and turning almost over. Through the grating we could only see the backs of their heads. "Besides," I said, "Dad's afraid of heights." Meena wanted to wait till they got off, but I refused. Dirty little sneak. We had to go meet Mrs. Olsen. Besides, I'd saw all the weird stuff I wanted to see for one day.

Just then a lady's shoe hit the metal platform above us with a clank loud as a bullet and bounced down the steps. Meena grabbed it and we ran, because the Rock-O-Plane attendant was yelling to bring it back, thief.

Everyone went bonkers that night: Olson and Olsen, Meena and her black patent-leather pump with rhinestones on the toes, which she said belonged to Dad's girlfriend, which was a fantasy she made up in the first place. So some poor Mexican lady had to hobble around on her stocking toe looking for her shoe, which Meena hid in her purse. Even though Dad wasn't home when we got there, that didn't prove he was at the fair horsing around. He was working late like he often did. California is lots more expensive than Oregon. My sister knew that. She was just feeling her hormones, like Aunt Debbie says, and wanted to cause trouble.

# 20

---

# Meena

Lights swirled around her in the air, blinking staccato streaks of red, yellow, white, yellow, red . . . like a time-lapse photo of streaming traffic, blurring into tinny music forced on her ears from all sides, numbing her senses, as though she had dived into ambient cacophony from a high board: barkers' shouts, girls' shrieking laughter, midway waltzes, Scott Joplin–John Philip Sousa racetrack razzle-dazzle . . . wallowing in hyperthyroid gluttony like a gaudy manatee rolling in shattered aural surf, exposing its vulgar belly, the whole naked vulgar underbelly of male thrill-seeking exposed below as they whirligiged in bright night air. Sailors with whoo-peeing grins at the sledgehammer gong, a great blinking clown face, its lobed nose glistening at the tip like the Frisian horse's thingy in Barn B; directly opposite in the gondola, Toby Olsen's jowlish face distending as octopus arms whipped faster-faster, tracing steel blossoms in the electric air, centrifugal force kneading flesh away from his teeth like macabre fingers, furrowing it around his ears, liquefying cheeks to a hideous tallow, until his skull burst through and lids slid away from his eyeballs. He leered.

Wind howled past her ears. Kids screamed. Octopus arms tilted suddenly, suspending them vertically above the midway. It was then she watched, alarmed and wondrous, Olson's hand hop from his knee to hers and slide under her skirt—as if that, too, was part of the thrill—while they hung upright, defying gravity in the cool night.

Perhaps it was a dream: She could not move, could not resist, an invisible hand pinned her against the seat back. Though her legs had clamped tight—double clamped with double gravity—so his fingers could not reach their prize, merely fumbled at elastic of her panties. Olson's sallow cheeks reflected Piggy Olsen's gelatinous grin opposite—the grossest dirty dog leer. It was best to ignore it, as Boney did, stare over Piggy's head at a giddy swirl of carnival lights: sky, midway, sky . . . believing it some aberration of dizziness, like the hollow nausea at pit of her stomach. Olson's fingers wriggled inward, tore at spider bristles. She sat helplessly until the car slowed to horizontal with the whining of a dying motor and righted itself—until the moment he prized her legs open and she moved instinctively, knowing (without Aunt Debbie, anyone, having taught her) the quickest way to call off a dog is to choke it. She clutched Olson back where he clutched: not his hardness, but spongy flesh beneath. His legs kicked out straight, hands gripped the air as if he was trying to climb ladder rungs away from her, mouth open—half howl/half moan. Toby laughed. Nosy-nerd Boney gawked her out—pretending not to. The world steadied, glided up alongside them in the form of a solid steel grating. Olson panted at her ear.

Later, too, she would remember the most beautiful creature she had ever seen, a black glistening Frisian stallion in Barn B, six and one-half hands high, of noble European blood, muscles quivering beneath sleek skin. His owner steadied him with a sure hand while she curried, while Meena stared at the glossy dark pizzle dangling to his knees. So vulnerable, she had thought. But knew better now. "That ain't nothing." Toby Olsen leered. "Wanna see mine?" The boys fell over each other. How is it possible that a thing of beauty can turn suddenly to ugliness?

"How did I feel?" she replied years later. "Disgusted and dirty. I wanted to puke. For such a thing to happen, for my own brother . . . because that sort of thing only happens to sluts. Again on the Fun House ride in ghoulish light, while doors banged open and angry people waited for us outside. Stupid punk-ass groping, that's all. Impressing himself. Nothing to do with me. He would've finger-fucked a spookhouse cat with the same zeal. But how could I know? How do you know? He wanted to *do* me is all; Olson was at war with all things prohibited. I slapped him and told him to stop, sensing Boney's ears burning in the car ahead. I was humiliated and confused, because it was exciting in some filthy, illicit way, then secretly delighted later when Dad brought Olson home from the police station, his eye swollen to a purple crocus where the fair attendant had slugged him. Though I'd already righted things in a way, or so I thought. I had my prize."

A black patent-leather pump, size 6½, rhinestone spangles on its pointed toe, bellying, run-over flanks, heel like a pig's dark nipple. Did Daddy pounce on the woman against the glossy web of the sky as Olson had done? Had she kicked the shoe off in her struggle? The vision was more troubling than her own humiliation. Boney insisted it wasn't Dad; it was just her imagination. Then he'd insisted they run away, probably fearing what his eyes might see. But she had ensnared the truth, wrapped the shoe in spider silk, which she collected with infinite patience from snow-spider webs—fine, elastic, remarkably strong— round and round the Mexican lady's shoe, hiding it in her cubby in the canyon wall (as trap-door spiders stash their inert victims), until that time she might need it. Mom wouldn't find it there, as she'd found Diana Tarantula's comb or Meena's collection of spiders: smashing specimen jars to bits, insisting her daughter "act normal."

What was normal? Olson's filthy fingers in her underpants? The odd unsettling sense of power his excitement gave her over a boy half her own blood? Was Wendy-Sandy's body obsession normal? (They caressed and oiled and coddled themselves like newborns.) Or Danner the Banana's slimy gaze which never left her breasts when he lectured her? The Weatherspoons back in Oregon were normal—the boringest, stuck-upest people in the world, next to Angela Vorpos. It seemed normal to water down Mom's new hooch stashes when she discovered them—in Karo molasses jars or a thermos right out in the open. Because Mom had broken her pledge. If it was normal for a lush to start drinking again, wasn't it normal for a spider to collect spiders? Was it normal for a father to become a ghost in his own house, coming and going at odd hours? Meena wondered if he knew—or cared—that Mom was drinking again. He preferred to be somewhere else.

She knew for sure the night Mom's fingers tucked covers under her chin. They were discussing Ms. Childlove, whom Meena had met that afternoon in Danner's office. "It's for your own good, honey," Mom said. "She's going to help you get off this spider kick."

"She's creepo. She smells like Dutch cleanser."

Meena felt comforted that Mom wasn't the midnight ghoul who perched on the headboard but plain old bitchy Mom who could never mind her own business. Then Mom's fingers brushed her skin, cold as the ice cube trays where she had once stashed her gin; her eyes held that old distracted glaze: sure signs she was no longer climbing the ladder to Tranquility. A vodka trace clung to her knuckles. Maybe others couldn't smell it, Meena did. Boney said lightning never strikes twice in the same place. But it wasn't lightning, more like creeping water. Still, thinking of the Mexican lady's shoe, Meena felt almost sorry for her mother.

"Tell me about Mama's hands," Ms. Childlove said at their first meeting in her spare office downtown. It read P.S.W. after her name on the yellow calfskin briefcase. "Why are they so cold, dear?" Meena didn't bother hissing, but curled up on the rug, the crown of her head touching her knees. Being her normal self. Spiders' legs grow from the cephalothorax, everyone knows that.

"We can carry on in spider talk if you like," Ms. PSW said.

Meena hissed.

Ms. Jerko got down on her nylon knees on the rug, tan skirt stretching taut across her ass, skirt crawling up her thighs. She glanced at Meena from behind an arm—one sulphurous yellow eye glaring—and hissed. Meena hissed back. Slowly, like crableg hockey in gym class, they maneuvered about each other. Hissing. Seeing Ms. PSW's shoe was off, the glossy stockinged flank of her instep, toenails Concord purple, Meena imagined it was Ms. Childlove's shoe she had snatched at the Rock-O-Plane ride. Leaping forward, she sank her teeth into the instep. Ms. PSW didn't flinch; she massaged her instep. "That wasn't nice, you left marks."

Meena grinned a wolf spider grin. "I can see your underpanties." Not white but glossy evil black.

Ms. Childlove's cheek flinched. "So *we can* talk, can we? We've been holding out. Tell me, don't spiders wear underpants?"

The spider frowned.

Ms. Childlove appeared suddenly distracted—as Mom sometimes did—rising to sit in the desk chair, swiveling side to side. A cold vacancy surrounded her. Who was she? A supercounselor from Guidance? A cat woman cop from the moon, like Boney said? Her hair the same dirty apricot as Mom's friend at Tranquility. Maybe they were sisters. She was nearly as tall. Meena was fascinated by the way Ms. PSW's upper incisor snagged her lower lip when she made an "F" sound. The liquid suggestion of a lisp. A generous mouth, Aunt Debbie would say. Huge. Meena pulled the band of her underwear up above her belt to show, then let it snap back. Ms. PSW smiled and picked up the picture Meena had drawn: frozen, dripping hands growing up out of ice cube trays.

"Are these your father's hands?" she asked.

Dummy. Did Dad wear a diamond ring? Her questions were purposely stupid—to throw you off guard.

"Mama's hands then. Frozen because she is angry at you? Why is she angry I wonder."

Meena stared. Four pairs of eyes to choose from—not the largest pair, which phosphoresced green and gave you away when you shined a light on them at night.

"She isn't angry. But sometimes you imagine she is. You imagine Mama is angry and doesn't love you, isn't that so?"

The spider hissed.

"Is there any reason why your mother shouldn't love you, Meena? Isn't that what mothers do?"

The spider yawned.

Ms. PSW smiled gimpily. "I'm not sure what you mean, dear. Yes, there's a reason or no there isn't?"

The spider snorted.

"Touchy business."

"Daws her bess," the spider managed.

Ms. Childlove's yellow eyes hopped. "Well, that's all we can ask of anyone, isn't it? And you, are you doing your best, Meena? Around the house? Helping out with chores, cooking and such?"

The spider nodded.

"Maybe you feel you're asked to do too much, haven't time for friends and schoolwork and things? Is that why you are angry? Because I think that's it, isn't it? You are very, very angry—"

The spider was silent.

"—You feel you do more than your fair share, is that the business? And it makes you mad. And your brothers, Meena?"

The spider started. For a terrible instant Meena wondered if Ms. PSW knew about Olson and the shoe. Our filthiest secrets fester and seep out like pus from inside us. Boney told her psychiatrists are trained to use their eyes like stethoscopes to make you transparent. (Is that what P.S.W. stood for: *Psychiatrist Secrets Witch?*) Ms. PSW's honey-colored eyes seemed capable of spider-witching the juice out of you. It gave Meena the willies. She bared her fangs in alarm.

Ms. PSW laughed. "I know what that means all right. You do your share and your brothers' share, too." Her brow creased. "I wonder, who else's share do you do, Meena?"

The spider climbed onto the couch, working spinnerets to anchor herself in place: index fingers growing from her rear. Ms. PSW rolled silently across the rug on chair coasters, hands patting the air as if some hidden irregularity between them needed smoothing (as Meena wished to smooth Ms. PSW's tangled eyebrows). "And Papa is pleased that you help out like this . . . like his second little wife?" Watching her intently.

The spider giggled. Dumbest idea she had ever heard: *His second little wife* . . . Dad, who couldn't hug her without pushing out his butt like a klutz, who sidled away when she snuggled up next to him to watch TV, before Mom snapped, "Are you out of your right mind?" She wasn't even his second little daughter. No more. But a spitting spider, Scytodida, who released a clever spray of mucilaginous venom from the poison glands behind her jaws, a sticky invisible lasso, pinning Ms. PSW in place, enzymes digesting her alive. Yuck. She tasted as yellow as her eyeballs. As her spongy hair.

"You don't have to tell me . . . not a thing you don't wish to tell. You know that, don't you, dear? No one is forcing you. But it's true, isn't it? You are a second little wife to Papa. Is that your secret, sweetheart? Haven't I told you we can trust each other? It's not such a terrible thing."

Dumbcough! Dad had a Mexican whore for his second little wife—whose shoe tumbled down out of the sky. Meena scooted forward and laughed in her face. Wasn't ladylike, Mom would say. Who cared? Who wanted to be a lady? Was Ms. PSW a lady with all the questions she threw out in a gaudy net?

Ms. Childlove's attention didn't budge from her, as a hopping spider's doesn't from a fly. "Such a terrible secret you won't share with anyone. Wouldn't dare. Mama would blame you for what happened. Isn't that what frightens you? You would be ashamed. Look! It's frozen Mama's hands. Frozen you inside a spider shell, Meena dear. You wouldn't dare tell. But I have a secret"—her voice lowered dramatically, she leaned forward exposing freckled tops of her breasts and the pale bald spot where her part began—"Me too," she whispered.

Alarmed, the spider gawked. Ms. PSW knew. Then the spider smiled relief. Which secret? She couldn't know them all. Mommy's thermos? Spiked iced tea which Sandy went inside to pour for Mom and Wendy (sipping from drinks as she emerged from the house, wobbling exaggeratedly)? Dad's rhinestone shoe? Aunt Debbie at Thanksgiving? . . . Olson's fingers? The night following the Del Mar Fair when she woke to a figure crouched beside her bed, a hand clamped over her mouth, another working nightie straps off her shoulders, two eyes glowing fervidly— like a trap-door spider's inside its warren? She thought him a rapist who had squeezed through her window web. His raspy laborer's hands kneaded and chafed her breasts. But then she inhaled Olson's sour breath. She struggled, but he was strong and sinuous as barbed wire, his hand doing what it wanted while his breathing came rapid and jagged. His body arched, stiffened, bucked; he left a sticky wetness on her sheets. "Tell," he hissed, "and you'll be sorry you were ever born." Which secret in a life built on them? The dirtiest? The most frightening? Which would she tell first?

"The sooner you tell, the sooner you will feel clean again." Ms. PSW smiled. "All the crazy stuff at school, bundles under your bed—" Her voice lowered. "I hear you, Meena. Loud and clear. But you must trust me. The real secret is—it isn't any secret at all."

Meena hissed.

Ms. Childlove's woolly-bear eyebrows arched theatrically, like Olson's back, or Dad's brow when Meena asked him if he would put a lock on her door.

Why on earth would she want to lock her door, Dad asked. "Your mom wouldn't like it. We couldn't get in to you if something should happen." What might happen? she asked him. "That's right! What do you imagine could happen?" His smile gimpy, uneasy. "You're safe, honey. Old Dad'll protect you from the bogeyman."

Did Dad know, she wondered. Is that why he had kissed her hard on the mouth? Maybe males could smell, see . . . sense it in a girl—as Olson had, as boys at school insisted they could spot a tramp, as Dad had his girlfriend. Seeing that mark now on his daughter, he was wary and unsettled by it. She thought they might work out a trade: the rhinestone shoe for her secret. Secret for secret. Maybe that way they would cancel each other out.

# 21

# Aunt Debbie

Jeff called to ask would I come for his birthday. I didn't think so, given my heavy flight schedule and all. Truth be told, I had no intention of setting foot in the same house with his dad. Trouble in Jeff's voice made me change my mind—telling me how neat it was down there, they had palm trees in their backyard, like a boy his age cares puke-all about palm trees. I went. Where family is concerned, resolutions aren't worth fish piss.

Meena had grown up in six California months. Spooky, I'll say. You could put a snapshot of Jerri beside her at that age and hardly tell the difference. Brooding dark eyes, silky dark hair. She was still a child to them: crawling about the house like a daddy longlegs. Two of three nights she did the cooking—if that's what you want to call TV dinners stacked in the freezer two dozen deep—while Jerri was next door at the pool with her pals Wendy-Sandy-Lindy (I never did get it straight), who wore

itty-bitty bikinis and matching shades. Twins, could've been. It
was nearly Christmas and warm as July. Not a trace of winter.

Meena lounged about the house in her negligee like a frowzy
housewife. Stark raving underneath. Maybe this topless thing
you read about. Down here they went natural and no one noticed. . . . Don did! Over his newspaper. Not like he could help
it, I'll give him that. She stuck out like sugar cones. It astonished
me Jerri let her go about like that. Wasn't like my sister one bit.
There's things you can count on—goldfish don't grow wings and
chirp outside your window. She'd watch her daughter with a
forced smile. "It's a phase Meena is going through, she'll snap
out of it. I'm being a good girl, I left my anger back at Tranquility." It had always been a house full of people fooling themselves, but it was getting out of hand.

At breakfast Saturday morning Jerri reeked of hangover. It
made me mad Don couldn't get her through six dry California
months. Wasn't like the family ignored her. They treated Mom
like a pet dog with a skin disease, more like. Olson, home from
school on break, looked like a Buddy Holly understudy—peg-
gers so tight I wondered his balls didn't atrophy. Tough-guy
smartass. Drowsy half-slit eyes roaming, daring us to a game of
first-wink-is-a-rat-fink. After I beat him three straight, Olson
pulled a rat-tailed comb from his back pocket and eased it
through blond furrows of his hair. Takes all kinds, I guess, but
I didn't like the type he was becoming. Meena appeared dressed
that morning. Never so much as glanced at her older brother.
While Jerri and Meena regarded each other through a deep slow
burn. You heard the fuse sizzling. Cozy, I'll say. So much like
Jerri and Sally all those years ago.

Jerri stood beside the table in a red velveteen robe, white chiffon up the front. It clung to her figure and picked up the red
sheen in her hair. A beautiful woman. I wondered Don didn't
notice, wondered if he noticed when she stood nude before him.
That was men, Sally would say: never grow up beyond the tast-
ing stage, like boys at Baskin-Robbins. While women can take
it or leave it. Solitary and self-sufficient as turtles. Sally maybe,
but I never could buy it.

Meena had brought a specimen to show her dad: a hairy wolf
spider, half an inch across, floating in alcohol. We admired it.
Jerri frowned and said we shouldn't encourage her. Olson mum-

bled something. When Don went to the couch to read the paper, I went over to sit beside him. Couldn't help myself. He had the employment section.

"Wha'cha reading, sport? Looking for a job?"

Don flushed and inched away. "No . . . well, thought I'd check. We could use another adjustor down at the office."

Tilting my head to read an ad. "Oh! Thought you might be seeking something in the sex offender line maybe."

"Deborah, for Pete's sake." Looked like a hound had treed him. Peeking over the paper at his family across the room. "Could we bury that?" he whispered. "I'd like to put it behind us. It happened, okay. I don't deny it. Let bygones be bygones."

"Sure. Abracadabra, presto! Forget it!"

"Look, we're making a . . . Jerri! . . . We are—"

"Whazzat? Speak up, Don, I can't hear you."

All dimples and stretched neck, motioning to keep it down. "Making a fresh start," he lipped.

"I'll just bet. California's full of fresh starts. I guess you'd never run out."

Jerri smiled from the dining table across the room, watching us over her coffee mug. "What are you two talking about?"

"Oh just—"

"Debbie tells me they've laid people off at United."

"Oh, have they?"

"Laid off? I'd say they've raped and ruined them." I glared at Don. He guessed I'd skewer him. Might have, but Meena bounded across the room and tumbled into Daddy's lap, crumpling the paper. Startled us both, the little fart. Rolled over and goggled her father. With a bit of imagination you could see extra legs coiled beneath her.

"Meena! For Pete's sake—"

I clapped my hands. "Get, Miss Muffet." Slapping her fanny. Not knowing why I should come to Don's rescue. She hissed at me. Jerri rose from the table and sidled us a look—Don's grimacing tan face. She went smoldering off. Don gimped me a smile. Gratitude I guess. Or fear I wasn't done with him yet, which . . . I didn't know. The thing is they just as well have stayed up north. A few degrees latitude doesn't change a thing. You learned that flying.

I remembered the Walnut Street morning I'd decided to move

out of my sister's house years ago. Jerri had burst into my room beneath the stairs and accused me of gang-banging fraternity boys for all she knew. Coming in at three A.M. She wouldn't stand for it, not in her house.

"I was studying," I had insisted, following my sister into a yeasty kitchen smell of cinnamon rolls, wondering what was eating her. Her eyes bulged under heavy lids, meshed in fine red lines . . . and damn, I wouldn't let her stare me down. Don arrived, shiny-cheeked from a shave, crisp white shirt and creased slacks. He pecked Jerri's cheek and slid onto the bench beside me, parking a brotherly hand on my knee. "Would you mind?" Don was all alarmed eyebrows. He could charm the drawers off Golda Meir.

"I'd like to know what you are going to do about her," Jerri demanded.

"Do about who, hon?"

"Your promiscuous sister-in-law."

Meena appeared beside the table in her Dale Evans pj's. Don lifted her whoop-peeing into the air, settling her on his bucking knee. "Mornin', pardner." Jerri was furious at the three of us. With hands on aproned hips, she demanded that Meena get into the bathroom and wash her face, "This instant, young lady."

"Give it a rest," Don mumbled. He hugged Meena to his chest and hummed "Smoke Gets in Your Eyes." Daddy's girl. Mommy's vexation. Jerri's eyes smoldered from them to me, like I was something that might fester if it wasn't cleaned up—bringing sexual diseases into her house for all she knew (though they had their own, God knows). Don patted Meena's fanny and told her to run wash up. Didn't Jerri think they ought to mind their own business, he asked.

Jerri guffawed. "Isn't that cute. He's afraid someone beat him to it."

I lost it then. The jealous bitch resented my freedom. She was unfair to her husband and lovely children. I told her so.

"Is that your professional coed opinion?" Jerri inquired when I'd done. She wound up with the glass percolator, letting fly. It exploded against the wall between Don and me, leaving a dark stain that remained until they sold the house and moved to the suburbs.

Now I see it wasn't me. Never was. Some crazy notion Jerri

got in her head: Don had shifted his affections to Meena. Maybe it wasn't so crazy. He couldn't keep his hands off his little girl. Pure daddy affection. Needy, just the same. I could see Jerri fighting the thing all these years. Not like it was her daughter at all but some dim shadow wandering between them in that house. The water hadn't changed any, only grown murkier.

Years ago, Meena had ridden in Jerri's shopping cart, Mommy's little girl, legs dangling through wire mesh. Jerri stopping at whatever caught their fancy, opening boxes, bobby-pinning cotton balls to Meena's bangs like fluffy snowballs, licking peanut butter from a finger Meena had scooped into a jar, cutting down disapproving housewives with a single flash of her dark eyes. (The Taylor Brothers never intervened; Jerri had the tastes of a rich man's wife.) School skunks together, having a ball. Inseparable as delinquents. What had happened?

Once, when she was five years old, Meena got lost in a Portland department store. A cosmetic girl told us she'd seen a little girl in a blue coat similar to Jerri's walk out of the store with an older gentleman. *Nooooo!* Jerri dashed for the revolving door, would've gone right through the glass if a customer hadn't been coming in, down a sidewalk oily-glistening in December drizzle, reflecting shop lights spilling across it. Christmas shoppers, a Salvation Army Santa leapt from her path. I kicked off my heels and pursued her in stocking feet over the cold wet sidewalk, dodging through umbrellas. A bulky man in a dark London Fog raincoat crouched to tackle me. "No—" forming my mouth. But Jerri had reversed and ran straight for me, eyes bulging like a runaway horse's. I caught her . . . nearly. Tumbled ass over elbow and cracked a rib on wet pavement. I remember the sidewalk splashed in a confetti of blue/red/green from twinkling lights strung over a tree vendor's stall, the greasy cold concrete against my cheek, its smell—fishy earthworm damp, sweet spruce, the wet-dog odor of Jerri's coat as she lay in my arms. While inside Meena sat safely in the security office, eating Almond Roca and hard Christmas candies. Jerri blathered that we had to hurry before she was taken away for good.

What starts as habit becomes a life. Jerri's vacuum woke me at four A.M.: same old house, cleaned as if by elves overnight while occupants slept—laundry folded, shirts pressed, dishes washed, a morning breath of Pine-Sol on the air. Because the thing about my sister, she had her pride. Don complained he didn't know whether they would eat at six or ten o'clock after Jerri finished kibitzing with her buddies. "Cook yourself," I suggested. That wasn't the point, she needed regular habits. But had them: a thermos full of hooch she carried to Sandy-Lindy's each afternoon and returned with it empty. (Iced tea was hardly my idea of a vodka mixer.) Each evening, doing the dishes, Jeff or Meena rinsed out Mom's thermos. The kitchen reeked of it. Don convinced himself she was taking a break is all. Short vacation from sobriety. It was a harmless little secret they were helping her to keep.

Jeff was still wary around his mom, as you might be around a dog that had bit you once. Still, she was Mom. For all he knew they were all that way. We only have one. He'd planted a veggie garden in back and spent hours weeding and watering when he wasn't reading a book. Funny kid, the habits of an old man. Don was mostly off playing golf or working at the office. All through Jeff's birthday dinner he sat low in his chair, eyes smoldering from Mr. Short, Donna's friend, to Jerri, getting pickled on ginger ale. Funny thing. Her eyes two small bloodshot peepholes to the soul.

Some crew, I'll say: Sandy-Wendy, Jerri's lush underwear-model friends from next door, tan as avocado pits; Donna from down the street; Piggy Olsen, who ate six pieces of chocolate cake, the last in two obscene bites, frosting squirting out between his plump red lips. Olson nearly split a gut. A pasty school friend of Jeff's, whose thick glasses panned like TV cameras as the night deteriorated, wide eyes sitting up on the couch behind. Jerri had made a few meager attempts at Christmas decoration.

"Call me Short," Donna's friend said when I introduced myself.

"Just Short?"

"Yes, ma'am."

Short men don't usually advertise, but he was dense, square and humorless as a cinder block. Donna took me into her perfumed confidence: "He dislikes first names . . . for grown-ups, you know. They're gimpy."

"News to me." Jerri shrugged. Short threw her a look.

Short was Marines. Korea. When Don said he'd been signal

corps, Short turned away and focused his attention on the
women. Dents like thumbprints above his ears, narrow forehead
bulging over his eyes as if thumbs were planted in his temples
at birth and strong linked fingers flattened the soft skull bone.
But his eyes were an ethereal peacock blue. Flashing green when
he became angry, like that flash above waves sometimes at sunset. I couldn't put it together—those eyes, that skull. When Don
offered him a beer and apologized he didn't have anything
stronger, Short shook his head. "No, sir, I'm of the Mormon
faith."

"Never touch the stuff myself," Jerri quipped, carrying things
to the table.

"Marines and Mormon, that about covers all the bases."

"You got that right." Short didn't return Don's smile.

Dinner went fine: Jerri's fried chicken and baked beans.
Donna confided she was an awful cook, you wouldn't believe.
"I bet you don't get a chance to do much cooking, flying and
all," she said. She'd already asked if I'd been married, like it was
something you might better get out of the way. That type.
Might've been pretty, but smile lines clotted with rouge made
her look eroded. She leaned close, I leaned away.

"Don't you believe it," Short said. "Donna is one fine little
cook." He looped Don a glance. "I guess you never ate Pusan
C rations. Makes canned horse meat taste like top sirloin. We
had to crush our so-called crackers with a boot heel before we
could chew them." The boys laughed. "But I'll tell you this,
fellahs, a man isn't no more than a Girl Scout he don't serve his
country in a fire fight." His eyes flashed green at Don, the half-
pint dildo. Wasn't anything didn't take him back to Korea, like
a flight kept circling above the airport to land.

Don let off little flinching smiles, Piggy stuffed his face with
cake, Donna stuffed hers with Short, chin leaning on linked fingers, Sandy-Lindy and Jerri gabbed louder and louder. Jerri's
sprawling laugh. Now and then, she threw Short a haughty chin-
tilted glance. Because I'll say this for Jerri, she could always spot
a turd. He squinted back as if through a sniper scope. Had to
remind himself he was sitting at her table receiving hospitality,
must've. Good Boy Scout. Still, I saw it coming.

Olson wondered how many gooks Short had killed. "You
don't keep track," Short snapped. "Fellahs, it's no darned fun."

"Of course it isn't," Donna told me.

"What's no fun?" Jerri asked.

"Killing people in the war," Jeff said.

"Sure! Killing's no fun. Only skinning the little shits alive." Sandy-Lindy, the younger, spewed liquid mist across the table. There were times Jerri made you half proud.

"That's not necessary," Donna scolded. "Why, Short served his country. He was purple-hearted."

He held up a hand. "Ma'am, it's some think so. Your red Chinese for instance. Skinned a whole village and stacked them up like cord wood. Froze solid."

"Wow," Jeff said.

"That's a true fact, I saw it with my own eyes. Women and children. We stopped them there at the Thirty-eighth Parallel else they'd be over here in Escondido now skinning your family."

"She doesn't mean Chinese," I told him.

He turned out his lips. "Heck, I don't know who she means. You fellahs going to let that cake go to waste? Your mama there's a fine cook."

Jerri laughed. "You don't want Shorty to skin you."

"Let it rest," Don mumbled.

Short glared across the table, not at her but him. Rubbing his hands slowly together as if they were cold. Donna looked worried. To set the record straight, I told him Jerri's—our—brother Chuck was killed in Korea. "If it makes any never mind."

"My condolences, ma'am." Short saluted Jerri. Then me.

Jerri turned away. That was that. I motioned to Don about her ginger ale bottle. Jerri downed wine goblets straight. He might've just reached over and removed it from the table, but decided to strike up conversation with Sandy-Lindy about school instead, like it mattered fish piss to him. Any excuse to gawk her cleavage without being caught. Meena sulked. You felt tension tingle down the line from their end of the table.

Before long Jerri slurred her words in a nonstop monologue—didn't matter pee-all we were there: dummy Don and his Corvette convertible, all the honeybaby, sugarbaby beach gals who kept him broke . . . hah-ah, get it? Broke! Like a stick. Cawing laughter. Wendy's cheek flinched, she smiled her underwear-modeling smile. Jerri swayed over her plate like she might fall in, a blob of frosting on her lip. We watched in that fascinated, helpless way you watch a smoking car at side of the highway . . . began talking all at once, laughing overloud: Meena, Jeff, Sandy-Wendy-Lindy, even Piggy Olsen trying to cover for Jerri. Wasn't any use. Short had left Korea and arrived in San Diego. The straighter he sat the more he appeared to slump. No use.

"*Limp dipstig,*" Jerri shouted. "*Don' you ged it?*" We watched like marionettes, Jeff's lips read *Happy Birthday* on his paper plate over and over. His pal goggled. Donna walked around the table and touched Jerri's shoulder. "Think you've had enough, hon, don't you? . . . The children—" she whispered.

"You bet your buck she has," Short snarled.

Jerri grinned at him. "Short wears short shorts, isn' that a kig." Squinting. "The U.Esh Marinshhh, saving the worl' for democra-shie. Three cheers for our big war hero!" Raising her glass in a toast. "Shordy shordpants . . . Chucky Chuck! Feel 'em, fuck 'em, forged 'em . . . I knowww youuu, bashtar'." She glared.

"Ma'am!" He pushed away from the table and stood at attention. Meena seized Jerri's glass and splattered contents across Short's pants—protecting Mom, or just emptying it, couldn't say. Jerri and Don tug-o'-warred for her bottle, Piggy's mouth sprung open, full of chocolate cake. I leapt up as Short charged my sister, lock-step—but must've reconsidered at the last instant and spread-eagled, arms cordoning off Jerri and Don from the table as they struggled out of their chairs, tussling for the bottle. Jerri weeping pathetic, Don growling, "Goddamn you, Jerri." Short's slacks looked like he'd wet himself. His chin bunched, eyes fixed in a sustaining green flash as I pushed by him. Afraid he'd do something couldn't be undone. He was that mad. Semper fi. "All right, honey!" I snagged Jerri under the armpits. Got her out.

Never a dull moment, I'll say.

Ms. Childlove, the psychiatric social worker, stopped by Monday afternoon. "Just to visit," she said. Never a dull moment. Phony as her name, you ask me—as tangerine-tint hair and the tight smile she managed shaking Don's hand. There's two kinds of people will slit your throat: them who smile with their mouth

alone and eye smilers whose mouths stay rigid. Short was an
eye-smiler, Ms. Childlove was a mouther. She had Don's number, I'll give her that. He played pocket polo with loose change
while she scrutinized him. Jerri wore large plastic-rimmed sunglasses and white hoop earrings to match. No sign of the looper
she'd hung on the night before. But Ms. Childlove's wide nostrils
worked as if she smelled hooch on the air. Nobody's fool.

Meena's principal had promised not to expel her if she re-
ceived counseling. (I laughed so hard when Jeff told me about
the spiders in the sloppy joe thought I'd pee. Wondered they
couldn't see the justice in it.) "She's doing fine," Ms. Childlove
said in a throaty, beery voice. "We're getting to know each
other." She chitchatted, asking out of the blue if they thought
Meena felt a "teensy conflicted, you know, caught between
Mama and Papa? Does that ring true at all?" Craning forward,
a gimpy coaxing smile. "Most youngsters experience a need to
choose between Mom and Dad. Some get hung up. Ring any
bells?" She watched Don like he might start caroling. Sly, I'll
say. Instead, he excused himself to get back to the office. Ms.
Lovelorn asked if I might leave her alone with Jerri. They needed
to chat. I smelled a rat. Like wasn't enough trouble in that house
already.

The next morning at four Jerri's radio woke me, the old
crooner, Roy Orbison. She was sitting at the dining table pol-
ishing silver, mouthing words to a song. Tears rolled down her
cheeks.

"For shitsake, Jerri." I turned the volume down.

"Hello, princess."

"Want to tell me what's going on?" I sat facing her, pulling
my robe tight around me. Every light in the room was on, over-
heads reflecting off the half-wall of glass, loud as the music.

"Know what"—rattling silver as she leaned across the table—
"I don't suspect you one itsy bit. Isn't that a kick?"

"All right, honey."

Her fingers polished with a mouse-gray cloth, round and
round. "How's your sex life?" she asked offhandedly.

"Funny question. Dormant mostly."

Jerri discussed her own, like I wanted to know about it. Jerri
Lee Simonet Tillotson's soliloquy. Or Jerri Lee's just plain. Has

a ring to it. How Don got on her like a boy humping a diving board—bounce, bounce, squirt. She laughed. *"Bounce, bounce, squirt . . . get it?"*

"That's how some do. It's not like he invented the wheel."

Cloth squeaked against a silver fork. She drew herself up and smiled. She'd stopped crying anyway. "Is that your expert opinion, Deborah? Deborah loaned her way through college on the student fuck program."

"Not funny, Jerri. I hope you don't talk like that around the kids."

She did one of those Jerri flip-flops, lips cinching. "Don't think you can poison my children against me, Deborah."

"I wouldn't do that, hon. Never."

"Never . . . nevermore, quoth the raven, she's a whore."

"Shush, you'll wake the whole kit and caboodle."

Her eyes narrowed. "You stay away from my husband. Keep your stewardessy little paws to yourself."

"I do my best, I guess you know."

She looked half crazy, eyes shining. "You plan to make off with my children? Is that what's in your liddle squirrely mind? You two?"

"Do you know how crazy you sound?"

"He's taken Meena." Her face collapsed. "Mommy's little sweetheart. She's Daddy's girl now. Mommy's an evil witch. Mommy is the crazy evil witch. Mommy is a cuckoo cluck."

"You sound crazy and that's the God's plain truth. Gives me the heebie-jeebies."

"Cuckoo-cuckoo—" She beaked her mouth and flapped her arms. Eyes glazed plastic. "You won't get my Jeff, Deborah. Over my dead body. I'll kill you first." Lip hooking like she meant it. I went across and slapped her, scattering silver. Jerri touched fingers to the red outline mine had left and cooed to herself. Reached to fill a glass half full from the thermos and threw back her head, emptying it. Dropped it shattering to the floor.

"Damn you to rotten catfish, Jerri."

We left it lie there: evil glistening shards.

"Don's fucking someone but issn' me. Issn' that a kig?" Not a laugh but a pained squeal. "Dirty liddle Mexican pachuco whore. Dummy me found her phone number in his jacket

pocket. Oh boy we had fun . . . Over my dead body." She'd begun crying in earnest, shaking her head. "It issn' that. It's the
other one—"

"What other, hon?"

"Your dad. Walter." Glaring. "You didn' . . . nobody, Deborah. Nobody. You think I made it up." Her cheeks candied,
tear-glazed. She unbuttoned her robe and pulled out a breast,
crushing and caressing white flesh, pinching a nipple.

"For pity's sake, Jerri. Put that away. Do you think I want—"

"That's what he did to me," she whispered. "And this—"
raking at the hem of her gown. I went for her, grabbing her
arms, leading her to the couch. She curled against me, fetal,
weeping. I buttoned the robe and coddled my big sister.

"Runs in fambalies," she squealed. "Meena and her dad . . .
*Did I notice anything unusual . . . The way Papa treats her? The
way he touches her.*"

"What are you saying? That woman suggested Don would do
that? That's fish piss, that's ridiculous. Don isn't perfect, God
knows, but he loves his little girl. Loves! The daddy kind."

Jerri laughed. "Tha's what Grandma Sally calls it. We know
all aboud it, don' we?" She stared blankly ahead. "I asked that
woman why would Meena want a lock on her door? Crawls
about the house like a creepy spider. Izzat normal? Do you know
what she said? 'You don' mind my asking, are you and your
husband sesually—' "

"Stop it, Jerri. Snap out. Whatever happened back then is over
and done. You can't mix that up, past and present. You hear?"

" 'How's y'r sess life?' " Jerri laughed. "Estra-normal."

I seized my sister's chin and jerked it around. "There's some
thieves walk right in the front door and take what they like.
She's sly as cold water. Isn't solution that woman wants, it's
your family. You're drinking again. Don't you realize . . . Listen
to me! You could lose your kids."

Jerri's eyes gone glassy-hard, resistant as obsidian. Sitting up,
she straightened the robe over her knees. Eyelids fluttering.
"What gave you that idea? I'm through with all tha'."

I stared stupid at her.

"We chatted, tha's all. We had a nice chat."

Unwanted, unbidden, there appeared the image of Don's uneasy glances at his daughter's breasts, Meena squirming in his

lap, baby-doll top yanked crookedly over her slit navel. So I
didn't realize it was Meena's round imp face reflected in family
room windows, rather than just a nightied specter out of my
own head. Her back against the short entryway wall. Eavesdropping. As quickly she was gone. Nothing could be trusted in
that house.

When Don asked me to meet him for lunch I couldn't help
wonder, What more? Like a cruddy soap opera I'd got addicted
to. Who's lying, who's telling the truth . . . tune in tomorrow.
Curiosity had got the better of common sense.

Main Street wasn't much: dowdy shops, cafés, a theater showing Mexican flicks. Hometowny California style. Palm trees
down center strip, Mamie Eisenhower mannequins in store windows—fashions ten years behind. Ranchers in jeans and Stetson
hats, thin, brown retired wives—wrinkly lizard faces and quick,
mistrustful eyes. Every other pickup said "Contractor." Broad-
faced fellows leaned out truck windows to whistle. Whoop-dee-
do. A warm breeze blew along Grand Avenue off the desert,
Santa Ana they called it. Sunlight so direct it came right through
my clothes.

El Papagayo, Escondido's finest Mexican cuisine. Authentic,
I'll say. White-washed room and leather-upholstered bar, bull's
horns and striped rugs on the walls. Don motioned me to a table.
"Feel safe?" Dimples dug in like pencil wounds in both cheeks.
He ordered beer and nachos. Tore shreds from a napkin and
discussed the quality of Mexican versus American beer. Motor-
mouthing how the Mexicans got a bad rap, must be fifty percent
of his customers of Hispanic descent. "They're honest, hard-
working people. We get along fine."

"So I hear."

Don boosted his chin forward like I'd goosed him.

"A joke, Don. Just joking." I frowned.

"Their ancestors were here before ours ever heard of America," he insisted. "Right now we're sitting in Northern Mexico.
'Aztlan' they call it. My friend Guillermo, the owner here, can
trace his roots back three thousand years in this region." Don's
eyes were going sleepy as he talked; the link watchband flopped
loose on his wrist. He'd lost weight, was almost gaunt. He
hardly touched his carne asada and tortillas.

"You asked me here to talk about local history?"

Don's Adam's apple played bobbing duckie in his throat; he leaned across the table. For a second I thought he might confess something I didn't want to hear. I'd become family confessor. The lot of them coming to me with secrets ripe enough to burst. Like anything addictive, secrets must be shared. That's half their power.

"I owe the IRS twelve grand; they've put a lien on the Oregon property," he said quickly, glancing about. "I'm behind on my alimony, Deb. Jerri's spending more money than I'm making. She won't see reason, for crissake. New drapes. The house isn't ours, but she's got to have new drapes."

"What else is new?" I didn't wish to sound relieved.

"They fired me is what. Didn't promote me to branch manager down here, they let me go."

"Fired you?" I wasn't expecting that.

"That's what I said."

"You came . . . Don, brought the family down—"

"Right, all right. I fucked up, I had to get out of there. Jerri was dry, I thought we'd make a new start. Afraid I won't be able to give the kids much of a Christmas this year. That's one thing you have to grant me, Deb. I've always put on a fine Christmas."

"Jerri knows about this?"

"What can Jerri do? Honestly, Deb, what earthly good would it do to tell Jerri? She can't handle the load she's carrying now." His eyebrows groveled sincerity.

"Fish piss. Nobody knows truth from dog pucky in that house. You're all half-buried and beginning to smell. Jerri's thermos and Meena crawling around like a loony spider, and Dad—"

Don sliced a hand at me. "Leave Meena out of this."

"Touchy subject." I studied the bald patch center of Don's head, backs of his hands beginning to crinkle, skin lifting in riffles like paint after remover's applied. What is it they say? Hands never lie. But what truth did they tell? "Did it ever occur to you Jerri drinks to forget a husband who treats her like a pet lizard?"

Don was offended. "I hoped you might lend me a little support here, Deborah."

"I don't have twelve thousand dollars to lend you."

"I don't want your money. I'm selling cars. Auto Park Way. Pontiac, Chrysler. Starting to make money, little by little. We'll make it, if Jerri doesn't screw up the works."

"She got you fired, I guess? You might sell me a lemon, Don, but you won't sell me that crap."

He shrugged. "You said so yourself, Deb, her drinking could hurt me professionally. Look, I don't know. I'm not claiming—"

"If self-deception was an Olympic sport, you'd win a gold medal."

Don went right on. Didn't matter fish piss what I thought. How they had it made after Tranquility, moved to a new environment . . . All for what? "We're right back where we started. It's a dream, that's all. A goddamned pipe dream." Fist clenched on the table. Might've half convinced me I didn't know better.

"You might be Saint Paul," I told him, "struck dumb and holy. Trouble is, I've seen it already: Mom Sally paying the bills, calling in an excuse when Walter missed work, always there for him to rest his drunk butt against . . . Enabler they call it. Believed she was doing what was best. Saint Sal the Enabler. Sound familiar?" My knees forced against his this time. Don was hopping mad. His knees jabbed back. Let him try, I thought. Let him!

"I didn't make her a drunk. It's in her genes, like you say. You saw her the other night. Insulting guests, for crissake!"

"Maybe you prefer it that way. Jerri's out of it and you're out of the house—no questions asked."

"Damn you, Deborah. I wanted to talk. Little friendly chat. Can't we manage that?"

"Tell me, Don, when you get it up for your Mexican gal, is that Jerri's do, too?"

A sleepy coiled serpent of flint blue embraced Don's irises. "You bet it is. D'you have any idea what it is to live with that, Debbie? Cold as a chilled vodka bottle beside you in bed? A man can't . . . he can't, Deborah. I do the best I can."

I frowned. "You're honest anyway, I'll give you that. For once you're honest."

The waiter cleared his throat, startling us. Who could say how long he'd been standing beside our table. Features taut with embarrassment. Sneering mustached men and blonde, dry, cigarette-smoking women turned away at nearby tables as we became aware of them, tucked smiles under their belts. I thought they might clap. The waiter raised a tequila bottle and shot glasses. "*Salud*," he said. "On the house." The owner waved from the bar, eyes glittering doggy bonkers. *Comprende?* Thinking me another of Don's gals brought to sup before he shtupped. Whoopdydoo. As my big sister might say, *Over my dead body.*

Later, Meena hung around while I packed to go. No trace of spider. A young woman, half-grown, smoothing my clothes as I placed them in the overnighter. "Easy, hon, I don't want them wrinkled." Head turned demurely, she asked if women could get pregnant the way spiders do, by the male rubbing his "you know" against the female's. In the spider it was called a "pedipalps," not a penis. I explained about the vagina, how the male had to penetrate and ejaculate. I'd been curious at her age myself.

"Jism is what makes the baby?" Meena asked.

"That's half of it. Who told you about jism?"

Her eyes jumped and bobbed. "Kids." She shrugged.

"Kids? You're sure?" Meena nodded. I thought of Don's snappishness when I'd mentioned her. "Is there something I ought to know about, honey? Some reason you're asking me this?" Meena shook her head. "It's nothing to be embarrassed about. Your body is a wonderful thing. Look at you!" Holding her at arm's length. "You're becoming a woman, a lovely young woman."

She smiled shyly. "That's what Ms. Childlove says."

"Listen, Meena, promise me something. Will you promise not to tell that woman about Mom's drinking. Maybe it's none of my business, but just don't."

Her shoulders tautened. "I already know."

Didn't occur to me till later I was feeding the dog with the hand that slapped it. Adding deception to what was there already.

I'd traded with one of the girls for the San Diego/Portland run. Doing the refreshment cart on the flight home, serving scotch and water to a baldy in tourist who'd said, "Sure, why not?" when I asked if he wanted a drink. Like it was an invitation. While I poured, he studied my fingers. "You have beautiful hands," he said. I frowned at Margie on the condiment side. "Oh brother, that's about the lamest I've heard yet."

"Yesterday a guy said I had sexy lobes!" Margie laughed, then winked at Baldy. "Wanna peek?"

Shielding my mouth with a hand. "This one's into hands."

He wasn't fazed. "Hands are my business." He'd taken one of mine and turned it over like it belonged to him, caressing knuckles with fingertips. Wasn't bashful, I'll say. Amazed me I let him do it. I stared down at his shiny naked scalp: secret bumps and swellings like a hairless pubescent mons—because it's odd what will occur to you. Half sexy. Not a whacham-a-call-it at all, a defect, like Don's bald patch, but an asset almost. Baldy's expression candid as his come-on. I stood in the aisle visualizing myself at Lindy-Sandy's pool in a string bikini the day before. Jerri ooo-la-la'd, but Don hardly noticed, preoccupied with Sandy, underwear model, brushing her blond hair, basking in his male leer, not bashful one bit. Crazy as it sounds, I'd felt jealous. Maybe I'd gained weight, my skin was going. Because there's feelings you can neither control nor find any way to explain, like relatives or bad weather. You disown them and stomp your feet, isn't any use. Margie motioned her head: c'mon, f'r crissake, curling a lip. My knees tingled. I told myself, *adiós* to this, but didn't budge until Baldy let me go with a promise I'd come back. Saluting with his scotch as I moved away down the aisle.

I sat in the seat beside him during quiet spells. Mort was a orthopedic surgeon from Portland who rebuilt hands.

"Rebuild them?" I asked.

"It's easier than starting from scratch."

It was one rule I'd never broke: fraternizing. I kept asking myself just exactly what the girls' wrinkle-nosed squints asked from down the aisle: What could I find attractive about a man with big ears, a loud voice and no hair on his noggin at all?

# 22

## Jeff

After seeing *The Mummy*, I dreamed the Mexican lady's foot walked around our house at night looking for its shoe. Nylon stockings, bunched up around the knee where her leg was amputated, made a rustling, grasshopper sound when it walked. One afternoon after school, Mom came in my room and asked what I was having nightmares about. She said I tossed and grumbled when she came to tuck me in at night. It gave me a jolt. Maybe I mentioned the shoe in my sleep. "Nothing," I said, trying not to look at her. "Just a mummy that wanders around our house at night and stinks like a corpse."

Mom smiled funny. "You mean a *mommy*, don't you?"

"That's okay, Mom," I mumbled. I was too old for her to tuck me in anyway. Right away I was sorry I said it; it hurt her feelings. But I was still mad at her for bombing my birthday. Guess you can't expect a person to stop being alcoholic overnight. Actually, her fermented breath in the dark did smell like a mummy.

Meena never stopped being mad at Dad after the Del Mar Fair. "Hypocrite," she whispered at him—some big-deal word she learned at school. Maybe if she acted her age none of this would have happened—stupid gonad, stealing people's shoes, wearing a skirt on the Octopus ride. At breakfast, my sister usually buttered Dad's toast, but one morning she threw it on a plate—dry and burnt around the edges. He smiled uneasily. "How about we rent some horses at Rancho Santa Fe this weekend? Be a lot of fun." Meena just wrinkled her nose like she didn't like the smell of his after-shave. But Dad didn't give up. Besides, Meena saw how irritated Mom got over his horseback riding plan and that cinched it. If there's anyone Meena gets along with worse than Dad (or Angela Vorpos at school), it's

Mom. They never stopped bickering over my sister's messy room, the purple lipstick she wore—copycatting Goona the Freak—which made her look like a junior witch. Mom got really pee-o'd when Meena dumped out Mom's thermos in the rubber-tree planter and you could smell sweet fumes all over the house. "Doctor's orders," she said, and Mom almost lost it completely. But ever since the plant was growing like crazy.

By Friday, Dad was saying they'd get up at six next morning. Meena wondered if they had any Frisian horses. Mom stood at the sink running water. When she turned around her face and hands were sopping wet. "Are you out of your right mind, Donald? Meena isn't going horseback riding with you."

"Why not? She's my daughter, for Pete's sake. We've been so busy at the office I haven't spent any time with her lately. We hardly had a Christmas." Christmas was a sore subject around our house. Mom had spent the whole day at Wendy's pool, because it was the warmest Christmas in recorded history, and Dad had been grouchier than before a vacation. I decided that Christmas and California were natural enemies.

Mom stood dripping water, her face all beaded, eyes puffy like she hadn't slept a wink. "You aren't thinking, Don."

"Look, we're not excluding anybody. Everyone can come."

"I need Meena's help this weekend." Mom firmed her lips.

"Jerri, don't do this."

"Do? What am I doing? The house is a pigsty."

"Bitch." Meena walked out of the room.

"Oh brother," Dad said. Mom put the water on harder, and I ran after my dumb sister to get her to apologize. She was going bonkers. She'd stole Olson's *Playboy*s and drew spiderwebs over every inch of Playmate of the Month. I knew she had hid the shoe somewheres, wrapped up in fake cobweb. I searched her room for it while she was at her weekly meeting with Goona the Freak. It had cast a voodoo spell over her, and I thought maybe if I trashed it she'd stop being jealous of Dad's so-called girlfriend who she made up herself.

Worst of all was how she had got even with Mr. Olsen, Toby's dad, after he accused Chester of shitting on his lawn. Aunt Debbie said Mr. Olsen looked like a "mustachioed turd" the day he came over to complain. He slammed his pickup door and marched up our drive, dragging Chester by the collar. "This your mutt?" he demanded, slinging him into the house when Mom opened the door. Poor Chester skidded on his knees and cowered in a corner. "Next time that sack of bones craps in my yard I'm gonna blow his head off."

"Oh, you are?" Mom smiled at Mr. Olsen like she could. "That's fine. And we'll sue you out of house and home."

That stopped him short. He looked from Mom to nutso Meena's fangs snagged on her bottom lip to Aunt Debbie with her arms folded. His hair jiggled—combed frontways on top like Frank Sinatra, back on the sides Elvis Presley style, all glued together with Brylcreem. "It's every word they say about you the absolute truth. You're crazy as ticks." He spun on his heel and marched back to his pickup. We laughed, even Mom, and told Chester he could take a dump in the Olsens' yard anytime he wanted—one for us too. He barked and boxed. I don't remember feeling so good since the house on Walnut Street. Until Mom hugged me tight around the neck and I squirmed to break loose.

After that, Mr. Olsen kept calling us up. "I warned you," he'd say, then hang up. Spooky. So Meena mixed a banana in Chester's Purina chow so he took the wettest dump in dog history; she wrapped it in Saran Wrap, then a baggy, then a box lined with aluminum foil, addressed it to Mr. Toby J. Olsen and sent it from the post office across town. That was her grossest trick ever—sending a dog shit in the mail for a Christmas present. Even Olson was impressed. "Pigso will probably eat it," he said.

One night when Meena sneaked out of the house I followed her: to Wendy-Sandy's first, where she placed the stethoscope she'd bought with baby-sitting money against their front window, then listened a long time at Sandy's bedroom. Next she went to the Olsens'. No wonder she knew everything in the neighborhood before it even happened. What was she trying to find out, I wondered. My sister had metamorphosed from a trapdoor spider to a Lycosa which hunts down its prey at night. Weirder even than Olson and Olsen.

I built a wigwam in the canyon out of eucalyptus branches and a palm-frond roof, like a hut on a tropical island. I'd escape down there to be alone. Lie on my back and listen to wind rustle the eucalyptus leaves and read mountain-climbing books. It was drier than our tunnel and less chance of suffocation, but not as secret. Rattlesnakes didn't worry me; I kept up a fresh supply of piss around the place to keep them away. Except it stank to high heaven when the weather was hot. I knew the bums whose camp Olson messed up wouldn't dare come up so close to our house.

Olson commandeered my wigwam on weekends and during semester break in January. He'd lie there smoking weeds and looking at the sky. "Bug off, punk," he said when he heard me coming. "I built it," I argued back, "it's my hideout." Olson would stretch and smooth back his greaser hair and grin: "Suck my yellow dick." Usually he hit me in the back with a dirt clod as I walked away. He'd turned mean since we moved to California. Wasn't really my true brother anyway, only the second grottiest person I knew next to his friend Toby Olsen, who told Meena he was going to cut Chester open and string his guts around our house like Christmas lights. Sicko. But what made her kick him in the nuts was when he stuck his finger under her nose and yammered, "Stinky pinky."

Kids were different in California. They all acted older than they were, like Sandy Beach next door. Grandma Sally says if you grow up too fast there's nothing to grow up for. But all my brother cared about was growing up fast.

I didn't have many friends like back home, just Sambo Silbertson, whose name was Sam but we called him Sambo because his dad owned the pancake house, and he worked there after school. I made a place between corn rows in my garden, where breeze rattled dry papery stalks and I could smell tart snap beans and onions. Olson never bothered me there. A huge brown-and-white-speckled spider had built a web between cornstalks. If you touched the web it ran out of its lair with its fangs wide open. Meena captured it and put it in alcohol, where it quickly succumbed, its legs jerking, and we examined it under her scope. "I'm naming it *Epeira olsonie*," she said, " 'cause it looks like Olson." It did, too: speckled blond hair and smartass mandibles grinning at us, bitsy eyes fading in the alcohol. She wrote *Olson* on the jar and stuck a pin through the spider's abdomen, twirling it in the air. "Poor liddle Olson spider," she cooed, making a kiss with her lips. I never saw her treat a spider so mean before.

One night Olson shook me awake. "Get dressed, dickhead," he whispered. "Don't sweat it, your old lady is passed out on the couch." Toby Olsen was outside. The night was chilly and moonless, like fall finally arrived in January. I was scared; I had a bad feeling in my gut. Olson said he wanted to take us to meet some friends of his. "Real people, not the dipshit kind around here." We walked single file down the canyon path. A night-hawk's jeering cry echoed along canyon walls; I could just make out Orion over the eastern rim. Piggy Olsen shined the light in my eyes and laughed. He said I was scared shit. We were going to the bums' camp, I knew, but didn't know why. They'd prob'ly kill us down there.

When we entered the side canyon, Olson held up a hand. We could smell smoke from their fire but couldn't see it. He pulled his pellet pistol from his belt and cocked it. "Just in case," he whispered. "Basically they're cool. No worrioso." He tucked it back under his belt and pulled his shirttail over it.

As we approached, two men lay on blankets beside the fire, talking softly. Flames lit up a lean-to behind them, a gleaming machete stuck in a stump. Olson clicked his tongue loud and they leapt to their haunches, their eyes glowing in the firelight.

"¡Qué susto, hombre!" cried the old one as Olson approached.

The other one blinked and waved away Piggy Olsen's light. He looked Indian—black hair combed back into a ponytail that gleamed in the firelight. The other had a stubbly beard and his cheeks wobbled as he talked. He looked more like a white person bum than a Mexican, except his eyes were dark and full of mysterious laughter. They talked Spanish, which Olson learned at school: es igual, saygooro and aquies miamigo and sientate . . . weird stuff, which I didn't recognize one word except "amigo" and "gracias." Olson was very polite and so were the men. They stood over the fire to shake hands with us; the old guy pointed at me and chuckled. "¿Cuantos años tiene tu hermano?" he asked Olson.

"Catorce, pero es un bebé," Olson said.

The men laughed and motioned for us to sit down by the fire. The old man gripped one hand around Olson's neck, the other on his biceps and told me, "You brother is friend." I had heard about seedy old guys who did weird things to kids; he looked like the type who might do that. I hoped maybe Mexicans were different. The young guy squatted on his haunches and stirred the fire with a stick, glancing sideways at us with suspicious

Indian eyes. He spoke low to the old guy, nodding at Toby. The old guy grinned. "¡*Verdad! Es un bruto.*" Toby glared back; he nudged my arm.

"Whaddaya get when you put two spicks in a washing machine?"

The men's heads came up at the word "spick."

"Spic an' Span." Piggy laughed.

"Shuddup, turdmouth," Olson said. "These cats are *mis amigos.*"

"So's y'r shitass dog whose balls I'm gonna waste big time." Toby cocked his index finger at the Indian. "Bang bang . . . dead."

The Indian's brow knit, he was ready to jump for the machete. Olson talked fast, sputtering to find the right words. The old guy nodded at Piggy Olsen, curling his lip in disgust. "*Un puerco,*" he said. They glared at him.

Olson started talking about me, waving his hands. They were gripping their knees, the Indian's lips forced together like he had swallowed something too big to go down. The old guy reached inside his shirt and brought out something gleaming. A knife! I thought. The young one spoke sharply and nodded at me; they argued rapidly back and forth; the Indian sliced his hands over the fire again and again like an umpire signaling "safe." I think he was saying I was too young to kill me. "¡*Peligroso!*" Gesturing with his eyes like cops were waiting in the bushes.

Then I saw it was only a bottle, which the old guy tilted to his lips. He nodded and passed the bottle to Olson, who tipped it back without wiping its mouth.

Olson passed it to Toby Olsen. He spit at it like he was blowing off germs. The Mexicans chuckled, liking him better after that. "Up yours," Piggy toasted them, his Adam's apple gulping. He came up sputtering, redder than the embers. "Shitawmighty Jesus! Tastes like fuckingay diesel fuel." The men laughed and slapped their knees.

"Tequila," said Olson.

Toby handed me the bottle. "*Hermano pequeño.*" The old guy grinned. The Indian turned away and frowned. The liquor was white as pure water, or Mom's vodka, only it had a sharp, burning wood-smoke smell that went right up my nostrils. I didn't know what scared me more—the old guy's germs, Piggy's slobber or the booze. I had promised myself I would never drink in my life. But they were watching. Olson gesturing: Go ahead, punk, be a man. Besides, Grandma Sally said Mom wasn't alcoholic: You have to drink lots to be alcoholic.

But I never expected it to taste like liquid jalapeños and come spoofing out my mouth and nose at once, burning something awful. They nearly split a gut, laughing and smacking their legs. Even the Indian was glad they let me try. "*Bravo*," he cried, "*bravo, hermanito. Un poco más.*"

Olson leaned over and whispered at the old guy's ear. They were watching me. Serious. Nodding. "Okay?" Olson asked.

"*Seguro.*"

"Y'r a lucky little dick to have me for a brother," Olson said. He pulled some bills from his pocket and gave them to the Mexican.

The old guy called back at the lean-to: "*María, ven aquí.*" Eyes gleaming from tequila as he counted the money.

Inside the lean-to, a figure threw off a blanket and sat up in the light of Piggy Olsen's beam. Sour-faced, muttering, shielding her eyes. Her hair scraggly. She knelt on her knees in bra and panties and yawned, stretching her arms. I'd never saw a woman with hairy armpits, blacker and thicker than any guy's at school. It turned me on and off at the same time. Toby Olsen whistled and blinked the light. She waved it away, her mouth mucked with sleep curd at the corners. Dark-skinned as Tokyo Rose, except older and potbellied. She dropped a sack dress over her head and shuffled out to the campfire in bare feet. Piggy Olsen nudged me, sweat bugs crawled down his forehead. "Save sloppy seconds," he said.

I was dead ready to bolt. Honest. Whatever they were doing, it was dirtier than Olson and Olsen's ammonia trick. All grinning at me but the woman. The hem of her dress was dirty; red-and-green embroidery around the neck line. She muttered Spanish to herself when she saw us. But the old guy slapped her leg with the money and she smiled at me, a gold tooth glinting orange in the firelight. Older even than Aunt Debbie, even than Mom. Prob'ly the old guy's wife. Skin hung in chicken wattles from her flabby arms. She walked around the fire and reached to take my hand. "*Ven. A ver si eres macho.*" I held back, my heart thumping like anything. But she was strong, she yanked me up and shoved me toward the lean-to, bop-dancing, jabbing her hips into me, while they laughed and whistled.

Inside, she gestured for me to lay down on the mattress. I shook my head, no. She pulled the dress over her head. Her bra glowed white in Toby's beam, grimy around the elastic where her breasts bulged. Skin on her neck sagged and wrinkled like skin on a pudding. I stared at dark splotches her nipples made, feeling all sorts of ways at once—scared, excited and confused. My dick didn't care how old she was; I had the biggest hard-on of my life. Except her eyes were so sad for a second I forgot how scared I was. She didn't like it any more than me. She reached to unfasten the bra: her nipples the color of red dirt we dumped over the widow's fence, puckered little mouths at center. The Indian said *"Basta"* in a stern voice and Toby's light went out.

She said, *"Mira,"* which prob'ly meant "dick" in Spanish, and unzipped my pants. Tingly electricity shot into my stomach when her hand grabbed my balls. She kissed me, ramming her tongue inside my mouth. Then she pushed me down on the scratchy blanket, cooing and massaging her palm around the head of my dick, so I didn't know if I was more scared or excited. She put my hand on her breast and squeezed, her nipple hard as a pebble, then shoved my head down: *"¡Besala!"* My mouth sucked all on its own while she guided my fingers into a moist hairy fissure inside her panties. I heard my own breathing—like my head was inside a bag. Outside, they'd fell dead quiet. All at once I knew what would happen. The Indian had stabbed Olsen and Olson, and the old guy stood outside with his machete: The second his wife got my pants off he would castrate my dick and balls in one whack. I tried to sit up, but she shoved me back down.

She was on top of me, grinding her underwear hard against me. Giggling. We wrestled on the blanket, my face in her armpit. I held my breath against a smell funky sharp as a skunk, sour-smoky, and sweet all at once. *¡Ven!* She squeezed my dick and balls. Then slid down and sucked my dick into her mouth, nibbling, ready to bite it off. *"¿Te gusta?"* She smiled.

I lunged and sank my teeth into wattling flesh under her armpit. Yanking my pants up and running—tripping through scrub, dodging eucalyptus trees—while her wail echoed off canyon walls behind me, bobbing like a stick on wild water. Cheering male voices bounced and ricocheted around it. Toby's whistle hung on the night as I rounded the fork of the canyon and sprinted for home.

# 23

# Meena

She was awakened by a rapid violent jerking of the string leading from the window web to her finger. She sat straight up. The window frame remained empty against the glow of the city on flats below. Just frog chirps, the far-off wash of traffic. Maybe she had imagined it. But when she pulled the line to test for tautness of her web, it was slack. Someone had cut the strands. There wasn't even time to feel panic before a shadow clamped a hand over her mouth. "*Silencio*," barked a hoarse male voice, "I slit you throat." Meena bucked and thrashed, fingernails raking his cheek with the fury of a wolf spider. He cried out. She managed to kick away at the waist, clear of the bed. He cursed and lunged for her, catching the hem of her gown, which sheared away in his hands.

"Incredible how strong you are when you're terrified," she told them later. "Trouble was the bookshelf . . . I'd forgotten that I moved it to barricade my door; I'd had to take the books out to move it, then put them back again. I snatched them away in both hands. Hopeless. I could make him out, crouched like a wrestler between me and the window, not much taller than I was. I screamed and lunged through the window headfirst, tucked and rolled, because we were practicing somersaults over the horse at school. I fled past the back fence, thinking how odd it was Chester wasn't barking. Numbnuts dog. He whined, his nose poking through fence slats. Some weirdo wanted to rape me and Chester yipped and wagged his tail. I scrambled up the slope over slick ice plant toward Wendy-Sandy's on the terrace above. But he was fast, he caught my ankle and we rolled down the slope.

"Maybe it will sound strange, but when you expect the unknown, the known can come as a relief—no matter how bad. I recognized Olson's smell. He was whispering, 'Hey, man, it's cool . . . Unlax, okay, Meena. Like I'm not gonna do nothing. No problema. I was playing a joke, that's all.' Very funny. Just Olson, my half-brother who enjoyed lighting his farts."

Fear passed. The bougainvillea twining up the fence was so sweet it left her woozy, petals blood red in motes of porch light slanting through fence slats. The grass cool on her bare legs, almost nice. Overhead, the sky blazed stars. Olson lay beside her in his swim trunks. He'd come in to see if she wanted to go up to Wendy's for a midnight swim, that's all; he couldn't sleep for beans. She thought it best to appease him. We can get Boney, too, she suggested, her heart beginning to slow. Olson snarled, "That little peckerhead's never going nowhere with me again."

She might have expected it. She'd been awakened the night before by a ruckus in Boney's room next door. When she'd gone in to see what was happening, Olson was straddling Boney on the bed, pummeling him with both fists, screaming about the twenty bucks you owe me, shithead. "I do you a favor and you make me look stupid." Dad pulled him off. Olson wheeled and walked out of the house. What favor, she wondered, would Olson do anyone?

"Okay, we'll go swimming, I thought, why not? It was one of Olson's crazy fun ideas. Swimming at two A.M.! All those flashing warning lights inside me I thought were just leftover scare."

Nights were when people became their true selves. Placing her stethoscope against his living room window, she listened to Mr. Olsen rant about Chester or punk college students who were "ruining the country." At times he seemed to confuse them, sending Chester off to Berkeley and bringing long-haired students to Escondido to shit on his front lawn. While Sandy-Wendy argued in their good-natured way about silicone breast implants. Sandy needed bigger breasts, she said, so she didn't have to spend her life modeling panties. "It's good enough for me," her mom said peevishly. Why couldn't mothers and daughters get along, Meena wondered, or husbands and wives?

Each secret she uncovered seemed to conceal a dozen others. Where did Mom go when she fled the house in her rages, squirreling down the horseshoe drive in the Ford wagon? Why didn't Dad stop her? Which was Mom's truer self—the lazy guzzling day self, or the dutiful housewife vacuuming early in the morning? Mom had reversed nature's pattern: snoozing half the day, awake all night. Although Meena often had to redo the housework Mom did the night before—like the house was a terminal domestic case requiring around-the-clock intensive care. Why did Ms. Childlove find this so fascinating? Why lately, when Donna visited, did Mom shove Meena into the entryway closet and crowd in behind her, a hand clamped over her daughter's mouth? In the close, rankling dark they listened to the doorbell ring and ring, Donna's muffled voice; Meena suffocated on the smell of Mom's hand lotion. Why didn't she attempt to break free? In California, lightning had taken a new guise: Closets must stand in for basements where none existed. Metaphors abounded. There were too many secrets to collect them all.

Soon Mom was hiding from everyone—salesmen, Jehovah's Witness ladies who arrived in a black Comet, Bibles under their arms. (They seemed to terrify her most.) Meena remembered times, not long past, when she had hidden in the closet away from Mom's anger, but this new portent gave her the creeps. What was Mom hiding from? Could she see things others couldn't see? Was she afraid people would discover she was drinking again? But everyone already knew. Only Mom—and dumb Boney—denied it. She threw a conniption the time Dad accused her of it. He raised both hands in a back-off gesture, "Okay, Jerri, have it your way." Meena couldn't understand why he didn't make her stop.

She wanted to ask Ms. Childlove why Mom hid from her friends in the entry closet. Didn't dare, because once you started, Ms. Childlove could unravel secrets from inside you like long coiled worms, gripping their sinuous hides, slinking them out bit by bit.

The day Meena hinted about her eavesdropping, Ms. Childlove sat forward on her swivel chair. "What is it you hope to learn, sweetheart?" Meena had learned to rotate her questions quickly, spewing out a mesh of silk gauze to ensnare them. "I already know," she said. "Everybody has dirty thoughts." Ms. Childlove's woolly-bear eyebrows arched surprise.

"You hear them talking about these dirty thoughts?"

Meena shrugged.

"Maybe you imagine? You've heard the expression 'Curiosity killed the cat.' Too much isn't a healthy thing." Stopping herself. "But it's wonderful that you shared this with me, sweetheart. Friends don't keep secrets from each other."

The spider smiled. It was a game, a nitsy-bitsy game of salt the slug; she didn't mind playing.

"So tell me, do you have dirty thoughts, too, Meena?"

Giving her your eyes was a biggo mistake. She would begin there, baiting thoughts like teensy wriggling grubs out through your eye sockets. She studied Goona's lips. Enjoying the small thrill of power secrets give—knowing things others don't know, dangling them just out of reach like Chester's Hershey bar, teasing, speculating how much they might have guessed. What others would consider ugly or shameful became her little joke on them. Let them learn her secrets—Mom or Goona—and they would turn the tables. Their eyes would ask: How could you have allowed this to happen to you? She would be ashamed. A secret was a sea wall holding back the world's censure. Ms. Childlove was hungry for her secrets, her yellow eyes burned like small furnaces. Meena wanted to change subjects. If Olson had mind-read filthy thoughts she hadn't even known she had, couldn't Ms. PSW?

"Boney's too big a nerd to have dirty thoughts," she said. "Like when I told him to lick a spiderweb. He said it tasted like acid. So I licked it, too."

Ms. Childlove smiled. "Did it?"

"They don't bite. Lorenzo hops out of his jar onto my hand to get flies and pieces of raw hamburger; he never bit me." Meena explained how spiders' stomachs were outside their bodies. "They don't bite people because we're too big to digest." Ms. Childlove rested her chin on linked fingers.

"Tell me, do spiders have dirty minds?"

The spider laughed.

"Well, I don't know. I rarely get a chance to talk to an expert. Maybe it's a human thing. Maybe that's what you like about spiders. No dirty thoughts."

"The brown recluse has a bitsy head, but if it bites someone their finger rots off."

"Who would you bite, Meena, so their finger rotted off?"

"My mom hates spiders. If she found Lorenzo she'd heave him in the garbage can."

"Are you afraid she might throw you away, too?"

"That's dumb." It made her nervous talking about Mom.

"Maybe that's what you want her to do." Goona looked very serious, elbows on bare knees, not ladylike, didn't keep her knees together. "Tell me, do Mama and Papa have dirty thoughts?"

Meena was bored with Goona's dumb questions about dirty thoughts and fingers she wanted to bite. She looked about the windowless room—a wall of books, purple couch and dark desk, tracks Ms. Childlove's swivel chair left across the carpet, like crisscrossing dune buggy lanes in the sand, a smell of book paste and Goona's fruity perfume. She had questions of her own (but knew Ms. Childlove would insist she answer them herself): Why didn't Dad ask Mom to make dinner on those nights she sat drinking vodka tea at Wendy's pool? Weren't husbands supposed to ask these things? He moped at poolside, hands dangling between his knees, brooding on his wing-tip shoes or Sandy's round breasts. Finally mumbling, "Doesn't anyone ever eat around here?" Stomping home for the TV dinner she had put in the oven for him, the women's laughter floating along behind him.

One night he wrapped a towel around his waist like a short-order cook and made a gooey mush of fried chicken and congealed flour in the frying pan. Mom materialized out of the greasy air, like an orb spider dashing over its telegraph line at first hint of an intruder. "Would I invade your office, Donald? Would I?" she shouted.

"The kids haven't had a decent cooked meal in weeks."

"This is *my* office. Go right ahead and smile, I know you despise my life, Don. You always have."

So it went, shrieking face-to-face. Nothing withheld. While she and Boney sat listening, afraid to call attention to themselves by escaping. Perhaps their parents didn't consider them children anymore. At what point do children cease to exist? When they are sufficiently anointed in the shameful, the undisclosed, the forbidden? When had they crossed the line?

A rental house, Mom cried, you brought me here to live in a tenement.

*What did she know about responsibility, she couldn't get dinner on the table. And the booze . . . You promised, Jerri.*

His lovers! He wasn't satisfied with Southern California, he was fucking Tijuana, too.

*The children, for Pete's sake! She'd always been insanely jealous. My own daughter, f'r crissake.*

You call that friendship? You think I'm blind, Don? . . . All over her, going off alone.

*Once! Horseback riding. What's wrong with that?*

Anything else . . . not that, she'd never thought him capable of that. Don't you dare . . . (her hand reaching for the skillet. His eyes sidling).

*Get control of yourself, Jerri. Do you want me to take a lover? Do you?*

I tried, I . . . really—her voice breaking—I never wanted to come to this hellhole. (Meena wanted to dash between them and cry, "Time out!" But Dad had found the neck of the wasp and leapt on it.)

*By God, look at you! Half the days you don't get dressed, you roam the house in a boozy fog. I doubt you'd know who was on top of you.*

The spider watches her mother lean back against the fridge's hard white surface as if lying prone, eyes glazed, a hand to her forehead. Hair tangled, clothes sloppy . . . Mom! Who'd always taken such good care of herself. He has hit deep, Meena knows, her pride, a place she has kept protected. He has hurt her. She never thought her father cruel before. Her ears burn as they had that other time, standing in the entry hall while Mom showed Aunt Debbie what Grandpa Walter did to her. *It runs in families*, she'd said. But it wasn't true. Only half. Olson's grubby fingers and hot damp threats at her ear so different from Daddy's smooth fingers kneading lotion into her back at the pool, fidgety quick, a smell of coconut oil and hot vinyl, drowsy delight . . . wishing it would go on forever. His nervous chuckle. Debbie's one-piece Jantzen swimsuit clinging to her navel in white scalding light off the house. No, a father could never be interested in his daughter that way. It wasn't human.

"I know there is something you aren't telling me, sweetheart.

Cats have claws and birds fly away, but spiders are dirty creatures that crawl on their bellies—"

"Spiders can go a long time without eating."

Ms. Childlove's eyelids batted.

"They don't hear what people say."

"What do people say, sweetheart?"

"Too many words."

Once she'd captured a wasp and dropped it in the mayonnaise jar with Lorenzo. The wasp buzzed furiously and Lorenzo ran out onto his twig. The wasp alighted on the floor of the jar, and they assessed each other, rigid in insectile avidity, until her patience wore thin. The wasp bobbed her deadly abdomen; Lorenzo did arachnid push-ups. He had the advantage of height and might have leapt onto Wasp's wire-thin neck, but the stinger waited. When Lorenzo leapt to cling deftly to the slick wall of the jar, the wasp rose, wings a menacing blur—a tiny hovering helicopter gunship ready to strike. Lorenzo retreated to his twig. The wasp clung upside down to the jar's lid. They stayed there, warily regarding each other, the wasp occasionally buzzing her wings, Lorenzo crouching, pedipalps working the air, prepared to spring.

Eventually one would doze off, Boney said. He was afraid it would be Lorenzo. They took the jar outside to release the wasp. At the last moment, Lorenzo leapt upward in a lightning stroke and sunk his fangs into the wasp's thin neck. They tumbled to the glass floor, rolling and buzzing, the wasp's stinger working, frantic to find its mark. Then it was over. The buzzing stopped. Lorenzo began eating.

Meena brought him to show Ms. Childlove, who let the spider leap onto her hand, tendons cinched tight at her neck. Meena had to assure her he wouldn't bite. Afterwards, moist globules of rouge clotted in creases of Ms. Childlove's forehead. "That was a big step for me," she said. "I'm a bit arachnophobic."

It surprised Meena when she let Goona stroke her lank brown hair, grooming her as if she were the pet. She tilted her head back to hiss, but it came out a purring sound. After that, Meena often brought Lorenzo, placing his jar on the desk. It was no longer a question of spider and hunting wasp, but which of them the pet, which the keeper. They fed each other tidbits.

Meena knew that everyone must have a defect if you're to trust them: Perfection is a cover for deceit. Boney, for instance, was naturally trustworthy. When he lied his Adam's filbert bobbed and ducked like a punch-drunk boxer. Ms. Childlove had her snaggle lip, crazy crawling eyebrows and yellow eyes. Enough defect for anyone. Still, the spider was cautious. Goona was quick and crafty as any wasp. Meena enjoyed the way dark caterpillars arched up Goona's forehead and eyes gleamed interest at her craziest doings. She learned which revelations enticed her most—anything to do with dirty thoughts. Never Mom's drinking. Ms. Childlove asked repeatedly about Dad, as if her therapist's feline eyes beheld some secret which Meena didn't yet fathom. It gave her power. In secrets, they both found power.

"Why did you ask Mama to put a lock on your door?" she asked one day. "Is there someone you want to keep out?" The question made Meena mad. Wasn't anyone's business but her own. It was a betrayal. "Not my mom, I asked my dad," she blurted.

Ms. Childlove looked puzzled. "You asked Papa to put a lock on your door. Why's that?"

"Mom's a liar. My dad, too. He wants to take back my microscope; he says it's too expensive. At Christmas he hardly gave me anything at all." Her bitterness alarmed her.

"Meena, who do you wish to keep out of your bedroom?"

"People."

"Which people?"

"Mom and my gonad brother."

"I see. Mama not Papa. And he refused to put the lock on?"

"I don't want to talk about him anymore."

Ms. Childlove smiled forbearance. "Do you have a secret you want to keep from Mama, sweetheart?"

Meena sensed danger and knew Ms. Childlove sensed it, too. She was sorry she'd opened her mouth. Didn't dare let on about the spook that had begun wandering the house again late at night. Or the other spook. But Goona was like a chess master who saw an advantage and pressed relentlessly ahead.

"I'd like to get this straight. You want to keep Mama out of your bedroom, but not your father? You want to lock the door?"

"Forget it, okay."

"You are angry because Papa won't help you keep your secret. Because it's his secret, too, isn't it, sweetheart? You're afraid maybe Papa doesn't love you anymore."

"That's dumb. I'm more of his wife than my own mom is."

Caterpillars leapt straight up. Ms. Childlove opened her desk drawer and reached inside. "What do you mean, Meena?"

She didn't know, really; it just came out. "I do half the cooking, even some mornings I help him with his tie."

Ms. Childlove crept forward on chair coasters the way Lorenzo did stalking insects, so slowly it was nearly imperceptible. "Wives and husbands sleep together. Are you his wife in bed, too?"

Meena was shocked. "That's spastic. They don't even . . . My dad always goes to bed first, Mom stays up late, I don't even think they do it anymore—*you know what*."

Shaking her head. "No, dear, I don't know *what*."

"The dirty thing—you know."

Ms. Childlove's face tensed. "Remember our agreement: no secrets. I want you to tell me about the dirty thing."

Meena shrugged. "People do it for babies—and fun, my aunt says. I don't see how it could be any fun."

"Why is that?"

"Because it's hard as a rock."

"What, sweetheart? What's hard?"

"His boner thing . . . disgusting."

So close now she could smell Ms. Childlove's spearmint breath; her eyes bulged, pressing out at the lids like letters too large for their envelopes. "He asks you to touch his boner thing? Your father asks you to touch it?"

It was a dirtier thought than Piggy Olsen's foul mouth at the bus stop, yet it titillated her in a strange incomprehensible way. Ms. Childlove sat perfectly erect, fixated on every word, as Meena herself once had lying under her parents' bed. It gave her a funny charge of power like a cup of coffee in the morning.

"Where does he touch you, Meena?"

"He doesn't anymore, I told you. He won't even hug me anymore."

"Before, Meena?"

"My breasts." She giggled.

"Your father touched your breasts?" A tremor seized Ms.

Childlove's cheek and worked into her jaw, tooth snagging on the "f" in father, hanging up on it.

"Accidentally. He always jumps like an electric shock."

"I see."

"He's funny. It makes him embarrassed, I think. It really beaks Mom off when I don't get dressed in the morning."

"And you want to beak her off?"

"You ask too many dumb questions."

"It makes you uncomfortable to talk about this, Meena? I think you are very angry at your father. Very, very angry. I wonder why you are so angry."

"He's got a girlfriend," Meena said flatly. "I saw them at the Del Mar Fair. They do dirty things. She doesn't want to but he makes her do it."

Ms. Childlove motioned for her to continue.

"He put his hand in her underpants on the Octopus ride."

It was as if she'd dashed Ms. Childlove in the face with icy water. "At the fair? You saw this at the fair? You saw your father fondling her?"

"I couldn't exactly," she hedged. "Olson says so."

"Olson saw it then? I must know, Meena. If we're friends you will tell me this."

"Olson says if she won't do it he'll make her pregnant and everyone will know she's a slut. He says if she tells her reputation will be ruined. They'll think she made it up, because she's nutso anyway." Meena was afraid Goona would notice goose-flesh crawling along her arms. She'd gone too far: The more she said, the more she had to say. Still, it served Dad right for squawking about the lock. The therapist watched her intently.

"Are you afraid people will think you are a slut? Is that what frightens you—that Mama will think it's your fault?"

Meena shook her head. "That's what Olson said."

Ms. Childlove regarded her as if she had run out of questions, or was searching through her collection for the perfect one. "You're his girlfriend, Meena. It's not the Mexican lady he threatens, it's you. Isn't it, dear?"

"That's a fat lie, and I have her shoe to prove it."

"Maybe I had better talk to Olson, don't you think."

The spider watched from the couch. "He moved away," she snapped. "He doesn't live with us anymore."

\* \* \*

On that night he had jarred Meena awake, Olson jimmied the lock on the shed and turned on the light in Sandy-Wendy's pool. A large submarine eye lit up the fragrant air; black lines shimmered and refracted along the pool bottom, rippling snakes twined off blue water in an evaporative haze. Here and there, a dark irregular shape hung suspended on the surface—floating leaves. The damp, acrid smell of chlorine. Olson stepped to the pool rim and dove toward the shimmering eye. White frog legs kicking, hair a sleek furrowed cap over his head. A spooky shadow followed above him, reflected off the mist. Meena leapt in behind in her baby-doll pajamas. The water was bracing, chillier than she'd expected. Chlorine stung her eyes. As she swam, wet fabric clung to her like tissue paper. Still, it was fun knowing Wendy-Sandy were asleep inside. Knowing Sandy would be all pissed off.

Olson goofed around, circling her with a hand planted atop his head like a shark's fin. He chased her, but she was a stronger swimmer. He spread-eagled before the pool's frosted eye, which projected his silhouette upon the screen of the night sky, grotesquely magnified, cheeks ballooning with air. When she dove down to hang against the light herself, he hovered before her, grinning underwater like a pale, sarcastic cod. His hands reached out and squeezed her breasts. She slapped back in slow motion, lost her purchase on the tiles. It was her body, Ms. Childlove had insisted; nobody could do anything to it she didn't want them to do.

They broke the surface, gasping. Her pajama tops floating around bare breasts. He could see everything through her baby dolls, Olson sputtered, like she was naked. His heat came right through the water. He pawed at her, snorting and panting, clenching her legs in a scissors lock. When she tried breaking free, he dunked and held her underwater until she came up gasping and flailing. "Be good." He hissed through clenched teeth. "You gonna be good?" He pinioned her to pool tiles beneath the diving board, the web of his thumb lodged against her windpipe, the pool's concrete lip forced cruelly against her skull. She'd lost the will to resist; she shivered and clung to the rim with both hands. She'd heard how people became very cold and just gave up.

"You gonna?"

Meena stared at claw marks on Olson's cheek—four puffy red welts bleached at edges. She nodded.

Olson fumbled in her clothes, doing what he wanted, while she watched water ripple across blue shattered light. Gripping the diving board overhead in both hands simian fashion, Olson jerked woodenly, stabbing his dick into her. At least there was chlorine to mask his sour breath. But she was afraid that his sperm would swim through the water up inside of her. Girls at school said you could get pregnant if you swam in a pool where a guy jacked off.

It was then she saw a figure watching from the far end of the pool. At first she thought it a tiki lantern, then it moved. A faceless shadow beside the pool shed, but she knew who it was. She shook her head for him to go away, avert his dirty eyes and mind his own f'ing business. Then Olson's head cut off her view—mouth ah-ah-ahhhing, skin ghoulish blue in the pool glow, like the ticket taker's ashen face at the Del Mar Fun House. When she looked again, the watcher crouched behind a chair nearby, a baseball bat raised over his head, ready to strike.

# 24

# Jeff

The Mexican lady at the camp kissed Dad all over his face, then I saw it was really the lady whose shoe Meena found. She grabbed me and started kissing. Pus leaked from her nose, her whole face was one huge scab. I tried breaking free, but we were on the Rock-O-Plane, I was strapped in my seat. When I screamed, someone screamed back—outside my dream in the actual world. It woke me up. I listened. Mom and Dad were fighting, I thought. Only it was spooky quiet. Just crickets and traffic down on Rock Springs Road. I heard a scraping sound in Meena's room next door and got out of bed, taking my baseball bat just in case. Meena's door was closed; the handle turned but it wouldn't budge, like somebody had jammed something against it inside. That worried me. I devised a plan to wait outside her window and crack their skull when they came out. I wanted to prove to Olson I wasn't chicken. Myself too.

I tiptoed down the hall. Mom was asleep on the living room couch, her head crooked against the armrest; she'd prob'ly wake up with an awful neck ache. I slipped out the front door and around the house. My sister's dumb spiderweb had been slit open. Inside, I made out her empty bed and bookcase crammed against the door, books splattered on the floor. It gave me the woolly willies. Whoever it was had to be strong enough to move her whole bookcase. It was weird, since Chester usually barked his head off even at a possum that came up from the canyon, let alone some creepo kidnapping my sister, but he hadn't made a sound. I thought I better get Dad, but there was a glow coming from Wendy's pool—an eerie turquoise cloud floating above it. I had a hunch.

Before even entering the gate, I saw spooky, shimmery, toad-leg silhouettes crawling in the pool spot, like weird figures in a finger-shadow show. Meena was pinned against the light, naked, I thought at first. A figure treaded water in front of her. Wasn't until they broke surface and I heard his voice I knew it was Olson. He dunked her a long time, the psychopath. Meena gasped, her head small and slick as an otter's, hair matted over her ears. Chickenshit Olson was beating up on her—a girl, just a kid. I edged along the pool-house shadow, its knobbly stucco surface prickling my back; decided I would sneak from chair to chair and when I was close enough to make a dash for it, I'd threaten to clobber Olson with the bat if he didn't let her go.

He hissed something. Meena nodded. Her hands gripped the pool rim either side and she let Olson feel her up inside her pj's, which I couldn't understand why she would. Like the Octopus ride, only grosser. Grottier even than my pus-faced dream. He hung from the diving board and humped her. (I only saw his bobbing white ass) like she was Tokyo Rose—made out of plaster or something. At Del Mar I told myself your mind plays tricks on you when you're dizzy. But now he was doing it right in the open. I couldn't watch but couldn't stop looking. Hypnotized by Olson's white bumping butt. Thought I would puke.

Pain jabbed my brain from the scar where Mom cracked my skull. *Over my dead body you will touch your sister again.* Now Olson was doing what she accused me of doing—but I never would. Meena's face winced in the pool light; it must've hurt. I knew what I had to do, there wasn't any choice. She was my sister. I had to protect her even if it was my own brother molesting her. I'd clobber him. Either that or run get Dad, quick, while he was doing it.

But didn't move. Like the time I tried diving off the high board at the high school. Kept urging myself: Now . . . okay, do it, no more chickening out. Now. But my feet wouldn't work. My heart chirruped like a bird in my throat. I wasn't afraid really, unless maybe embarrassment is another kind of scared. My sister was looking at me. Our eyes locked while he poked her. A shiver ran along my spine, almost like I was doing it myself. Meena shook her head no. *Forget it,* her face said, *forget you ever saw it.* I started forward like that was the signal I was waiting for all along. Because you've got to take a stand sometimes. Because I knew I'd hate myself forever for just watching and letting him do that.

I dodged from chair to chair, looking straight ahead at his slicked blond hair, my bat ready. Then Olson gasped, his mouth yawned. He'd shot his wad. He let go of the board and slipped underwater. I turned and ran. A huge sticky orb web snared my face like a wet handkerchief. I caught the spider in my hand when it tried escaping across my shirt. At home, under my bed lamp, its six eyes gleamed inside my fist. I knew then why my sister had become a spider.

Sometimes something awful has to happen and you didn't prevent it before you decide you won't ever let a chance go by again. For me it took three tragedies in one week. First Meena. Which I tried erasing from my mind. But I kept seeing Olson's bumping white butt before I fell asleep.

Chester's murder could've been stopped easy if only I let him sleep in my room. I could've snuck him in my window, easy. After he was missing three days and nobody in the neighborhood had seen him, I searched the canyon again for the third time. Except now Chester's smell led me right to him. He laid on his side under a bush, his belly bloated and legs stuck out stiff. Flies swarmed like a glistening black carpet over his eyes and butt-hole, a column of ants crawled in and out of his black rubbery nostrils my sister always liked to kiss. Worst of all, his belly had broke open and his whole insides was full of wriggling black-headed maggots which made a crinkly sound in the hot putrid air. I turned away and barfed. Then I ran uphill bawling like a kid. Everybody bawled, even Mom, who never liked him, and Dad when he got home—just in time because I was worn out from trying to keep my dumb sister in her room. Each time she tried to rush past me to see Chester, I shoved her back and warned it would make her sick. "He's my dog, too," she shrieked. "I have a right to see him." The jerk kept looking at her cobweb window, which she had repaired out of glistening copper wire, like she might try breaking through it.

Dad helped me bury Chester beside the wigwam, then Mom and Meena came and put up a cross. Meena got down on her knees and promised Chester that she would get even with Mr. Olsen, that shitass murderer—because we knew that's who poi-soned him. Mom wanted to call the cops, but Dad said we couldn't prove anything. "Give it a rest, Jerri; it's just a dog, for Pete's sake."

"I loved him," Meena shrieked. After that she was as mad at Dad as she was at Mr. Olsen.

In a funny way, Chester's murder brought Meena and me closer. Since the swimming pool, we wouldn't hardly look at each other. She prob'ly blamed me for not stopping it, like I did myself, like it was my fault as much as my psychopath brother's. Olson had woke up the next morning as if nothing had hap-pened. No big deal. When Meena didn't show up for breakfast, he said she was prob'ly on the rag, then did a double take at me for staring at him. Maybe he had been sleepwalking or maybe he thought it was only a dream. I would have been glad if he never came home from school on weekends again.

The night after I found Chester, Meena and me stayed up late talking on the patio, planning revenge. We never mentioned that certain night; we forgot all about it. Meena said we should tell everybody at school Toby Olsen was homo and pour Drano on Mrs. Olsen's prize tomato plants and put a black widow in Mr. Olsen's car. Put a stink bomb down their chimney, I thought, and call the telephone company where he worked and report

Mr. Olsen for a communist. Finally Mom came out and said we better hit the sack. Her eyes red and puffy but she hadn't been drinking, which proved my theory she wasn't really alcoholic. She and Dad slept together that night in their bedroom. Tragedies are a good way to bring a family together. Unless you cause them yourself.

Next Sunday Dad and me went fishing up at Lake Cuyamaca, where the season just opened. We rented a boat with a seven-and-a-half-horse Evinrude, went out in the middle and wind-drifted. Dad had his fly rod; me only my spinning reel—which Dad said no self-respecting Oregon trout would fall for that outfit, but California rainbows might not be so choosy. I liked the way his line whip-snaked overhead when he cast, coils piling high above him, stretching out like a long easy finger to touch the water. Olson had stayed home. He said nobody went fishing except bald-headed bozos in rubber booties. Still, everything might've worked out okay if Dad didn't ask me if I had a girlfriend.

"Fess up, pal, you've got those famous Tillotson good looks. I'll bet you're breaking some little gal's heart."

I shook my head. "I've got better things to do."

"Like fishing!" Dad laughed, then frowned at where his line glistened across the water like a spider strand. "What's the rush? Your brother doesn't have anything on his mind but sex. Twenty-four hours a day. Hey, everything in moderation, that's what the Greeks believed." Dad scuffled my hair. "This is the life, isn't it, buster."

Suddenly I was asking, I don't know why, the question popped out of me. "What do you call it where a brother fools around with his own sister? That's scuzzy, isn't it, where a brother does that?"

Dad whipped his line off the water and lashed it overhead, aiming for a rise thirty feet away, hitting the ripple dead center. I thought maybe he didn't hear me. The boat rocked gently. He let his line go slack, his eyes looking ahead, glowing almost turquoise under his cap brim in light off the lake. "What are you telling me, pal?"

"No, naw . . . nothing."

Dad gripped my chin and pulled it around. "Don't give me that nothing stuff. What's on your mind?"

I hemmed and hawed, but he had me hooked good. So I told,
bits and pieces. Dad's lips stretched thin and purple, eyes narrowed, drowsy like Olson's when he was mad. When I hesitated,
he knuckled my knee and said, "Go on, all of it. Spill." So I
told: the carnival ride, Olson's fingers in Meena's undies, the
pool and his white bobbing butt. "Why in the hell didn't you
wake me?" Dad demanded. He was furious, upper lip jittering
against his teeth. I couldn't answer, I was confused. I hadn't
expected Dad to be so angry. His anger scared me. I knew then
I'd done an awful thing ratting on Olson.

Dad's eyes blinked from sweat coursing down his forehead,
like someone dumped a glass of water under his cap, though it
wasn't hot but breezy and overcast. He cranked the stick around
and gunned it, humping for shore. We didn't hardly talk on the
road home, just wound down through the canyons past huge
cactuses and tilting boulders, the tires squealing furiously around
turns. My gut nervous as a paper bee's nest hanging in a tree.
Why'd I open my stupid mouth? First, I chickenshitted by not
stopping Olson at the pool, then chickenshitted by ratting on
him.

When we entered town, Dad pulled to the curb and slapped
my knee. "You did the right thing telling me, Jeff. Don't worry
about it. I want you to swear to me, pal, never tell your mother
about this. Never. Do you hear? Never. A deal like this could
put her off the deep end."

So I swore I wouldn't, I'd die first, and meant it, too. We
shook on it, his strong hand encasing mine and squeezing. It
made me feel solemn and strange: I'd never shook hands with
my dad before.

# 25

## Meena

"I was gratified at the start, but it went on and on. Daddy burst into the house in his fishing clothes and snagged Olson by the stringy long hair and threw him on the bed in the back bedroom. He used his open hand like a club, not caring where his blows landed—face, chest, groin. Olson curled up in a ball to protect himself. Both were screaming, Dad loudest. *'You know what this is for, scumbag.'* Boney and me huddled in the hall, listening to flesh strike flesh, Olson's wails. I was terrified Dad would come for me next. Because I knew—I knew why he was so mad, just like Olson did. Olson was promising he wouldn't ever again . . . *Please, Pop.* The turd. Out in the hall, Boney shook like Chester had when he was cold, mumbling he hadn't meant to, honest, it just slipped out. I knew then that Dad was doing this for me. Not that I asked for it. Let him take Olson downtown and dump him naked on Main Street, that would have suited me fine. Not a beating.

"It was Mom's turn to call off the dogs. She and Wendy ran in from next door, smelling of sun lotion. Most likely you could hear his screams all over the neighborhood. 'I'm fed up' was all the answer Dad would give her.

"Boney holed up in his room for days after, mourning it seemed. After Olson's bruises yellowed and his puffy right eye opened enough for him to see, Dad drove him off to a new school in Orange County. Fort Defiance Military Academy. 'Specializing in the toughest cases,' the ad said. No muss, no fuss, no home leave. Good old-fashioned ball busting. Olson kicked Boney's door on his way out of the house and said, 'You'll get yours, dickhead.' Dad cuffed the back of his head. No muss. No fuss. He was gone."

Afterwards, Daddy wouldn't look her in the eye. He grimaced

a curt "Morning" over breakfast cereal, so Meena waited until he'd left for work before dashing down for a piece of toast. A conspiracy of silence gripped the household: grim clinking of silver against dinner plates. Meena pulled steaming chicken pot-pies from the oven and placed them on plates in their gleaming aluminum trays, a sad salad in a wooden bowl. "Well, isn't this cozy," Mom said on a rare occasion she joined them. She'd begun slurring words, self-degradation having finally reached her tongue. Sometimes her chair went over backwards with her.

Meena understood that in his passive, unconscious way Dad blamed her for Olson's weakness. If only she hadn't developed so quickly, if she were more discreet, if she didn't act out at school and sneak about the neighborhood, confront her mother with a wall of unbreachable insolence, if she didn't crawl around like one of those small ogres with their unfathomable appetites, if she hadn't used a bookcase to barricade her door, if her boobs didn't stick out straight, if she weren't such a sassy, headstrong little beast, if only, if only . . . his eyes fleeting out of reach. She had expected that if anyone discovered her secret it would be Mom; she hadn't expected this. Yet it wasn't Dad's judgment she feared. There was always the Mexican lady's shoe—tit for tat. Besides, he would forgive her. Didn't he love her! It was Mom who would never forgive her for making Olson lose control. Meena had overheard her telling Aunt Debbie how a girl could be loose without realizing. Meena had known since the Del Mar Fair that she could never tell Mom. Never. Though she wanted to tell—had rehearsed telling often enough. But couldn't. Mom would think her a slut. Meena would rather Olson came into her room every night and did what he liked. Good girls didn't let such things happen to them.

Meena eavesdropped on her parents whisper-arguing behind their bedroom door, desperate to know what Dad would reveal. She crept into the attic crawl space above their bedroom through a ceiling hatch in the utility room, crawling from creaking joist to joist, bare two-by-fours leaving notches in her knees, but she made out only fragments, Mom's bitter laughter: "Aren't we the dutiful daddy all of a sudden." It seemed he wouldn't reveal her secret. But if Ms. Childlove guessed, couldn't Mom guess, too?

After school Meena sat cross-legged in the dust atop Chester's grave, placing Lorenzo's jar on the crossbar of the crude cross,

listening to breeze crackle dried palm fronds on Boney's wigwam
and tickle leaves of a cottonwood grove nearby. The sky remained a washed, specious blue, surreal to an Oregon girl: winter without rain, without even clouds. Lizards came out from
hiding to watch her—their lidded eyes. She didn't go home until
dusk filled the canyon, a last pink grimace fading to an opaque
frown over the western rim, and she heard the first screech of
nighthawks overhead. Mom's laughter trickled like liquefied
glass from Wendy-Sandy's bright patio on the terrace above, a
single light on in Boney's room, otherwise the house was dark.
He'd be reading, the gonad, or playing the electric football he'd
got for Christmas, announcing touchdowns in a cawing voice
from back in his throat. She would yell from the kitchen: Did
he want a turkey or ham dinner. Dad rarely came home for
dinner anymore. "It's a slow economy," he told Mom, "I'm having to work more than I want to." Likely story.

Nights, Meena kept watch on the Olsens. Getting out was
easy; Mom sat up in bed watching Johnny Carson, thermos at
her side, laughing and talking back to the TV like she was one
of Johnny's guests. Meena went straight over and pressed her
stethoscope against the Olsens' living room window. Mr. Olsen's
complaints about Chester had ceased. Now it was those "college
punks" and "Martin Luther Mouth," or "that little bitch down
the street who's pinching my mail. I'm gonna put a rat trap in
there," he insisted, "a big old rat trap." Meena would ring his
doorbell and run.

Bad luck comes in threes, Boney told her. Like the three
Fates—who were spiders, too, weaving the web of life. Or Ol-
son's three favorite words: "boss," "buttfuck" and "balls."
Three times in a row that week she was caught spying. First, by
Mom as she emerged from the attic in the utility room, then by
Mr. Olsen, as she poured pee in his gas tank, finally by Dad . . .
Sandy Beach really. Though this last time she wasn't spying, only
searching for jumping spiders among fat succulent ice plant
leaves matting the slope below Wendy-Sandy's pool. Meena had
sexed Lorenzo and discovered that *he* was really a *she*; she
wanted to find her a mate—who would double as husband and
nutritious meal if he didn't split fast enough after they "did it."
She looked forward to watching the mating ritual. Using his
pedipalps, he would deposit sperm in her epigynum, she would

seize him with her front legs and sink fangs into his cephalothorax just behind the eyes. Later would spin her wondrous silk cocoon.

Meena crouched near the fence on the lookout for distinctive cream stripes along spiders' abdomens, six eyes in a trapezoidal arrangement. It was a glorious Sunday morning; spring had arrived. So she wasn't surprised to look through fence slats and find Wendy-Sandy lounging by the pool. However, it surprised her to see Dad sitting with the neighbor women (though Wendy's patio was like their own family room, where they all lounged about in swimming suits, dark as polished luan). Mom was asleep, she knew, and wouldn't be up until long after noon. Desultorily, Meena watched them sip screwdrivers. It troubled her to see her father drinking. One lush in the house was enough.

"Hows about a little fresherupper?" Wendy asked.

"Sounds good, babe." Dad patted Wendy's bony fanny as she bent for his glass. Sandy pursed her lips in a knowing smile. Meena edged up closer to the fence on slippery leaves.

Wendy disappeared into the house and Sandy dived into the pool, crossing its length in a few brisk pulls, doing a racer's tuck and returning, climbing the chrome ladder in one continuous movement. Dad reached a hand to help her up. His gleaming white teeth, her gleaming blond hair. She came up dripping, giggling, the bitty string bikini slipped half off her breasts, creeping six inches below her navel, reminding Meena of that song: "Itsy Bitsy Teenie Weenie Yellow Polkadot Bikini," except Sandy's was glossy black. Sandy shook out her hair coquettishly, lips firmed in a sarcastic moue, while Dad leered. The blue nylon pocket of his swim trunks bulged hugely. He yanked her against his bare chest and kissed her hard on the mouth. Sandy laughed a brash little tinkle. "Down, Rover. Naughty, naughty." Shoving him off. He bent forward and kissed the white tops of her breasts.

Meena seized fence slats, her stomach gone jelly. Right here! Right in this very place! With a girl little older than herself, Daddy did what Ms. Childlove insisted he did to her. Meena pressed fingers to her lips, which seemed to burn with physical memory. The shimmering blue pool like a glittering eye revealing the lusty, priapic hearts of men in her family, a window to their jaded souls—or a sapphire that held them mesmerized.

Sandy ran a hand back through her slick hair and smiled at the sky. Her eyes snapped at Meena. She slapped Dad's shoulder and leaned toward his ear. He turned abruptly, his face a brazen ringing alarm when he made brief eye contact with his daughter. So unlike Boney's beseeching, frightened eyes beside the pool house, but hard and angry and altogether alien. In his dash toward the gate, he collided with Wendy coming out of the house. She twirled and landed with a whump on a lounge chair, drinks level in her hands—half empty of sticky yellow fluid that had splashed over her legs and stomach. Her half-dopey underwear-model's smile. Dad crashed through the gate and Meena was fleeing before her father's rage.

He chased her into the canyon. Meena dodging shrubs and boulders—like some childhood game of time-out tag come true. But once she could cry "Time!" and Daddy would stop, his ghoul's claws frozen midair. Now, in real life, his footsteps gained on her, he shouted, "Meena! Damn it, stop! Would you." She tripped on a root and fell headlong, skinning hands and knees. Dad's fingertips stooped like hawks' talons from behind and yanked her to her feet, wheeled her around into his fiery vodka breath. Not giving a damn. A blue bulge in his swim trunks. Not caring. Shaking her. "Damn it, Meena, you've got to respect people's privacy. Darned little sneak." Each word delivered in a moist angry packet like the venom of a spitting spider. Not giving a shit. "Sandy's like a daughter to me, you know that. Can't I show my daughter some healthy affection... huh?" His fingers dug in. "We were horsing around, that's all, baby. Goofing off. Didn't mean a thing, little tomfoolery at the pool. Whaddaya say?" His fingertips gouged at soft indentations by her shoulder blades. "Oops, sorry, baby. Gee, didn't hurt you, did I?" Seizing her hand, he saw skin peeled away from her palm. He patted his hips for pockets—a handkerchief—then flushed. "Not wearing pants." Dad made a prissy scissoring movement of his knees.

She might have forgiven all this. What she could not forgive was the lie he insisted she share: to pretend she'd seen nothing at all. Presto! Like Olson. Presto! Like Mom's drinking. Presto! The truth gone. Hypocrisy is a kind of furtive, festering hatred, she knew. Like Diana Tarantula's gimpy smile when they passed in the hall at school, or Danner the Banana's simper when she entered his office, lip corners jerking like fishhooks had snagged there. A smile that didn't forgive but threatened.

"I think we can forget all about it, huh? Whad'say?"

She didn't speak. Staring at a germinal palm tree that had taken root in a fissure between granite boulders—stiff green chitinous fingers. She could smell her father's sweat, acrid and sharp. Moisture glistened in a mist across his chest, in whorls of hair around his nipples. He'd gone craven and conspiratorial, promising her a microscope, one-hundred-fifty power, how's about it? Would she like a puppy? Hoping to strike a deal like she was some whore at the Del Mar Fair.

She broke away and sprinted to the canyon wall where she had hidden his girlfriend's shoe. Spun and threw it at his feet. "Wife cheater," she shrieked, "you can give it back now."

He stood in swim trunks and sandals, staring. He tore away cobwebs and turned the pump over in his hands, brow furrowed in puzzlement—as if she'd pulled some archetype of his life from the earth. He hadn't shaved that morning, his cheeks vaguely blue. Gradually, comprehension cleared his gaze. Alarm. His thumbs traced rhinestones—likely remembering how his girlfriend limped beside him arm in arm as they circled the Rock-O-Plane. "Some kid took it," the attendant had surely told them, "some fuckin' kid." She had limped, laughing, clamping an arm around his waist. What a crazy idea. Who would want to steal a shoe?

"It's just a shoe." He laughed. "A woman's tacky shoe."

"I saw you, Dad."

"Saw me . . . Saw me what? Don't be a little fool."

Dad turned the shoe over and over, his left eye flinching spasmodically. For a terrible instant she wasn't sure what he might do. Then she was talking rapidly: how the shoe dropped out of the sky at their feet, Boney saw it, too. Dad's eyes went drowsy with fear. His mouth tore open. "Sneaky little slut," he muttered.

"Y'r the sneak. I hate your guts."

Ms. Childlove worked fingertips over rhinestone fleur-de-lis on the shoe, frowning to herself. She placed the pump on her desk and squinted at Meena under the crotch formed by heel and arch, much as Dad had done the day before when Meena confronted him with it, only Dad turned the shoe over in his hands like some secret portion of himself that had been torn away and presented to him, his head shaking denial.

"I grabbed the shoe and ran," Meena told her. "Even Wilma Rudolph couldn't have caught me. Dad was shouting I better not do anything stupid. But he couldn't run uphill too good in his sandals. I was scared he wasn't my dad at all. I knew I couldn't hide the shoe in my room, it had to be someplace he'd never look. I thought of Mom's shoe bag in her closet she never uses anymore, and I hid it in there. Mom was snoring like crazy. I was going to get in bed with her, but I sneaked under the bed. I heard Dad come in the back, whispering 'Meena,' dumping stuff out of my drawers, then he went away. I went in and put the bookcase in front of my door—just in case. A while later he knocked and shoved a note under my door."

"Mama was asleep all this time?"

"She likes sleeping in Sunday."

"She must be a heavy sleeper. What did the note say, dear?"

"It said whatever I thought I saw I should never tell my Mom. She would go off the deep end if I told her."

"What does he mean—the deep end?"

Meena shrugged. "Like in a pool. I don't think he even cares. He doesn't love her anyway."

"Okay, sweetheart, I'm trying to understand this. You confronted Dad with the shoe because you were mad about Sandy. Are you jealous of her?"

"I hate his guts," Meena hissed.

"You say he'd been drinking. Did he strike you, sweetheart?"

She shook her head.

"But he struck your brother."

"He isn't mean, just a hypocrite. At least Olson isn't a hypocrite anyway. Only a gonad."

"Tell me, what did Olson do to make Papa strike him?"

Meena looked away. "He's a gonad fruitcake."

"Was Dad drunk that time, too?"

"He never drinks at home, only at Wendy's pool."

"Why is that, dear?"

Meena shook her head.

"You don't know or you don't wish to tell?" Goona twisted

the spiked heel in her fist, making a squeaky sound. It looked brand new, barely scuffed on the sole. "Papa has a drinking problem?" she persisted.

What you must do is lie squarely in the person's eyes, never swallow or fidget your fingers, although it isn't easy lying into unblinking feline eyes, lacquered yellow. The choice, as Aunt Debbie made clear, was being taken from home and put in foster care. "Not anymore. Since my mom stopped."

"Has Mama started drinking again, too?"

"I said she stopped," Meena snapped.

Ms. Childlove leaned forward. "Do you know that when people lie a small balloon inflates over their forehead. Most people can't see it. Policemen can. And child psychiatrists. We're trained to see. It's only hard-core liars who can keep from inflating their balloon." Meena stared as Goona scooted toward her on silent coasters. "Now I want you to tell me about Mama's little secret. I know, Meena, I'm not blind."

"She's cured now," Meena said hoarsely.

"But it isn't really Mama's drinking we're talking about, is it? When Papa drinks he likes you to play his little wife, doesn't he? That is why you confronted him with the shoe—to tell him how hurt you are. How very jealous."

Goona's questions bewildered her: so nearly true, so totally bonerhead dumb. Like Steve Weatherspoon back home, right and wrong at once. There was a sulfurous smell in the room. She wondered if Ms. Childlove farted. Her nose was nearly as thin as Madame Chevaux's, but humped. Impossible to imagine it twitching. With each mention of Dad, Meena's anger throbbed like an open ulcer. Her love for him, which had always seemed solid as the rock in the Long Loops' cave, was fragmented now as if a California quake had broken it to pieces. She hated this place. This new life.

"I hate my dad to shit," she said.

Ms. Childlove swiveled around and seized a broadsheet from the bookshelf and opened it on her desk: a cherubic pink man and woman in precise anatomical detail. "He touches you here." Ms. Childlove touched her own breast. "Does he touch you here, too?" indicating her crotch. Gimpier than health class—except there they used "anatomically correct" dolls. (*This, girls, is a penis.* . . . ) She laughed in Goona's face.

"I know, sweetheart," Ms. Childlove said intently; it seemed capillaries would wiggle like blue worms from her skin. "I know about these things. And he asks you to touch him—here!" Touching her pencil tip to a pink, half-tumescent limb dangling from the illustrated man.

"That's his dick," Meena said.

"I know what it is," Ms. Childlove said sternly. "Victims have balloons, too. They surround us like transparent globes. If we don't puncture them we suffocate inside. Our hearts shrivel and die. This is something you must tell me." Her grape lips formed every perfect word. They fascinated Meena. She knew what Goona wanted her to say. But why should she tell what everyone knew already? The girls' sly, knowing smiles at school, whisperings behind her back. At the bus stop, Toby Olsen crowed an incessant limerick:

> There once was a girl named Meena
> Who loved to suck on my wienah.
> She'd lick all along
> Every inch of my dong,
> That's how it got so much cleanah.

All of them. Except Mom. Except Boney, who leapt on Toby the pig's back one morning and got in two good punches before grunthead knocked him to the ground and straddled him. She'd got hold of Piggy's hair and twisted until he screamed. They were saved by solemn, doleful Reverend Smith, the bus driver, who didn't put up with any crap on his bus, making the kids ride as quietly as if they were seated in pews of his church. Let them think what they wanted. What you didn't tell couldn't hurt you.

"I know," she persisted. "Don't you see. I know how you have been hurt. The truth is a wonderful thing. Like pure clear water, washing away all the muck and confusion inside. I hear you, sweetheart, I know how desperately you are crying out."

Insisting that Meena level with her, like Danner the Banana, who called her into his office each time something was missing from a locker. "What's important is that you level with me," he would say, eyes lined in gray ashes, wanting to find in her the solution to each of the school's petty thefts. Her honest denials infuriated him. They weren't convenient. It wasn't the truth adults sought but handy lies that would settle the matter and let them rest easy again.

Ms. Childlove was offering something—some quid pro quo— her words soft, but her demeanor as aloof and disapproving as Madame Chevaux's. Something about Mom's drinking, how one illness in a family brought on others: If the root disease was cured it would cure them all. She understood Meena was in trouble again at school. Meena grinned quick at the memory of it. She had gone to the door of Piggy Olsen's shop class with a piping hot apricot cobbler from home economics, shouting, "This is for Chester, asshole," throwing it at him. Steaming peach slices crawled like orange slugs down Piggy Olsen's cheeks. It burned him some; but worse, he was working at the wood lathe at the time and it could have torn off his thumb.

Ms. Childlove leaned close, each labiodental sound accentuated by the crooked upper tooth snagging her bottom lip. "Very, very serious," she said. "You know the difference between suspension and expulsion. This is for good. It will mark you. It will break Mama's heart." She might use her influence to convince Mr. Danner to give Meena a second chance. "I think if he knew why you are acting out, if he knew about *your little secret* and Mama's drinking he would be sympathetic. But you must level with me, Meena. If I can't trust you, we can't expect Mr. Danner to trust you. I'm sure he will want to help. It's when Daddy is drinking, isn't it?" She took Meena's hands. "Darling, I know he molests you. I want you to tell me all about it."

"Once," she mumbled, hoping to put an end to her pestering. Trying to remember. "At Wendy's pool . . . he put his hand in my bottoms."

Ms. Childlove's eyes closed. "Tell me, darling."

She was in a state of suspension, all of her focusing on Meena's lips, her brow deeply incised. But her eyes soft now, fawn-yellow and seductive. Meena's heart beat furiously; it was as exciting as that instant Lorenzo had leapt onto the wasp's neck. She felt a giddy authority—knowing the truth was whatever she wanted it to be. And relief. The weight shifted from her shoulders to Ms. Childlove's. Revenge, too, yes. Ms. Childlove jotted down each word, her fuzzy eyebrows making "go ahead" motions when Meena halted.

Meena might have told her she had seen Chester in bed with her mother, or there were horns under Boney's long hair, or that her father's prick was as big as a Frisian stallion's, jet black. Ms. Childlove would have dutifully written down each word. And been satisfied. It didn't occur to Meena that Ms. Childlove was offering her a bribe—like her father had. Or that she was accepting it, trading her own culpability for her parents'. Not at all. Because children can be selfish or capricious, but they can't fathom the fury of adults. They're helpless before it. Meena just wanted Goona to leave her alone, with her secrets.

But it became fuzzy. She saw herself rising from the water in her baby dolls, blond hair shimmering, but realized it was black bikini panties he was trying to push down her legs. A kind of dream. He kissed her lips hard, then the tops of her breasts . . . Who did?

"He dunked me if I wouldn't, so I let him," Meena said.

"Your father tried to drown you." Ms. Childlove's face cincturing taut like a drawstring bag.

Meena shook her head. "He helped me up, then he kissed me."

"On the mouth, dear?"

"He always does."

# 26

---

# Jeff

I remember gas bubbles rising in the pond at La Brea Tar Pits—blurp, blurp—everywhere! Like the earth had a bad case of gas. Natural gas, Dad said, the same kind when you light your farts. The whole pond seethed on cold boil from gas pressure down below. Tar gunked along the shoreline, making slick funky-dunk rainbows with candy bar wrappers and paper cups stuck in.

"Pretty crudso," Mom said. There were small tar puddles on

the grass like black miniature tar pits, and Mom said we couldn't walk out there. She was scared the whole lawn would collapse or we'd get a foot stuck in and get pulled under like the mastodons.

A thin crazy man followed us around. His glasses frames were taped together by masking tape. You knew he was nutso because he never stopped talking and his eyes were as close together as a robin's. He told Mom how much he loved the smell of asphalt. Meena giggled. Mom whispered he might be dangerous, but Dad got a kick out of him. There was a huge empty pit underneath California, the crazy man said, where they pumped out all the oil. Someday the whole state would sink into the tar like the mammoths. "Certain and inevitable," he said.

"Donald," Mom scolded Dad.

But Dad was preoccupied by "the Eighth Wonder of the Natural Known World," the crazy man called it. A bishop pine tree with oil soaked up its trunk like God dunked it in tarry chocolate. Tar seeped out of the tree between fissures in the scaly bark like black pitch and hardened in glistening dribbles down the trunk. It burbled in a slurpy mass at the tree's base—looked like the whole tree grew out of a tar pit. Higher up, regular clear pitch dripped out and turned the hot afternoon piney-smelling: sweet and sour (from the tar). Dad and the crazy man discussed how it must've brought tar up through its roots by osmosis. Dad said he wouldn't have thought that possible.

The crazy man said he was an atomic physicist who they fired because he told the truth about how all the molecules in the universe are headed toward critical mass collision. Dad nodded. Mom took Meena off a ways, frowning and motioning at Dad to go. Suddenly, the crazy man turned to her. "Makes no difference whether you stand with us or against us," he said. "For the right or the left. When it sinks you will sink with it. Tar will swallow you up with a sound and a fury."

Back then I thought he was nutso, but now it seemed his prophecy was coming true. Tar was rising up out of the hole under California and swallowing our whole family alive, like the dire wolves and American camels and saber-tooths and *Mammut americanum* and condors that swooped down to eat them. You never realized you were sinking until it was too late.

\* \* \*

Goona the Freak picked Meena up from school. She looked like a tall witch walking out to her Volkswagen, stooped with her hand on Meena's back; sun glistened off the white part in her hair. It scared me maybe Danner had expelled my sister and Goona the orange-haired freak was driving her to reform school. But when I got home Meena was sitting on the couch staring at her feet. Mom paced before her, grinding a fist into her belly like she had a stomachache, muttering that she had known this would happen, she had always known. It was her own fault. Mom's hair all messed and tears cut red trails down her cheeks. Every once in a while she ran over to hug Meena. "Why didn't you tell me, darling?" Meena just shook her head like she couldn't speak, couldn't look at Mom. They didn't even notice me come in.

By the time Dad got home Mom was more plastered than at my birthday party, glugging straight from a white Purex jug, which scared me she might drink bleach and not realize. I knew something awful would happen. Dad seemed to sense it. He stood in the entry hall, head cocked, listening. When I tried to warn him Mom was blotto drunk, he held up a hand for me to be quiet. A funny grimacing smile on his face when Mom charged around the corner holding the cast-iron frying pan over her head, cold grease sludging down on her bouffant hairdo.

"Don't, Jerri!" Dad's voice broke. "Take it easy." I grabbed Mom's waist. Wasn't any use. She let the pan fly and shattered a frosted glass panel beside the door. Dad bolted outside.

*"Don' you ever come back in this houz,"* Mom screamed, *"Mons'er . . . filt'y mons'er."*

After she calmed down, I led Mom back to her bedroom and put her in bed. I'd already decided to stop any more craziness in our house, because you're either part of the problem or part of the solution, like Aunt Debbie says, and I was already part of the problem too long. She sat up the second I took her shoes off. "I haf to protesh y'r sis'er," she slurred.

"I will, Mom. I'll protect her."

"Sush a sweedhard. Y'r sush a swee . . . " Her head flopped on my shoulder and tongue dangled from her mouth. I couldn't help remembering what Dad said about her not taking care of herself, and I felt ashamed. She was beautiful really, deep down.

Mom tried to get up. He wasn't going to touch her again, she said, over her dead body. Just when I thought she was too strong for me, she'd fall limp again, eyeballs bouncing against her brain like rubber balls. Last thing she said before passing out was "Sex upender," under no circumstances was Dad to enter our house— ever again.

Dad was leaning against the fender of his Corvette when I went out, arms folded and his head shaking, bewildered. "What's it about, Dad?" I asked him. Because it was like at La Brea—everybody was sinking into tar by himself.

"She's not coming out here, is she?" he answered.

I told him he better go to Wendy's; when Mom woke up she'd prob'ly forget all about it and I would come get him. He shook his head. "She's not going to forget." Then he looked at me, startled. "You don't believe this crap, do you, son?"

"I don't even know what it is."

Dad gripped my shoulders and said he didn't know how much more of this a man could take. "You see that, Jeff? Sometimes I think she's out of her right mind. What am I supposed to do?"

"It'll be okay as soon as she gets sober."

"Sober!" He laughed bitterly. "When was your mother ever sober?" It embarrassed me to hear him talk about her like that— his own wife!—like she was a stranger or something.

"What'd you do, Dad?"

"Do?" He hunched his shoulders. "Damned good question."

Meena wouldn't tell me what happened either. She hissed at me like she was a dumb spider again. She gripped her knees and rocked on the bed, hair hanging in a snaggy curtain over her eyes. I swept up broken glass and put cardboard over the entry-way window. About dark, Dad knocked softly on the back door and whispered he was staying the night at a friend's. "I can't stay here, your mother's likely to brain me." I was glad anyway I didn't have to tell him he couldn't come in our house.

Late that night it started over again—with Meena this time. Mom dragged her out of bed, whispering *Quick*! They had to escape while your dad's asleep. Meena was groggy and grumbling as Mom shoved her into the wagon. My sister slipped out the passenger door while Mom ran around to the driver's side. The tires squealed as Mom backed down the drive, sideswiping a bottlebrush tree on the way, didn't even notice Meena wasn't in the car. All you could hope was there weren't any trucks coming on the county road.

We went looking for Mom at dawn. We knew all the dives where she usually went when she split like that and the best route to take on our bikes: Night Owl Tavern, The Glass Eye, which, officially, they closed at three A.M., but vague shadows moved inside. We scratched on bubbly frosted champagne glasses on the window and Sam came out and told us, "Sorry, kids, haven't seen y'r mom tonight. Sure wish I could help you out." He looked like a cadaver, his features squashed close against his skull like he had been wrapped in a mummy bandage.

"Hypocrite," my sister hissed. She hated bartenders as much as Piggy Olsen.

We circled down to El Norte Parkway and the golf course, because one night by accident we found Mom's wagon parked in the empty lot and Mom strolling a fairway singing to herself. Telling us look at the stars, weren't they lovely, even though they mostly had disappeared. This time we nearly rode past, dodging rain puddles, but I noticed tire tracks veering off the road across number thirteen fairway like tank treads. Meena and me exchanged a look.

We followed them up number nine toward the green, over a little rise, which Mom tore up pretty good aiming for the flag pole, crushing it flat. The green was a muddy mess. Mom's County Sedan wagon was nose-dived in a sand trap beyond, the driver's door slung open. Mom was lying on her back in the sand, her head resting on the grassy lip. We stood there looking down at her. It was quiet except birds hopping about looking for worms after the rain and early cars going to work on Country Club Road. "Mom!" we called from the green. She didn't move; we thought she was dead this time. We dropped our bikes and ran down, scared shitpiss she'd be all bloody underneath and her brains spilled out in the sand. *"Mom!"* we yelled. She didn't budge a wink until Meena got close and Mom sat up and hugged her, pulling her down in the sand. Meena shrieked.

"My poor li-ah baby," Mom blubbered. She'd searched for her everywhere, she said. Sand clung like tiny glistening jewels to Mom's nylons and leaked out between buttons of her blouse. Her hair was full of sparkly grains, her skirt twisted up; one nylon bunched around her bare foot. I could smell booze ten feet away, like she'd went swimming in it, too. She kept saying we better run, "They'll comink baaa'."

"Who, Mom, who's coming?"

"Y'll Gran'pa Waller an' th' unner un."

"She's bonkers," Meena said, scared and disgusted both at once. She sat up and brushed damp sand from her clothes.

Mom seemed content to just lie there. Maybe she couldn't get up, maybe her back was broke. It was all she could do to just lift her head. "Take y'll sis'er, Jevrey. They'll going ah rape 'er . . . they'ah . . . Jus' like y'r Daaa'."

"Okay, Mom."

"She's bonkers in the head."

I told Meena to shut up. We had to get Mom out of there before greenskeepers arrived for work and found she'd tore up their golf course. Though I saw it wasn't any use, the wagon was high-ended on the transmission hump, its front fender buried in sand like it had fell from the sky. We each took Mom under an arm and tried to stand her up. She slumped back down. Then poked her head up, looking left and right like she wasn't drunk at all. "Honey, go on. They'll be back shordly." Just then we saw Jeep lights bounding along the fairway toward us.

"Hurry," I cried, but Mom wouldn't cooperate. I grabbed Meena's hand and ran to hide behind the wagon.

It was two greenskeepers in faded green uniforms, a middle-aged white guy whose pink scalp showed right through his thin blond hair, even his eyeballs were pink, and a Filipino guy who looked like Mr. Villanueva, our shop teacher at school, who saved Toby from getting his thumb tore off when Meena threw the cobbler at him. Only this guy had mean, laughing eyes. He thought everything was funny. Mom yanked down her skirt when they drove up, and he whistled and laughed.

"How's Sleeping Beauty?" asked the old guy, his face prune-wrinkled from working in the sun. I was scared they might rape Mom or something.

They squatted beside her. "Been a little more loaded you might'a made it clear across the course," the older guy said. "Peekaboo!" He lifted Mom's skirt. She slapped his hand. They laughed and hoisted her under the arms. "Uppsydaisy. Sheriff will be here in a minute. I believe he wants a word with you."

They fireman-carried her to the Jeep, her heels dragging in the

sand. Mom was screaming; she scored with a blow in the short
guy's balls and he bent over. Meena and me watched through
the car windows, scared stiff. My sister kept poking me with her
elbow. The big pink-skulled guy, whose woolly wrists were thick
as tree limbs, cursed and tried lifting Mom by himself.

"Look here, bitch," he said.

I ran out and told him, "Leave her alone."

Then Meena ran over.

His mouth fell open. "Where in hell'd you come from?"

"She's our mom. Don't you touch her."

"Yes, sir."

Meena pointed a finger at him. "We saw you, dirty pig."

"Now hold on right there. Your mom is been remodeling our
golf course. Drunk as a gawdamned skunk."

"I saw what you did," Meena persisted.

"Now, gawdamned it, you didn't see one damned nothing."

"Hey, le's go, Johnny," said the short one. "Okay? Le's go. I
don' want no trouble." He was still stooped over.

"We're gonna pull her outta that sand trap," the other huffed,
so red he might pop like a firecracker. "Then your mother's got
some explaining to do."

"She gonna fix that." The Filipino nodded at the green. "Hey,
kids, we called a ambulance. Don't got to worry." He slipped
under the wagon and hooked a cable from the Jeep's winch to
the wagon's frame. When the old guy hit the lever, it did a slow
turn in the sand and came out onto the grass slick as a whistle.
No damage except a busted headlight. The Filipino guy winked.
"She gonna be all right," he said. "Don't got to worry."

They decided to bring the ambulance to pick her up. "We
gonna jus' go back and bring him. Don't go nowheres." He
grinned and jangled Mom's car keys and jumped in the Jeep
beside the white guy, laughing. They sped off. I could tell they
never had an alcoholic mother or a sister like Meena who knew
people's secrets, including where Mom kept spare keys in her
purse. We told Mom to hurry up unless she wanted to go to jail.
Somehow we got her into the wagon and Meena hightailed it
out of there, throwing up a huge divot around the green, following Mom's tracks back to Country Club Road, swerving like
crazy because she couldn't see too good over the top of the
wheel. Still, she drove better than me.

We were on El Norte, swinging right onto Nordahl Road when we heard sirens in the distance. Meena drove like nobody ever invented a red light, looking straight ahead, nearly swiping an old farmer in a pickup who slammed his horn and swerved sideways down the middle of the road to miss us as Meena ran a light and hung a left onto Rock Springs Road. One thing you had to say about my sister, she drove good for a dumb spider.

# 27

# Aunt Debbie

I told my supervisor: "Fire me if you've got to but I need family leave."

"Damn it, Deborah," she said, "I've got three girls out this week. We'll be short-flighted to Houston and Boston."

Girls, I told her, is what she didn't have—but grown women with families and responsibilities. We nearly got into it. Truth be told, I didn't want to go one bit. I had my own life . . . or might've if I stopped postponing to attend to someone else's.

Like a bad movie, I told Gloria, who flew with me on the Portland/San Francisco run, only grottier than what Hollywood produces. Jerri calling to tell me Don had molested Meena. Sexually molested, Meena told the social worker—Ms. Lovechild, the apricot-haired family eater—and now the Child Protection Team, something or other, was seeking a court order to get Don out of the house, or else Meena would go into foster care. Just like that! Because you have to protect an incest victim. Proof or no. Just like that.

"Hold on," I'd told Jerri. "Slow down. D'you think maybe you ought to find out if it's true first?" Jerri started shouting. Didn't doubt it one minute. She was drunk, I'll give her that, words glommed together like cornstarch. No court orders, I insisted, no hysterics, I'm on my way. Seemed it was habit forming. "D'you know what it's like to play family nine-eleven?" I asked Gloria. "Like stringing salmon eggs on a clothesline or shoveling out the whacham-a-call-it stables with a sand shovel."

"Fun and games," she said.

"If it wasn't for the kids—"

"Somebody else's," she reminded me.

Don picked me up at the airport, came around the car with a hand extended. All his teeth. "Give me a fighting chance, Deb, that's all I ask." He looked rugged: long-eyed, first I'd ever seen him without a healthy tan.

"Meena says I molested her, can you imagine?" Asking not me but the horizon as he drove. A jet throttled overhead from Miramar Naval Air Station, shook the windows. Don didn't flinch. "Jesus, what's happening to us?"

I watched him drive, eyes squinting from tension, cheek dimples sunk to hollows under a five o'clock shadow that looked permanent. "Did you do it, Don?" I asked.

He turned on me. "My own kid! What do you take me for?" Squinting, developing a tic. The thing is, you couldn't be sure. I recalled how angry he'd been the morning Meena leapt in his lap. Flushing furious. Just maybe he had adopted his daughter's bed like he once tried mine. Despairing of his wife's. It happens.

I pieced it together best I could: Meena told the social worker that Don molested her at Wendy-Lindy's pool, and she'd informed the police, but Meena was confused at the sheriff's questioning, so Don hadn't been formally charged—not yet—and the public prosecutor wouldn't decide whether to press criminal charges until after a formal interview with Meena, which had to wait until the validator, who handled abuse cases, returned from a trip to Guatemala. Complicated, I'll say. Meantime, Child Welfare had petitioned the court for an injunction to bar Don from his own home—to protect his daughter. But the judge had refused to ban a father from his home on a mere allegation; he needed formal criminal charges. At least someone in that town had some sense, though he agreed it would be best if someone stayed with the family. Enter Deborah. Don was a criminal in his own house, and I was his jailor.

That social worker had sunk her teeth in good, I'll say. Meena? That's the part I couldn't understand. You don't idly accuse your father of a thing like that. No girl would.

Home was something else. Shoes, coffee mugs, magazines,

towels left where they were dropped, a Q-tip on the living room rug, blinds half-open, garbage rotted in the kitchen. Like they'd up and abandoned home without leaving the house. Don stayed away mostly. Jerri stayed shitfaced. Just tore her up: The husband she thought was sleeping around was sleeping with her daughter. The kids had stopped trying: Jeffrey devastated, Meena withdrawn. Their parents had abandoned them. Each of them lived separately in the same house. I think Don had made up his mind I would side against him. Grandma Sally was his single ally—outraged some outsider with a peculiar name should tear the family apart. Not that I blamed her.

Jerri holed up in the bedroom she and Don once shared. Don and I took the front rooms. Meena rarely left her room, avoiding her dad. It was a nest, littered with clothes, crisscrossed by fishing line strung wall to wall; tinkling alarm bells hung everywhere, so you had to duck and squeeze to get inside and still set them jangling like harried sleigh bells. Meena crouched in a corner inside a gossamer tent woven of fish line that she called her "cocoon." Wanted to metamorphose into someone else, I guess. Jeff alone passed freely between different spheres, nearest thing to a link holding that disaster together. He brought Mom plates of food and sat stiffly on a patio chair to talk to his dad. A roving ambassador between them. He sprawled in an emotional stupor when we were alone, blaming himself for his loony family. "Meena's a dirty rotten liar," he confided, but wouldn't let on how he knew.

On the afternoon I arrived, he led me back to his mom, motioning me close outside her bedroom door. "She says weirdo things sometimes. It doesn't mean nothing." He stood taller than me. Shocked overnight into that gawky adolescent stage, like his sister on my last visit. His dad's Adam's apple stuck out like an extra gonad at his throat, stretched boy's face with its long, thoughtful forehead, his mother's heavy-lidded eyes, the nerdy, side-parted haircut. I touched his arm. "We're going to have to change your hairdo."

From Jerri's room came a smell like an animal died and turned to cheese in there. Drapes shut, Jerri stretched in rumpled shadows in a filthy gown, green metal thermos on the night table, dishes scattered over bed and floor. A portable TV flickered on her vanity, the picture rolling. Great God and little fishes! Most dogs had more pride. I took a breath and threw open drapes, a window. "We're going to clean up this peehole."

Jerri sat right up and ordered me out of her house.

"You asked me to come down, hon," I reminded her. I got mad then and dragged my big sister into the shower, clothes and all. She'd better pull her act together, better detox, better talk to Don, better damned well get a grip. "The shits have come into your life and family and y'r dead drunk. They'll chew you up, hon, you'll lose your home, your kids. . . . Is that what you want?" By way of answer, she upchucked on me. I could've drowned her on the spot. We soaped down, clothes and all, stripped and soaped again. Like two school-girls in the bath.

Funny how things come. Maybe she'd got it all mixed up— or Meena, with the social worker planting crazy ideas in her head . . . her mom, too. I remembered Meena's weasel face fixed in the playroom window that night Jerri demonstrated what Walter had done to her. Remembered something else, vaguely, like misty fragments of a dream just after waking: a claw-foot bathtub, two giggling sisters sudsing each other, the older warn-ing solemnly how we'd die of lead poisoning if we licked where enamel had chipped away; so we had to lick, of course, after a dare. Daddy's balding forehead loomed overhead, thick fingers soaping between our toes—where, he said, they cut off the web-bing when you're born. We laughed and splashed. He dried Jerri first with a fluffy white towel.

*Don't, Daddy, it feels funny.*

"Don't!" he whispered. "I thought you'd like that."

Or Sally cried: "Don't! Don't you dare."

The door had burst open and she led him off by an ear. We were forbidden to bathe together ever again. Punishment, I sup-pose. Until now! Our toes mealing in grains of Jerri's vomit. My sister who never vomited from drink. But maybe from memory. She was still beautiful, despite scraggly hair and puffy skin. Still, after all these years, I felt ashamed I'd let him dry her first.

They say when an alcoholic relapses she drinks twice as hard. A metabolic thing, where cells don't function right without booze to feed them, something about membranes. Or her blood won't process any but wet calories. Truth be told, wasn't a thing to do with hooch and never is. Take away the drink from a drunk, Alcoholics Anonymous says, you still have a drunk. Something was drunk inside my sister, booze or no.

That house was tense as death row before an execution. Don slept outside on the back lawn in his sleeping bag, afraid Jerri might come for him in the dead of night. "I don't want anyone uncomfortable with me in the house," he said. "Until we clear this nonsense up." About noble as he could get without splitting in half. He alternated between defiance, hostility and plain hurt. Refused to vacate the house. Let them get a court order. Jumpy each time the phone rang. He begged me to plead his case. Couldn't they all sit down and talk it out. No outsiders! No goddamned male-hating child psychiatrists. But it was too late for talking. By a long shot.

"It might've happened," he admitted one day, "but it wasn't me."

"What might've happened?" I asked.

"Whatever . . . abuse! Isn't that what they are calling it? Meena has confused things somehow. Look, I've said enough already." It was an environment nourished on deceit, like maggots on spoiled flesh. I did my best to reserve judgment.

You could see the pressure building in Jeff. He didn't wish to abandon his dad or betray his mom. When he asked me which of them I thought was telling the truth, Dad or Meena, I shook my head and suggested we clean the house. Fresh smell, fresh start. Afterwards, I saw him enter the canyon behind the house. He spent hours alone in his wigwam beside Chester's grave. There's a great empty cavern under California, he told me, where they pumped out the oil. Someday the whole state will collapse inside. "We shouldn't never have moved down here. Oregon was safer."

Sally wanted to come down. Over my skinny ass, I told her on the phone. "Easter is coming," she whined.

"Not here it isn't."

"I'd like to come nevertheless. Jerri could use my help."

"Mom, you don't want to see her."

"Well, she's confused just now. Meena, too. Why any child would say such things against her father, I don't know. It's that woman with the sneaky Pete name is who it is, nutty as a pecan pie. Can you imagine!"

"It happens," I said.

I would give Don the phone, and the two of them commiserated. It was an ambience so similar to what I grew up in I felt I might turn around and there would be a steamy-cheeked girl in her flannel nightgown trailing behind me.

Meena and Jerri were allies one minute, enemies the next. Alternately protecting and accusing each other. Strained and formal. Disapproval poured off Jerri like a foul sweat: Meena's eye shadow made her look cheap, her clothes were too tight. *She was a slut, who tempted her own father* (I knew Jerri wanted to say, but didn't quite). Fabric stretched thin between them at that moment two women should come together. When Jerri reached out for her, Meena withdrew. Recoiled was more like it—insolent to the point I wanted to slap her cheeks. What was in that small head, behind silky lashes and brooding dark eyes? Did she blame Mom for all this? . . . If only she'd stop drinking, if she was a better wife, if she'd stop picking and protecting and looking me the twice-over like I'm a streetwalker—those dark eyes flashed. *Just leave me alone.*

Jerri, my poor crazy f'ing sister, erupting without notice. Who knew what might set her off: a thumb-smudged mirror, the Tampax Meena had hidden under her vanity sink. A woman's black pump, spangled in gaudy rhinestones, like a hooker's, which she found in her shoe bag. Jerri threw it into Meena's room, tinkling through bells and trip wires. Where had she stolen it? she demanded. Some girl's locker at school? Meena pounced on the shoe and tucked it away in her cocoon quick as a wink. Gave me the woolly willies. A shoe! What could she want with a shoe?

Later, I caught Don outside his daughter's door. I froze seeing him there, not knowing what he intended. I hadn't heard him come in the house. His mouth to the door crack, a band of light striping his face like a tribal marking—eye, cheek, chin. "Let bygones be bygones," he whispered. Seeing me, he leapt skittishly away.

"What bygones are those?" I asked.

"I wanted to talk, that's all. She's still my daughter, I wanted to talk to her, Deborah."

Meena spun her cocoon from bookshelf to desk to window ledge, creeping up the wall. Driven by some silent anger. Squatting beside a bed lamp inside, reading a book, she looked as if some huge spider had woven her in as a meal for its young. Threads shimmering in lamplight, a gleaming gossamer halo around her. Any girl has her fantasies—horses or autographs or foreign places—but this was fish piss. After months visiting a headshrinker, she was screwier than a mayfly.

I went in for a closer look one day while she was at school. A clever little ape, I'll say. The cocoon's inner layer a finely woven tent of silver thread, fine as silk, the outer a broad mesh of clear nylon monofilament, hundred-pound test. Its strands anchored to desk and walls, forming a support for the rest. At center was a mayonnaise jar and inside that another weave, more snare than web. A fine silk ball hung from its side. Hanging upside down beside it was the spider queen: glossy black, a red hourglass center of her abdomen. I snatched my fingers away, afraid she might come through the glass. At that moment, I didn't know which of them was screwier: my sister or my niece. Crawling about in her own private world, not looking you in the eye, keeping black widows for pets. Runs in families I guess.

I went in later to sit on her bed while Meena huddled in the cocoon. "I want you to come out of there and be a person," I said. "I'd like to talk to you."

"If I can bring Avenger."

"Listen, honey, black widows aren't pets. She can kill you."

Meena laughed. "She doesn't bite." She emerged from her hidey-hole and sat beside me. Slowly opened her fist. The black widow spider crouched in her open palm, legs coiled beneath her. I nearly shit, I'll say. Scared spitless. Meena touched my arm. "Don't excite her," she whispered. How long would it take, I was wondering, before toxin reached her central nervous system. Meena bent over and breathed on the spider. Avenger outstretched her legs pair by pair, long front legs stroking the air. "Isn't she beautiful," Meena said. I might've thought so if I didn't have to worry about losing control of my bowels. Mirror glossy, tiny multiple eyes peering up at us, I swear, aware and watching. She crawled over Meena's palm, trailing a gleaming strand of silk behind. She was a *Latrodectus hesperus*, Meena explained, common locally, not so poisonous as *Latrodectus mactans*. (After all, what was a black widow to the daily dangers of that house?)

She had become tired of her old pet, Lorenzo, so she'd put

Avenger in his jar one day. But the real reason she had got her was to put in Mr. Olsen's mailbox. "That's why I named her Avenger." She grinned at me.

I walked right over to get the mayonnaise jar, tapping it with my nails. "Put her back." The moment she did, I seized her arm. Little shit, she would do no such thing. "Or we're going to squash her right now."

Meena's eyes clouded. "He killed Chester."

"So that makes it right to kill him, is that it?"

She shook her head. Who had hurt her, I wanted to know. Was it Dad? Mom? That whole crazy f'ing . . . I wanted her to tell me what had happened with her father. The truth! She watched my lips as if I spoke a foreign tongue.

"I told Ms. Childlove."

"Told her you slept with your dad?"

She shook her head, reluctant to look me in the eye.

"You didn't tell her?"

Meena was vague, restless, turning the jar in her hands, watching Avenger pick her way through tangled twigs inside to reposition herself upside down under the snare: purposeful, steadfast. Maybe that was the attraction.

Didn't she know what was at stake here? People's lives, her own father's, her family's survival. "Your dad might have to go to jail." She stared at that damned poisonous spider. Exasperated, I shook her. "Meena, will you listen to me. Will you speak up."

"I told her the truth," she mumbled.

"And what is the truth?"

"I got molested at Wendy's pool."

I didn't realize how shaken I would be to hear it. Like an icicle was plunged into my chest. He did that. The bastard really did. The f'ing fuck. He actually did.

# 28

---

# Aunt Debbie

Fog covered the lawn and Don in his sleeping bag. Not a blanket but a fat squashed pillow. Morning dew silvered spiderwebs in the rosebushes and persimmons. I prodded Don awake with a toe. Not friendly, I'll admit. He rolled over, arms folded across his face, expecting Jerri. "Your daughter's in deep shit," I said. "If you had one ounce of decency you'd find yourself a motel room."

He sat up, blinking, fuzzy-edged and ghostly in the fog. "You've got this all wrong, Deborah."

"I don't think so."

Don clambered out of the bag in his shorts, finger speared, "You're outta here. Today, Deborah."

I glanced casual at his boxer shorts. "You ought to take care of that. It looks unhealthy."

Funny, could'a been: Don hopping about with a wake-up erection, pulling on his pants and cursing. Self-pity poured off him like foul air.

Sally arrived that afternoon. Walked right in with her suitcase. "Where's my daughter?" she asked. "I come to talk some sense into this household."

Jerri appeared on cue, frizzy-haired, eyes like two red-hot discs. "Well, looky who the cat dragged in."

"Lord almighty fishhooks," Sally exclaimed. "You look like something they forgot to haul away in the trash."

"Thank you, Mother. You always did have a way with compliments."

"Well, doesn't she?" Sally asked me.

"This is starting out fine. Regular old-time family reunion."

"Doesn't she have any self-respect?" Sally persisted. Skin quivered around Jerri's lips. She turned and walked back down the dim hallway. "Well, my God!" Sally said.

"Yeah. My God! Shut your fucking mouth, Mother."

She tried, I'll give her that. Eight hours maybe. Then she sat her granddaughter down and asked what this nonsense was about, did she wish to ruin her family? Jerri swept Sally off to the bathroom. Couldn't care less who heard—her kids, neighbors, the governor in Sacramento. "You leave Meena alone," she insisted, more rational than she'd been in days. Sober nearly.

"I won't. Not to ruin her daddy's good reputation."

"Which reputation is that: child molester or retired insurance executive?"

"Why, Don wouldn't do a thing like that, you know very well. What would become of you if he went to jail? Did you consider that, Jerri? How do you intend to support yourself?"

"Aren't we cozy. Make my daughter his little whore in exchange for his support, is that what you're suggesting, Mother? Isn't that what you did? Isn't that egg-sactly what you did?" Jerri smiling like she did, right up in Sally's face, I was afraid it would go physical.

"Hush. Why, look at yourself. Go on! Don't you see! They will take your children. Mark my words. Do you think, Jerri . . . In your condition—"

"Not mine! Not my daughter. Over my dead body will I do what you did, Mother. I won't. Maybe I'm a screwup, but I won't have her despise me her whole life for pretending it didn't happen."

Sally drew up and patted her hair. "What are you saying? I'm sorry for you, Jerri, and that's the God's truth. Sometimes a person must be strong and accept the world—ugly as it is."

"Is that what you call it, 'acceptance'? Playing pimp for your own little girl?"

"Hush up. I guess you don't see. You can't sit down and talk to your own husband. It's all the booze."

"You call that a husband—the man who finger-jobbed my baby? How sweet. How lovely cozy."

"My goodness!" Sally cried as if she'd been clobbered by a stick. Retreating from the bathroom, Jerri slammed into me. I could've been a wall.

Ms. Childlove called Thursday afternoon. She had found a

Family Court judge in San Diego who was willing to place Meena in protective custody until her formal interview if Don didn't leave the house at once.

"How thoughtful of him," I said.

She assured me it was the best she could do. The judge wanted to talk to the family first: Meena, Jeffrey and Mama *on her best behavior*. "Do you understand me?"

"What do you mean exactly, *best behavior*?" I asked.

"Don't bullshit me. I know that family better than it knows itself."

"Wouldn't take much."

"Four days ought to give her time to sober up, d'you think?"

"Are you asking or telling? Who exactly do you work for— the Sex Gestapo or the California Thought Police?"

"Do you understand? It would be a *sober* choice."

"Maybe just yourself, because that's what I think. I think you've got your own little private home-wrecking industry going."

There was a pause. "You're the *aunt*, aren't you?" she asked smugly, her question just dripping slime.

"I'm not blow-jobbing my nephew, if that's what you mean."

"Do you think that is funny? Do you think this is a joke?"

"Listen, Miss Lovechild, whatever you call it, your holier-than-thou act doesn't impress me one bit. You may be right about my brother-in-law. Maybe not. But I love those kids. Nobody—d'you hear me!—nobody with all the PSWs and state bullshit licenses on earth is going to tell me what is best for them. They are my family. Flesh and blood."

She snorted as if I'd said something ridiculous. "We'll see."

"That's the joke. Just plain. What trouble there is in that family, you don't know the start of it."

"Maybe you'd like to tell me," she said sweetly, the smell of grape lipstick coming right through the line.

"Tell the Devil maybe! I'd like to know what my niece told you. We're in the dark here."

"Better you don't know. We wouldn't want anyone accused of coaching her. We must protect Meena's interests."

"Coaching her!" I laughed. "What are Meena's *interests* exactly, if I may ask."

"Monday, ten A.M. sharp, Mama sober." She hung up.

Sure thing! Tie Jerri to the bed, fill her full of Freon.

Sally had that much right anyway: They walked into your home, tried and convicted whomever they pleased. People complained about Russia!

We managed somehow to convince Jerri to get a grip. No telling what that judge might do—take her kids if it suited him. I measured out booze, six ounces a day. You couldn't expect a drunk on such a roll to go cold turkey, she'd get the DTs. Some picture: The three Simonet women sitting in a row at the dining bar, me pouring, Sally eyeballing, Jerri bottoms up. Her two kids watching like solemn monkeys. "Mom's on a cure," she told them. "Soon as this thing's over she'll quit for good. She promises."

Sure thing. I think she half-believed it.

After the hearing on Monday, Jerri stood staring out at the backyard, an overgrown rosebush in one corner, snagged branches and thorns, an apricot tree sprouting bright green leaves, bougainvillea a tangled chaos along the fence, invading ice plant in a deadly mutual stranglehold where it met the slope to Wendy-Lindy's above. Maybe she saw her own predicament in that slow green death march. Don had twenty-four hours to vacate the premises, else Meena would go into protective custody—an emergency-care psychiatric facility for kids. Push had come to shove. There was no going back. Maybe she had her doubts. The judge said it didn't look like anyone in the household was fit to raise children.

"Can you imagine?" Sally was scandalized. Easily.

That night as we sat together on the patio, I told Mom about Mort. It was a balmy evening, full of crickets and mock orange perfume. You wouldn't guess there was a house full of anger behind us. Don refused to leave; his lawyer advised *under no circumstances*. Last I looked, my sister lay facedown on a fluffy throw rug in her bedroom. Any luck, she might inhale enough synthetic fiber to asphyxiate. The kids were asleep. The house seemed normal almost.

I told Sally how Mort had complimented my hand bones. Corniest come-on I ever heard. "He's an orthopedic surgeon from Portland who specializes in hand reconstruction. We got to exchanging stories about great come-ons. Him at the hospital, me flying. I'd go away and handle the cart awhile, then come back and tell him about my keys: the a-hole from Dallas who asked me did I know what they meant by 'Longhorn State'; I said I wasn't sure, but didn't they say the more a man's wife sleeps around the longer his horn grows. We got to laughing. Mort's favorite was a surgical nurse who specialized in plaster casts of new interns' penises. The whole hospital was in on it. They'd cast bets on how new doctors would respond when she approached them—kept a tally board in the nurses' lounge listing the 'pricks' and the 'prudes.' Pretty soon I was plain ignoring a party of turdheads across the aisle. Lawyer types, drunk and obnoxious, flying to a football game in Seattle. Whooping and hollering about how they needed a drink. I told them they'd had enough. 'Do you believe her,' they'd say. Mort winked and said, ' 'Atta girl.' Would you believe I gave him my phone number? Imagine! Me dating an MD."

Sally pursed her lips. "I don't know why not."

I told her I'd had enough. Fed up to here with my sister's family. Couldn't say who was more selfish—Don and his slick lawyer or Jerri and her bottle. What's the use? They don't intend to save themselves, can't anyone do it for them. They couldn't care less about their little girl who was about to be put in a loony bin.

"You can't blame Don for refusing to confess to what he didn't do. Well, it don't surprise me any." She frowned. "You've never given a thought to a person in this world beyond yourself, Deborah. That's your whole trouble."

Predictable, I guess you'd say. Strangely, it didn't bother me one bit. Let her believe what she liked. There would be a hearing and all this nonsense cleared up, she said. Family room light a glowing nimbus in her puffed silver hair, illuminating gargoyle glasses frames, catching the white of an eye. Give her another life and opportunity, Mom would've made a politician. She had a regular genius for sweeping things under the rug. I told her so. Then leaned over to kiss her forehead, surprising her.

"Well, it's my generation," she said, bashfully. "What use exaggerating our troubles. Trouble attracts trouble."

" 'Damage control' they call it now."

I went to sleep in Olson's room. Packing my suitcase, sorting his drawers where I'd put my things, I discovered a bra stuffed away in a corner. Some girlfriend's, I supposed. It was a house full of secrets. I stuffed it back into a jumble of old T-shirts and underwear and shut the drawer. I was washing my hands. I had my own life to live.

# 29

---

# Jeff

We sat around the hugest table I ever saw, half an acre of dark shiny walnut. Nothing on it but just a name tag at the head: HON. HENRY M. SILVER. Leather-bound law books all around the walls: California Penal Code. Olson would prob'ly say they listed the size of every guy's penal gland in California, but I knew it was really law books.

"All rise!" barked the clerk when Judge Silver entered. He dropped his jacket over a high-backed burgundy leather chair and sat down with a squawk. He wore red suspenders, which surprised me. He had a gravelly beard and thick amber-tinted glasses. Didn't look at us, only nodded, and we sat down. He looked a lot like I imagined God might look. But I saw from Ms. Goona Childlove and the lawyer lady we shouldn't look at him. Except Meena did. And Mom in her sunglasses. All gussied up in a white suit with blue piping around the sleeves and collar and her white oyster hoop earrings which matched her sunglasses frames. Meena wore an Eastery yellow dress that made her look like a sunflower. I had to wear my suit.

We didn't dare drive Mom's wagon to the courthouse because of the golf course incident; we took Aunt Debbie's rental car instead.

On the way, Grandma Sally warned Meena not to "speak a word against your father, not in my presence." Her and Mom started yelling. It was all I could do to get them to cool it. Now they sat side by side looking straight ahead. My gonadal sister stared furiously at the judge. Really dumb. A judge could lock you up and throw away the key. Grandma Sally blurted out how she admired his library. "Shhh," the clerk hissed. She was an old lady who looked like Danner the Banana's secretary. Later, Grandma Sally called her a "clucky old coot."

Judge Silver said "Proceed" and the clerk read something about the court being in session, though wasn't any courtroom or jury or anything. Grandma whispered at Mom to take off her glasses, Judge Silver shot her a look, the lady lawyer cleared her throat. It was worse than detention in there. A trickle of rouge-colored sweat rolled down Mom's cheek and clung to her jaw. I watched, wondering when it would drip off. Goona watched, too. The part in her apricot hair was white as a bone; it fascinated me. I couldn't decide whether I hated Meena more for starting rumors about Dad, or Goona for putting her up to it, or myself for ratting on Olson in the first place—because I figured Meena did it in revenge for Dad beating Olson up.

Goona's yellow eyes bumped at me, and I looked away fast. It was like a vacuum cleaner reached into my brain and sucked out the old contents: me wiping scrambled eggs off Mom's chin, hangers jangling all by themselves in the entry-hall closet, Mom sinking thumbs in my shoulders and saying she knew I had a secret I was keeping from her (but I wouldn't tell even under torture), even Olson's letters threatening he would cut off my nuts . . . Goona smiled like we were allies. Then she watched Mom, scared maybe her speech would slur, like Lily Lunchcakes, the lady bum in Millford. But Mom wasn't any Lily Lunchcakes. Nosy witch. Who gave her permission to investigate our family?

Judge Silver asked the lady lawyer why Grandma Sally came.

"I'm representing the father," Grandma said smartly.

The judge's forehead knit. "You are his legal counsel?"

"No, sir, a plain ordinary free American citizen."

The judge frowned, the lady lawyer cleared her throat and said she was petitioning that Goona be appointed guardian ad litem for Meena; I didn't like the sound of it. He raised a hand. "First things first." He turned to my mom. "Is the girl often alone with her father?"

"N-no," she said. "Not anymore."

He was studying Meena, twice as stern as Danner the Banana. His lips thin as razor blades (Aunt Debbie says never trust anyone with thin lips). "Is she eating well? Sleeping? Showing signs of—Would you mind removing those silly goldarned sunglasses! It's like talking to a mirror." Grandma Sally snatched the glasses off Mom's nose.

"I'm waiting," he said.

"What does he want to know?" Mom whispered at me.

"Mrs. Tillotson, are you under the influence? Your eyes look like glazed apples."

Goona and the lady lawyer exchanged a glance.

"My daughter put that behind her," Grandma Sally said.

"Strike that," the judge told the clerk. He glared at Grandma. "I'll have her speak for herself."

"Yes, sir." Grandma's nostrils widened.

"Mrs. Tillotson? I'm waiting—"

Mom tilted her head back. "Never touch the stuff. Maybe I had a bitsy problem once."

"Bitsy, did you? Look at me when you answer, young woman."

Meena looked up with a startled smile, then turned to glare at me. She'd hated me since I blitzed her room yesterday—after Grandma and me tried talking sense into her thick head, how they would put Dad in jail. She was a total douchebag if he had to move out, and I would hate her guts. She had just sat there in her so-called "cocoon," holding Lorenzo's jar between her knees, stroking it and playing deaf and dumb. I couldn't figure her out. She knew she was lying, she knew it wasn't Dad that night at Wendy's pool (Dad wouldn't never do anything grotty as that), she knew it would ruin our family, but she wouldn't come off it. So I got mad and ripped her dumb cocoon to shreds. While Grandma said, "That'll do, Jeffrey," and my sister just sat there, covered by gauzy cobweb strings like the Crypt Lady at the Del Mar Fun House, whispering at her dumb spider bottle: "We'll get even, don't worry." Now her fingers picked at lace-work around her dress collar like it was a spiderweb.

Judge Silver asked the lady lawyer did the family have a history of alcohol abuse. "We believe there are more pressing concerns," she answered. "We're requesting Meena be placed in protective custody if the father doesn't leave home at once." Judge Silver said he'd decide which issues were most pressing. He didn't like bossy women. But didn't mind when the lady lawyer spoke for our family like he had when Grandma Sally did. Really weird. She kept saying "we," though none of us ever saw her before in our life. They talked mumbo jumbo about a "brief amicus," and Mom snapped the clasp of her purse with a tiny metal pop.

Suddenly Judge Silver swiveled toward me. "Young man, has anyone at home touched you in a way you didn't like?"

For a second I panicked. His eyes were unblinking thumbtacks pushed into his face. I stared at his peppery eyebrows and tried not to gulp. "No," I said in a small voice, "only I slipped on the bathroom rug once and cracked my head on the toilet by accident." Mom studied her nails, Goona the Freak watched me with a gooey caramel smile, Judge Silver squinted an eye. None of them believed me. His eyes were like jellied fish eggs with hooks waiting inside. Ten thousand times colder than the deputy sheriff's when they called me down to the office over the PA system. I thought it was about the golf course, but the deputy asked did I ever see anything funny at home? Did Dad ever go swimming with my sister at night? No, I said, the God's truth. So he got less suspicious.

"Have you witnessed anyone touching your sister?"

"Of course he hasn't," blurted Grandma Sally.

The judge's finger shot out. "I won't tolerate these outbursts. Once more and I will hold you in contempt." Really pee-o'd.

"Well, you don't expect—" Grandma broke off.

"I expect the truth, young fellow."

My sister glared at Judge Silver, the jerk, right in plain public.

"What's the hesitation? Are you listening?"

My voice creaked like an old door, 'cause it was like lying to God. "Waw-once I saw Toby Olsen . . . you know—"

"Know what?"

"Goose her," I whispered.

"Have you ever seen your father *goose* her?"

"No sir, I didn't."

"Tell me about your mother's drinking." The judge swiveled and leaned back with a squawk of his chair.

My mouth barely had spit to talk. "No, sir, I can't."

"Can't!" He laughed and squawked forward, his head bigger even than Grandma Sally's, eyes magnified behind tinted glasses. I knew any second he would ask about the golf course. (Kids at school were all talking about how a drunk lady tore up the course, and two kids helped her make a getaway. Biggest crime in town. They said it was Mexicans, because everything got blamed on the Mexicans. Mom kept her Ford in the garage ever since, but Toby Olsen was suspicious; except all you had to say was "cobbler head" and he turned red and started sulking.)

Judge Silver folded his arms on the table. "You don't want to talk about it?"

"No, she doesn't drink anymore, I mean. Except iced tea."

Judge Silver chuckled and opened his hands at the lady lawyer. "Who doesn't like iced tea?"

My armpits were soaked, my throat so tight I knew I couldn't answer another question. I stared so hard at a calendar behind him that Judge Silver turned around to look. Maybe I'd just spill it, I thought. Get it off my chest. I wasn't used to lying for real. Truth tiptoed out on my tongue like a determined kid on the high dive. The very next question I knew it would jump. But the lawyer lady saved me, reminding the judge that the amicus plea applied only to the girl.

"I'm aware of that. Is it your intention to preside over these proceedings then, Miss Pasternak?"

"I assure you it isn't, your honor. But we feel as long as the father is in the home it isn't a fit atmosphere—"

"I doubt either parent is fit." Judge Silver turned to Mom.

"Nonsense," grumbled Grandma Sally.

"Pardon?" snapped the clerk. The judge glared.

Grandma ducked and patted her throat. "Just clearing my pipes."

The judge aimed a file folder at her. "You're lucky I'm in a good mood this morning, young lady."

Meena laughed, because Grandma was older than him. His chair squawked. "I'm getting to you, Miss Tillotson."

Meena slumped down and glared at him, playing first-wink-is-a-rat-fink, her face barely above the table. He didn't impress her for beans. I was never so amazed by my sister in my life. Maybe playing spider strengthens a person's character. But when Judge Silver asked us to step outside so he could talk to her in private, Meena looked spooked. As we went out, I heard him say, "Would you sit up straight so I can see you, Miss Tillotson, please."

"I'll be right out here, honey," Mom said.

Outside his chambers, the lady lawyer introduced herself: Louise Pasternak, special prosecutor. Smiling an honest-to-goodness smile, not like Goona the Freak, with her creepy-crawly eyebrows and orange hair with the perfect white part down the center, like she was made up of spare parts from the fun house. Ms. Pasternak told us she'd been away in Guatemala. "I'm studying the child-raising methods of indigenous peoples," she said. But Mom stared at the judge's chambers door like she expected The Mummy to walk out any second.

Grandma Sally asked why couldn't they sit down and talk reasonably together like adults. "There isn't any need to tear up the family. Don isn't what you take him for." I could see Ms. Pasternak didn't want to talk to her. She said it was best to remove Meena from home if there was even the slightest possibility. "I'm staying there," Grandma persisted.

Ms. Pasternak apologized to Mom for postponing Meena's interview so long. There were lots of cases backed up and it wouldn't be for two more weeks. "Meena will be one of our first children to be videotaped," she said. "Closed-circuit television is a powerful new prosecuting tool in child-abuse cases."

"That's not fair," I blurted. "What if she's making it up and everybody's watching?"

Ms. Pasternak laughed. "Not that kind of TV. Only in the courtroom."

Goona the Freak stooped into my face, smelling of stale coffee and grainy rouge. "You know children don't lie about important things, Jeffrey. Small things but not important things."

I gawped at her. Maybe she wasn't never a kid or never had to make anything up.

"I don't want blood," Mom said. "I just want *that man* to stay away from my little girl." I guess she meant Dad.

"We wouldn't wish to see him put in jail," Grandma insisted.

Ms. Pasternak didn't want to discuss it. After the interview, they would decide whether to press charges. "I came down to meet Meena today. I find it helpful to have a relationship with a child before I interview her, to establish trust. Beyond that, I like to keep an open mind. I assure you, we're very sensitive to the family's wishes in incest cases." She smiled at me.

"Oh pee hooks," Grandma Sally said. "You don't care ten cents about the truth. You already have him tried and convicted and locked in the hoosegow."

Just then Meena came back out.

"See, that wasn't so bad," Goona said.

"He's a pukehead," Meena replied.

The grown-ups laughed nervously. "My sentiments exactly," Ms. Pasternak whispered. I could tell Meena liked her. A bad sign already.

That night our house was like tag-team wrestling: Grandma Sally versus Mom and Aunt Debbie. I went out and sat in my wigwam beside Chester's grave, trying to figure it out. It was a half-moon out—creepy and beautiful at once, making ghosts of the eucalyptus and mesquite trees. Crickets sang in the brush around me, but all I heard was thoughts tumbling in my head. If I hadn't ratted on Olson, Dad would never have got so mad; and Meena wouldn't have got so mad at Dad for beating up her boyfriend—even if it's sicko to have your half-brother for a boyfriend, but Meena was weird like that—or mad because she thought he blamed her for making Olson horny, or mad about the girlfriend whose shoe she stole. Dad was mad at Mom for boozing; Mom was mad at him because of Meena. Grandma Sally was mad at Mom for believing Dad really did it (which made me mad, too); Mom was mad at Grandma for taking Dad's side . . . or just for being her mother, because girls are spastic that way. I was pee-o'd at Meena because of her dumb accusations, and she was pee-o'd at me 'cause I blitzed her cocoon. It was complicated. It made my head ache thinking it out. But mostly it made me sick thinking I started it all by squealing.

Then I had an awful thought: Maybe Dad's girlfriend really was Meena. That's why she got so jealous at the fair and Dad got so pissed at Olson—out of jealousy. Like rival boyfriends fighting after school. Maybe my sister was telling the truth. If her own brother could do that, why couldn't her dad? No! That was stupid. But after you think something scuzzy it catches like a cocklebur in the folds of your brain and you can't get it out. In my mind, I saw Dad hanging from the diving board and couldn't get rid of the image. Then it hit me.

The image wouldn't erase until I told everyone what I really saw, because guilt is like a boil which won't heal until you lance it and relieve the pressure. If I told, it would start a chain reaction of truth, like it started a chain reaction of lies when I ratted on Olson. If we all told the truth the chain would break. Mom would admit her boozing and Dad would forgive her; Meena would tell the truth and Mom would forgive Dad; Olson would whale on me so I didn't feel guilty anymore. We were stuck in a web of lies and wouldn't be free until we cut every single strand.

I ran up the path to tell them my discovery. The house glowed like a fluorescent tube in the moonlight, brighter than I ever saw it before. I would burst into the family room, interrupt the fighting and tell them the secret to saving our family was secrecy itself. Grandma Sally would laugh her crinkly laugh, Dad would chuckle, Mom and Aunt Debbie would remember they were sisters again and hug each other, while my spas sister hop-hopped across the floor, plunk into Dad's lap. Then we'd remember it was Easter tomorrow. Mom and Grandma would boil eggs; we'd get out dye packets and dipping hoops and Dad would show us how to do swirly cool psychedelic patterns by putting salad oil in the dye, while Meena held her nose against the sharp vinegar smell.

But the house was dark inside, Dad's car gone, Mom's door closed, Grandma Sally snored on the couch. It was already too late. By next morning Aunt Debbie had left. Meena was packing. Soon Goona would pick her up to take her to Riverside. Grandma sat on her rumpled covers looking like an old lady.

On Monday, Toby Olsen and Daryl Fox cornered me in the boys' lavatory. All I could think was the time Daryl cracked a kid's head against his knee and threw him unconscious into a urinal then peed in his face. But Daryl only pinned my arms while Piggy Olsen slugged me. I didn't feel nothing but blood-red explosions inside my brain, sending out angry spasms each time his fist landed. A line of startled faces blurred behind Toby's head. "This one's for your brother, rat fink, this one's for the peach cobbler, pansy fuck. . . . " I understood they were Olson's avengers, evening up the score. So I stood and took every punch until Piggy was panting too hard to continue. I knew Meena prob'ly told Olson I was watching that night at the pool to make him stop, but I wasn't mad at her. They were breaking the chain of lies.

"You're brave for a coward," Daryl said, when he let go of me. My knees gave out and I slumped down on the dirty floor. Some kids helped me down to the nurse.

Dad was hopping mad when he came to pick me up. Couldn't even look at my face, only slammed his fist in his hand and spoke without opening his lips. He wanted to crack their punk heads together. But I said they were visiting wrestlers from another school. They already left on their team bus.

# 30

# Meena

The hall was lined with clowns' faces and black horses with sad turquoise eyes, weirdso-nerdso drawings sketched in charcoal: women with crazy shattered hair and lopsided eyes.

"Retros do them, mostly," Tiffany explained, leading Meena along the hall to Cottage C where she would sleep. Tiffany's upper lip curled eloquently as she spoke, hunched and crawled. She halted before an earless elephant. It had a dangling blue rubber trunk—a finger cut from a glove—and long sexy eyelashes. It made Meena's skin crawl. "Ork that shit! Gotta be Alvin Zit," Tiffany exclaimed, "A-one bona fide fruit loop. Show him a zit, Alvin'll pop it for you and suck out the scuzz. He lives for it. Like he shouldn't be here at all but over in permanent. Riverside's for temporaries and freak-outs, not air cadets. What you in for?" Gum-chawing, blasé brown eyes rolling at Meena.

"Child molestation."

"Ooh-la. Naughty naughty."

"The other way I mean."

Tiffany shrugged. "BFD, like who isn't? Y'r mom or y'r dad?"

"My dad," Meena managed, scandalized.

"Like you wanna let it torpedo y'r life or what? Rule number two"—Tiffany seized the Rubbermaid trunk and amputated it with an elastic pop—"Isn't serious unless it's Code Blue and dripping blood out its anus. Right? In here you don't keep priorities straight you go potatoes."

She had decided Tiffany was boss. At school, girls like Tiff never paid her the slightest attention. Here they were already best friends. Meena ground the trunk into the floor with her shoe heel and smiled shyly at her new friend. Tiffany clamped fingers to her nose and flattened against the wall, motioning Meena to do likewise. "Bowel control alert! Aliens!" she snorkeled. Meena gripped her nose just as she was hit by the sweet smell of human shit. A phalanx of shuffling, open-mouthed retards approached—bulbous heads and round eyes turning to gawk as they shuffled past. Balloon-headed space creatures, Meena thought. Gave her the willies. Tiffany copped an attitude as she watched them trudge on—nodding, lip crawling: "Think you got problems, ork them bananas. Shows the patheticity of the human race." She shrugged. "Can't help it, they're born that way. Brain zero."

Ms. Childlove had parked before a great complex of low buildings spread out in a kind of maze. The lawns brown in places, not nearly so ample as Tranquility Acres. "It's homey inside," Ms. Childlove had assured her. She took Meena to meet Dr. Langerhorn, a brisk, chubby, curly-haired woman, who sat her down with two tests (she called them "instruments"). The Thematic Apperception Test: Dr. Langerhorn showed her weird pictures and Meena made up stories about them. She answered carefully, guessing if she flunked they'd never send her home. The second was easier—Forer Structured Sentence Completion Test:

"*Sometimes she wished she* . . . turned into a tarantula."

"*At times she worried about* . . . being a slut."

"*Nobody knew that she* . . . knew everybody's secrets."

Dr. Langerhorn glanced over her answers and nodded. She summoned Tiffany from cottage. "Tiffany's an old hand here."

Dr. Langerhorn smiled, putting an arm around the slender, pretty, dark-haired girl when she came in. "This is her third visit with us."

"Would you mind!" Tiffany shrugged her off and copped a stance—feet apart, gum-chewing. "Rule number one: Never trust a doctor. Especially sike-eye-atrists, they're the worst." Meena was fascinated by the lip doing gymnastics over Tiffany's perfect white teeth.

Langerhorn laughed briskly. "No one can make 'psychiatrist' sound so much like a curse word. I love it." Going serious. "I'm counting on you to teach our new sign-in the ropes, kiddo. No bull."

Nodding, chewing, lip in peristalsis, Tiffany gave Meena the once-over. "She'll do."

No matter the lawns, artwork, brightly painted rooms, Meena wasn't fooled. It was a barless prison. Scorched California mountains watched relentlessly in the distance. No matter you could say anything you liked in group—*I'm gonna cut off my dad's dick and feed it to him in a bun*—and Dr. Langerhorn or swami Assami just looked at you. Other people sinned against you and you were locked up for it. *C'mon, vent! Spill! Release!* they'd cry at evening "clear out" sessions ("psycho-babble," Tiffany called it), while Doctors Langerhorn, Sanger or Assami scribbled notes on tiny spiral pads slipped in and out of jacket pockets. "What are they writing?" she asked Tiffany early on.

"You don't wanna know."

Dr. Assami mumbled into a tiny Sony recorder.

"Hey, man," kids would cry, "Assami's writing you up." Assam the Assassin, so mild, cool and dogged.

It made Meena nervous. No secrets! It was like a near-fatal dose of honesty after the secrecy of home. The two most disorienting weeks of her life. Threatening to transform her from a spider to a fly. Twelve kids to a cottage. Acute care. Meaning they were there because there was nowhere else to send them. All of them abused somehow—depressed, suicidal, antisocial, substance abusers, "behavior disorders," like Tiffany.

"I loved that," she told the others years later. "Somebody else's behavior fucked you up and *you* were 'disordered.' The place brimmed with society's early success stories. Not tragedies, not accidents, not fuck-ups. Victims every one."

Donald tried to hang a kid at school. Crissy Crabmeat beat up on her kid sister. Always smiling, that one. Cottage mascot. She got her nickname from pudgy Dungeness-pink cheeks round as elf buns. Meena's first night, Crissy slipped down her pajama bottoms and showed where her mom had scorched her ass with a hot iron: hard wrinkled weals of red-purple skin glazed like plastic bags melted together. Riverside was a crash course in the world's strangeness. Crissy loved to flash her wounds—proud and horrified at once. "Mom stopped doing it after she got caught," Crissy said, like that made it okay. Tiffany was almost wholesome. She'd been thrown out of five Sacramento high schools. Pretty boss, Meena thought. "I'm a tramp, a vamp, I make 'em damp," Tiffany boasted. Bobbie was borderline Alien, a living contradiction: Down's syndrome and brilliant. A retard who wrote incredible poetry. Tooth braces and an ungainly, gatelegged stance. In for threatening her stepmother with a butcher knife. When her parents visited, Meena saw it all: Dad was a sour old man, the stepmother a meek Mongolian idiot (like Bobbie's own mother). All of them were front-line casualties of what the simpletons called "family values."

At first Meena sat quietly, feeling out of place at nightly "clear out" sessions with Doctors Assami or Langerhorn. Orderlies came and went, dispensing zombie pills from tiny paper cups. Tall, tough Kim, whose hair was cut in a Mohawk, and who'd adopted Meena as a pet, doodled hearts and daggers on her jeans. When, rarely, she had something to contribute, it came in brief, violent outbursts. Meena would watch Kim's biceps tense beneath rolled black T-shirt sleeves. Peace symbols and slogans—"Meth Kills," "Eat Shit and Die"—tightened across her denimed thighs. Softly, Kim would say, "I'm going off, I need time out." Or she'd just blow. Orderlies appeared out of nowhere to rush her to the crisis room. "Anger grows inside my stomach," Kim explained, "like a sun is scorching my guts and I got to go off." Tiffany said Kim had one forward speed: "pissed-fucking-off." Kim wouldn't tell what made her that way.

The walls, floors pulsed with raw emotional energy. At first it terrified her. There were no breathless whispers or euphemisms, none of Ms. Childlove's hints or Mom's tense, conspiratorial silences. Everything was right up front. Ten-year-old Sydney talked about candlesticks inserted up his asshole. No one blinked an eye.

"Birthday or dinner tapers," Tiffany asked.

"Suck mine," Sydney answered. His cousin blow-jobbed him, he said, when he visited Seattle last summer. "All's I want to know is am I queer?"

"Obvious question." Donald laughed.

"Did you enjoy it?" asked Crissy Crabmeat.

"What's that prove? You can enjoy taking a crap without being an asshole," Tiffany said.

"All right, that's enough," said swami Assami.

But Meena knew what Sydney meant. She'd often wondered the same thing. Molestation didn't just happen to you; there had to be a reason.

Fourteen-year-old alcoholic Monica, who possessed Mom's incipient puffiness of eyes and mouth, her same smoldering melancholy—only Monica's hair was brown and perfectly straight—insisted she had a right to kill herself and she would try again.

"That's corny," Bobbie yelled.

"That's fucked," said Donald.

But Monica persisted in a monotone so like Mom's it gave Meena the creeps. "I've already lived my adulthood and I'll tell you something, it sucks. I'll kill myself if I feel like it."

"Big deal," Jessica said. "I got cheated out of my childhood, too. It isn't any reason to kill yourself."

"You planning to be a social worker or something?" asked Tiffany, gum smacking, lip furling.

"Ease off on the personal," advised Assami.

Kim doodled in her dark way, muttering to herself.

"My father molested me when I was five years old," Monica said. "And he never stopped."

"So what. My dad molested me, too. Doesn't mean I can't have a good life. Like you gotta rise above it, h'ya know, got to leave the past be past and forget about it. Make your own self-image by yourself."

Dr. Assami wanted to talk about that. Meena studied the girls, trying to detect outward signs they had been molested.

Monica glared at Assami. "My parents don't give a damn about me, I don't have any parents. You know who's my family?

The bums on Jay Street. Like, if I do them, I could share their bottle."

"Bummer," laughed Donald. "You suck bums?"

"Retro! For a bottle of Lancers?" Tiffany's lip furled. The others were impressed. "Case in point," Tiffany said coolly. "You think it won't like raunch her life, somebody like her"—nodding at Monica, Jessica, Meena—"her and her! Their life is already predicted. Hundred percent! Jessica's gonna marry like a replay of her dad who molests his brats. Monica's kids will be lushes. Sydney's would be fags if he had any. And Meena! Whaddayathink?" She shrugged. "It's all like genes and astrology and like that. Zipporooni you can do about it. Aliens produce Aliens. Lushes beget lushes. Scientific fact."

Everybody protested at once. Bobby waved her arms, shrieking, "That's corny." Shep, the new boy, watched it unfold, wide-eyed, subdued—as Meena did. Beside him, Kim etched her arm with a ballpoint pen: A bright bead of blood bloomed and trickled into a rut. She smiled at Meena, her eyes bright and wild. "I'm going off," she whispered. Visions of yellow-shirted goons loomed in the room. "Chill out," younger kids chanted. Meena tried to comprehend what Tiffany meant by that glib, gum-clacking "whaddayathink." Though the answer seemed obvious enough to everyone else.

"That's what really pisses me off, h'ya know," Jessica was saying. "Most people don't got to grow up so fast and lose their whacham-a-call-it—innosense. We never got to be kids."

A small riot of agreement. Bobbie grinning her horrid metal grin.

"What do you think, Meena?"

Assami's question startled her. She had never known kids like this. The kids she knew were preoccupied with bra sizes and *American Bandstand*; they wanted to lose their innocence as fast as possible, they weren't bemoaning its loss. She had never felt like one of them. They were looking at her, waiting.

"Spiders have hundreds of babies," she mumbled. "Maybe some women, too. Maybe we're all really brothers and sisters from the same family, but they split us up 'cause they were scared to keep us together, so they sneaked us into different hospitals and told our fake mothers we were their babies. But when they saw we were different they took away our childhood to punish us. Now we're back together again." The others gawked at her, Tiffany's gum-smacking stopped, Kim looked up from her self-mutilation. "Far out," whispered Shep; Bobbie made a joyful gurgling sound in her throat (Meena was afraid she would lurch forward and hug her). "Fucking fuckinay," said weirdo Donald. Dr. Assami smiled. "I agree . . . metaphorically, of course."

Meena was as astonished as anyone. She had no idea what was riding around in her own head. Later, Shep asked if she wanted to watch TV with him. She sat beside him in the cottage common room, stiff as a new shoe, pleased when he slipped his arm around her, liking the way he tossed a brown lock of hair out of his eyes. Her first real date. If only Mrs. Clark, their cottage mother, would leave the room, he might kiss her. Meena stared ahead and saw nothing but a spiky cardiograph picture of her own heartbeat pulsing across the screen.

Later, she couldn't sleep. Oddly, she missed the familiar craziness of home, shut away among freaks in a craziness more indomitable, destined, she was sure, to spend her life locked up among Aliens who whisper-spittled in her ear: *Feelings are corny. I hate feelings.* A swath of yellow light from the open door striped Crissy Crabmeat's cheeks. Tiffany tossed and muttered on her cot. When Meena closed her eyes, tattooed snakes twined up fleshy poles, bleeding heart-eyes leered at her from sunken sockets. But she couldn't keep them open for fear Bobbie's flashing braces would appear in the door crack—a butcher knife in her fist. For an instant, a huge steam iron flattened Crissy Crabmeat on her cot, steam hissed out from beneath, filling the room with the odor of scorched flesh. Then it was gone. "Dear God"—she was praying—"I'm really sorry. Tomorrow I'm calling Mom and telling her it was a mistake. Please, I don't want Alvin to suck my zits. Please let me out."

"I lay my cheek against the cool plaster wall and felt suddenly serene. The wall was glazed like the rock in the Long Loops' cave, slightly moist. I knew it was 'the Rock'—mine—its feet resting against the earth, and all I had to do . . . Getting carefully from bed, watching to be sure Mrs. Clark didn't trudge past in the hall, I grabbed a pencil stub from the desk, crawled under my bed, caring nothing about dust mice or the dried snot turds of former inmates. Carefully, I scrawled my secret in tiny letters: Proof, when the time came. *Dad never touched me.* Under there, I lay my cheek against the cool wall and fell asleep."

They called her "Spider" and Kim said she was bitchin' and tattooed a spiderweb on her back in black ink with Avenger poised at its center. It was a work of art. Aliens stopped to ork when she passed in the hall. A boss sign of respect, because Aliens are wise inside their balloon-headed spasticity. She often thought Boney was half Alien. Bobbie asked Meena if she would pretend to be her when Bobbie's parents visited, nearly peeing her pants in glee. And she did actually impersonate Crissy Crabmeat when cops came to take her to court. Except the trick was discovered before they got out of the parking lot. "Shit city," Tiffany said.

They sat around the cottage dining table one night trying to decide on Shep's initiation. Fake a schizoid, Tiffany suggested. "Pretend you're seeing hallucinations, walking eyeballs and stuff." Nah, Shep said, he saw crap like that all the time. Jessica, who was nervous as her dad's trial approached, suggested he fake suicide. Monica proposed he play Alien lion tamer in gym when Mr. Eisenglass went out for a smoke. When Eyeglass returned, the Aliens would all be up on chairs balancing on one foot and growling. Shep threw back his blond hair and said cool. A tall, gentle boy. You'd never guess he was in for punching out a teacher. A boss idea, they agreed. Girls volunteered to donate bras for a whip. (They'd taken away their belts to keep them from hanging themselves. "Retro stupid," Kim said. "If you want to hang yourself nothing works better than bras tied together.")

When the boys left, table talk turned to sex horror stories. The girls tried to outdo each other: golden-haired Katie's communal travels with her mom, aunt and assorted hitchhikers in a hippie microbus—they traded sex for dope and traded Katie, too, if anybody asked; Jessica had played little wife to her father since she was nine; Monica of the straight brown hair and nerdso glasses, who looked like a junior college professor, grossed them out with stories of winos whose clothes reeked of vomit, shit and sweat. Nobody could outdo Monica. Yet she seemed perfectly normal. If such things happened to them, Meena wondered, why couldn't they happen to her. Perhaps they had. Ms. Childlove thought so.

After telling of her own sex-ploits, Tiffany goaded her, "Speak, kiddorooney, last of the Meenicans, like spill." Their bright, eager upturned faces, as if they were discussing a school dance. Kim looked up expectantly from the Corvette she was tattooing on her biceps to match the one she'd tattooed on Shep—that two-timing dork. *He's mine, you bitch. All mine. I engraved his heart on the rock under my bed; I wrapped his comb in thread and put it in my shoe.*

So she told how her dad kissed her on the mouth when she climbed up the pool ladder, then her breasts, and when she dived in to escape, her older brother pinned her against the bottom. First he, you know, down there . . .

"He fucked you on the bottom of the pool?"

"Then my dad. I almost drowned. His dick looked like a fish."

"Men suck scum," Kim snarled.

"Impossible," Monica was saying, "not humanly possible."

"Y'know, up on top while I held the pool rim. Swear to God! My younger brother watched the whole thing. You can ask him."

"A family affair," cried Tiffany. "Farrr-out."

They were impressed, orking, freak-out city. Tiffany giving her the high five. Awwwwright, Meena.

"That was just once," she told them. Status comes in every-sized package. There it came kinky, twisted, the wrapping torn away and spoiled goods revealed inside. Meena basked in their respect. Except she couldn't remember where the fiction ended and truth began. She remembered Ms. Childlove's furrowed brow, her face cinching up like a drawstring tobacco bag and her own giddy, drunken sense of power as she played any tune she wanted on her keys. She was feeling that same power now. Revenge was like a bitter, caustic wine, satisfying and dyspeptic at once. She had no idea what the consequences would be.

She remembered looking into Olson's reptilian eyes, warning, "Boney's watching." To end it. Cotton pajama top floating like seaweed around her neck. She wanted to run back to shower and peel off her skin. Ms. Childlove's threats later: She didn't dare get expelled from school; Mom would have a conniption. An exasperated sheriff's deputy seated across a narrow table from her. "Who did this to you?" he demanded. "Someone in your family? Your father?" He couldn't bring himself to say what they'd done. But he was convinced of it. "Young lady, I need a *name*, I've got to have a name." Pencil poised above a form, cheeks folding into jowls.

She never gave him one. "Don't call me 'young lady,' " she sulked.

He told Ms. Childlove, "I don't know what we have here." Anyone less intrepid than her would have given up there and then.

That night, Monica and Tiffany distracted Mrs. Clark and Shep slipped into the dorm with Meena. *A vamp, a tramp, I make 'em damp.* Drinking in his kisses, his earthy hayfield smell, Meena guessed it was his first time, too, by the wondrous way he touched and nibbled and giggled—fumbling with the catch on her bra. It wasn't the groping, slamming she'd known before. Hurrying for fear Mrs. Clark would appear, they got tangled up in pants legs and sleeves. The rubber he had carried in his wallet for three years was brittle; he went limp trying to roll it on. She loved him all the more—his shy snuffling laughter when she tried to help. LOVE IS A DAGGER read Kim's biceps. Now she understood.

"Two weird kids," Tiffany said when Shep emerged, looking down the hall both ways, tucking in his shirttail. Here everything was shared communally. They were family, after all.

Kim was in the crisis room when she passed, seated on a wooden bench directly across from the largest, angriest-eyed, blackest woman Meena had ever seen. Kim's hands folded in her lap as if she sat in church. She wore a beatific expression—while the woman glared uninterruptedly at her from behind a plain wooden desk. Her skin gleamed like polished stone. "She's my guiding angel," Kim explained later. "She helps me keep control."

Ms. Childlove awaits her in an interview room. All smiles, kissy smacks. "I know how relieved you must be feeling, sweetheart," she exclaims.

248    WILLIAM LUVAAS

She has come to coach Meena for the formal interview, to insist how important it is she tell the truth. "You can't bargain the truth, Meena. Nothing in the world is as important as the truth. I know you are scared your father will go to prison, but we'll see that Daddy gets help. You have my solemn word on that."

She wears hokey brown shoes with square toes, her face paler than tissue paper—purple lips and cinnamon eyebrows that seem dyed into the skin as if Alvin pimplesucker painted them on. How could you trust anyone with square shoes?

"What is the truth?" Meena asks her.

Ms. Childlove blinks rapidly, orks her fingernails. The syrupy smile cracks and falls away, beneath is a Crissy Crabmeat flush. Her eyes are Olson's, but yellow instead of brown. She seems to have a strange fever. She leans close.

"We know the truth, don't we, you and I? It's ugly, yes, and you imagine it is something you saw in a dream. But it is real, Meena. Every word. *Every word you've said.*"

Meena's arms chill, blood trembles in her brain. She suspects that Ms. Childlove knows the story she told the others. One of the girls must be a spy, or there are hidden microphones in the walls. She sees herself pinned down at bottom of the pool. Dad and Olson float past like huge fish. She wonders if just saying something makes it so, like in a book. Ms. Childlove smiles a Crissy Crabmeat smile that says *You are about to do a wonderful thing, Meena. You must do it for everyone, because they haven't courage to do it for themselves.* "That should make you very proud, that you have courage to face this monster alone, Meena. Doesn't it make you proud?"

Meena nods her head, just to be rid of her.

On Family Day, it's Grandma Sally's and Boney's turn. Grandma apologizes that Mom couldn't come; she isn't feeling well. Likely story. They sit together on a bench beneath a huge live oak tree, her gonad brother orking the Aliens who play catch with a beach ball nearby. The point is to let it smack them in the head then fall down, hooting gleefully. "Don't stare," Meena scolds. "They're people, too."

"I know," he says.

She turns to Grandma. "People in here are normaler than people outside."

Grandma Sally smiles uneasily and asks if that unpleasant woman has been to visit. "I imagine she wishes to influence what you say next week at your interview." She won't ever forgive herself, Grandma warns, if her father goes to jail. "How will your mother survive, I'd like to know" . . . blah blah . . . until Meena clamps palms over her ears and begins humming, watching Grandma's mouth open and close like a gap between buttons in a red flannel shirt. "Goodness sakes alive!" Grandma Sally grabs at her hands, her mouth angry. "I want to know what you intend to tell them, young miss."

"Why didn't Dad come? Other kids' dads come and they molested them." Meena points at Theresa and Monica.

"Well I . . . I . . . " Grandma's mouth opens, white talk curds at the corners. "Now you wish to speak to him, when you might have spoken to him at home all along."

"I didn't want to then."

"My Lord! If it isn't Princess Grace of Monaco."

But she needed to talk to him *now*. Ask why he blamed her for her brother's sins, as if he wanted to beat her, too—with love instead of his fists. Why he had called her *little slut*. Why he didn't tell them the truth, keeping the blame all to himself. Who was it he wanted to protect—Olson? Sandy Beach? She couldn't understand it. Or did he—just maybe—did he think it was true?

She remembered his hard wooden kiss that time he came home from California, the smell of his after-shave so much like Olson's hair oil. The memory alarmed her.

What is true, she wondered, lying in bed, staring at a yellow penumbra of light thrown across the ceiling through the cracked door, a wedge of illumination split mysteriously by a darker triangle into a light zone and a dark. Which of those markings she had etched into the wall under her bed, using only fingertips to guide her:

> *he did*
> *he didn't*
> *he did*

Each, in turn, scratched through with a line. Possibly, she would tell Ms. Pasternak the truth. She was a nice lady. But what was true? *My parents love me / My parents don't*. Could both be true at once? Maybe truth is a dream. The moment you have pinned down place and events, it switches and becomes something else. Maybe every thought you have is true, because *it could be*. Because lies, when you need them, are more compelling than reality. Like a reversible shirt: true on both sides. Truth is only an idea.

She lay awake, afraid she might turn inside out and become lost inside herself—which is what Shep said happens to fruit loops. Not knowing what she might say when Ms. Pasternak asked her to tell the simple truth. Which truth did she even believe? Was she fruit-looping out? You could slip on a truth, as on a bathroom throw rug, and split your skull open and never know what was true again, like Boney had.

Meena lay arguing out loud to herself, while Crissy Crabmeat slept beatifically and Tiffany tossed and mumbled. Once, Tiffany spoke into the dark, like she'd been eavesdropping on Meena's ruminations all along. Her theory, she said, was that Aliens were normal people in their past lives, but they went retro and started confusing dreams with reality; weird, dough-faced people invaded their sleep, like images of themselves to come. "Hey, kid-dorooney, you gotta watch out. Do you want to reincarnate as an Alien? Like are there any dough heads in your dreams?"

"Only my mom," Meena whispered.

"Ooh-la. Shit city."

Meena imagined Tiffany's lip curling, though she couldn't see it.

Next night, just two days before her scheduled hearing, Meena called home to talk to Dad and demand he tell her the truth. Crissy Crabmeat complained of a stomachache, giving Shep and Meena time to slip in to use Mrs. Clark's private line. Shep dialed in case Grandma Sally answered. The phone rang and rang. Just as he was going to hang up, an unsteady voice answered.

"My mom—" Meena gasped, not hearing but seeing her voice. Staring in horror at a snaking ring finger that insinuated through holes in the mouthpiece and coiled around Shep's throat, the large diamond in Mom's ring bearing down on his Adam's apple. "Hang up," she was mouthing. "Hang up."

"Is Mr. Tillotson senior at home?" Shep croaked.

"No," Mom said, "Mr. Tillo'son no longer resize at this residence. Who is this?"

Meena snatched the receiver from him and slammed it down. Mom's presence was swallowed back into distance and space. At the last instant, Meena heard her whisper: "I'm coming, honey." A panic so palpable soaked into tissues of her brain that it would take years to rid herself of it. It filled the room—not with the familiar vague sweetness of vodka but the black fetor of a grave.

Meena saw her mother walking down hallways in her nightgown, stopping to peek in rooms. Though she grabbed her lips to still them, her mother's words came out: *Mommy's been naughty, she didn't come visit, wasn't that dummy of her? But she's going to protect you, honey.* The words slurred, Meena tried to still them, biting down until she tasted blood. Then she stumbled and fell into a dark hole at the back of her skull and lay there, her shimmering gown just visible from the entrance. Her enemies gathered at the cave's mouth, their doughy ashen faces looking down inside her.

They found her curled on Mrs. Clark's hook rug, blood foaming from mouth corners, receiver clutched so hard in her fist she had cracked its plastic casing. An epileptic fit, the duty nurse decided. Poor Meena was epileptic.

# 31

# Jeff

A mockingbird woke me up, singing outside my window in the pecan tree, imitating four birds at once: a robin's tweet, a blue jay's squawk, a thrush's whistle, finally the sharp call of a bobwhite. A very confused bird. Any second now Dad would yell "shut up!" and a rock would clatter in the branches, then the mockingbird would scold him and fly away. It was seven years' bad luck to kill a mockingbird, but Dad kept a pile of throwing stones beside his sleeping bag in the backyard 'cause it drove him nuts to be awakened by a mockingbird every morning at four A.M. But no stone clattered; between rounds of the bird's song, it was spooky quiet. Then I remembered Dad had moved across town to a silver Airstream trailer in Cassidy's Retirement Park. I had helped him move his stuff just yesterday afternoon.

Now he had to pay rent on a house, a trailer and our mortgage in Oregon at once. Nutso. He said it was only a trial separation. "Your Grandma Sally and Grandpa Walter separated regularly. You know the saying: Separation makes the heart grow fonder." His grin wasn't convincing. He turned away to a box he was packing. "Your sister has suffered enough with all this. They'll let her move home now that I'm gone."

The trailer was furnished with fusty old people's stuff: a linoleum dining table and rusty-legged chairs, a couch that smelled like cats. "Not much." Dad smiled grimly. "But it's cheap." His eyes were baggy; lately, he looked tired all the time. "Hey, what say you stay here with me awhile, pal? Couple of bachelors. We'd have a great time." I told him I couldn't, I had to stay with Mom. "I know you do, buddy." Dad's eyes misted, mine bumped around the trailer like it interested me—the tiny bathroom in back. I already promised myself I wouldn't blubber. Dad needed me to be strong. I did too.

But when he dropped me at home his mood changed. He glared at the house and told me he had the best darned lawyer in town. "I'm going to get you out of this mess, don't worry, son. If that's the game your mother wants to play she'll get all she can handle."

Why not just tell the truth about Olson, I asked him. Why should he take all the blame? Dad became stern as Judge Silver, his eyes squinting. "We don't want to involve your brother in this mess. They'd only think I was trying to pass the buck. Hang in there with me on this one, son. That's not asking a lot, is it, one small favor for your old man?"

I nodded. I knew lying only added to the mess, but telling the truth was wrong, too. Somewhere between the truth and a lie I'd got hung up. My dad, too.

When I came in, Grandma Sally was balling out my sister on the kitchen phone. She hoped Meena was satisfied now she had run Dad out of our house—maybe she'd picked up a few other tricks besides from those loony birds. Mom came flying in and they wrestled over the phone, Grandma's glasses flopping on their leash, both grimacing down to roots of their teeth and eyes popping. They looked like twins that way, just the opposite of Wendy-Sandy next door, who only looked like twins when they weren't fighting.

Lately, there was always an angry atmosphere in our house. Mom and Grandma never stopped screaming at each other. Crazy stuff. Grandma called Mom a "nutjob . . . and your daughter's no better."

Mom yelled back, "D'you want me to unzip his pants and hold his dick for him? Would that satisfy you?" I'd go outside so I didn't have to hear. This time Grandma Sally said she'd had enough. "Well, I've tried, Jerri. If you want to destroy yourselves, isn't a thing I can do to stop you."

I stood at the door of Olson's room watching her stuff clothes into her old-fashioned straw suitcase, throwing them in off hangers any old way. Usually, she even folded her dirty laundry. But everyone kept changing lately, like the weather in Oregon—Dad, Mom, Olson, Meena, Aunt Debbie, now Grandma Sally, who hated quitters worse than anything. Now even she was quitting. You couldn't depend on anyone being the same person from day to day. It was like they all caught a personality virus. Like a mockingbird, never knowing whose song it would sing next. It scared me I would catch it, too.

"I hope you can talk sense into your mother, Jeffrey," Grandma Sally said as she left the house. "Though I doubt anyone can. I've tried all her life and she won't listen."

"Will we make it okay, Grandma?" I asked.

"Don't be foolish. Why, of course you will." But all the color had drained from her cheeks; she looked guilty. I watched her walk off down the road toward town, lugging her suitcase. She had promised to send money if we needed any. But it wasn't money that worried me. We were on our own now.

I wanted to get up and throw a rock at that dumb bird, but it would only fly to a higher branch in the pecan tree. I needed to pee bad, but it scared me I might see my face in the bathroom mirror and I would be changed to someone else. In spite of myself, it creeped me out to realize I was alone in the house with Mom. Then I remembered Meena was back home and I felt relieved.

Yesterday, when Goona the Freak brought my sister home, I told her Mom was out shopping—although I could hear hangers jangling in the entry closet behind me and I was afraid Goona heard them, too. She told us not to worry, "We'll get your papa some help. Mama too."

"They don't need any help," I told her.

Goona's smile fell apart like brittle toast. "We'll see." She looked at me like she thought I needed help, too.

Meena was sullen and quiet. When I went in to talk to her, she lay on her bed with her hands folded behind her head and talked crazy-people gobbledygook: "ork" and "retro" and "You need your tubes cleared."

I said I was sorry about her cocoon.

She shrugged. "You can't stay spastic your whole life." She sighed, her eyes rolled around the ceiling. "I hate this place, I wish I never left Riverside." Stretching. "I'm outta here anyway as soon as Shep sends me some cashola."

"Who's Shep?"

"He's none of your business, that's who."

I had hidden Lorenzo's jar in a cubby under her bedroom sink. Meena grinned and said he was going to have babies. Really dumb. Though there was a round egg sac in his jar with a nipple at the top, like a tiny baseball with a ripe zit. Lorenzo hung out beside it, huge and shiny black, his long front legs cuddling the sack. In our house even spiders changed. Meena had changed his name to "Avenger."

The mockingbird sang, forlorn and lonely, calling to its mate. (Maybe Dad killed the other one.) The wind came up and I drifted in and out of sleep, watching branches sway like hands across my curtains. Creepy. Suddenly one reached out and shook me awake. I cried out and scooted back in the corner. Mom yelled, startled by my scream. I was afraid she had the fireplace poker. Her breath poured over me: vodka and pepper. Her hair was all mussed. Her velveteen robe glowed rosy pink in the light coming through my curtains. She kept shaking me, whispering weirdso stuff about Dad's car was parked down on the road; him and his lawyer had come to steal us kids from her. "Hurry and get dressed," she hissed. "Get your sister."

When I peeked out the living room curtains, it wasn't Dad's car at all but a pale green sheriff's cruiser parked at foot of our drive; up top, its bubble-gum machine glowed pink with the color of the horizon, like Mom's robe. "It's the sheriff," I whispered. "Prob'ly come to arrest us for the golf course."

"Golf course? Don't be ridiculous. It's y'r dad and that lawyer bastard." She clawed her fingers into the meat of my arm. "Wendy's in it with him. Quick! Pack your clothes. Meena!"

I made out my sister's figure beside Mom's, almost the same height, one rosy the other pale. "Mom's going retro," Meena sulked.

"Just do it," I said.

We got our suitcases into the garage. Mom ran back and forth across the back patio from house to garage heaving armloads of stuff into the wagon: towels, blankets, coffeepot, lamps, any old thing—like we were going weirdso camping. She planned to make a run for it, I think, past the sheriff. It wouldn't never work. I said we should go down and hang out at my wigwam until he left. Maybe he was only casing us out. But Mom was sure they'd find us. Maybe he was here to guard our house from Dad, I said. Mom laughed a loud hysterical whinny. Meena barked at her to shuddup. Outside, it was growing lighter, the mockingbird had stopped singing and the birds it imitated started. Roosters crowed down at the citrus farm. Suddenly, squad car lights snapped on and the car started up the drive. We made a dash for it out the side, down the path into the canyon.

The moon was still up, sliced in half. Down there it was darker and cool, but you could already tell it would be hot from the hazy paleness of the sky and the taste of dust in the air. Crickets chirped around us in the brush. You could imagine their bitsy eyes watching from shadows.

After a while, I sneaked up to see what was happening. The squad car was gone; there was no trace of it. Wendy-Sandy's house still sound asleep on its terrace above ours. And our house looked like someplace I never lived—its row of penis trees and grapefruits growing like big yellow apples, and whiskered palms

like party favors God blew up into the pink sky one morning
when he had a hangover—like someplace only half-remembered
from another life.

Quick, I got Mom and Meena. In her rush to get out of there,
Mom crashed right through the garage door which we forgot to
open. Fortunately it was flimsy and ready to fall off anyhow.

# 32

---

# Jeff

Mom was singing. She gripped the steering wheel in both hands.
Her face glistened and sweat ran in a trickle between her breasts
and under a tiny pink rose on her bra clasp. Her tan had faded
from chocolate to yellow almost, and she was developing a pot
above the waistband of her pedal pushers. She was hauling: Cars
we passed flapped by in a blur like birds' wings.

"She's going a hundred," my sister's hot breath said at my
ear. All I could think was what if she got stopped for speeding—
drunk and in only her bra?

Mom turned to me and smiled. "Feel better, honey? You had
a nap." She lifted the thermos cup from the holder on the dash
and chug-a-lugged.

"Cute, Mom. Drink and drive, why don'chou," Meena said
from back.

Mom ignored her; I wondered if she knew how fast she was
doing.

"It's hotter than a pee hole in here," Meena said.

"Don't you dare talk that way around me, young lady."

"What's so special about around you?"

Mom swiveled around to slap my sister. The wagon swerved
toward an eighteen-wheeler in the next lane. "Mom!" I shouted,
and grabbed for the wheel, but she veered away at the last moment—so close the truck's vacuum caught hold of us a second

before letting go. We wobbled like a drunk top across the center line, the semi's air horn blasting behind us.

"Cute," Meena said, holding her cheek. "Real cute."

Mom slowed to ninety and started humming again. Hot dry wind slapped our faces through the open windows; sagebrush shot past. Burma Shave signs so fast you could hardly read them: WANNA SEE . . . HOW FAST . . . SHE'LL DRIVE . . . BETTER TO . . . ARRIVE ALIVE . . . BURMA SHAVE. Aunt Debbie says there's some people think if they go fast enough bad luck won't catch up. Maybe Mom was one. But I was worried about cops.

"Why'd we leave Escondido so sudden like that?" I asked her. Wasn't the golf course, I didn't think. Maybe it had to do with Dad.

Meena dropped back against the seat with her arms folded. "To skip out on my dumb interview, that's why. BFD, I don't even care." Her hair danced like sea grass in the breeze: cut in funny tufts, bleached blond at tips, what Grandma Sally calls her "loony-bird chop," 'cause her friends at Riverside cut it that way to recognize each other when they got out.

"Is that right, Mom," I asked, "is that the reason?"

"What's that, dear?" A tiny smile froze on Mom's lips, what Olson calls her "calm before the storm" smile. I knew Meena was right. It didn't have anything to do with the golf course. Judge Silver said Mom was unfit to be a mother; she was scared they would take us kids away. Or maybe she was scared Dad really would go to jail and we would be destitute.

We passed an Airstream trailer beside a stack of irrigation pipes on a huge plowed field; the furrows extended as far as you could see. I remembered what Dad had said: It was up to me now, I was the man of the house. Everything would go to hell in a pee bucket if I didn't hold it together, because you couldn't say which of them was loonier, my mom or my sister. I didn't want to go loopy with them.

"Slow down, Mom," I ordered.

Mom's chin jolted forward, a small furrow formed between her eyes, her foot lifted off the gas, then pressed down harder. I reached across and buttoned up her blouse. Then her foot lifted again. We slowed way down and I didn't know why until we went under an overpass and I saw a black-and-white Highway

Patrol car up there. One thing about my mom: She has built-in radar detection. You got to if you're going to drink and drive.

Oregon felt like scenes from a home movie which you recognize but can't believe you really lived there. The house looked dark and foreign and didn't seem like home anymore. Just black windows staring out at us. Seemed like we left home behind in California. Dad's Christmas lights hung in a tattered necklace around the blue spruce out front, bulbs busted out. Mom's rhodies were clotted with dead leaves. She moaned when she saw them. We stood looking at the house like we couldn't decide to go in, surrounded by the old familiar smoky smell from slash burner tepees at the sawmills, the air damp and heavy. Mom firmed her jaw and nodded. "All right, we'll look."

Inside was a destruction derby: holes in the walls, deep ruts across the cork floor like somebody did razor-blade wheelies, the downstairs bathroom smelled too foul to go inside, but bedrooms weren't hardly touched upstairs—except Meena's, where someone drew obscene pictures on the walls in purple lipstick.

Mom walked from room to room slapping her arms in exasperation, mumbling, "Great God and little fishes, who would ever . . . " Finally she sat on the bottom step leading up to the bedrooms with her face in her hands. *It's okay, Mom*, we assured her, we would clean it up. It would be back like it used to be.

"What kind of animals did that idiot rent to?" Mom muttered. Meena and I looked at each other, scared she might lose it after we came all this way. I motioned for my sister to move in front of the plate-glass window in case Mom did something dumb. We kept telling her it would be okay, but she sat crying and cursing my dad.

There wasn't any electricity, so we had to hurry and clean up before dark—sacks of broken beer bottles and trash, a mattress and old sleeping bag, which we hauled to the foot of the drive. Buck came over to help. He wasn't surprised to see us back; it was like we just saw him yesterday. He'd grown his hair out in a princeton like Olson's, combed back greaser-style at the sides, but so short on top his scalp peeked through. He still stank, but from after-shave now instead of dirt; he must've poured it over his head. He wolf-whistled at my sister, and we exchanged the

Long Loop handshake. But Buck told me, "The Long Loopth ith dithbranded."

"Except for us," I said.

He nodded. "I gueth Mom didn't like California." He glanced nervously at her—sitting on the step with her face in her hands and rocking.

The place didn't look too bad after we finished, almost back to normal. Buck told us after the renters moved out some fraternity friends of Ginny Seamore used our house for a party pad until Dr. Weatherspoon called the cops. He brought over a Coleman lantern. When he came in, Mom caught a hand to her mouth and stared like she hadn't never saw him before. Her eyes flashed white in the lantern glow. "He's the spitting image of my dad," she gasped. "Y'r Grandpa Walter."

"It's just Buck," I said. Our voices echoed spooky through the rooms like in gym at school.

Over the following days, neighbors stopped by with chairs, a gateleg table; Steve and Dr. Weatherspoon carried over a bed they had in the attic, which we put in Mom's room. Widow Grazziola brought leftover spaghetti and apple crisp; she just happened to make a little extra. It was like the Christmas we had almost forgot to have.

Dr. Weatherspoon took Meena and me aside and asked what the situation was. He had a stern way about him; you couldn't look him in the eye if you had to bee ess. It was a trial separation, we explained, but didn't tell him the rest.

"Is your mom all right?" His eyes tippling so we knew what he meant.

"No problema," Meena insisted. "Everything's copacetic" (one of her dumb loony-bin words).

We didn't fool anyone. They knew Mom wasn't copacetic. She ran to her room when they knocked on the door and refused to talk to them. After they left, we had to coax her out of her bedroom closet. Her mouth worked in the shadows: "Dirty-minded shits. They just love it . . . Over my dead body." After Buck's dad brought a half truckload of reclaimed furniture from his department store, we thanked them very much and said it was enough. We'd be going down to California soon and pick up our own stuff.

At school, girls had filled out, boys had grew into horny toads.

Compared to them, it seemed like I'd stayed frozen. Deborah
Cooney, who I used to like, squinted right through me like I was
a smudged window. It was weird. Even in Oregon everyone had
caught a personality virus. At the bus stop, Walt Whitaker and
Jerry Stitt, who used to be Double Dutches, stood talking to
Buck in low tones and smoking cigarettes. But Steve Weatherspoon, who was getting fat like his dad, grinned his sneak-a-
peek eyes at my sister's tits and said he had X-ray vision.

"Tough tit." Meena squinched her lips. "I'm wearing a lead
bra." Steve wasn't much competition after Piggy Olsen and the
loony birds.

Dad's checks began arriving the second week. I don't know
how he knew where we went. Grandma Sally maybe. We took
down the FOR SALE sign out front and got the lights turned on.
When Mom was sober enough she drove us to the store. Otherwise Meena drove, wearing one of Mom's floppy-brimmed
hats and heavy makeup, so from a distance she could pass for
old enough. Soon she started dressing that way all the time. It
made her look cheap. The first couple weeks, Mom dressed and
did the housework. She said we were making a fresh start and
didn't start drinking until late afternoon. Still, her and Meena
fought constantly.

One day at the store, we met one of Meena's school friends.
Mom was a bit polluted, her blouse was crooked on her shoulders. Meena pretended she didn't even know her. Mom stepped
up beside her and smiled. "Aren't you going to introdouche me,
Meena! Are you embarrash of little ol' Mom?" My sister was
talking fast, spinning her hands in the air. Her friend stared uneasily at my mom; she prob'ly never saw anyone like her before—except Lily Lunchcakes maybe.

"Isn't that a kick. Embarrash of y'r own mother."

Meena kept talking like Mom wasn't there at all.

"*Isn't that a riot!*" Mom let out a yelp and swept her arm
across a shelf of pickle jars, which came smashing to the floor.
Glass and pickles wiggling out like fat green grubs under our
feet.

"*Embarrash of y'll own motherr!*" Mom shrieked.

I grabbed her arm to steer her away from the glass in her
thongs. Meena's friend turned and fled. Mr. Taylor came hus-
tling up the aisle and said he was awfully, terribly sorry. "Mrs.

Tillotson, you've been a fine customer, really, but I'd prefer you took your business elsewhere." Mom began shrieking how dare he and kept hollering all the way out to the car. Meena called Mom a drunk bitch, loonier than Monica at Riverside who fucked winos. Mom waved at passing cars that slowed down to watch. Somehow I drove home, though I could hardly drive worth beans. But I was learning.

Mr. Akroyd the alkaloid was suspicious because we had come back with only eight weeks left in the school year. It was a ball bust to catch up. In Oregon we were doing history of the Pacific Northwest, geometry and Willa Cather, but in California we had been doing South America, algebra and John Steinbeck. It was all completely different.

Meena didn't care if she flunked out. Every night she dumped her homework on my desk and shrugged, like *Okay, if you want to be a nerd.* So I did both of ours. Sometimes Mom knocked on my door late and said I should go to bed. But how could I? We would talk awhile, Mom and me, and she seemed almost normal again. I thought if we just hung in there things would get better. She would forgive Dad and go back to Tranquility for a cure.

I'd wait in the hall at school to walk Meena to her next class. Kids we'd known all our lives did a staggering drunk's stumble in front of us; they placed thumbs to their mouths and tipped back their heads like it never wore out being funny. Dumb, bored Oregon lumberheads! Meaner than kids in California, which I couldn't believe was possible. I bit my lip until I tasted blood and walked stiffly beside my sister; it took all my self-control to keep from losing it. Meena clutched her books to her chest and looked right through them like clear glass. Sometimes Buck walked shotgun, his square head sweeping slowly side to side. Nobody bugged us then.

When Mom suggested we make a short stop at Lee's Drugs (so she could run into the lime-green Liquor Control Commission store next door), I felt like every eye in town was watching. I heard their skittering whispers, like mice in a closet, and stared at the wide felt brim of my sister's hat, pretending we were gangsters waiting for our partner to run out of the liquor store with the loot, then Meena would screech away from the curb in a clean getaway, like at the golf course.

Meena got called into the office one day because her English teacher noticed the handwriting on her last book report wasn't hers. She had to dictate her report to me, she said, because she sprained her wrist. Dismissal rang and I was waiting for her out front. Bob Corduroy and a bunch of them, including Gary Seamore, stood by the bus lineup. We had to walk past them to our bus. Bob Corduroy smirked as we approached, so I knew he was planning something. He was a big dumpling of a kid, like Toby Olsen but baby-faced and not so fat, just big all over. Even his eyes and fingernails were oversized.

"I hear your sister licks your dick," he said.

A flashbulb popped off in my head. I rushed him in a head butt to his gut before he chopped the back of my neck and floored me. Every shoe in the world was kicking me at once. I curled up, covering my head. I saw Gary Seamore's nose bunch up angrily before he kicked me in the stomach, and thought I would throw up then, more because we used to be friends than because it hurt. Meena was screaming and swinging her purse around her head like a bola. She landed a blow in Gary's face.

Feet came clapping; Buck and Walt Whitaker and Jerry Stitt came running from behind the school, tossing cigarettes away like men in the movies. They kicked ass. Jerry Stitt pinned Bob Corduroy's arms behind his back. He looked like a wiry terrier with a greaser haircut who had tangled up a badger twice his size.

"Do him your best shot, Jeff," he told me. But Bob's face already looked like a pepperoni pizza.

"Nah," I said. He was hurt bad enough, but I warned him, "Don't never say another word about my sister again." I saw by his eyes he wouldn't.

The world is a peculiar place; I learned that when the truck ran over my head. Half backwards. For no reason, except passing circumstances, friends become your enemies and enemies become your friends. Your own parents become strangers. What was once your home becomes foreign territory.

Sometimes when Mom was in a bad way we didn't go to school at all. She'd got worse than Meena in her spider days, always hiding—downstairs in the lawnmower cupboard, the broom closet, under the utility-room sink in a scatter of dead bugs and mice turds. The slightest thing sent her hiding, just a car turning outside in the loop. She would fall asleep in there. We'd come home from school and find her frozen stiff from being in one position too long, the booze thermos empty beside her, barely able to walk when we helped her out of her hidey-hole. Who knows how long she'd been in there. It wasn't healthy.

One day I found her in the clothes hamper in the upstairs bathroom, which I didn't see how she got in it. She smelled like stale, fusty clothes and was pee-o'd at me for finding her when I came in to take a pee. "Mom needs some peace and quiet," she scolded. "Can't you do that much for her?"

"Okay, Mom." I backed out of the room just as she went into the shower in her nightie.

Leaning against the bathroom door outside, listening to the shower, I realized Mom had entered her own tunnel—a dark secret place where no one could enter behind her, where there wasn't enough air exchange, so she would asphyxiate if she stayed down there too long. Wasn't any use refusing to stop by the liquor store; she would walk haughtily down Rogue River Road in her filthy bathrobe, chin thrown back, smiling at the staring people like it wasn't nothing strange at all. Like Lily Lunchcakes. You had to know exactly where to start digging to save a person from a tunnel like that.

It scared me to think we couldn't protect her. When I found her standing at my window, looking down at the empty drive-way, whispering she knew Dad was waiting in his car around the loop for Meena to walk outside, it wasn't hard to distract her—show her my biology project or ask for her potato-salad recipe. But she'd return to the window and stand for whole hours, hair scraggly and nightgown crooked on her shoulders, while I did homework under the lamp at my desk.

She forbid Meena to go outside. If my sister was in a good mood, she'd laugh it off. "Retro Mom," she'd say, "BFD." Other times she grabbed her jacket and walked defiantly out of the house, stood in the loop and gave Mom the up-yours fist pump while rain flattened her spiky hair. Still other times, she'd smile sadly and brush Mom's hair with gentle strokes to remove the tangles, whispering like she was her child, while Mom stood with a palm against cool glass, a funny smile pulling skin taut

across her cheeks. You couldn't say which was less predictable—
my mom or my nutso sister.

As I stood listening to the shower, Mom humming like everything was hunky-dory, "sweetness and light," like Aunt Debbie
says, I had an inspiration. I ran out back through the arborvitae
hedge into Mr. Ashcroft's empty lot—maybe the only lot in
Oregon which they forgot to build a driveway into. It was an
island with houses all around where nobody but a suburban
hermit could live.

When I was a kid before we moved to California, I thought
it was huge as an empty desert behind our house. Now it wasn't
only half as big as a football field, pocked with big red gopher
mounds like a bad case of acne clear down to the widow's fence.
A thick jungle surrounded the compost heap; I had to stomp a
path through to reach the tunnel opening—a mound of dirt
overgrown with grass like the hump atop a grave. The Long
Loops had closed it over to keep some kid from falling inside. I
worked doggy fashion, clawing dirt back between my legs until
I hit Olson's trapdoor.

A musty ancient breath, fishier even than Grandma Sally's,
swiped me across my face like a wet tongue; I thought I would
puke. Just a ragged hole leading down into the dark, nastier than
Mom's hiding place beneath the utility sink. I couldn't imagine
why I liked it as a kid. Then I remembered the rock and mysterious handprints we left in the cement walls and I had to crawl
down there. Knowing I'd get my pants and shirt mucked up, I
stripped to my shorts. The tunnel bottom was squishy, roots
tickled my shoulders and gave me the creeps. In places, dirt had
collapsed from the ceiling and you had to squeeze through a
small passage. I lit my first match when dark was so thick it
wrapped like a wet glove around me. The match flared just long
enough to see the tunnel widen ahead where cement began.
Roots had become millipedes crawling over my arms and shoulders. I slapped them off, so creepy-jeepied I couldn't move. Every
inch of my skin broke out in goose bumps. Still, I pushed on.
Cement walls scraped my shoulders, water puddled under my
knees. Down there it smelled of old comics which the pages had
got wet and mildewed.

Lighting another match, I saw strange markings on the
walls, like something out of an ancient Indian burial cave. A

wet breath blew out my match. I couldn't tell if I was shivering more from cold or jittery nerves. It was as spooky as an Edgar Allan Poe story. I remembered how we used to work without our shirts on, how I used to stretch out on the floor and peer at a vague glow like a star echo from the entrance. The chill never bothered me then. Now the air was heavy, I had to suck it into my lungs. A spooky-profound idea occurred to me: Even if we dug it, it was no longer our cave. Mother Earth had taken over control and turned it down to the temperature of buried glacial boulders and the ice age. She turned it over to the sow bugs and millipedes and gophers. Then I remembered I was maybe twenty feet down, three times deeper than a grave. I thought of crumbly sandstone we'd dug through and tons of wet heavy soil piled atop me, and I freaked. It didn't seem like a refuge anymore. The mud squishing under my knees was the same mud cavemen's flesh and bones rotted into a hundred thousand years ago. A living person was better off up top.

In my last match, I saw a cave-in five feet ahead: dirt and concrete chunks, jumbled-up strands of cable and rusty re-bar tufting out like hairs from a mole. I couldn't never reach the rock. The match went out like wet fingers snuffed it. That instant I beheld Mom's face clinging to the wall, just like I'd seen it before: eyes bulging, hair tangled in a nest of snakes, bare clenched skull's teeth. I shouted and crawled out of there so fast it left my knees red and scraped and my brain dull from lack of oxygen. Up top I could breathe again. I covered the hole with dirt, burying what I'd seen the best I could. I got dressed and ran back to the house, which—nutso as it was—at least the roof wouldn't crumble and fall down on my head.

That night Avenger had babies. "Definitely alien," my sister said as we watched spiderlings escape from the gray egg pouch by the dozens, crawling over each other and straight up through breathing holes in the lid like they knew exactly where they were going, tumbling down the sides onto the rug and fanning out. "Isn't that cute," she said. "Now we'll have a whole house full of baby black widows. Survival of the fittest."

"Stomp them," I yelled, and began mashing them with my shoe. My sister went bonkers, hammering me with both fists at once.

"Murderer!"

"They'll get all over the house, you jerk."

"They have as much right to live as we do."

We were standing up wrestling like we were doing the tango, while I tried to mash spiderlings headed toward the door. But my sister was strong as a monkey and fought twice as dirty. Every time I started getting an advantage, she gouged sharp fingernails into my arm or jabbed me with her tits. Unfair fighting.

Mom came in and must've seen it all at once, 'cause she dropped to her knees and began smunching baby spiders in her fingers. I ran over and pulled at her. "It's black widows, Mom."

She seized Meena. "Get out of here. Get out of this room. Are you out of your right mind!"

We smashed as many as we could on the way out and slammed the door behind us. Mom stuffed the door crack with newspapers so they couldn't get through. We'd call the exterminator in the morning, she said. Meena was furious. It was her bedroom, she had all her stuff in there, Mom had no right to lock her out of her own room. What was she supposed to wear to school?

"What you have on, young lady."

"Y'r always out to get me," Meena bitched. "If it wasn't for you we wouldn't even be in this shitty mess."

Mom's eyes blinked. "This is the thanks I get. I whisk your sister off in the middle of the night to protect her from her dad. Mom sacrifices her life and her home . . . Over my dead body."

For a second I thought she was back to her old self, smiling the madder she got. But it's like the air leaked out of a bag: Her eyes went glassy and her words tripped over each other. But Meena's eyes were enamel hard and sharp as her fingernails, lips tight and bloodless. Ever since California, she was like a simmering angry pot on the stove—steaming and steaming until all the liquid boiled away and nothing was left but a scorched black sludge. She grabbed the throat of Mom's robe and pushed her face right into hers. Close up that way, they looked like sisters— only Meena furious and Mom afraid, leaning away.

"D'you think he would've touched me if you weren't such a drunken bitch?" my sister hissed.

"Cool it, Meena," I shouted. "Just cool it."

"Don't, honey," Mom murmured.

"Don't sweat your drunk little butt, I'll never be like you. I'll never be a witch like you and make my husband screw his own—"

Mom shrieked.

I locked my sister's arms behind her and pulled her away, yelling: "Dumbass shitfuck peehead, just shut up your puke mouth, isn't it enough already? Isn't it bad enough?" But Mom had fled downstairs. I swatted Meena across her lippy mouth with the back of my hand until it was bloody and she'd started to whimper.

Each of us went off to be alone, me sick to my stomach because I'd never got so mad at her before. We were all enemies now, a family full of enemies, just when we needed to be friends. I sat at my desk and wrote Dad a letter, explaining all that had happened. Later, I went in to Mom, sprawled on the burgundy chaise lounge Buck's dad had brought. The floor and bed littered with dirty clothes, lingerie, shoes, old Kleenex, deodorant bottles, newspapers, pictures of kids she'd clipped from magazines stacked in small piles here and there—the only thing arranged in any sort of order. Filthier than a pigsty. It made me mad to see her living like that, her gown mussed and cheeks puffed like she'd been crying, eyelids drooping, staring off into a black hole. She used to be tidy, she got pee-o'd at Olson and me just for leaving a sock on the floor. Always neat and fashionably dressed.

"Why not clean up, Mom," I said. "Maybe it would make you feel better." I wanted to warn her about what I saw in the tunnel, warn her to be careful. But I didn't know how.

She rolled her head on the lounge back to look at me. "D'you thing Mom likesh living like thish? D'you thing she wan's to live like thish?"

"I just think maybe if you cleaned up you could get some pride back in yourself again," I argued.

She stared blankly like she didn't know what I was saying.

"It's like all the clothes got dumped out of your closet."

Mom looked around as if she hadn't noticed. "How will Mom clean ub?" she asked in a wilted voice. "She'sh made a mess of everyshing." She hugged chin to knees, bare naked underneath.

"Mom," I snapped.

"Clean ub, clean ub," she chanted, ripping off handfuls of newspaper from a stack, throwing it around like confetti. "How can she clean ub?" She charged past me into the bathroom.

Maybe an hour later Meena told me Mom was in the shower in her nightgown and wouldn't come out. That's not weird, I said, she was washing herself and her nightgown at the same time, which needed it. But she had been in there an hour. We went in and Meena pulled on the shower door with both hands, yelling at Mom to come out. Inside frosted glass, her wavery form clung hold of the handle. "Help me," Meena insisted, "she's gone totally retro."

"Mom wan's to clean hershelf," Mom piped in a shaky hysterical voice that sounded like somebody else's.

"Let go, Mom," I ordered, knowing it was up to me to get her out since I started it. We went inside in our clothes and led her out, and I wished I was blind then and couldn't see her breasts under transparent wet cloth, nipples large and dark as the Mexican migrant lady's. I wrapped a towel around her, 'cause no kid likes seeing his own mom naked—unless he's a pervert like Olson. The skin of her face was shriveled in pale wrinkles, all the color bleached from it like a living corpse.

We led her to the bedroom; my sister said don't be a jerk and help her pull off Mom's wet gown, which we had to scrape off like a wet sock. Shameless, as Grandma Sally would say, like she fell naked out of the sky onto her mussed bed, knees wide open, the skin of her sex brown and wrinkled as elephant skin. "Only what was natural . . . ," I told myself, not knowing why I should be so grossed out.

"Why don'chou ork her out or something." Meena sneered, throwing a blanket over Mom. "Gonad pervert."

# 33

## Meena

Boney said he was sick and tired of cleaning up after Mom, wiping gravy off her chin. The next time they came home from school and found her passed out on the floor he was outta there; he would hitchhike to California. When they went to the grocery store, he always ducked away down an aisle if he saw anyone he knew approaching, leaving Meena to keep Mom from toppling into a freezer case. "It isn't natural for kids to take care of their own mother," he insisted. "It's all backwards."

But Meena no longer believed in escape . . . to what? To Dad? When the whim struck her, she would help her mother dress, or sprinkle Pine-Sol against the stench permeating the house, or take her into the shower. Really retro: having to wash your own mom's tits and ass—while she leered shamelessly at your nakedness like you had turned into someone else.

Mom was tuned to a channel no one else could receive, smiling for no reason, crying. She'd begun sleeping all day and staying up all night, regressing to Walnut Street days, convinced Aunt Debbie lived in the utility room. Once, when Meena emerged with a load of laundry, Mom grabbed her arm and whispered that Debbie was a bad influence. "She wants to sleep with y'r dad. Isn't that a riot?" Just another of her nutjob notions—like showering in her nightgown or the photographs of kids she clipped from magazines, scalps trimmed so closely you couldn't tell boys from girls. Mom dressed—when rarely she did—in mismatched plaids and patterns: a bright madras-print blouse with a polka-dot hip-hugger skirt, round-collared purple dress with a shiny green belt, paisley scarf and red pumps. She plowed through clothes she had emptied from her closet, holding things up to her shoulders and discarding them until she found the right combination, not noticing how wrinkled things had become from all the dropping and scooping up. It seemed natural to Meena that the disarray of Mom's mind should be reflected in her dress, but it freaked her out good when she came home one day and found her whispering dirty names at Aunt Debbie through the utility room door. Any kid knows that's true craziness.

There seemed no end to what they learned to tolerate. A light bulb flashed out and Mom rushed them to the garage, insisting they remove their belts, as she had on Walnut Street. They couldn't convince her there was no cellar, let alone no lightning. "Listen to it, you idiots!" Thunder rolled so loudly in Mom's head they could almost hear it.

"I was afraid I would spend the rest of my life looking after her," she told them later. "My mother had thrown away her own life, now she wanted mine. I would lie on my bed and plot her murder: how I might mash sleeping pills into her food, or slip Avenger between her sheets. Once when Boney was at Buck's, I took Mom downstairs for a bath and brought a chair along. My plan was to pin her down underwater beneath the chair legs and sit on it until she drowned. I sat beside the tub until the water grew cold and my mother's flesh turned to turkey wattles; I couldn't work up the courage."

Lying nearly concealed in steam rising up off the water, Mom yammered, studying Meena's lips as she spoke, but looking vaguely away when her daughter looked at her. Because eyes are perilous swales: You can plunge into them and be lost. Meena was picking up her mother's habit, looking away when she spoke to people. It was safer. Mom had slipped inside an egg sac, pulled over her like a body stocking, a cocoon of pain tightly woven and impenetrable. It frightened Meena to imagine what terrible birthings gestated inside it, threatening to burst forth like a gang of bastard spiderlings.

Occasionally, Mom showed up for dinner, actually dressed, her hair sculpted in a retro bouffant, like some gear in her had temporarily popped into neutral. She sat at the table talking in a nonstop monotone: how the neighbors compared notes, she wasn't that dummy. *Mom drinks too much. Isn't that rich? Poor pathetico Jerri! Pot calling the kettle black. Mom hears you whispering behind her back, Jeffrey! Isn't that a riot? Mom knows.* (Boney's eyes popping up in alarm) *Grandpa Wal'er . . .*

*hah! Old man in wader boots. Great Gods and little fishes, over my dead body . . . That old man!* (teeth clenched, exposed to roots) *Hah-ah. Mom hears them. . . . Looka' her! Heaven forbid. Looka' the bags under her eyes.* (yanking at loose skin) *Isn't that a kick?*

"Okay, Mom! Cool it." Meena threw a glance at Boney—because if he bolted, if he left her . . . What then?

*Hip ho rally squad kid, hip hip hurray. Jerri Jumpkick, splitarooney kid! Junior Miss Oregon. Hah-ahhhh, isn't that a kick-aroo?* (Tears dripped from Mom's chin into food which she pushed off her plate with a fork and mashed in an ever-widening orbit, nibbling desultorily at her tears.) *Mommy hears them. She isn't fit to raise children.* (seizing Boney's hand across the table) *What is it, darling? Mom knows. You can't hide a thing from her.* (whispering intently) *She made you—y'r liddle nose and eyes. You used to love her so, so much . . . She knows.* (tearing open her collar) *If only we could breathe, darling.* (Stroking Boney's hand, while he sat tense, bolt upright, staring down at it as if the hand belonged to someone else.)

*Just shuddup, Mom. Shuddup y'r retro mouth.*

Boney snatched the hand away, anger bunching against his eyes, Adam's apple bobbing wildly as he swallowed. He stared intently at his plate, trying not to lose it.

Later, over dishes, Jeff insisted he was outta there, tonight! Hitching south. Dad asked him to come. "It's not wholesome up here, not for a boy, a girl maybe."

He was a dickhead retromorph. What did it have to do with being a girl? "I'm the one who can't leave the house, 'cause my pervo Dad is waiting outside in his car to rape me. I'm the one she shoves into the closet and breathes down my neck with her booze breath when Mrs. Weatherspoon rings the doorbell. I'm the one who should leave, not you."

"He's still my father and I miss him," Boney sulked. "A guy who spends all his time around women goes fruity. Doesn't even know how to think like a guy anymore."

"I miss him, too, you know."

Jeff stared at her, astonished. "You—"

"Sometimes. But he needs his tubes cleared."

Meena threatened to abandon Mom, lock her in her bedroom to die of hunger and the DTs—until Boney agreed not to leave without her. His eyes had begun to contract from that froggy, wide-eyed openness to something more furtive, to bag like Mom's; Dad's Adam's filbert jutted obscenely from his throat. He was caught between them, pulled both ways. He had to keep busy, dashing from task to task. Let himself be idle a moment and terror overwhelmed him. His constant fear was that Olson would show up at their doorstep with his clamshell grin.

But there were limits. Meena found hers when Mom's station wagon screeched up to the curb in front of the junior high one afternoon after school, horn blaring, blocking the drive. Mom flung open the car door and ran toward them, waving her arms and shouting: a female harlequin in a motley of clashing colors and patterns, a flounced hoopskirt (relic of square-dancing years), tight, sequined bolero jacket with long formal sleeves, cheeks rouged beneath the broad-brimmed lifeguard's straw hat she'd often worn at Wendy's pool. Boney stiffened and would have bolted back inside if Meena hadn't caught his sleeve. Kids moved away, giggling or wondrous, openly gawking at Jerri's disheveled face. Meena turned haughtily to those fuckheads. Mom had been a knockout compared to their doughy dishrag moms—before her hair lost its luster and went frizzy, before her cheeks puffed out like old pillows, cushioning exhausted bags under her eyes.

She ran toward them shouting, "Hurry! Before your dad arrives. C'mon, darling—" Glancing fearfully back at the cars lined up behind her wagon. "Meena! Jeffrey! He wants to kidnap you."

Bob Corduroy made a farting sound with his lips, girls snickered, Boney's eyes darted every which way. Meena was terrified he would break and run. Or she would leap forward and seize her mother's throat, ride her to the ground and crack her skull against the pavement. She might have if their eyes hadn't met— Mom's, Meena's—terror moving in a current, an electric familial pulse between them, as it had through that phone at Riverside. She beheld, as from a distance, two small smiling children running toward Mommy, squabbling to be first in the backseat. Buck and his buddies to one side—a trio of smoking Huckleberry Finns, shuffling their feet uncomfortably, because children know. Her stomach poisoned to stone, her heart to steel. *That son of a bitch! He won't do to Meena what Walter . . . Over my dead body!*

"C'mon, sweethearts," she cried. "Daddy wants to kidnap you." She shoved them into the car, then jammed the accelerator and squealed off, peeling rubber, taking out a small cherry tree in a crackling explosion of leafage. Boys whistled, Mr. Akroyd stood like a Marine sergeant out front, arms folded. All of it fishtailing away behind them.

Later, a police car pulled into the drive. Two cops got out and stood looking at the house. She recognized them from the time before the move to California. "Hide," Boney whispered when the doorbell rang. Mom was passed out across her bed upstairs, so shitfaced driving home she was in the oncoming lane as much as her own. They'd come to arrest her: For the tree at school? The golf course in Escondido? For skipping out on the hearing in California? To take her children away?

"Millford Police Department!" she heard them calling from the front. "Just want to chat." She and Boney clung to each other in the downstairs bathroom. She'd been expecting it. Ms. Childlove wasn't the kind of person you could run away from. "It's locked, everything's locked," she heard a cop say just outside. Then silence.

Boney said they would get a search warrant then come back and break down the door. "I'm out of here."

"You can't just leave Mom," she whispered.

"I can't stand it anymore. Pretty soon she will come right into our classes. How'd you like that?"

"I'm coming with you."

"Dad molested you," Boney reminded her.

Meena shook her head, whispering, "I never said so, I never said he did. Ms. Childlove said . . . and Mom, and everybody."

"You did too, Meena. You said so yourself to Mom."

She shook her head. "I never said he did."

"Yes you did," he shouted. "You said it's Mom's own fault."

"It's her fault he screwed around, that's what I said."

"You said it's her fault he screwed his own . . . You said—"

"Doesn't matter what anybody says. People hear anything they want." Because everyone put words in her mouth, believing what they wished to believe. She said one thing, they heard another. The truth was whatever they wanted it to be.

Boney was flabbergasted. "You went along, Meena. You never said he didn't. That's the same thing."

"He fooled around with Sandy. I saw him."

Blood swelled capillaries in Boney's cheeks. "You lied. You made our dad move out of the house. You got us into this shitty mess."

"It was already a mess. Mom's been retro ever since she was born."

"You're retro. You're a dogdickhead. You fucked up our whole family and you don't even give a shit."

"Little boys shouldn't swear."

"Slut," he shouted. "You already ruined Olson's life. Why'd you have to ruin Dad's? Shitty whore."

She was alarmed by her brother's rage. "If you kept your rat-fink mouth shut it would never have happened."

"Slut liar!" he shouted. "You ruined your parents' marriage. Are you happy now?"

"Shuddup, Boney, you'll wake her up."

"I don't care. *Mom*," he screamed, "*Meena's a liar.*"

She flew at him, covered his mouth. He bit into the meat of her thumb. There's nothing for viciousness like a down-and-dirty between siblings. They slugged and bit and gouged, as if fury had pent up inside them and never found a proper target. A raging beast was released from someplace inside Jeff where he had kept it caged. She could only contain it by squeezing his balls until he gurgled. A trick Tiffany had taught her, but meant for a rapist.

Afterwards, they blubbered and hugged each other, went together into the bathroom to clean their wounds—his black eye, her bloody nose—as they'd done that other time. Couldn't care less if Mom found them together. There wasn't any rubbing alcohol, so Boney led her down to the kitchen. In a ghostly swatch of refrigerator light, he sterilized their wounds with lemon juice—reasoning that if rubbing alcohol smarts, then lemon juice, which bit fiercely into open flesh, must disinfect even better. There wasn't much in the fridge: a dozen eggs, a quart of milk, lemons, which Mom bit into whole, discarding the husks like a spider does the carapaces of its victims. Lemons were her primary nourishment. Mom's regression had reached rally squad days.

Sitting together in the dark living room, they confessed their sins in a litany of "If only I hadn't's," divvying up guilt between them—Mom's, Dad's and Olson's. How else could they comprehend what was happening to them? Meena tried to explain what she didn't understand herself: how powerless she had felt once accusations began . . . and powerful! Gratified in some strange way. How astonished when others were so eager to believe Dad had molested her: Ms. Childlove, Mom, the kids at Riverside.

It was her own fault. Wasn't she the girl? Some girls brought it on themselves. Like female spiders, putting out a scent the male can't resist . . . Whoever he is, he's still male. It could've happened, since it happened with Olson, which was nearly the same thing. Could have, considering the kiss Dad once gave her—right on the lips. She was *that kind of girl*. Even her own mom thought so. Besides, if you could imagine it had happened, wasn't it almost the same as true?

Boney frowned and turned away, troubled, saying they'd better get out of there before the cops returned. But they didn't move. Fear or loyalty or well-worn love weighed like a hand upon them. Mom would wake up soon, would be thirsty. Maybe, with any luck, the police would return and enforce some order on their lives. Though Meena doubted it. Nothing is less reliable in this world than sensible authority.

Boney went across to Buck's to call Aunt Debbie, certain they could count on her. But burst back into the house shortly later. "She's not coming," he panted. "We're in a shit heap and our aunt has to go off to Europe with her boyfriend. She couldn't care less."

They looked quietly about, as if seeing their predicament for the first time in its stark reality: counters bare of homey clutter, kitchen smelling of garbage (Mom's kitchen had always had a redolent crock of beans baking in the oven, suffusing the house with molasses sweetness), walls bare of ornament. More austere than Riverside.

"I told Debbie you lied," Boney said. "She already knew. She said she'd come see us when she got home. 'Honey, much as I'd like, I'm not your mama,' that's what she said." His eyes glistened angrily. Meena didn't want him to cry. Shout, scream, kick holes in the walls, but not cry. "Fucking bitch. I'm never gonna love her again."

They put TV dinners in the oven and sat at the dining bar. Boney tore a page from his school notebook and said from now on they had to take care of themselves, his eyes glistening determination as he sketched out a plan: They would pack Mom in the wagon and dump her at the main gate of Tranquility Acres on their way south, abandon the car at state line—before the fruit inspection station—and hitch from there to San Diego. They wrote up a list of rules Dad would have to follow if they agreed to live with him.

"What about Ms. Childlove?" Meena asked.

"You got to tell her it's a lie about Dad."

"They'll make me a permanent. Tiffany says if the court removes you from home they put you in foster. That's ten times worse hell than staying with Mom."

His eyes lit. "We'll hide out . . . get a job. You didn't do nothing, Meena. They can't arrest you for not being molested."

"They already did."

She and Boney looked at each other across the table, understanding at that moment that fate is a blind maze rather than an open road. We choose our destiny unaware that we are choosing it. Unwittingly, they had acquired a taste for insecurity. They drifted off to their separate rooms. Mom would wake soon, and Meena would go in and coax her to eat something. She was all white fat from booze calories, potbellied and wattle-armed, starving herself on vodka and lemons. Boney sat at his desk under the harsh yellow penumbra of the desk lamp, staring at book pages.

When car tires squealed into the drive, they both ran.

"Dad!" Jeff cried.

Neither of them thought "police." However, the man who stepped from the car on the driver's side in a London Fog raincoat—long lean face illumined by green dash lights—disoriented them a moment. Then Aunt Debbie got out. "My two favorite orphans," she said.

Next morning, when Mort and Boney were out getting them something to eat, just after Meena professed her father's innocence—in a tiny voice, staring down at her feet—Aunt Debbie told Mom something that made her go alien: shrieking crazy, fleeing the house in a panic.

While Meena confessed, Mom leaned back on the couch, vaguely smiling, chin tilted as if listening to something she alone could hear, beyond the tittering of rain against patio windows.

"I got confused," Meena insisted. "I didn't mean to. . . . I got confused, really, Mom."

Mom shook her head. "No, honey, wasn't y'r dad. It was your Grandpa Walter. In his wader boots . . . Remember, Deborah? He always wore a cap and red flannel shirt that itched like hell's fire ants against your skin. His pants bagged like a skirty skirt around his knees." She laughed unhappily.

"All right, Jerri."

"His balls hung down ten inches, one below t'other. Hah!"

"Damn you, Jerri."

"Bumpety-bumped against his knobbly knees. Isn't that a kick? Clopping about house in his shirt and waders, that carrot sticking out between his shirttails."

"Shuddup!"

Mom glared at Debbie, mouth crimped, lips crawling away from teeth. "He stuck that in cows' rear ends and children, Deborah! Anything that couldn't run away."

"Damn you to holy hell." Debbie leapt up.

Meena held a hand to her mouth, staring feverishly at her mother; Debbie seized her wrist and led her from the room, while behind them Mom's voice called, "She knows, darling. Mom knows everything."

From the entry hall, Meena picked up snatches of the sisters' low, intent dialogue in the other room: "Maybe you're drunk crazy, maybe you're plain crazy. You haven't a thing better to do in this world than kill yourself slow. . . . One or the other," she heard Debbie say. "You have to make a choice."

"You want to take my children?" Mom cried, her voice more bereft and forlorn than Meena had ever heard it.

"I want them safe," Debbie answered.

Then muffled sounds, as if they spoke with sacks over their heads. When Meena looked into the family room, Mom had Debbie up against clerestory windows; they tussled, gripping each others' arms, rocking side to side as if Indian-wrestling,

breath coming in quick gasps. Then Meena saw it propped up
on the hearth, the poker thing, thinking as she seized it she didn't
know which, which of them she would . . . which she wished to
protect, her eyes fixed intently on those two dark heads, one
raven black the other lit by gleams of inner fire. Just as Meena
saw her contorted face reflected back at her in plate-glass windows, Mom seemed to see it, too. She turned and fled past her
daughter, out of the house into the drizzly morning, whimpering:
"Over my dead body, Deborah . . . Over my dead body you will
take my children."

But Debbie did.

# 34

## Jeff

Aunt Debbie said we were supposed to stay at Buck's until she
got back from Europe. Under no circumstances were we to return to our house. Meena said it was permanent. She said Mom
and Debbie had a low-down drag-out fight, and Mom lost it
completely when Debbie said she was taking us away. But my
sister says lots of stupid things.

Aunt Debbie left Mom a note—since she'd took off before me
and Mort got home with breakfast—but didn't tell her we were
staying across the street. Buck's mom said it wasn't any trouble;
I could sleep in Buck's room and Meena could sleep on the
couch. But it made her nervous, I could tell. Her and his dad
were gone all day and didn't get home from the store until late.

We kept a close watch on our house. I was worried about
Mom, since no one was there to take care of her. The house was
totally dark; we weren't even sure Mom was at home. But
Meena said she was, because she saw her driving into the garage
in a dream. Meena said Debbie and Mort weren't coming back.
That's gonadal, I told her. But by the fourth day—two days after
my aunt called us from England—I was getting nervous, too.

The house looked totally forlorn and gave us the willies when we passed it coming home from school: so dismal and forgotten. So I said I would call Dad to come get us, but first Meena had to confess to him he didn't molest her.

"That's retro," she said. "He already knows."

"You accused him, Meena. Now you got to unaccuse him."

She scrunched down in the overstuffed couch and sulked at TV. "You tell him. I don't want to." She was prob'ly too embarrassed.

Dad laughed loud on the phone when I told him, like it was a joke. "I suppose she was angry at me for some reason," he said.

"You're not pee-o'd at her?" I was amazed.

"Water under the bridge, pal. Why don't you put your sister on."

Meena shook her head; she was sitting beside me at Buck's kitchen table. "She doesn't want to, Dad. Not yet."

"It's up to her." He sounded hurt. "How's your mom?" I told him Aunt Debbie had taken us away to scare Mom into sobering up. Dad was pissed. "Who gave her permission to do that?"

"I thought she told you."

"She sure as hell didn't tell me."

"Uncle Mort doesn't like it either," I said.

"Who the devil is Uncle Mort?"

"Her boyfriend. He's not a fruit or anything. Just a doctor."

"Some character named Mort?" Dad snorted. "Good deal, Debbie hooked herself an MD. I wonder if Dr. Mort knows he's kidnapping. Likely Debbie wouldn't; she's always been half-cocked. Runs in the family."

Dad wanted us to take the bus up to Grandma Sally's.

"Meena won't go. She hates Grandma Sally's guts."

"Hasn't your sister caused enough trouble in one family for a while?"

"Okay," I said. It seemed weird he was so hot under the collar, after all the times I had called and told him how we had to feed Mom and drive her to the liquor store and coax her out of the shower, how the kids called me a "son of a boozer." And all he ever said was he was working on it. "You never wanted to come before, Dad. What's so different about now?" I asked him.

He got pee-o'd then and said no one gave Debbie permission to take us kids away from home. "If Meena won't go to her grandma's, you had better come down here. Can you get to the bus station all right? I'll wire tickets."

I suddenly changed my mind. "We better not, Dad. Mom might need us."

"What about the old man? Doesn't he count? Son, I love your mother—I guess you know—but her needs have about swallowed this family whole."

"I know, Dad. I better get off now."

"There comes a time you have to declare it a lost cause. Comes a time you have to think about number one."

"I got to get off, Dad."

"Listen, Jeff! You're tangled up in a lot of women up there. And this Mort! I dunno. A guy can't go all watery-feely, can't let his mother's half-cocked notions, or his aunt's—"

"Sorry, Dad, I got to go." I hung up on him. In the dial tone, I thought I heard him calling my name over and over.

"We aren't going to Dad's," I told Meena.

"Mom's in trouble," she said in a low drone that wasn't her normal voice. She sat cross-legged on a chair and spoke in a swami trance—staring at the refrigerator like she could see Mom there. Gave me the willies. "She's sitting on a pile of clothes in her closet holding a knife. Every light in our house is on, every single one!"

"You don't know." I laughed. "You're guessing."

She shook her head. The kitchen overhead tinted my sister's face pale yellow like a Sphinx, hair hung in bundles over her ears. All of a sudden she looked like Mom, except her cheekbones harder, like Aunt Debbie's.

"Sometimes I hear her thoughts."

"You're making it up, Meena. Don't be a douche bag."

She turned to me. "It started at Riverside."

"The loony bin," I snorted. "What's she scared of?" I asked huskily.

"Dad. And Grandpa Walter with his carrot sticking out."

"Bug off, Meena, that's totally and completely retro."

"BFD." She sneered. "You don't even have one. I'm the one she should be scared of, 'cause I know what I'll do if I have to." The way she said it—eyes and voice narrowed—sent shivers down my spine. I told her it wasn't funny; some things you don't never joke about. Meena rubbed her bare arms; they'd gone goose bumps. Must've been contagious 'cause mine goose-bumped, too. I called to Buck in the living room. No way I wanted to be alone with my sister when she was going bonkers.

"I think y'r mom'th having a party," he said.

"A party? My mom?" I asked, amazed.

"Every thingle light in your houthe ith turned on."

I gaped at my sister, who was smiling weird. We ran outside to look. Our house glowed like a luxury liner afloat on the dark lawn, blazing light out of every porthole. Nothing—not Widow Grazziola sunbathing under the moon or when my head was cracked on the toilet—nothing ever creeped me out so bad. Mom had took possession of my sister's mind. Everybody had caught the personality virus. Meena worst of all.

Our keys didn't work 'cause Mom had thrown the bolts inside. That freaked us good. She didn't even want Meena and me coming in. When she didn't answer the doorbell, we went around back and knocked on windows. Then stood underneath her bedroom throwing pebbles against the window, yelling that it was safe for her to answer, it was only us. It was getting dark. Clouds hung like a heavy gray tarp across the sky; our voices hung off our lips like smoke. Above us, the house blazed light from every pore—except Mom's bedroom window, the only dark room in the house.

We got the extension ladder from the garage and put it up to her window. Buck's theory was if Meena got closer she could tell if Mom was okay—like radio reception, the closer you are to the tower the better it comes in. He was impressed she could read Mom's thoughts. She told him don't be a jerk-off.

"I only can sometimes. Now it's a blank."

"Maybe she's lying on the floor in a coma," I said.

I climbed up and knocked on her window. Nothing. Buck said we should call an ambulance, but I wanted to try getting inside first. Then I would make her check into a hospital; I was sick and tired of her games. My sister's bedroom window was open enough to pry it. We climbed the ladder and crawled into the familiar cherry Lifesaver smell of Meena's clothes and the fishgut stink of garbage leaking in from the hall. Somewhere a radio played. We crowded together in a huddle by the window, waiting for someone to go first. I had the same jittery, foreboding feeling as when I escaped from the hospital and Mom attacked me with the fireplace poker.

"I don't like it when she's so quiet," Meena breathed, clutching the chisel we used to pry the window.

"Don't be retro, Meena," I whispered. "Give it here. You going to stab Mom or something?"

She shoved me. "Go ahead, chicken .... It's only our sweed liddle Momsy doll."

I stepped out into the hall. We crept along with our backs to the wall, hands planted beside us, like on the Roundup at the Del Mar Fair and centrifugal force flattened us against the wall. Buck, who was never scared of anybody at school, looked spooked. His eyes big as fish bowls, pupils swimming back and forth. With his hair combed back, he looked like James Dean in *Rebel Without a Cause*; hair stuck out in greasy handles from the sides of his head.

"She prob'ly heard us break in anyway," I whispered.

"Yeah," he said softly.

"Talk normal then," Meena said in her normal voice.

We jumped. Inside Mom's closed door the radio played Lawrence Welk dance music. We smiled relief. No wonder she couldn't hear us. I knocked on her door. "Mom! It's just us: Meena, Buck and me. We came to see if you're okay."

No answer.

"Okay, Mom, you can open up." I knocked harder.

Just loud waltzy music.

"*It's us, Mom*," Meena shouted.

Still no answer.

We were all knocking and shouting: "Mom! Can you hear us?"

Music, only just wocky music, like ladies whirled inside in their white gowns and men in tuxes. We were all scared she might be dead or something, but didn't want to admit it. Buck looked expectantly at my sister.

"It's a blank," she insisted. "*Are you alien or something?*" Meena screamed at the door.

I grabbed her arm. "She prob'ly passed out."

Buck turned the knob and the door cracked open, wasn't even

locked. We tapped at each other—Meena, Buck, me—like three dumb monkeys. "It's our mom," I whispered, "it's only our mom." Pushing the door farther, I stuck my head inside with my biggest smile. Dodged back. Something tumbled through the air and slammed the door a whanging thud. Buck spun away, hands over his head. Meena rushed past me into Mom's room, the chisel raised. I went in after her. But we stopped short.

It stank in there as bad as the animal rot Chester used to bring up the canyon after he'd rolled in a dead animal. I gripped my mouth and gagged. The bed was mussed, fouler than ever. Back in shadows, a figure huddled, gripping its knees. Wasn't Mom. Couldn't have been. A ray of hall light pierced like the beam of a movie projector, lighting the person's chalky white knees. Their hair was cut in a short tufty crew cut; spikes stuck up in back and on the sides. She had Mom's eyes only puffier, like a boxer's swelled up after a fight, but the ears were too big, a purple birthmark across one cheek. It was Mom's crazy sister who they didn't never mention, who escaped from an insane asylum and killed our mom and put on her soiled nightgown. Behind me, Buck made that same sucking sound in his throat he had made that night at the widow's fence.

"Mom . . . ?" Meena asked in a tiny voice.

The figure beckoned with a hand for us to come closer. We crept forward, touching each other.

"Run, Deborash," she garbled, "y'r sis'er will protesh you."

Dumb Meena had approached nearly to the bed, her head craned forward in wonder. I touched her shoulder to stop.

"Mom," I said, "is that you?"

She jabbed a finger and sprang forward on her knees. She had the antler-handled carving knife Dad used on Thanksgiving. I cried out and slammed back into Buck, conking heads.

"Don' try, monsher! Ged away! Ged away from hersh. Deborash . . . " Mom—because it was her—seized my sister's arm, while Meena poked at the air with the chisel like she wanted to carve a space between them. Mom dropped the knife and grabbed Meena's other arm. They wrestled, my sister thrashing and twisting, Mom on her knees on the bed, too strong for her, pulling Meena onto her lap. She leaned over and bit my sister's wrist to make her drop the chisel.

I stood petrified, sure this crazy Mom would slit Meena open.

But she only cuddled her, rocking and cooing, stroking Meena's face. "Don' be sillish, y'r sis'er will protesh you."

"It's Meena," I said. "Mom!—It's Meena."

She scooted back to the corner on her butt, hugging Meena like a doll. Meena's whole body heaved in terrified sobs.

"Please, Mom, let her go."

"Don' you toush 'er." She rocked side to side, her free hand tousling my sister's hair, while the other wrapped around her, holding the knife blade flat against Meena's back. My sister made gurgling baby noises, her face buried in Mom's neck. In a strange, throaty, sober voice, like the voice of the insane sister who had taken over her body, Mom said: "Dad, y'r not wearing y'r cap. Isn' that a kick. Put that pole away. You can' go fishing withoud y'r waders."

"Please, Mom, let her go," I begged, trying not to get her excited.

Just then she must've saw Buck behind me: She let go a blood-curdling scream, her eyes rolled white. She clutched Meena harder, the knife digging against her spine. "Ish only y'r brozher Chuck," she whispered crazy to my sister. "Ish on'y brozher Chucky an' Walder. We'll cud off 'is carrod. Hah." Motioning me with a crooked finger. "C'mon, Daddy Dick, Chucky Chuck Chuck . . . Come an' geddit. Izzis whad you wan'?"

Heaving Meena aside, she pulled up her gown. She was bare naked underneath. "Izzis whad you wan'? Izzit? Take id an' leave ush alone. *Leave me alone!*" she shrieked, her eyes crazy popping light bulbs. Panicking me . . . what she did next, more than all the nutty years put together.

Hallway light flashed off the knife blade, the rough antler handle and two evil silver horns at its base. Seizing the blade in her left hand, Mom yanked aside her gown and bucked her hips, grinning insane. It was nothing, nothing I ever wanted to see. Blood curled off her buckled fingers and rolled down the silver blade.

I barfed. Turned and collided with Buck, sonuvabitch, who stared at what my mom was doing to herself with a knife handle. I slugged him with both fists and shoved him into the doorjamb. Into it again. Behind me Meena was screeching. Pulling the knife out of Mom's bloody fingers, shrieking: "*You crazy fucking stupid retro-assed bitch*! You gonna cut out y'r alien guts?" She heaved the knife clattering against the wall and slapped Mom with both hands, struggling to break free. "I'll kill you. I promise I'll kill you, you crazy witch."

I ran to help her. My mom. To break it up. Trying to get between them. Seeing at the last instant the chisel in Mom's bloody hand, stabbing for my stomach. And would've bought it if my sister didn't grab her arm. It only nicked me, taking a gash of shirt and skin. I rolled away across the bed.

Mom hugged Meena tight. Try hard as she could, my sister couldn't break free. Mom's face leaned toward me, inches from mine. I stared up at her chafed, cracked lips, eyes bright as twin moons in a wedge of hall light. "Walder," she said solemnly, "over my dead body you will damash that girl again."

I scrambled off the bed and backed out of the room, trying to remind myself it was only Mom. My mother. Once she was. You couldn't mistake your own son for your dad—not that close up—unless you were completely cracked.

We ran outta there, Buck and me. Across to his house.

His sister was in the kitchen fixing tea. "Buck, Jeff, what's got into you boys?" she asked. We leaned against the door panting and shaking our heads, avoiding her insistent green eyes.

"Are you fellows in trouble again?"

"Hith mom—" Buck began.

"She's okay," I cut him off. "Meena's saying good-bye." Because it hit me in a flash what I was going to do.

Buck looked at me like I was . . . like our whole family went totally bonkers.

When his sister left the kitchen, I called Dad collect. No answer. I knew it wasn't any use calling Grandma Sally; she had washed her hands of us. Besides, she'd make Mom even nuttier. I told Buck I was hitching down to my dad's. He would come and help me get Meena outta there and check Mom into the hospital. Buck said I better call the cops before Mom cut Meena up. But I knew they would put us in permanent, would lock Mom up in the loony bin and throw away the key. I knew she wouldn't hurt my sister, except the smell, and Meena was used to that. I told Buck to tell his Mom we took the bus down to our dad's. Everything was cool. I asked him to keep a watch on the house.

"If anything crazy happens, call the cops."

"What'th crathee if it ithn't crathee already?"

He was right, I knew. He loaned me his bomber jacket to make me look older and a pack of cigarettes to offer people who gave me rides. With any luck, I figured, I would be in Escondido by late next afternoon.

# 35

# Aunt Debbie

She wasn't going to take Europe away from me, my sister. All my life I'd wanted to go. All my life! Goddamn Jerri to holy hell. But she did take it in the end. Same old story.

"You get to feeling like a one-person clean-up crew," I told Mort on the flight home. "The minute you get a break, there's crude oil spilled all over some fragile shoreline. Come quick!"

Truth be told, I didn't enjoy a minute of that trip, knowing I shouldn't have left Jerri in her condition. A voice barked at me in the London underground, Charing Cross station, when the train pulled in: *Mind the gap*. I took it as a personal reproach. By Paris, on the fourth day, I told Mort I had to get back.

"Something's gone wrong, I sense it. I shouldn't have left Jerri alone in the first place."

"Then we'll go back," he said. "Europe can wait."

When I called, Buck's sister told me the kids had taken the Greyhound to their father's. Wouldn't you know, Don wasn't home when I tried. I called Sally and asked if she'd heard from them. "Why, you know I haven't. Jerri hasn't spoken to me in weeks." I asked her: Did we have a history of mental illness in our family. Sally was scandalized. "Of course not. What kind of question is that to ask clear across the world?"

"Just curious," I said.

I was haunted by an image of Jerri the night we had driven down from Portland; I'd walked right upstairs into her room and blinked the overhead. My sister looked ten years older. Gave me a fright, I'll say. I badgered her from bed to the vanity mirror, supporting her arm. "I wonder if you know, Jerri! You look like honest-to-God shit." Cruel medicine, but sometimes there's no choice. The vanity was a marquee in the red-light district, bulbs burned out. My sister's face lined and puffy. When our eyes met in the mirror, she shrieked. Scared the lumps off my tail. Jerri scrambled back to bed, shielding her face with a pillow, peeking out at me. God knows what she saw.

I grabbed her thermos from the night table, rifled drawers and closet. Same old same old: an orange juice jar full of hooch. Jerri crouched on the bed, eyes following me like a large vindictive family pet. I raised the bottle. "One move, Jerri, I swear I'll coldcock you. You haven't the sense God gave a dead mule." I dumped the bottle in the hall, called Meena to bring up a piddle pan and water. "Don't even try coming out," I warned my sister when I shut her door. She could DT, hang herself from the closet bar, I didn't care. Europe or no, I was going to dry her out enough to talk sense—feed just enough booze into her veins to keep her from detoxing too fast.

"This takes a hospital," Mort admonished me. "It's tricky business. Her gut's hard as a football, her blood pressure—"

"Try it my way first. If it doesn't work, we'll do it your way. She needs more than a hospital."

I imagined her huddled inside, listening, feline eyes glowing in the dark. We sent the kids to bed and Mort sat up half the night, me the whole: lying on couch pillows in Jeff's room, imagining the vigil he'd kept these past weeks. Chastising myself for it. I wondered does a person have any right to their own life when all hell has broke loose next door? Those kids had lived like this all their lives and me next door to it—knowing they did, wishing to believe they didn't. Offering water to a body that needs blood. Maybe that had to change.

Mort went in at dawn to examine Jerri. I came in on him listening at her bare back, telling her, okay, she could raise her gown. A near stranger who had walked into her bedroom; he had that way about him. By noon Jerri was up and dressed, want to call it that. "Good to see you up," Mort said. I told her she was looking chipper, wondered if it was Halloween, considering her outfit: Little Orphan Annie and Barbarella in one. Jerri's eyes fixed on Mort, dark and puzzled. She whispered in my ear that he had molested her this morning.

"No, hon, he's a doctor."

She was edgy, eyes roaming from kitchen to Mort again, in search of her thermos: bumpy, twelve hours without a shot.

"We're going to do this in pieces," I told her. "Nobody expects you to cold turkey."

Jerri regarded us coolly. Old stonewall hauteur. Drinking problem? Hadn't a clue to what I was talking about. I went into my suitcase and got the bottle, poured two fingers in a glass of orange juice. "Hair of the dog." Jerri wolfed it, hands trembling. She looked up at me, expecting more.

"Step by step," I said.

When Mort and Jeff went out for food, I asked if Meena wanted to tell her mother the truth about Don or if I should. She sat primly in a wing chair speaking toward her tartan plaid lap, hair falling in a fringe over her eyes. Might have been her mom twenty years earlier, prettiest gal in class. She had Jerri's hair, Don's squinting eyes.

Jerri smiled politely as if Meena were discussing some silly school project instead of family crimes. Right then—seeing my sister confuse her daughter's pain for her own and Don for Walter—I knew the time had come to get those kids out of the house. Jerri would have to make it as best she could on her own until we got home. Because she wasn't taking Europe away from me. Not on a bet.

"Booze or your kids," I told her. "Make a choice. You can't have both anymore, hon. I'll see to that."

Jerri went cold sober. "You're going to take my children?"

"I don't know how else to reach you."

"You want my children?" she asked softly.

"I want them safe—until you can prove you want to be their mother."

"You always wanted them, Deborah. First my husband, now my kids. All along." Moving in on me.

"Turkey piss. I want you to come to your senses. When you've good and decided you want them back, we'll see."

She came forward into my face, crouched at the knees as if about to spring. "I found your shoe in my closet, Deborah, the spangly one. He fucked you, too. Isn't that cozy?" Her finger shot out. "Don't you dare." One wing of her blouse collar had buckled under. Her fingernails scraped the kitchen door post, gouging out curlicues of paint.

"Let's don't do this, hon. Let's try to be dignified."

She had walked me against plate-glass windows. God almighty fishhooks. Scared, I'll say. Her mad stumbling words: something about a man in wader boots and incest bastards didn't count. Eyeballing me, furious, like I better didn't contradict. I studied Jerri's clenched teeth—jacketed in brown overcoats—eyes gone blistering mad, wild as Nez Percé horses. My shoulders flat against cold glass. I wondered how it was possible . . . two sisters? Blood kin! Then we were wrestling upright, fingers clawing into biceps.

Over Jerri's shoulder, I glimpsed Meena gripping the fireplace poker, knuckles white as bleached daylight. She crept forward, the poker raised above her head. I moved then—because sometimes you must. Chopped my sister behind the ear, leapt forward as she staggered and steered her away from a daughter with cold murder in her eyes. Jerri broke away with a strength I couldn't match. I'd heard of that: the strength of madness.

"Over my dead body, Deborah; over my dead body you will take my children." She bolted for the entry, colliding with Meena, clawing at her. "Hurry, honey, we have to find your brother."

Meena struck out wildly with the poker, just missing Jerri's head, sinking the cruel curved end of the iron deep into wood paneling. We heard Jerri's car squeal into the loop, a furious shriek of tires. All was normal at the Tillotsons'.

"Bitch," Meena hissed, "I'll kill her."

I didn't doubt she might.

I took the kids to stay at the neighbors' across the street. It scared hell out of me to realize I wasn't bluffing. Where it might lead: courts, hospitals, custody battles. But love is like an old person, not worth a damn without its teeth. Someone had to act, that's the thing.

On the flight home, I told Mort it's like you've waited all your life for something to happen, knowing it must. All your life you sense it coming, though can't say what you expect exactly. And though you haven't any name to call it, you know when its time has come. Just do. A blood thing. A truth in the blood, call it. You know.

I should've gotten those kids out of there months back. Children can't sit and watch their mother deteriorate. It eats them up. Meena was hanging out with a tough crowd. Dressed like a slut. Wouldn't surprise me she had sex for the asking, like she wished to fulfill something. There was this dependency thing between them: Jeff did her homework, Meena washed his clothes. They looked out for each other, but it wasn't healthy. Each needed the other to complete themselves. Mort covered my hands with his long miraculous fingers and told me to get some rest.

I slept fitfully, like you do on planes. Jumped up once to catch a passenger's buzzer. Forgot I wasn't flying myself. "Greenland does that to you," one of the gals said after they'd stopped laughing. "Someday I'm gonna buy it over Greenland, I just know it," she said. I told them I preferred dry flights. Decided right then and there if I ever did Europe again I'd take a ship— me! With ten years on my feet in the air.

Millford was clear skies, tepee burners glowing like cigar tips, half pretty from above. The puddle jumper's wheels squeaked as we touched down; as cozy a sound as a voice you love entering the house when you've flown all these years.

The taxi dropped us at Rodeo Loop. House rising pitch dark above the boxy lawn, suburban gothic, might say. Tower of London ranch style. Stars twinkled above the ragged ornamental spruce, strands of Don's Christmas lights like cobwebs against the sky. I started up the steps, imagining Jerri might be waiting by the entry clerestory, peering out at me as she had that other time. Mort called from below, saying he heard voices in back. We went around. Don's Corvette was parked in Dr. Weatherspoon's drive next door. As we passed below the kitchen window, we heard glass shatter. Mort reached out a palm against my chest as we approached the side porch. Men's voices just ahead. Flashlight beams.

"Hullo?" I cried.

"Deborah? That you?" It was Don.

We waved flashlights out of our eyes. Don was about thrilled as duck piss to meet Mort. "Where are my kids, Deborah? I'd like to know what you've done with my children."

"I thought they were with you, Don."

"They sure as hell aren't with me." His breath in my face; he'd been drinking.

"Calm down," Mort said.

"Sure, Doc. No problem. You got any other advice after kidnapping my kids?"

"That'll do," said Dr. Weatherspoon. "Buck tells me Meena is here with her mother. That so, Buck?"

I hadn't noticed the boys, Buck and Dr. Weatherspoon's son, standing in shadows by a rhododendron.

"Couldn't be," Don insisted. "She would have answered the door. I've been here over an hour." His voice tight as elastic stretched near to popping.

"Meena'th Mom hath a knife," Buck said, stark and startling. "Jeff hitched down to California to get hith dad."

"To get me?" Don snorted. "But here I am!"

"Doesn't make sense," Dr. Weatherspoon agreed. "If you kids were in trouble you could have come to us."

"Not unleth it wath an emergenthee."

"Well, for Pete's sake."

"We going to stand here arguing when God knows what's happening in there?" Don demanded. Mort tapped Dr. Weatherspoon's shoulder and angled the light into Don's face, wishing to confirm what his voice told us. Don's cheek flinched—features cinched tight from fear, drink and lack of sleep.

They'd broken a window to open the utility room door since Don's keys wouldn't work. "Let me go first," Mort suggested.

"You!" Don snorted. "Big chance."

We all went in, moving cautiously room to room, turning on lights as we went, calling in eager voices. Mort motioned at me to get Don away before he saw a great splotch of dried black blood on Jerri's bed sheet. There was more smeared over the shower door and bathroom counter. "Jesus Christ." Don tested it between his fingers as if trying to tell whose it was. Scared, all of us, I'll say. Half sick with worry. I'd never been much good at praying, but I was trying my best. Looked like thieves had rifled the house: furniture toppled, clothes spilled from drawers, the air saturated with a rotting, gangrenous smell. Dr. Weatherspoon stood over the bed shaking his head, saying they should've hospitalized that woman long ago. A large, melon-headed man with a small boy's haircut and an abiding faith in Richard Nixon. "Keep it to yourself," I told him.

The boys were calling from downstairs; they'd found what we should have noticed first off but hadn't in our eagerness to search the house. A clerestory pane shattered and glass splashed across the patio as if someone had run right through, a drying puddle of blood inside. Mort dropped to his knees and dabbed a finger in; it came away sticky, long dark spidery filaments stringing from it. "Within half an hour, I'd say."

Don shook his head. "Couldn't 've been."

We searched in earnest then—inside garage storage doors, beating the arborvitae hedge, calling hesitantly, then boldly as we all took it up, voices soaking into the night air:

MEEEENNNAAA . . . JERRRIIII

Scared spitless, truth be told. Half guessing already what we would find. We'd gone into the empty lot in back that extended to the widow's fence. I thought of the time Buck and Boney dumped dirt into her yard. Something clicked in my head but didn't quite turn over. We stood in a huddle, the glow of flashlights illuminating our faces like a campfire: boys' eyes wide and eager, Don's fleeting. Early crickets scolded us from the grass. "What exactly are we looking for?" Dr. Weatherspoon asked— the type always has to say what no one else wishes to. His answer came waddling across the empty lot toward us.

"Hellooo," it called timidly. "Hellooo there." It was Widow Grazziola. She had seen Jerri just before dark, she said. "Scurrying along, you see, she and her daughter. Acting peculiar, tugging one another this way and that. They went into the brush there—" She pointed. "I thought, well, isn't that odd. Don't you think? You see, I didn't wish to be nosy."

"Tugging?" Don asked.

"Yes, in an odd sort of way. The girl's mother was dragging her. Well, I didn't wish to nose in." She blinked, shielding her eyes from the light Don shone in her face.

"She dragged her into those bushes?" Mort asked.

The boys were whispering, arguing about something. Dr. Weatherspoon's son piped up, "That's where we dug our tunnel."

"Rat fink," Buck snapped.

We glanced at each other, all remembering at once.

"Tunnel!" Don cried.

"God almighty fishhooks . . . You don't think—" But I'd already plunged into the brush, Mort and the boys behind me.

# 36

## Jeff

My first ride left me off in Weed. It was cold and desolate in the mountains. Wind whistled past my ears and cut through Buck's bomber jacket like a sharp wet tongue. Out on Highway 5, trucks blasted past, throwing cold walls of wind in my face and gritty sand that stung my cheeks. Some slowed but kept on going; I wasn't sure if I was more disappointed or relieved. I had a weird feeling Meena was hitching with me, though I couldn't see her. I walked in circles slapping my arms, kept looking over at bright warm diner lights, surrounded by a sea of trucks; but whenever I considered going over for a hot chocolate, I saw Meena huddled on Mom's bed. I heard my sister's voice hiss at me to get my ass in gear.

A lady in a pickup stopped. She was Aunt Debbie's age, dressed in faded blue jeans and a frilly buckskin jacket. Her truck interior was upholstered in thick lamb's fleece and the seat in old jeans—pockets, zippers, everything. Pretty cool. She looked me over. "You a runaway?" I told her I was going to my dad's in San Diego. She nodded, her face lean and tough-looking in dash lights, full of old pimple scars. "I run away at twelve," she said, "ain't been back since." She smiled ahead down the road. Country-western music filled the cab like warm bathwater, and Joy tapped rhythm on the steering wheel. "Makes you feel free." She lit up a thin brown cigarette, the smoke sweet and musty, like the smell of our basement the time Olson set it on fire. I leaned against the door and fell asleep, would've gladly rode clear to San Diego like that, but she stopped south of Red Bluff and said, "End of the line, cowboy. I got people to meet and bills to pay."

One taillight kept winking at me until it disappeared over a hill. Then I was alone. Just an arc lamp and a green sign: SAN FRANCISCO 186. There was a gas station at a crossroads under the overpass, dark except for the light in a pay phone out front. I went down to call Dad. The phone rang and rang with a hollow echoing sound on the far end. Where was he at two in the morning? Up on the freeway, a station wagon hummed past at about ninety. Mom! I thought, and ran around back to hide.

I sat against a stack of old tires in a heavy, drowsy smell of motor oil, looking across a fence at open range and the dark outline of hills to the west. Far-off shapes, which I took for bushes, kept moving. Cattle, I decided. It made me less lonely to think it was cows. Wind moaned across stacks of tires like breath across the mouth of an empty bottle. I thought of the weird sister who'd took over my mom's soul and Meena holed up in our house with her. I didn't want to think about it. My sister could take care of herself—that's what I kept telling myself.

I was freezing my nuts off. I struggled to keep my eyes open. If you fall asleep in the cold you're a goner; everyone knows that. Stars were bright as lanterns over western hills; they shimmered and made me dizzy. I slapped my arms and fought drowsiness, my eyelids heavy as pig iron. Slowly, bushes beside the fence turned into fawn-colored cows and grazed close around me. . . . Grandpa Walter's cows—Guernseys like the one pulled Dad down the river. They gathered and watched me drift off.

Next thing I knew, Mom lunged with the antler-handled knife. Meena stopped it with her hand, the thick blade pierced right through the hammy part behind her knuckles. My sister turned her hand this way and that, fascinated by the blade stuck through, then pulled it out with a wet gristly sound and plunged it into Mom's chest. My teeth chattered too hard to scream. A cow's skull mounted on the gas station wall grinned at me, then turned into my sister's face. Her mouth opened: *I'm gonna kill that bitch*. But Meena's teeth were a grinning tire-pressure gauge, lips coiled like a red insect tongue.

Something awful had happened. Meena's mind reached out to me from up north, like when we were younger and I knew she was spying outside our tunnel. Mom had closed her in a closet and the weight of clothes on top of her was like a stack of tires twenty feet high. Meena couldn't breathe.

An old Buick fishtailed up the hill. A beer bottle flew out the window, spun and glistened in the thin blue air. High over my head, tires leaned like the Tower of Pisa. Amazing they didn't fall down on top of me. I noticed every detail: black grains of sand on my white sand pillow, a dandelion weed broke through asphalt inches from my nose, yellow petals grubbed in oil, Camel cigarette butts crimped in letter "L's." The light was orange-lavender, just being born. I forced myself to sit up. But when I tried to stand, my legs were ice blocks and I tottered like an old man.

My first surprise: Instead of walking up the on-ramp to I-5 South, I passed under the overpass and went up the other side and stood under a sign: PORTLAND 455. Didn't know I was going back until then. It was beautiful, if your teeth weren't chattering nonstop automatic and your ass pins and needles. Western hills salmon pink; to the north, Mt. Shasta's cone glowed fluorescent purple, its top gleaming icy white in the first sunlight. A lavender mist hung over range lands; the sky overhead so clear and blue you could tap it with a hammer and it would ring.

It took me four short rides before I caught a lift with a trucker going to Portland about noon. I dreaded getting home, afraid Mom would still be crazy, not knowing what I would do when I got there. I tried remembering the good times: long ago on Walnut Street before Mom went retro, how we made homemade blackberry ice cream in the hand-crank ice-cream freezer, packed in ice and rock salt, turning the crank till our arms wore out. It was sweet and delicious. Deep down, Mom still had that sweetness inside, but she'd got locked in a jacket of ice and needed to break free. I knew we could never return to Walnut Street days, but maybe we could go back to how it was in California before I ratted on Olson.

It was getting dark as we climbed the Siskiyous, the driver's face lit up in the green glow of dials and gauges on the instrument panel like a Martian astronaut's. I cupped a hand to my mouth and whispered into it like a CB radio—close enough for Meena to pick up reception. I listened for her while the truck engine whined and the quiet landscape rolled by outside. No answer. Nothing.

The trucker dropped me at the foot of Rodeo Loop. It was only just a day since I left, but seemed like a month. I hurried past familiar houses. Stopped dead in my tracks at the top of the loop. Cop cars and an ambulance were parked in our driveway, a fire engine out front, its bubble-gum lamp flashing red-and-blue wedges across houses. Every light in our house was on, like before. "What's wrong?" I asked out loud, then started to run. Did Mom try to set our house on fire? Did they come to arrest her for the golf course? Or my sister for skipping her interview? When I saw Dad's Corvette parked at the Weatherspoons', I was never so relieved in my life. Everything was hunky-dory. Copacetic. He came to bail Mom out, that's all; the ambulance would take her to drying out. My bonerhead sister prob'ly called the fire truck by mistake.

I ducked under yellow police tape they put around crime scenes and ran up the front steps. The front door was open. "It's me," I shouted. Nobody answered. I wasn't scared, not at all. Everything was under control. Dad was there and the State Police. No problema. "Mom . . . Meena?" I called, going upstairs to look in their rooms. Nobody answered. Like the *Invasion of the Body Snatchers*. Everyone had disappeared. There was blood on Mom's sheet from where she cut her hand. They should've washed it by now, it would stain. Nobody downstairs either. My heart was pounding.

I stopped at the living room door. Then I heard my sister's voice tell me to go on. She tapped my shoulder and I crouched down beside the ugly striped couch Buck's dad loaned us and turned over a cushion: all splotched beneath where Mom stained it with coffee—so looped she had fell and spilled it. I followed my sister like on the road, through the kitchen where dirty dishes still filled the sink from before Aunt Debbie left, overflowing garbage, a row of empty booze bottles lined up on the counter. Beside them a bandage; blood soaked through the gauze, rust red and mucousy at center, yellow-orange at the edges.

I stopped right there in the garbage smell and said I didn't want to go any farther. It was stupid. Nobody was home. Half the cop cars in town were parked in front. It was a bad joke. But I could make out Meena standing beside clerestory windows in the family room, pointing down at shattered glass—a jagged hole where it looked like somebody ran through. She knelt and placed her hand flat on a splotch on the floor, lifted it to show me her bloody palm. "No!" I cried, "I won't go in." Dear God, I prayed, if only they're okay—Mom and Meena!—I will do anything, God, just if she's okay. I'll never leave her alone again, my sister either. Never. I promise.

Don't be a jerk. I walked into the family room, smiling, because I figured it out. They were waiting for me around the corner by the fireplace. *Surprise!* they would shout.

But the room was stark empty. Cool air poured through the broken plate glass—with voices and the roar of heavy equipment! Beyond the arborvitae hedge, spotlights lit up Mr. Ashcroft's compost heap, aimed down at darkness spilling from the ground in a smoky vapor, snaking dust which we once carried in gunnysacks to spill over the widow's fence. I realized then that I knew they would be there all along. I knew . . . just didn't want to admit the truth to myself. I had seen it long ago, burned like a prophecy into the tunnel wall. Steve called me a spas. But even then I knew. Knew why we dug the tunnel in the first place.

I closed the door behind me and trudged across the yard toward lights and voices. My legs stiff, my body shivering like the morning's chill had never left me. Knowing I had to see what I didn't wish to see. The truth was out there waiting.

# 37

# Meena

Mom licked blood off her sliced fingers one by one, tongue poking at creases, diligent as Chester's. Retro fucking nutcase! She stank like rancid hamburger. Meena led her downstairs after the boys had fled and held her slit fingers under tap water over a sink full of dirty dishes, since bathrooms stank too much to enter, the toilets clogged with shit. Water curled pink along contours of white plates. Mom opened her mouth, leaned her forehead against her daughter's shoulder, but didn't cry out. Hardly any taller than me, Meena thought. She ran into the bathroom for gauze and tape. Something had to be done. Even Aliens learn to flush.

She lay Mom on the couch—eyelids flagging, cheek slumping against an armrest—and sat facing her, wondering what now. Chickenshit Boney had run away. Call the hospital? Say screw her and flee—across lawns into the arms of neighbors who'd surely been alerted by her brother? Instead, she fell asleep sitting up in the bright room. When she opened her eyes, Mom stared at her, ghoulish, as if fingers had stretched down her lower eyelids. Bloody fingerprints intertwined across her filthy gown. A wooden hand squeezed her heart. Meena knew the signs: DTs or plain fucking nutcase retro freakination. But this time was different. Meena saw them too: worms wiggling grublike out of floor cracks, crawling up their ankles, tumbling off and writhing in coiled balls at their feet, over Mom's toenails on which flecks of red polish clung like a tawdry remnant of her former self. Their eyes were facing mirrors across an empty room.

"Deborah?"

Meena watched her walk into the kitchen and dive under the kitchen sink, knocking things out onto the floor. Fucking retro would drink liquid bleach or her own piss if she thought the alcohol content high enough. Let her. *Let her kill herself before I do myself. I'm outta here.* Now! Dodge out the door into the night. Instead, Meena lined up empty bottles on the counter, sloshed two fingers of water into the first, swished it about to get tailings, poured from one to the next under Mom's hungry gaze. Mom swilled down the tag end and grimaced, expecting stronger. Meena promised to take her for more. Better that than have her walk half-naked down Rogue River Road.

In the bright glare of kitchen lights before the window, she seized the neck of her mother's funky gown and ripped it vertically like an old rag—before watching eyes of the neighborhood . . . Except no one watched. No one cared. With a dishrag softened by suds, Meena scrubbed streaks of grime from Mom's pasty white deflated breasts and flaccid skin about her navel—a body which, six months ago, gleamed pecan-brown beside Wendy's pool, hadn't a loose pinch of flesh anywhere. Mom waited to be dried, obedient as a poodle. Meena sensed the tension in her tightening buttocks; Mom's eyes swiveled to the utility room door.

"No one's in there," she barked.

"Your brother—Chucky Chuck. Isn't that a riot!"

"My uncle Chuck, who got killed in Korea before I was born."

Mom trembled, her skin gone goose bumps. Meena guided her upstairs, repeating like a mantra to herself: *I'm in control, in control* . . . because Tiffany swore it worked, because she had to be. She retrieved a crumpled organdy blouse from the closet floor. Mom let herself be dressed, a tiny smile on her lips. Orb spiders throw loop-the-loops around their victims to pin them down, bitsy eyes gleaming. "I'm going to brush your hair," Meena said, as to a child. "When we get back, I'll do laundry."

*Then I'm outta here. She'll pass out drunk on clean sheets and I'm outta here.* She would call the alcohol retro squad, hitch to Tiffany's in Suckramento, split to San Francisco. *There's a million runaways in San Francisco; no one will find us.*

But something had happened, she knew—was hit with it before Mom slammed her hard as a Roller Derby blocker and sent her sprawling into closet doors. One teetered and whumped to the rug on a cushion of air. Meena limped behind into her room, where Mom stood at the window in blouse and underpants, peeking through a curtain crack, pantyhose halfway down a leg.

"It's y'r dad," she whimpered. "Don't let him see you."

From the window, Meena could see Buck standing in the dark driveway below, looking up. He waved. Before Meena could wave back, Mom yanked her away, speaking hotly in her face, more filthy-mouthed than Monica at Riverside: his wader boots, tobacco-smelly fingers, stiff yellow dick stuck out between red shirttails . . . every grotty detail. Teeth scissors snipping out words. She grabbed her daughter between the legs. Meena slapped her, she slapped back. "Over my dead body, Deborah." Seizing her daughter's hair, she dragged her to the bathroom, heels skidding along the hallway rug. Too strong! The strength of psychosis. She could break down a door. When Meena screamed for Buck, Mom clamped a hard hand over her mouth;

Meena opened, Mom's bandaged fingers slipped inside and Meena bit down to bone. Wounds bloomed open, flooding her mouth: Mother's blood, almost her own. Still, the mouth wished to throw it up.

Mom dragged her into that shit smell, pinned her to the sink counter with a hip and yanked open the laundry hamper. Paying no attention to Meena's "Mommy please's," she lifted and plunked her inside. Meena knew the icy sound of metal doors clanging shut, solid oak doors thumping, but never anything to match the sinister hiss of that hamper on its wooden guides, the thump of its closing reverberated through her skull, a slithery liquid noise as Mom tied it shut with pantyhose.

The first terror was claustrophobic—boxed in, knees buckled to chest, neck crooked against the underside of the counter—then suffocation: in her own sweat stink, the stale, tired odor of soiled laundry, something vaguely sweet—Mom's cologne—plywood and paint, slowly overwhelming all, the shit stink leaking in around her. No, she wouldn't suffocate, except in outrage.

*For years afterward, I was phobic about my bodily functions. The whisper of Dr. Langerhorn's nylons, shifting in her chair, wheeled me into terror. We started with sounds. Then smells, until we hit on a combination: shit, soiled clothes, sweat, cologne . . . the smell of soil. But what about the rest of it? Had she tried to strangle me with her pantyhose? Did smells follow us underground—cologne, dirty jeans, my own sweat, the stink of dirtying myself in fear?*

Later, when she heard Mom's car start in the garage below, leaving her locked in that bin, room, house—for hours? days? for good?—she shrieked and rattled the hamper on its guides. When the first panic passed, she concentrated. Mom had gone for beer to Mason's All Hours, she'd be back. The image of Mom walking in barefoot in her underwear to the delight of winos and late delivery men was nearly comforting.

She prayed. Not to God—whom she'd long since disavowed for the fucked-up world he'd plunked her into—but to Boney. (After cursing him for deserting her; she'd thought he was different, thought it was thick and thin between them.) She tried locating him on a vague mental map. *Come back quick.* When Mom's wagon squealed into the drive, she knelt silently on her cushion of clothes and prayed that Mom would forget where she'd hidden her.

Milky light leaked through vent holes beside her left ear, projecting a polka-dot pattern against the back wall of the hamper. Raw breaths of excrement leaked in. She alternated between bouts of frenzied rocking and fitful sleep; she couldn't feel her toes; small chisels carved at her neck. Once, Mom came in to pee, squatting in the shower stall. When tap water ran overhead, Meena begged Mom to let her out. The sink drain clanked shut beyond Meena's right ear. Maybe Mom disliked the plumbing talking to her. Her bare feet squeaked away over bathroom tiles.

She'd lost all sense of time. Had hours passed? Days? She was thirsty, aware of tap water just overhead. She placed hands against a crossbar at back of the bin, trying to reposition her numb legs; a jabbing pain shot up her spine, she jerked involuntarily, something snapped, nails creaked, she slammed against the front of the bin and it broke free. Meena toppled out onto the floor.

Pins and furious needles. It was long before she could straighten her legs. She quenched her thirst from the tap. Then poured two fingers of green Drano crystals into a glass—Shep had taught her—filling it half full of water: sodium hydroxide! Lye! It sputtered and fizzled like witch's brew. She promised herself she wouldn't use it unless she absolutely must. It was quiet, so quiet. She hobbled down the stairs, glass cocked to one side, evil and sizzling. She would walk straight out the front door. No way Mom would stop her this time. No way.

Mom knelt in the living room peeking over the windowsill. Meena ducked back into the entry, but Mom had sensed her presence. She motioned Meena down. The front door was three steps away: outside! Freedom from that crazy retro skunkdrunk witch.

A car door slammed. Mom whisper-shouting: "Ged down, ish y'r daaa, ish y'r daaa." Crazy loony lushbrain. Not this time. Meena cocked the glass. *Try, bitch, just try.* Foam piled along sides, a flotsam of green pellets on its roiling surface—filthy as the river that time Grandpa Walter's cow drowned. She visualized caustic green scum catching Mom's face and peeling down skin, sizzling to clean white bone.

"Debo-rash, ish y'r daaa, the man in wader boosh."

Crazy fucking loony loon. But the car in the drive caught her attention through plate glass: familiar tail fins of Daddy's Corvette "fuck mobile" (Olson called it). Dad stood beside it looking at the house. She shook her head violently but his image remained: crumpled blue sports jacket, white shirt unbuttoned at collar, tan face and scattered, boyish hair. Outside, it was the pearly white time of morning—or twilight . . . she wasn't sure. He was walking toward the steps. Instead of the joy she might've expected upon seeing him, cold fear gripped her. She rubbed fists in her eyes, but he refused to become who he really was: Buck's dad or the gray cop with tallowy lips. Mommy had opened her mind's laundry bin and come inside.

"It was as if she had invaded me somehow," Meena would remember later. "I felt my cheeks bloat to accommodate hers, my breasts and hips swelled. I was terrified my skin would split open like a dead frog's. A residue of stale beer at the back of my tongue, thoughts slurred in my mind, I stumbled toward the window, afraid I would fall through. I saw at the last moment that Dad wasn't wearing a sports jacket at all but a red flannel shirt. He was coming. For an instant, I knew my mother's terror."

Something slammed into her, taking her with it upstairs. The glass fell from her hand and broke. *Who could throw acid in her own face?* She followed room to room, looking down on his thinning hair from windows as he circled the house—ringing, shouting, knocking—while a voice whispered a nonstop narrative at her ear. They clung together like twins, stroking each other's cheeks, promising to protect one another . . . *Over his dead body.* Their twin eyes peeked over the windowsill, watched him open the car trunk, glancing up at them—that lusty, smoldering need that possessed him at the pool when he clawed away her baby dolls . . . standing in wader boots in lacy green strings of watercress that beaded on wet brown rubber, lifting his shirttails, asking her to lift hers, shoving thick fingers inside her cotton panties. "Don't tell, now. Mother will be angry." The taste of tobacco at back of his throat as he kissed her mouth to silence.

Carefully, he folded the coat and put on a checked mackinaw, removed a tire iron from the trunk and turned it over in his hands. To break in, she realized, to break in the house.

"Grandpa Wal'er." Mommy smiled sheer horror. "Our belovah fathar . . . Isn' thad a kick?" He slammed the trunk.

They fled downstairs into the family room, didn't hesitate—Mom first—crashed through, hands shielding their faces. Glass exploded slow motion into the air, a sparkling momentary spray of light. Mom leaping through—Jerri Jumpkick! Then Meena into the jagged gap she'd left behind, into a hail of shards that nipped at her like a school of tiny shimmering fish. Across the lawn through the arborvitae hedge: They knew where they were going. She saw an image in Mom's mind of a cave entrance more accommodating than it possibly was, all of them huddled inside while the storm raged overhead.

But breaking through the hedge, seeing it wasn't morning but dusk, seeing the mother-of-pearl sky lose its sheen, seeing that angry tangle of crab apple, wax myrtle and blackberry vines beside the compost heap, something in her cried: No! She wouldn't follow Mom down into moisture and mold. The man at the front door wasn't Grandpa Walter or Chucky Chuck but Dad, who had come to rescue her, while Boney waited in the car. Her own daddy who wouldn't think of touching her that way. Meena resisted. Mom pulled her, thrashing, into brush, her heels peeling divots from soft ground.

"Blind terror. My own . . . hers—whatever it was. I didn't know what she would do to me in there. Because isn't it the same, really, our fear that someone else will have their way with us against our will? Rapist, lust-drunk brother, crazed mother, what's the difference really? It's the same violation."

Just before the thicket swallowed them, Meena saw a figure wriggling like an upright worm across the lot. "Hullo there. Yoo-hoo." A hand shielded eyes as if from the moon's glare. Meena was shrieking. Mom chopped her hard behind an ear. "Shush, Deborash!" She began to claw away dirt and debris.

Woozy sick. Looking up into Mommy's pale straining face, eyes bugging, tendons taut at neck, Grandma Sally's crow's-feet beside her mouth—smile lines, she called them, but Meena couldn't recall when her mother last smiled. Had she ever? Hers was a face inspired by sadness. Even Mom's baby pictures were melancholy . . . rally squad snaps beside her giggling friends—Jerri Jumpkick's solemn, downcast eyes.

"We could try to forget," Meena begged her mother, afraid she would have to remember her like this—on her knees, clawing sod back under her butt doggy-style, bare legs smeared with dirt, looking old and haggard in the weak light. "It's only Dad."

Mom laughed.

"Nooo," Meena shouted as Mom stuffed her headfirst into a gaping hole, down into oozing mud, root hairs and debris fallen from the walls. Over her shoulder, she caught a last glimpse of her mother's grim lips, cheeks taut with the serious work of madness.

She crawled in near total darkness past gopher burrows and mole balconies into a smell clean and new and old as time. Mom shoved from behind, but she crawled on her own volition, squeezing through a passage narrower than she remembered. Air moist and suffocating. How deep, she wondered. Did that retro loony loon think they could dive into the earth ocean and swim away? She heard Mom's labored breathing and wished to tell her to breathe shallowly, make oxygen last. Then sensed the tunnel widen; her fingers touched gritty walls. They had reached what had been the reinforced section and had to pick their way over jagged chunks of concrete fallen from the ceiling. Pressure ceased behind her.

"Y'r safe now, darling," Mom's voice vaporish, incorporeal in the close dark. "He things y'r in the broom closet. Isn' that a kick? Ish safe in the bashemen'. I love you," Mom said softly, with a sober finality that inspired terror.

She was moving away, Meena heard her, shuffling back to the entrance—to bury her daughter alive.

She caught her mother's ankle. Mom slapped back at her, ragged fingernails lashed her cheeks. Strange, the strength fear can give. Meena was atop her, pummeling, bare knuckles scraping cement walls. Over my dead body, she kept thinking. Mom slammed her against the jagged wall, she slammed back. Mom shoved a hand in Meena's face, against her nose, sharp pain stabbed behind her eyes. "Deborash, be nice," Mommy said. "Be nice."

But didn't know how or what! . . . Maybe trying to pull herself ahead, Mom caught protruding re-bar. A muffled crack, a huffing sound; earth groaned like a stomach rumbling. The world collapsed. Something hard slammed Meena's head—a chunk of ceiling. White lucid light. Suddenly she knew why they had come down. (Tragedy, they say, is plotted ahead.) And knew she wasn't knocked out, just covered in dirt and rubble. She'd wait a moment until all had fallen.

Beneath her, Mom's legs spasmed, tattooed her chest in a violent, epileptic staccato. "Cut it out," Meena said, getting a mouthful of dirt. Because she didn't . . . only half understood what had happened. "Relax, Mom, you jerk." She twisted and wallowed free, shook dirt from her hair. Darkness was total. Her hands worked rapidly, garnering impressions of soil, stone, flesh. Where Mom had been was a rubble of cement chunks and moist packed clay. The world had slid down atop her, sealing off the cave.

Buried alive. Buried. What she planned to do to her daughter had happened to her. Meena's first reaction was hiccuping wild laughter.

Served her right. Buried. Just her bare legs sticking out. She wished Boney could see. Buried living . . . buried alive. Then it struck her. She started to dig, frantic, clawing aside dirt and concrete chunks until her fingertips were raw. She hit a piece too large to budge, lying transverse across Mom's body, ribbed with re-bar like a lizard turned inside out. Where Mom's chest and head should've been was packed unyielding earth. The cave shook again. She didn't hear only felt it.

Mommy's legs lay still now. Meena gasped for breath. Hysterical, crying, scraping at concrete. Each inhalation pulled through a straw. She slumped atop her mother, too exhausted to continue digging. Daintily, she brushed dirt from her bare legs, brushed them clean. Mom's hand was there, reaching back out of the packed dirt, surprising her—the hand that had shoved Meena back and saved her life. So familiar, so pliant and seemingly alive. She caressed veins strapping across the back, like Dad's.

"When we dig you out we will detox you, Boney and me," she whispered between smooth fingers, thick jagged nails. "Don't be scared." She cradled fingers to her cheek in the darkness. "We won't leave you ever again. I'll call Dr. Langerhorn at Riverside, she's expert at child molestation. You'll like her, Mom. She's going to help you out of your hole, word of honor." Her own voice sounded alien in the darkness.

Couldn't say how long before Mom's fingers went stiff as the clay from which they extended. Meena tried to warm them between her hands, knowing it wasn't good to become so cold, knowing, too, that Mom's head stuck out the far side of the pile. Safe. Soil covered her midriff like a heavy blanket; maybe had broken some ribs, but she could breathe, that's the important thing. They might have to amputate her legs, they'd grown icy, skin taut as leather. Meena took off her socks and worked them over Mommy's toes. She tickled soles of her feet to cheer her up. Couldn't expect her to react. She was in poop soup, like Olson says. She had more air up there. Even if they had to amputate, it didn't make you alien. It'd be a lesson she wouldn't forget.

Water trickled somewhere. The earth ocean had shifted dirt around them like the sea shifts sand. Meena sat in a puddle. Her fingers discovered a trickle down the wall. Placing her tongue there, she tasted the basement on Walnut Street, Boney's breath when truck tires rolled over him and he got pushed down so deep he swore he saw China; it tasted of the flooding river, the matted pelt of the cow Olson switched to shore. Water frightened her more than earth. Mom was okay with her head facing the entrance, but Meena's own grave would fill slowly with cold water, until her mouth sucked at the cave vault for dregs of air.

"Breathe shallow," Boney's voice warned her. "You got to breathe little sips, make oxygen last." Buried alive. That's what you get when you kill your mom. Centipedes creep from their lairs and nibble your flesh. . . . No! Mom wasn't dead. Jerkhead! What good did Boney think he could do now? She saw him hurrying from room to room, peeking around corners, calling for her in a scared voice. For Mom. She's dead, stupid—below the waist. Entering the bathroom, he stops to finger Mommy's nylons, knotted between hamper handle and hot water faucet. "One of Meena's dumb spider tricks," she hears him mumbling overhead. *I'm here! Down in here!* she screams.

The dumbcough walks on into Mom's bedroom, calling, "Mom, it's just me, I'm not Grandpa Walter." He sees old blood on her sheets, turns and goes downstairs, following a tiny cord of faith that never breaks. Chattering hyper to himself how Dad took Mom to the hospital, they were going to be a family again. Retromorph. She shows him where Drano ate away the nap of the living room carpet, empty bottles on the kitchen counter. . . . Blood, she insists, when he kneels before the shattered family room window. Coffee, he replies. *Blood, mine or mom's.* Spilt coffee! She sees him rubbing it between his fingers. *Gonadotrope!* Seizing him by the nape of the neck: *What's that then?*

Bright lights in back, shouting voices, the clatter of a backhoe. What's the use of such a brother? Always believing things will work out. Never learning. Insisting, even as she becomes groggy, that someone tried to break in their house, that's all, and Dr. Weatherspoon called the cops.

She pushes him across the backyard through the hedge, points out police spots, the backhoe working cautiously, a fireman in the trench beside the bucket, throwing up a hand, shouting, "Wait!" Nearly chopping his spade into Mommy's face, slicing off a sheaf of red-black hair. Other men leap into the pit beside him and throw out spadefuls of dirt. Dad shoves them aside, plants his mouth over Mom's and breathes.

Boney turns. He's been looking spellbound at his mother in a trench twelve feet deep. It isn't Buck who taps his shoulder but a figure in a cowl, planes of his skull gleaming white in the glare of klieg lights. Boney makes a chortling noise back in his throat, like years ago when they fled from lightning. She plants a hand against her brother's chest as they lift Mommy's body from the trench. "Don't look, we've seen enough already."

"No," she shouts into darkness. "No, she isn't."

Water trickled along my calves. I was so sleepy, I rested my cheek against Mommy's cold knee and decided to let the water cover us together. They wouldn't find me. My mother had taught me to hide. I detected a vague softening of darkness far at the cave's end, and knew I could crawl out whenever I liked—lift the hatch and go outside. I would lie in tall grass above, looking up at a universe which had regressed to swirling gases. Safe! For I'd bring the cave up inside me. It reached out tributaries and spread to all my hidden corners, blotting out secrets, taking possession. For now, I was planted in clay. I wasn't afraid, I felt peaceful. It was easier to stay down there with Mom than to try to guide her out. Darkness was safer.

My flesh was taut, covered in gooseflesh. I decided to strip naked, because it's easier to die of cold than to suffocate, I reasoned. My body disagreed; muscles cramped and wouldn't do my bidding. My stomach grumbled so violently it shook the walls around me. Darkness brightened. My eyes blinked protest against scalding light brighter than a sun. Exposing me. All at once—in a single infusion—my brother's idiot hope invaded and took me. Hands reached down and jerked me out of safety into the terrifying world.

*She's alive*, they shouted. *She's alive.*

But they wouldn't find me, I was beyond their reach, I had brought the cave up inside me. My mother had taught me to hide.

# 38

## Aunt Debbie

We crowded into the tiny clearing, flashlights directed down into that hole, little more than a badger den. Dirt scuffled away around it. Looking at each other and shaking our heads. Faces eerie in the yellow glow. "That'th weird," Buck said. "We thealed it up." Don dropped to a knee and called down inside. His voice swallowed up. "Why would—" Dr. Weatherspoon began. "No one in their right mind . . . "

Buck slithered into the ground headfirst like a groundhog. Wasn't gone a minute before Dr. Weatherspoon called after him. Didn't like such business, you could see: People swallowed in the earth or huddling in the dark. Not that I blamed him. Buck reappeared dirty as a boy's elbow, his eyes glowed. "It'th tholid dirt down there and concrete all packed up. Gave me the spookth."

"That's it then. It'll be the golf course," Don said, relieved. "Jerri always finds a golf course."

"Afraid not." Mort's tone about froze the jelly in our spines.

He held up a hanky. Opaque red in the light, stiff as a tin plate.
Don grabbed it and worked cloth in his fingers.

"Jerri's," he said.

"That's blood," Dr. Weatherspoon said, as if we didn't know.

"A bandage," I guessed.

"What are you getting at?"

"Buried alive," Weatherspoon's son answered, staring at the
hole.

Mort was poking in bushes. Without warning, Don hit him
at the waist and sent him sprawling into blackberry vines. Went
in after him, pounding with his fists. "You killed my kids," he
screamed. Took all of us to pull him off. Dr. Weatherspoon
jostled Don away with his huge gut. "Get a grip on yourself, for
goodness sake." A barrel-bellied man who considered it his
rightful place to give orders. "You boys get shovels. Don! We'll
call for help. The doctor can stay here."

Boys went running. Mort drove his car around through yards,
illuminating the thicket in his headlights, projecting misshapen
shadows through the foliage. Creepy, I'll say. Mort's shirt was
spotted with blood. Wouldn't believe blackberries could be that
cruel. I tried cleaning him up a little.

Soon as the boys arrived with shovels, they hacked away
brush and began digging. "Too slow," Mort insisted, though he
was in a hole up to his knees. Don grabbed the shovel from him
when he returned. Mort let him have it, though it worried me
Don might take off his head. His eyes white and wild in headlights. We traded off, digging till one was exhausted, then another leapt in. Except Don, who wouldn't give up his spade.
Water dripped off Dr. Weatherspoon's chin; wasn't good for
much more, you saw.

"Too slow," Mort kept saying. "Shuddup your goddamn
mouth," Don answered. But Mort knew about such things: how
long a person could hope to live in a hole in the ground. Dr.
Weatherspoon went down the road for a man with a backhoe.

"What are we looking for?" a sheriff's deputy asked when
cruisers pulled up, radios crackling, spotlights glaring.

"My sister," I told him, "and her kids."

"Down there? Jesus, Mary and Joseph."

Don shrugged off the cop who tried to spell him, shouting it's
his children down there, so pooped his spadefuls of dirt caught

the lip of the trench and slipped back inside. His bare chest and shoulders a tattoo gallery of blackberry welts. He shook like a dog pulled from water when we got him out; I wrapped my coat around him. I'd never liked Don until that moment. Never saw as much in him to like. I liked his fear, guess it was. Just wondered why it didn't occur to him sooner. Don was an aging boy running out of time and playfulness.

Paramedics arrived, then the backhoe, creaking on its treads— bright cyclops eye in front and Dr. Weatherspoon riding shotgun on the running board. The operator cleared away brush and dirt piles, planted stabilizers and dug straight down along the course of the tunnel shaft, which looked, in cross section, like a large winding burrow. He scooped out bucketfuls of dirt that came up black, then brown, finally red. "Bless my soul," the widow cried, "so that's where they got it." A hand pinned at her throat. Likely she expected the operator would bring her deceased husband up in his bucket. I hoped so! Anything but what I feared he'd find.

A small crowd had gathered: police, medics, firemen, their yellow sou'westers glistening under the lights, faces smoky beneath helmet brims. A vague ring of neighbors whispering in the shadows.

The hoe bucket hit something solid, a loud metallic clunk. The operator stood up over his controls to look. "Tha'th concrete," Buck said, telling us how they'd shored up the tunnel. Bless their clever hairy little butts. The shaft disappeared in rubble and the operator said he'd best go slow, motioning a fireman down in the trench. He scraped and probed with a spade—just to be sure—before the operator sunk in the scoop. The smoke of his breath drifting up in lights. It looked less a rescue hole than a mass grave, ten feet deep.

We moved close around the trench. Arms folded across our chests, hearts kathumping. Mort's arm around my waist. At times, we made out the outline of the tunnel, like an archway to the underworld, then it disappeared again.

"Wait!" cried the fireman. He dropped to his knees and brushed dirt away with both hands. I focused on his muscular shoulders, ribbed, sleeveless T-shirt, scotch white under the backhoe beam, shoulder blade knobs and tiny dips before triceps began, musing how I'd once gone for his kind of fellows—because it's funny what you think at a time like that—but Jerri never had. There's the irony right there.

The fireman shouted, "Good Lord, I almost . . . That's her!" He held up a fistful of Jerri's dark hair which he'd sliced off with his spade. I cried out and spun away.

Don leapt into the trench, skidded on his knees between the fireman's legs, clawing dirt from Jerri's pale blue face (cyanotic, they'd taught us at flight attendant's first aid: the mask of asphyxiation). I knew right then. But Don didn't. Men in uniforms swarmed around him. Mort elbowed through cops and firemen, shouting, "Doctor here!" I couldn't manage. Don was mouth-to-mouthing Jerri, spitting up mud. They pulled him off. Mort and a paramedic squeezed shoulder to shoulder above her in that narrow space, scooping packed dirt from her mouth and nostrils, bruise-blue lips. Uniformed men called back and forth, radios crackled. Above all, a piercing anguished cry which I thought was in my own head. Down below, the medic knelt forward to give my sister mouth-to-mouth. Mort touched his shoulder. And I knew. He looked up at me, his chin bunching.

Firemen freed Jerri from where she had just as well be left, bringing her up on a stretcher, waving at us to make way. Don plunged back into the trench through a cordon of men in leather armor. "Meena," he yelled. "My little girl's down there. For crissake, *Meena!*"

Me along with him. *Meena.* Tears coursed down my cheeks.

"*Meena . . . Jeff!*" we cried together.

"*Daaad,*" a voice answered. "*Moooom . . . Meena!*" it wailed.

Looking up, I saw Jeffrey standing at the lip of the trench. Mouth stretched wide, hair leaping like flames off his head. Just dropped down that way from nowhere.

I'd started for him when a shout went up in the trench below. The widow shrieked. The backhoe operator leaned far over his controls to look.

Before our eyes, a ghostly hand reached out of the hole from which we pulled Jerri, groping about as if to find its bearings. White as sheep gut, fingernails caked with mud. Don seized it, and Meena broke head and shoulders from that earthen womb—birthing strange, more dead than alive. Rags clung to her back, dirt crumbled into her lap. She looked at us as if fearing what she saw, eyes wan as Lazarus's might've been, blinking, blinking.

Her distorted face scarcely recognizable at all. Skin no earthly color: pale pearly blue.

I waved arms before my face, thinking we had committed a violation to bring her up. Then Don hugged her to him, spun her round, painting her face with kisses. We shouted joy and wonder. Miracle! Like years ago, when Boney rose from tire ruts. But nothing the same, that's the thing. She had returned to us alive but unwhole. Having entered the hole her mother vacated.

Mort wrapped her in a blanket and gave her oxygen, while I kneaded warmth back into fingers cold as Jell-O, combed dirt from her hair. "You're all right, honey," I cooed. "You're safe now."

"My boy?" Don demanded. "Where's Jeffrey?"

"Here! Safe, Don," I cried. Meena's eyes bulged above the oxygen mask—so like Jerri's it was spooky. She pushed the mask away. "Grandpa Walter's dead," she spat.

"It's going to be fine," Don was saying. "We'll be a family again. Won't we, Deborah?"

A fireman shouted, "All clear, no one else below." Because they'd gone down to check.

Beside a backhoe tread, paramedics toiled over Jerri, violating my sister's cold body. Something sprang up in me. Call it indignation. "Enough!" I cried. "Don't you know when to quit?" Any fool could see: features frozen in a death cringe so I hardly knew them, lips grimacing away from teeth—not horror, but like you'd flinch from a slap—one eye screwed up, her head twisted to the side as if she'd heard a voice. One elbow flexed in rigor mortis, palm up as if attempting to lift a weight from off her. That's what got me. "Jerri," I whispered. "Honey, I'm here." I wiped her face clean with a hanky, attempted to smooth a cheek to rest.

Mort touched my shoulder. I shrugged him off. Sensing a presence behind me, I turned and found Jeff peering over my shoulder. "Mom's dead," he told me as if I didn't know. Maybe I didn't. Really. I leapt up and held him.

Fate affords us only so many miracles, and they'd spent theirs early. Meena's one last miracle was afforded with the family's end. Jeff let it go, all that he'd pent up inside, shaking with rage and grief . . . and relief. Because that was part of it, too.

Meena skipped over to Mort, who was kneading her mother's features with knowing thumbs. "That's retro," she said. "Mom's drunk. Don't you know when she's drunk? She's sleeping it off." She reached into her mother's open mouth and snagged out a lump of dirt.

"Is that so?" He watched her warily.

"You can't ever wake her up when she's sleeping it off." Cocking her head to the side, looking down at her mother with mixed affection and annoyance. "Mom!" she shouted.

"No," Jeff said into my chest. He wiggled, I held him close.

"Really retro, Mom," Meena scolded. "Sleeping it off in Boney's cave. Really dumb. You'll catch your death." She crouched and whisked clots of clay from Jerri's matted hair.

"Well, goodness," I heard the widow say.

Mort and Don seized Meena by the elbows and pulled her away. "You wish she was dead," Meena shrieked, "but she's not. She always does that." She thrashed furiously and nearly broke free. Kicked her dad viciously in the shins. Then smiled and stroked his cheek. "Chucky Chuck . . . asshole."

She followed the gurney as paramedics hurried Jerri's body to the ambulance, insisting they were taking her mother to drying out. "Just like you wanted," she sneered at Jeff.

"Our mom's dead, Meena," he told her.

"She's drunk, butthead," she shouted, seizing hold of her mother's hand which hung heavily off the gurney. They'd got front wheels onto the ambulance apron, but Meena clung hold and wouldn't let them push her inside. Jerri's body strained against restraining straps, lifting grotesquely toward Meena as if she meant to rise. All of us—cops, firemen, Mort, Dr. Weatherspoon, Don—were a little afraid of Meena's gay, desperate laughter. So like her mother's. She had thrown the sheet off Jerri's ice-blue face and they laughed together.

Meena jabbered rapidly: "I won't let them touch you, Mom, I promise. Over my dead body."

"Going in," snapped a stocky female medic, losing patience.

Meena turned, displaying her small white teeth to me. "It's your fault. You breathed up all the air."

"That'll do." A sandy-haired cop gripped her shoulder.

"You're retro," she shrieked; he flinched away. Jerri's beaked upper lip curled up from her teeth—that grin-grimace I could mimic myself—but wasn't any mimicry. Suddenly, I recalled Meena standing behind her mother with the fire poker—threatening to kill her. Impossible! Just erase the thought.

"Going in."

It was Jeff who broke free from me and approached her, his mouth set. "Shuddup, Meena. Mom's dead. Mom's plain dead." He hugged her. When she struggled to break loose, he held on. "You got to cry now, Meena. It's time you have to cry."

The medics heaved the gurney inside with a clanking of wheels and slammed ambulance doors. I steered those two toward their father. It seemed Meena might cry: brow knotted, eyes creased. Seemed she might let it go, erupt, all of her, in her brother's arms. Maybe it was the sight of her dad. In that nightmare glare of headlights and spots, rising vaporous breath, her eyes flashed from brown to the fiery black of Jerri's at moments of agony or rage. She glared at Don as if what she beheld wasn't a man swamped in grief and need but something altogether alien. A truth we could not know and wouldn't wish to accept.

We buried my sister one drizzly morning in the cemetery beside the river. Some markers remained caterwhumpus in their green gums like teeth worked loose by the flood. A few were missing altogether. The funeral home had put up a striped tarpaulin beside the grave. We stood under it listening to rain pelt down in a solemn dirge. One of those drizzly spring rains that seemed it wouldn't never stop. Just the kids, Sally, a few friends. Pastor Nordstrom read the service. Not that Jerri gave duck piss about religion, but I wanted to give her a fighting chance. Though doubted either Satan or St. Peter would want to keep her in booze for eternity. Sally sobbed like they were pulling out her guts. Great heaving. And Jeff. Meena watched the pastor intently, her face smooth as glass, listening, it seemed, for him to make a mistake. She laughed out loud when he said, "Dust to dust, ashes to ashes." The pastor's brow knit consternation.

"Don't you dare," Sally snapped.

I led Meena off to read names on old markers. She dropped to her knees on slushy turf and traced a finger over carved script, staining white stocking knees mud brown, just as pretty and frivolous as Jerri had been at her age. She placed a cheek against the wet gray stone and shut her eyes. "I was buried once," she said. "I liked it better."

The hollow thud of dirt falling on Jerri's coffin came across to us as the diggers shoveled: two men in yellow slickers. Just as well we missed that part. Meena watched them dry-eyed. Underneath, she told me, there's an ocean and bones sink to bottom.

"Do you know who they are burying, honey?" I asked.

Meena tilted her head, working a finger along a v'd groove of chiseled script. "She drinks too much."

"She's dead, honey. Y'r mom's passed on."

Meena pursed her lips. "Life sucks anyway."

"Do you understand me, Meena? Because I can't tell. Do you know who I am?"

She laughed, wet burnished cheeks turned up toward me, face shining as if bathed in pure light. Hair a flat close cap over her ears. A little terror crept into her eyes.

"I'm Debbie, your aunt Debbie." I reached to help her up. "You'll catch your death."

"That's retro. Nobody runs fast enough."

We walked back to the small caravan of cars above the grave site. "Been swimming?" Mort asked us. Because that was Mort—even at a funeral. He dried Meena's head with a golf towel from the trunk and shooed her into the warm car. I took Jeff aside under canopying branches of a Douglas fir. Overnight, grief had resculpted his face, eyes gone hollow and puffy at once. He had his dad's prominent Adam's apple, but not the chin. His was bold, with the nose. He wouldn't look me in the eye.

"We shouldn't never have dug the tunnel at all. It's like I killed my own mom."

I dragged his chin around. "Isn't a thing you did! Or could do. Listen to me, Jeff. Isn't a thing . . . any of us! We want to find blame. That's human nature. Blame is the only reason we know, and we must find a reason. And blaming ourselves is easiest—your sister, y'r dad, me! If only I hadn't gone on that trip . . . if only, if only—no end to it. Terrifies us to think there isn't any reason at all. But there isn't any, hon. It just happened."

He looked at me then. "Will they put Meena in permanent?"

"Over my dead body they will. How'd you like to come live

with Mort and me, you two? I think your mom would like that. Mort's the decent sort of fellah she didn't believe existed. Just like her son."

"What about my dad?"

"You can visit. He agrees it might be best for a while."

"Can we wait till they're done?" His eyes flashed at grave diggers.

"Your dad will want to come," I said. "And Olson."

His face hardened. "Why didn't they come when she was alive?"

I shook my head. "He couldn't stop it. It's a thing you will learn. Some planes crash, and might be yours. Isn't a thing anyone can do to prevent it. We aren't given to do that for each other."

"I will." Light caught whites of Jeff's eyes, lingered there. He wasn't either of them—his mom or dad—or the two combined. But someone altogether different. I saw that.

"Would you like that? Would you like to give it a try? Portland is about wet as fish piss."

He nodded. "I want to help put the sod on top. Like a blanket," his voice breaking, "on top of her."

"It's just only her husk. Her empty shell, hon."

"We always covered her, even when it wasn't Mom but just her body."

"We'll cover her," I said, knowing his digging had started long ago.

He looked me straight in the eye, unembarrassed by grief or need. "Can we call you Mom, Aunt Debbie?" he asked.

I nodded.

But Jeff had touched a nerve already raw: if I'd done this differently. Or that. There's no end to guilt. Goodness never counts for half as much. You keep hoping it might. Because though it is true that we can't always save others, it is also true that we must try.

It was Jeff who refused to give up on his sister. I'd find them sitting in the dark upstairs in Meena's bedroom, Meena staring through the skylight at the Big Dipper, her brother patiently waiting, telling her the day's news. Knowing a time would come when she must speak, must bring up the truth from her mother's grave. For words twist and thrash in us and finally must speak themselves. He knew madness is stone you must wear away little by little. Like grief or fear.

They'd walk together to the park below Mort's house when Jeff visited from college, years after we'd adopted them, after their dad was little more than an obligation Jeff fulfilled each Christmas, going south to visit. One year he decided not to go and Mort argued with him about a son's duty, till I reminded him he was barking up the wrong family tree. Jeff returned that year with stories about the hippie gal living with Don, how they partied and smoked pot, and she bossed Jeff around—a wanna-be stepmother young enough he might've slept with her himself. Next year Jeff didn't go and Mort didn't say a word. It worked out in the end that Meena forgave her dad but her brother never could. It's all a riddle: family and all that goes with it. As Meena's surfacing was a riddle.

After years of analysis and drugs and her brother's steadfast faith, she came down to breakfast one Sunday morning with a photo of the three Simonet girls—Meena, Jerri and me—sitting on the bench around the huge amphaloola tree in the backyard on Walnut Street. All of us in summer dresses Jerri had cut from the same pattern, a checked yellow gingham. All grinning like cheerleaders for Don's Kodak.

"Do you remember this, Debbie?" she asked. "When you came to live with us and we did a garden—" She broke off, for I'd leapt up and sent things clattering, coffee to the floor.

"Take it easy," Mort said. "It's only a photo." But his eyes sparkled. A decade in darkness and she'd decided to emerge.

"There's Mom." Meena reached across the table to show Mort. "The famous tree house where my jerk mother tried to freeze to death in the rain."

Mort nodded. "I've heard stories."

Her brow knit. She seemed suddenly less the young woman who ventured out two nights a week to French class than the girl who preferred being a spider. "How long ago was that?"

"You were six years old." I steadied myself.

"Seventeen years." She was thoughtful. "I remember Mom lying on the ground. But I don't remember how she fell. Dummy me."

My hands shook as I collected broken shards of coffee mug.

Sally had bequeathed me her gnarled knuckles. Some things we can't disinherit, as Meena might her mother's madness. "No honey, it wasn't—" I glanced up at Mort.

He held a finger to his lips.

"I believe it was suicide," she puzzled.

"You have her hair," I said.

She seemed pleased in that. "My real father lives in California," she told Mort. "It's been a long time since I've seen him."

"All in time."

We began leafing through family albums. "La Brea Tar Pits," Meena exclaimed, "Grandpa Walter's farm . . . Gimphead Olson—" Darkly pondering before her brother flipped the page. They were laughing, discussing me: a girl sunbathing on a blanket in a strapless Jantzen one-piece which left little to the imagination. Me thinking I would kill for that figure now.

"I never thought Aunt Debbie would get married and become middle-aged, stodgy and normal," Meena teased.

"Oh turkey piss."

"I used to think I'm going to be like her—free, beautiful, unmarried. Flying for the airlines."

"Collecting a-holes' apartment keys," Jeff quipped.

"How glamorous."

"Or that she would have kids, I would never have believed that."

"Or the kids would be us." Jeff laughed.

"Thanks, Mom," Meena said, so soft and solemn we gawked at her. She was speaking to a picture of her mother on a swing in Grant's Park. Jerri was maybe eighteen. Toes stretched skyward, hair fanned out behind her. It was the kind of thing her brother never would say, though he might think it.

I understood then that my sister's death was a last desperate gift to her children. The only way she knew to break through the web of neglect, deceit and unhappiness that ensnared them. The only way she knew to free her children and herself. A mother's last selfless gift.